RITUAL DUES

A WITCH OF THE DEMESNE NOVEL

B.L. BROWN

GOOD INTENT PRESS

Book Cover by GetCovers

Illustrations by Fantasy Sprite Studios

Map Illustration by Lindsey Staton

1st edition 2024

ISBN 979-8-9900634-0-2 (ebook)

ISBN 979-8-9900634-3-3 (ppbk)

It was only a matter of time.

To Ana – Sorry I killed you. Or did I?

To every square peg forced into a round hole: may you remake
the world to fit *you* and not the other way around.

Ritual Dues is book two of *Witch of the Demesne*, a series within the World of C.R.O.W. The suggested reading order of all books within the shared universe is:

Ritual Income

Stitching Palms

Ritual Dues

Shady Depths acts as a prequel. For the best experience, it can be read at any point following *Ritual Income*.

Content Warnings

Depression, self-harm, on-page sexual acts (consensual), PTSD, anxiety and panic attacks, mental and emotional abuse, self-medicating with controlled substances, gore, profanity, witchcraft

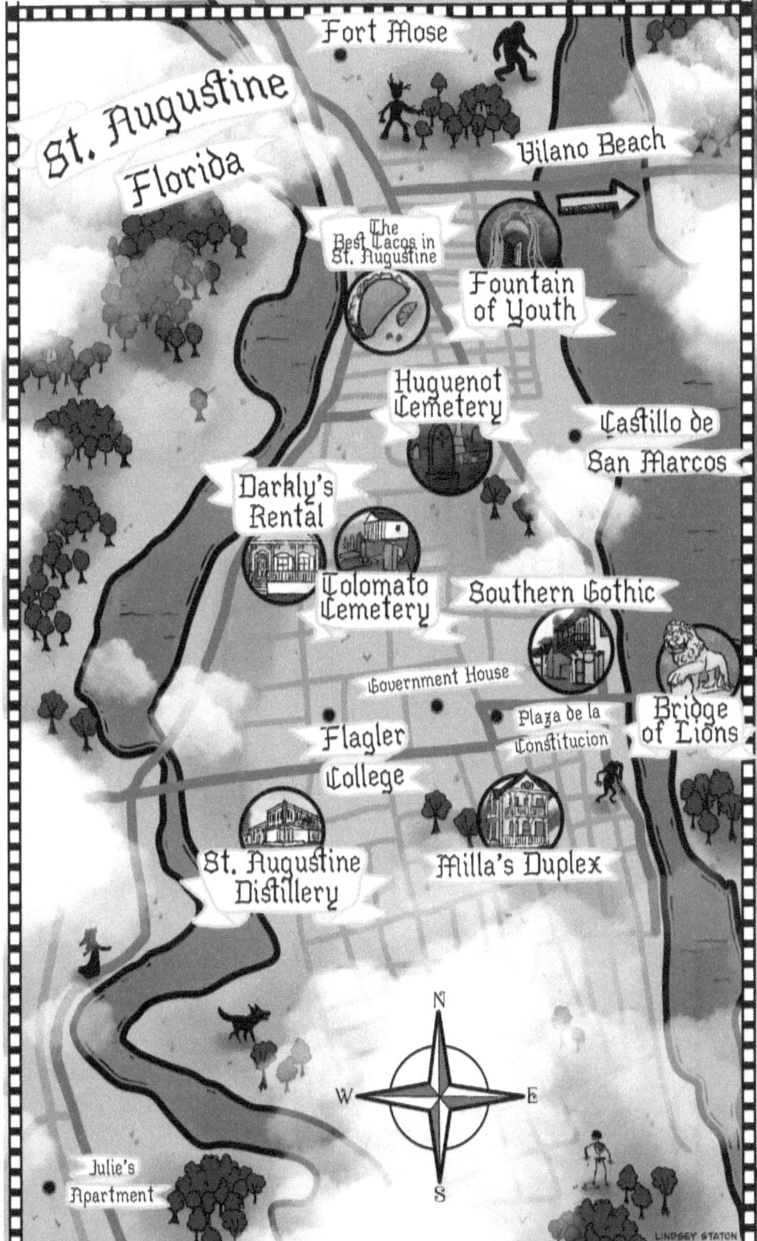

St. Augustine Florida
Fort Mose
Vilano Beach
The Best Tacos in St. Augustine
Fountain of Youth
Huguenot Cemetery
Castillo de San Marcos
Darkly's Rental
Tolomato Cemetery
Southern Gothic
Government House
Flagler College
Plaza de la Constitucion
Bridge of Lions
St. Augustine Distillery
Milla's Duplex
N
W
E
S
Julie's Apartment
LINDSEY STATON

BELTANE
1
2
3
4
5
6
7
8
9

LEGEND
1. Limbo — Campground P
2. Lust — Fertility Rites
3. Gluttony — Food Trucks, Beer Garden
4. Greed — Coven Tents
C 5. Anger — Sex Magick
C 6. Heresy — Casting Ranges
C 7. Violence — Illusions
C 8. Fraud — Music Tents, Art, Sculpture
9. Treachery — Ritual Stage

Ways
Fine and Faire

Aragon

Audiomantic *sound*
Augurist *crystal witch*
Chiromantic *Fortune tellers*
Chronomantic *timey-wimey*
Hippocromantic *doctors/nurses*
Meteomantic *(Donny)*
Obfuscari* *weather witch* *mind witches*
Obnubilari*
Technomantic
Vinefica* *poisons + potions (Rai)*
corpomantic*

Čeſký-Krumlov

Green Witch *good herb*
Kitchen Witch
Light Witch *soul, truth*
Pastýř *animal handling (shepherds)*
Vestic *diviners*
Spalování *flame witch (Toby)*
Stitch Witch
Svítilna* *wee sparks*

Ways
Forbidden and Foule

To be reported immediately to C.R.O.W.

~~Corpomantic~~
Dark Witch *Master of shades*
Death Witch

* numerous historical incidences identify the marked Ways as At-Risk. Witches of the noted Ways are observed closely by their demesne's Aural Insurance Adjusters and assessed for Fine and Faire aura every five years.

Only those who will risk going too far can possibly find out how far one can go.

T.S. Eliot, Ink Witch

THE NEITHERWORLD

He walks in darkness, in a world that is neither here nor there.

Subtle and smooth, toeing a path none can see save for him.

The wind is relentless, harsh, and cold. It bites at his skin, burns his cheeks, and after an hour, a day, a week, he no longer feels it.

The cold has become a part of him, nestled in and among his bones with the Darkness that was always there.

Sometimes, he hears a voice, a wail calling his name, but the wind steals it away in the same gust that drives him deeper and deeper into the expanse.

At some point, his legs give out, so he leaves his body behind to become a passing Shade, and the expanse solidifies with each shadow step he takes. The path becomes cobbled, and the suggestion of brick buildings loom over his head. Others fall into step behind him, beside him. They bow their heads and bend at the waist for the boy who walks with Darkness.

"Keir!"

The voice wails again. He pauses at the edge of a dead field, looking back down the road to where a pin-point of white light bobs and weaves in the Shade, a will-o-wisp tempting him to leave the Darkness—his Darkness.

"Keir, come back to me! This instant!" the voice calls again. The light bobs closer, and Keir steps into the field.

"She wants you to go home."

He stops at the sound of a small voice at his side. Silk tangles around his ankle and winds up his leg. A small hand slips into his, tugging the boy out of the field and back onto the cobbles.

"Who?"

"The Light," that little voice replies, blunt and brusque. "Obviously."

"And who are you?" he asks, stunned to be addressed, to be touched in a world that is neither here nor there.

"Just a little shadow." The hand in his squeezes again and the boy thinks he sees, for just a moment, a little girl at his side. She vanishes as quickly as she appears, leaving behind a Shade and the whisper of a hand in his. "They want you to come back."

"I don't know how," the boy admits. He left his body behind an eternity ago.

"I can show you," the little voice giggles. "I've done it before; come on!"

They run, the little shadow leading him through his neither-here-nor-there world. She stops beside a fallen form and pulls at his arm before pushing him down down down, and then Keir stands in the body he left behind.

"How did you …"

"I told you, I've done it before." The little shadow stomps a foot that isn't there and points an arm of empty night to the will-o-wisp, dimmer now. "You don't have much time in here. Not in that body. You should run."

"How far is it?"

"Almost a kilometer." The shadow curls around his wrist, tying itself in a knot. "Come, I'll show you the way."

"What if I fall in again?"

"I'll find you," the little shadow hums, "and I'll drag you back out again."

Part I
As above,
so below

One

"COME ON, YOU PIECE-OF-SHIT chain."

Milla focused on the tingle in her fingertips and the warmth pooling in her palm, easing her Way out bit by bit. Too much, and she would pass out again. Too little, and she'd end yet another day screaming her frustrations at the palm trees and startling the birds.

Patience was key. Patience and focusing on the ritual.

All magick was a ritual, from major castings requiring full covens to minor summons any witch could perform without thought, and a ritual required three things: intent, desire, and sacrifice.

Her desire was clear: rust the iron link without tipping headfirst into her Way and waking up with a hangover. But metal was tricky, and her Way worked best with organic matter. She could do it, rust was within her Way, but the purpose of this exercise wasn't to get blackout drunk before noon. It was to control her Way, rust the iron, and reverse the corrosion.

And as for the sacrifice, Horned God, hadn't she sacrificed enough time to this Goddess-forsaken swamp?

So it was the intent she was missing. Intent was tricky—it had to be tied to the desire, but it could not *be* the desire. It was the core of the ritual, the aim, the goal for which a witch stepped into her Way and appealed to the Triple Goddess.

And Milla's intent was to rust the chain.

"Wait." She sat back on her heels and swept lank bangs from her forehead. "I'm sacrificing time, and my *desire* is to rust this iron so I can leave the swamp. Or—no, my desire is to leave to swamp, and the intent is to rust the chain …" Which she could do. She'd done it before, again and again over the last few days, suffering headaches and nausea and all the other fun after-effects of stepping too deeply into her Way, so was her intent to rust it slowly? To avoid the hangover?

She dragged her hands down her face and glared at the fat chain strung between hefty wooden posts. The unrusted chain.

Heat fizzed in her arms, sizzling and burning into her palms as her frustration rose.

All she intended was to rust that chain and be standing afterward. All she *desired* was to leave this swamp without flinching in fear anytime anybody got too close to her. And Horned *GOD,* hadn't she already sacrificed enough?

"*Koroze.*" Milla flexed her fingers, palms hovering over the iron links, letting her frustration fuel the corrosive hex. Magick coursed through every vein in her body, and as she channeled it into her hands, heat rushed down her arms, flooding her palms. She clenched her teeth, restraining the tide of magick to a fine trickle—slow and steady like Darkly had advised. Too fast, and she'd burn through her Way, but if she kept control, she could rust the iron, reverse the corrosion, and argue her way out of this tick-infested swamp.

She was sick of hiding, sick of day after boring day in the sweltering heat, and the nights weren't any better. The hut had not been that oppressively warm in her memory. It had been cute and quaint and welcoming, hidden from prying mortal eyes by the look-away hexes Ezra had cast on the walls and roof. A witch would have to know the hut was there to find it, making it the perfect hideaway for two witches looking to lay low and get to know one another.

But Darkly wasn't here, and Milla would be stuck here unless she could rust this stupid chain and reverse the damage without passing out.

"*Koroze.*" She released her hold, just a little, just enough, to eke out more of her Way. The tips of her fingers grayed with ash, the skin withering to decayed, blackened points. Magick burned in her veins and still that Horned God–damned iron link remained untouched. "*Koroze.*"

A bird chirped overhead. Palms rustled in a sticky-thick breeze. Sweat trickled down her spine, collecting on the waistband of her shorts, and the damn iron did nothing but remain completely oblivious to the witch trying not to corrode it into a pile of oxidized dust.

"*Koroze!*" Magick filled her palm as Milla's frustration finally won over her patience. The ash crawled down her fingers, bony tips revealed beneath the rot, and finally—*finally*—a speck of flaking brown appeared on the iron, crawling outward like lichen over a stone. She gnashed her teeth as Way bled from her veins. Fast, too fast, heat dripped from her arm, and her head grew light, but she was doing it. It was working. She had control of her Way, she was rusting the iron.

"Hoookay," Milla exhaled, focusing on maintaining the flow. "Nice and easy."

That was the trick and where she'd failed time and time again. Nice and easy. Slow going. Channel the magick to her hands, but don't let it slip through. She could almost hear Darkly whispering in her ear, his rolling accent, and the thick slang she was just beginning to understand.

"Hold on," he would say. "Dinnae get excited, hold your Way, and let it out easy."

But Darkly wasn't here. He was *elsewhere* as he'd been all week, only to show up at the most random times to lecture her on magick.

This was not what she'd had in mind when she told their vampire detective-turned-chauffeur Dies-well to head south, but neither had she anticipated her magick going weird and that weirdness stemming from the Dark Witch. But it had, and it did, and Milla wanted to go home.

"Easy," she repeated. "Easier said than done."

Still, the circle of rust spread, crawling steadily across the surface of the iron. Milla curled her fingers, frowning at the bony tips. Her Way frothed in her palm, pressing against the webbed scars, wanting to burst free and consume the metal, corroding the iron and dragging Milla down with it.

"You control your Way, *leannán*." Darkly's repeated words ran through her mind. "It doesnae control you."

"No, it doesn't," she muttered.

As if needing to prove her wrong, a rush of heat bled down her arm, boiling in her veins and leaving her hand before Milla could form a fist. As fast as it had every damn day since the Loa, and the Fountain of Youth. Since she'd taken hold of Darkly's Shades and hauled them from the Neitherworld, summoning the only thing she could to destroy a revenge-bent Voodoo spirit and spare the women of St. Augustine from untimely death and a multi-level marketing scheme.

The rust surged outward, engulfing the link in flakes of reddish-brown. A divot appeared, deepening to a saddle in the ever-thinning metal. Thin flecks fell to the sandy earth as the iron crumbled beneath her Way.

"No! Nononono." She gripped her wrist, the gesture useless. She needed to reverse the hex. To switch her intent and re-focus her desire before the link rusted through. This was what she had been trained to do. By the Morgenhexe and a revolving cast of would-be Enforcers. It was the groundwork Ezra had worked off of, molding Milla into a witch of his own making. She could do this. She *needed* to do this, needed to *control* her Way, or else what was the freaking point?

The world blurred into swathes of muted browns and greens. Sour spit pooled on her tongue, and her stomach gave one warning swoop.

"*Obnovit*," she grunted. *Restore. Renew. Triple Goddess's tits, reverse!*

The saddle of rust collapsed on itself, a cloud of dusted metal rising as the link tipped to the side, barely balanced on the next link in the thick chain.

Her head spun, the ground tipping off-kilter as Milla's Way took its cost. She grunted, dropping to one knee. Bile rose in her throat as she forced out one last, "Horned God-dammit, *obnovit!*"

Magick rushed into her leg, up her thigh, searing through her belly and torso before surging down her arm into her casting hand as the reversal took hold. It was too much, too fast, and Milla could not catch hold. Like a weighted rope slipping through her palms, the renewal allure ran free, winding around the link and, just as quickly, reversing the damage of the hex. Flecks of rust rose from the dirt, the brownish cloud sank back into the iron. The saddle filled until it was a divot, a dent, and then nothing at all. Not a seam or a speck of rust to be seen on that link, or the one next to it, or the one after that.

Milla staggered to her feet, clenching her fist to cut off the flow of magick. Goddess, it was too much. It was the Shades all over again. Her Way had taken control, using Milla as a vessel to be filled until it overflowed, uncontrolled.

She stumbled back, too Waydrunk to think of a hex, an allure, *anything* to seize control and stop her Way from rotting the world. An impossibly cool breeze licked up her spine, and a hoarse cry tore free—from relief, from fear. She had no idea other than the world tipped to the side, her legs turned to jelly, and the last thing she thought before hitting the ground was, "This's gonna *hurt*."

Milla jolted awake, hurtling upright and caught by strong hands at her shoulders. She gripped the worn blanket, her brain only half-registering that she wasn't lying in the dirt beneath the palms but in a bed, in the ramshackle hut she called a safe house.

Hidden deep in Tomoka State Park, north of Daytona, the one-bedroom fisherman's shack was not much, but it was hers. Restored by bored adolescent witches, it had an artesian well for fresh water and a gasoline-powered generator she had added on a weekend camping trip during college. For all it lacked in luxury, it had been comfortable enough for Milla and Ezra and now secretive enough for her and Darkly.

"Easy," Darkly soothed. "Hasnae been near long enough to sleep off the effects."

"Darkly?" His name was thick on her tongue, and a troubling roil in her stomach followed. Soft flannel crumpled in her palm, disintegrating to nothing until her nails pinched the scars on her palms. She groaned and dropped her head, leaning into his comforting grip. "Didn't think you'd be back today."

"Got here just in time," he answered, his voice tight. His right hand slid along her shoulder to cup her neck, thumb and forefinger gently massaging the tendons. "Hate to think how long you'd be laying in the dirt if I hadnae."

"I had it," she mumbled.

"As well as a slotted spoon holds water."

Milla snorted and raised her head, sending Darkly a bleary smile. Dim light bled through narrow cracks in the western wall and cheap curtains, but not so dim she didn't notice the strain on his face and firm set of his mouth. His eyes were trained on her, the green obscured by wafting shadows, and his normally styled hair hung in lank waves as though the witch had been repeatedly running his hand through the ginger mop.

His eyes darted over her face, lingering on her eyes. He frowned at whatever he saw there, and tipped his head forward.

"Alright, *leannán?*" he asked, voice dropping into a low rumble.

Milla's belly flipped and she nodded. "Better," she answered, turning her head to press a kiss to the back of the hand still at her shoulder. "Now that you're here."

Darkly hissed, a sharp, pained sound. His fingers flexed against her arm, and the motion snapped Milla out of her drunken haze, awareness rushing in all at once and far too late.

"Horned God, Darkly!" She scurried away from him, legs tangling in what was left of the flannel blanket. "Do you have a death wish?"

"There's a joke there." He straightened and flexed his hands, unable to hide his wince or the rising blisters. "Ken it's something like, 'nae, but I've got a death *witch*'."

"This isn't funny," she snapped. "You can't keep doing that."

"Doing what?" He dropped his arms, eyes darkening. "Helping you? Keeping you from passing out drunk in the dirt?"

"*Touching me.*" She threw a hand in his direction, and this time, Darkly couldn't hide his flinch. It hurt, but nowhere near as much as the hurt she'd caused him. He wore the same black v-neck she'd last seen him in but had traded his Enforcer blacks—tactical pants fitted with an absurd amount of zippers and pockets—for a pair of grey joggers. His shirt was rotted through, a diagonal swathe of moldered cotton from the top of one shoulder down across his chest and torso, and the skin she could see through the desecration was raw and red, rotted everywhere her body must have pressed because, of *course,* the idiot witch wouldn't leave her lying in the dirt.

Her eyes dropped to his palms and the inside of his arms, the skin there a puffy, swollen violet speckled in pale blisters. Evidence that he had hoisted Milla into his arms and brought her back to the hut. "Look at you."

"I'd rather not," he said.

"Goddess, what were you thinking?"

"I was thinking that my Death Witch pushed herself too far, *again*, and that she might prefer waking up in a bed rather than a festering crater."

"Yeah, well, what did you expect me to do?"

He stared at her. A long, hard stare silently implying all of the things he had expected her to do, like not overexert herself while stranded in a swamp at the ass-end of Daytona while he was off in St. Augustine doing Horned God knew what. "Milla…"

"I'm fine, Darkly."

"You're nae fine, *leannán*. It's been days, and I cannae touch you without risking my hand rotting off."

"It's not my fault your Way is a freaking battery for mine." And who in the nine rings could have predicted that? Like, what were the odds? "Which," she raised her voice, "one hundred percent, would have been nice to know before I summoned those Shades!"

"And how was I supposed to know?" he hollered back. "Even if you had warned me what you were gonnae do, which, one hundred percent, you didnae, how was I to know how our Ways worked together?"

"And you think I knew? Neither of us is supposed to exist!" She threw her arms wide, swaying slightly. Darkly darted forward, reaching out, ready to catch her, and Milla pulled away. "I don't understand why it's so *hard*."

"It's only been a week, Milla. Seven days, and you're attempting to master what takes a witchling months to get ahold of. This is normal, so normal that C.R.O.W. has legislation protecting witches in your circumstance." He sent her a soft smile, and she scowled in reply. "It will come, Milla. You just need to be patient." Her scowl deepened. Darkly put up his hands in surrender. "Though it is surprising the Morgenhexe never taught you how to do it."

"Morgen taught me how to hide my Way beneath hand-to-hex, not how to maintain a delicate balance of self and magick to keep from rotting a fencepost." She curled over her knees and buried her face in her hands. "This would be easier if I had my tea."

"No." He stepped close, looming over her. She splayed her fingers, watching his shadow extend beyond his person, wrapping around her ankles and crawling up her legs to hold her in the only way he could. "That shite's poison, Milla. I cannae watch you do that to yourself again."

Again.

"There's no need to keep drowning your Way." A wisp of cold traced her chin, urging her to look up. She did, her anger washing away under his gaze. Absent the smoke, jade green gleamed brightly at her, and a faint smile curled the corner of his mouth. "It will get better."

"When?" It was unfair of her to expect him to have an answer, but she'd been gone from her demesne for a week. She needed to get home and run the streets, tending the Ancient City as only she could. She had sacrificed her anonymity to protect St. Augustine, calling every Enforcer in the region to her city when she'd dropped headfirst into the furthest reaches of her Way. But she'd done it to save Darkly and countless women from a vengeful Loa running a pyramid scheme. The idea of losing her demesne now, after giving so much to keep St. Augustine safe and *hers*, was unfathomable.

"Cannae say." The shade at her chin wafted lower and curled around her throat, tracing a lazy path along her collarbones. "From what I saw, you rusted that chain thoroughly."

"How long were you there?"

"Long enough to see you fight against your Way." More shadows stretched across the floor, crawling up Milla's legs, soft as moth wings fluttering against her skin. A sigh escaped, and she edged back onto the mattress, meeting Darkly's heated gaze.

It was a distraction and a welcome one. The few moments they spent together in this hut had been filled with bickering, sleep, and distraction. Then the sun rose, and Darkly was called away by his Enforcer sister, leaving Milla alone to fight with her Way. So she'd take the distraction, embracing a few moments of ill-advised peace before it all started over again.

He stepped closer, green eyes bleeding black. "Long enough to see you call it back faster than you did yesterday."

"Not fast enough."

"Still an improvement, Ludmilla." He rolled her name over his tongue. A shiver that had nothing to do with the Shades pawing at her knees and tracing her thighs ran down her spine. "You cannae push this too quickly. Endurance is earned over time; move too fast, and you'll continue to burn out."

"How am I supposed to gain endurance if I don't push myself?" she argued. His Shades gathered at her waist, prodding gently until she lay back and stretched out on the bed. The edge of the mattress dipped under Darkly's weight as he knelt, a knee on either side of her leg, careful not to touch her skin.

"A drained aquifer refills all the more quickly, *leannán*."

"Oh, my Goddess." She rolled her eyes. "Do not start with that Mister Miyagi bullshit."

"Isnae bullshit." His eyes dropped to her chest, and his Shades followed, rolling over the curve of her breast. She gasped as they slipped beneath the low neck of her tanktop, teasing her nipples until they tightened into buds. A whisper of pleasure, the suggestion of a pinch. Enough to have a low throbbing build between her hips, but not enough.

It was never enough.

These ghostly touches, his intense, hungry gaze, only left her wanting more.

He inched further onto the bed and Milla widened her legs, easily falling into the motions they had discovered days ago. The only way to sate the need to touch, to feel, to *be* together when she couldn't hold him close. Couldn't feel his strong hands on her hips and her waist or those clever fingers driving deep into her, for fear of losing control of her Way.

His knee pressed against her groin, and Milla gasped at the delicious friction—tangible and real when the Shades were a cruel tease. She rolled her hips, a whimper building in her throat and escaping when he asked, "This alright?"

"Yes," she hissed. They would have to strip the bed. Her tank top was going to be a wreck. Already she could feel the heat building in her veins, but Goddess, she wanted more. She wanted him to throw her further into the bed. Wanted his fingers digging into her hips, her arms, her wrists, but this would have to do. The blanket and her clothes would rot, and the mattress would decay, but she wanted this too badly to care.

Shades trailed her jaw and traced her lips, engulfing Milla in Darkly's phantom touch. Over her, he bit his lip, flexing a hand at his side. Every muscle taut, as though he employed all of his restraint to keep from reaching out and touching her.

"*Leannán.*" His voice deepened to a growl, rolling over the walls of the hut and vibrating through her bones. A demand that Milla was all too happy to obey. She cupped her breast, rolling the nipple between her thumb and forefinger as she slid her other hand down her front. Shades followed, teasing Milla's exposed midriff and swirling between her thighs. A muscle twitched in his jaw, those black eyes trained on her every move and gasp as she drove her hand beneath the waistband of her shorts, circling her clit as Darkly watched on. "Good witch."

Milla shivered at his praise and the caress of his Shades rolling against her. She moaned, and Darkly tipped his head back, cupping himself as he cursed. He spat into his palm, nudging Milla's legs further apart as he thrust his hand into his joggers. Color rose in his cheeks. More Shades wafted from his body, writhing over her thighs and into her shorts, joining her fingers and the Shades already lapping against her center.

"Darkly," she pleaded, knowing he couldn't give her what she wanted and asking all the same. "More."

"Demanding," he half groaned, working his cock in slow, steady strokes. Milla reached for him, her fingertips barely dusting his thigh and leaving streaks of decayed cotton in their wake. "Touch yourself, Milla."

"Controlling little witch." She half-heartedly glared at him, slipping her hand beneath the waist of her underwear and swallowing a cry at the zing of pleasure.

His Shades kept their steady pulse and roll. She circled her clit, hips twitching, seeking out more touch, more pressure, and Darkly answered her silent need. Shadows shot from his person, blanketing the hut in midnight and driving against her pussy, their cold chill pressing against Milla's fingers. Urging them to dive deeper and seek out the wicked spot that had her crying out his name.

On and on, they drove against her, throbbing and pulsing, imitating the flick of a tongue against her clit as Milla's fingers crooked and bent until the heat in her arms puddled in her belly. Her core tightened, the tidal wave of sensation too much to contain, and she burst, pleasure tipping her over the edge right as Darkly grunted and gasped, "Milla."

He tipped forward, catching himself with a hand at the last moment. They held there gasping and staring at each other, the comedown bittersweet without his arms wrapping around her. Without his touch.

Slowly, the Shades retreated, bringing the room back into early twilight. Slowly, the green reclaimed his eyes. Darkly gazed down at her, his hand curled into a fist beside her head.

"Too much?"

Milla pressed her lips together and shook her head, willing her heart rate to settle and slow before she answered, "Not enough."

Two

"WHEN WILL YOU BE home?" Diego's voice crackled over the line, sounding far more distant than he actually was.

"I don't know," said Milla. "Darkly says they're almost done at the Fountain of Youth, but even if C.R.O.W. left tomorrow, my Way is still being weird."

"That ha—ot gotten—er?"

Milla pulled the phone from her ear, squinting through the cracked screen at the bars—or rather, the lack thereof. "Diego, can you hear me? You're cutting out."

"It is th—ower," he answered. "The serv—rrible."

"Same here." Milla kicked off her checkered slip-ons and scanned the tiny beach, perched on a narrow peninsula at the furthest edge of Tomoka State Park. Once the site of a Timucuan village, the land now hosted several miles of multi-use trails, campgrounds, a complex of ten ancient shell mounds and a web of smaller middens, the remains of a plantation, and two witches in self-imposed exile. None of which had the makings of decent cell service. "Hop on the wifi."

"She turned it off," Diego answered, voice still faint, but no longer cutting out. "When you left for college."

"Of course she did," she grumbled. Setting her phone on the warped armrest, she shoved someone's damp towel to the ground and unrolled her own, gritting her teeth as the cotton loops brittled beneath her hand. "Try heading up A1A toward New Town. The service on Duval can be tricky, but there's an Irish Pub on Flagler. Shanna something, they'll have wifi you can use."

"Bruja, you realize everything you just said to me was nonsense, ¿sí?"

"Just borrow a bike and head north." She eased into the beach chair. One of the back slats bowed and Milla glanced back, frowning at the rotting wood.

"If it is so easy, why do you not do it?"

"I told you, St. Augustine is crawling with Enforcers. I've barely even seen Darkly. When he *is* here, he looks like he's about to keel over from exhaustion, and then he's gone again before dawn."

"And where is *here*, ¿exactamente?"

"In my own private Idaho," Milla stated.

Diego chuckled, and in that warm, comforting sound she felt every mile of the distance between them. He should be here, with her, instead of stuck down in Key West with her foster mother. Not that Milla begrudged Morgen for whisking him away to the Keys. The Morgenhexe had heard the rumblings of a witch Forbidden and Foule in the Panhandle, and her first thought had been to grab Diego and get him to the safety of her demesne in Key West while Milla was chasing down rumors in New Orleans.

"One of these days, pequena bruja, I will understand these references. But today, we have just discovered Annie Lennox."

"Into the Ls!" Milla pumped her fist, even though he could not see her. "Nice. You're going to love her early 90s stuff."

"Whatever you say," Diego laughed, and Goddess, did she wish he was here. "Are you alright, Milla?"

"As good as I can be," she admitted. Though they had only known each other for a little over a year, having Diego was a balm. Even on her worst days, she accepted his disapproval and adhered to his guidance, knowing what he had endured, both in his first life and accidental resurrection, were ten-fold her troubles. If any witch could understand her desire to hide and heal, it would be him. "I just need to accept that this is going to take more time than I anticipated, as much as that sucks."

"I can see how that would be frustrating." Goddess bless this witch and his patience. "The key is in control; you own your Way, bruja, it does not own you."

"Oh my *Goddess*, you sound just like Darkly."

"Good," he said. "That means two of us are talking sense."

"Okay, sure, fine." Milla adjusted her seat, careful of the rotted slat. "I'll just forget years of highly specialized training in hiding my Way and master absolute control overnight." She snapped her fingers. "Easy peasy."

"That is not what I meant, Milla."

"I know, tío." She dropped her head back and sighed. "I just want to go home."

"Entiendo," he said. "I want to come home as well but it is up to Morgen. She says we must wait until, and I stress this is quote, 'the crooked noses of C.R.O.W. stop sniffing around your demesne'."

"She sounds like Darkly," Milla said, "but with ten times the anti-semitism." That earned a half-hearted chuckle, so she doubled down, more to convince herself than Diego. "It'll all blow over." She had to believe that, because the alternative was too depressing to consider—that she might never get back to St. Augustine. That she might have to live her life in hiding avoiding mortals and witches alike. Becoming a Baba Yaga bog witch of legend hiding in the swamp. A thing of local folklore and fairy tales.

"I hope so, sobrina." Her heart warmed at his calling her niece as easily as she called him uncle. "Keep working at it, it will come," he added. "I recall the lessons with my sister. I was so afraid, working so carefully to remove infection for fear of causing further damage. Have faith in your Way, it will come."

"Thanks, D," she said, doing her best to pack away the panic and shove it down, down, down to focus on what she could do in the here and now.

Which was abso-fucking-lutely nothing.

So she did just that, ending their call with a stilted goodbye and a promise to chat once he got somewhere with better service. Diego was safe in Key West. Morgen was looking out for him and, by extension, her, which freed Milla to worry about herself.

She slathered on sunscreen, adjusted her sunglasses and floppy black sunhat, and tried desperately not to think about the mess she'd made of things. Darkly promised it was only a matter of time, Diego swore she'd acclimate to the new bounds of her Way. She had to believe them, with their years of experience both within and without C.R.O.W., or else she'd burn herself out trying to bludgeon her Way into submission.

Humid, midday warmth blanketed her skin, and the easy, slow waves of the Halifax River lapped at the pebbled shore, lulling Milla into a not-quite sleep. That space of soft awareness where dreams crept along the fringes of consciousness, teasing her with whispers of a voice she left in the dark.

Millapet.

Birds called from the trees, and a rabbit or a lizard rustled the undergrowth. Out on the river, a boat motored by as kayakers called to each other.

Millapet.

A cool shadow fell over her legs and Milla smiled. "You're back early." Eyes still closed, she rolled her head along the creaking chair back to face the source of the shadow. "Sun's still up."

"Excuse me?" The voice that replied was deep and crisply accented. With the wrong accent. She opened her eyes, heart racing as she fought to keep her body still, relaxed, and took in the stranger.

Tall, tanned, and trim, he was close to Darkly's height, though where the Dark Witch boasted muscled shoulders and defined arms, this stranger wore the long-armed build of a rower or swimmer, trimmer all around but no less athletic. Water beaded down his chest and stomach, dripping toward a pair of deep red swim trunks that clung to his thighs. Sun-bleached blonde hair was swept away from his forehead, and he stared down at Milla with glacier blue eyes and a faintly amused expression.

"Can I help you?"

"Ja," he said. "You are sitting in my chair."

Milla blinked, startled anew by his accent and how he formed the words. Clipped and brusque, clean like a mountain spring. Like Morgen.

She scrounged her brain for any German she knew, coming up with 'gesundheit', 'wo ist der Hauptbahnhof?', and "'ein Bier, bitte', so she settled on, "And?"

"My chair." He crossed his arms, glaring down at her with all the clinical cool of a man who thinks he's in the right. "You have taken it."

Milla curled her lip, glancing around with over-exaggerated awareness. "I didn't know this abandoned beach took reservations."

"Was it not obvious from the towel?"

"The towel." She glanced around genuinely this time, stilling when she spotted the damp towel she had shoved off of the chair. "Ah," she shrugged and sat back, watching him out of the corner of her eye. "Sorry."

"Tch." A muscle in his cheek twitched in annoyance. "I placed my towel there earlier to reserve my place, and now I find that you have stolen my chair and ruined my towel."

"In what world does abandoning your towel on a chair mean you've staked a claim?" Milla scoffed. "And even if it did, how do I even know that is your towel?"

"I assure you it is my towel, and by right of property, you are sitting on my chair."

Milla stared at him, awed. Just awed by the presumption. A needle-like headache pinched the side of her head, and her palms tingled, her Way itching to rot the chair and see how this audacious German liked that turn of events. Instead, she grabbed the sodden towel, stood—"Here, fine, take your stupid towel."—and tossed it at him.

It smacked him in the face with a damp squelch. The stranger backed up, grunting in surprise as he pulled it away. She dropped heavily in the chair, tugging on the rim of her sunhat and crossing her arms over her bare stomach.

"And the chair?" he prompted with a whisper.

"Are you for real?" Milla glared at him. "I'm not giving up my chair."

"But … I reserved it."

She dropped her gaze to the towel in his hand and scoffed. "What are you going to do, Baywatch? Arrest me?"

The stranger's mouth twitched upwards, bright eyes flaring with interest.

No, not with interest.

An icy chill raced down Milla's spine, and she sat up, transfixed by the twists of blue flame in his eyes, recognizing the tell-tale burn of a spalování fire witch and realizing that she may have made a very, very huge mistake.

"Funny you should say that." He grinned, his hands burst into flame, and Milla lurched from the chair and ran.

Three

SPALOVÁNÍ Flame and combustion witches; House of Český Krumlov

BAREFOOT AND IN A three seasons out-of-date bikini, Milla sprinted across the loose pebble beach, barely avoiding the long-armed reach of the spalování. She darted down the narrow path through the trees, legs churning over uneven terrain, but she wasn't fast enough. She'd never been fast enough, good enough, strong enough, and now she was going to be arrested in a Horned God-damned state park wearing nothing but her bathing suit.

Low-lying coastal shrub on her left burst into flame. Milla glanced back, spotting the spalování hot on her tail. Literally.

"How in the *fuck* did you find me?" She surged for the trees only to be knocked off her feet by a wall of wind rushing in from the river. Out of the corner of her eye, she caught sight of kayaker with their arms extended and had the passing thought of, "Oh shit, a meteomantic."

Her back hit the rocky ground, and the wind siphoned from her lungs. Milla gasped, working her mouth like a fish out of water. She scrabbled onto her hands and knees, crawling forward.

She had to keep moving, had to get away, but she couldn't breathe, and that *spalování* was right behind her.

Rocks and twigs dug into her palms, her knees. Her lungs screamed for air, her chest growing tighter and tighter. Twigs snapped, and leaves rustled, the *spalování* coming close, and in the very last second before she passed out—her Way flared to life. Heat flooded her arms, and stones crumbled to dust wherever her skin touched the ground.

"*Zem*—" Milla wheezed, sweeping her casting hand across her throat. "*Zemřít.*"

Die.

She clawed her hand at her chin and mouth, pinching and scraping the suffocating hex away. A thin stream of oxygen filled her lungs, and she struggled to her feet, staggering as fast as her heavy legs could carry her.

She had to keep running, get under the cover of the trees, get to the wards of her hut. Ezra had set those wards. He had coated the little shack in layer after layer of look-away hexes, ensuring no one but a witch who had been there could ever find their hideaway. If she could outrun the *spalování* and get to her hut, she could hide and then … *what?*

Wait them out? Hex them all into shambling corpses and desecrate the remains? Prove to C.R.O.W. that she was exactly what they thought her to be?

Milla was a Death Witch. A thing Forbidden and Foule, but she wasn't a *murderer.*

A ball of fire flew over her shoulder and crashed against a tree. The stink of burning hair and greenwood filled the air, making her gag. She pressed her speed, veering to the left, the right. Zig-zagging through the trees as more blue fire crashed against trunks and moss, setting fallen leaves to flame and melting sand to glass. Half a dozen conjured tornadoes rose, slicing Milla's skin with shells, rocks, and fine grains of sand like the keenest blades. Blood ran warm down her arm, a leaf like a razor blade sliced across her cheek, and still she ran. Left, right, left. Cradling her right hand to her chest until her Way could no longer be restrained.

"*Zastavit!*" Flinging blind, Milla threw her arm back and sent a flash freeze hex at the flame witch.

"*Feuer.*" He responded with another fireball, landing it less than three feet in front of her. She skidded to a halt, a passenger to the instincts and muscle memory trained into her by a decade under Morgen's care. Sliding into a spin, Milla swung her wounded arm, shouting a wicked hex without thinking, her intent and desire composed by the words "don't" and "die."

"*Moje čepel!*"

An arc of her blood spun out as a scythe. The spalování's eyes widened, and he dropped flat to the ground, covering his head with his arms. The bald cypress behind him took the brunt of her hex, bark shearing from the trunk as a curtain of Spanish moss wafted to the ground, the gossamer strands still in the tree stained red and cut at a harsh angle.

"Oh, nonononoooo," Milla moaned between pants, staring wide-eyed at the damage and well aware of what she'd just done in flinging that hex.

A textbook hex, Forbidden and Foule, cast in plain sight of a C.R.O.W. Enforcer.

Because what else could he be?

It was stupid, so *stupid,* to give in to her panic. To not stop and think for a moment. She could have siphoned off the spalování's intent and twisted it into dreadfire, or ash, or *anything* but a

Horned God-damned *blood blade*. But she hadn't, and she didn't, and she was *fucked*.

"Triple Goddess's tits!"

Milla whirled, staggering back when she saw a stocky russet-haired witch in Enforcer blacks rushing through the trees. His buckled and multi-pocket rip-stop pants were wet to the knee and clinging to his calves. That, along with his chapped cheeks and wind-blown hair, marked him as the meteomantic in the kayak. He raised his arm, and Milla braced herself for more wind. Leaves kicked up at his feet, whirling around the witch in a dervish as palm fronds trembled and thrashed overhead. He opened his mouth to call out his intent, and the world went still.

Utterly still and silent save for the rasp of Milla's panicked breathing.

She spun in place, sand crunching beneath her bare feet. The sound echoed off the trees, magnified by the silence surrounding her. The meteomantic stood frozen a dozen feet away, encircled by leaves, twigs, and other detritus blown up from the ground. To his left, a green witch was tucked among the trees with a handful of bulbous green pods. Another witch wearing a cross-body bag, a tablet in his hand, stood beside a mind-fucking obnubilari with blood running from his ears as he covered the arrest with an illusion. And just a few feet away, the spalování lay flat on the ground, hands clasped behind his head as flame-licked eyes stared at her.

"What the …" She whipped her head around in search of more Enforcers, and the motion threw her equilibrium. The woods spun and blurred, and she wavered, the drunken effects of her Way increasing with every second.

Movement overhead pulled her attention to the trees, where a grackle flapped its wings in dramatic slow motion and then not at all. Blue-black feathers rippled like oil over water as the bird hovered in the air, its taloned feet grasping for a branch it would never reach.

Milla closed one eye, then the other, to make sense of what she was seeing while her brain utterly refused to join the party. She cocked her head at the frozen witches, and the cost of her Way slammed down like three shots of fireball on a Tuesday night, sending her from pleasantly inebriated to flat-out shithammered.

"Oh, uh oh." Milla clamped a hand over her mouth and lurched for the nearest tree. In a half step, the world blurred, and her body seized, gripped in a sticky molasses feel. Milla lunged for the tree again. Again. Throwing her body forward only to find herself right back where she'd started, caught in a hex on the verge of vomiting her guts out and unable to break free.

Fuck.

Her eyes wheeled in her skull, nausea drawing out a sticky sweat to coat the back of her neck.

Horned God-damned chronomantics.

Milla was no stranger to the time witches, thanks to Morgen ensuring she sparred against them at any chance she got. They were rare and powerful, the only witch that could pose a true threat to a Death Witch, or so her foster mother had lectured. Twisting time and taking the cost upon themselves, their appearance couldn't be trusted. A white-haired, crook-backed chronomantic could easily be a young, fresh Enforcer on their first assignment, while a baby-faced witch could knock the Advoccultant General himself on his ass.

And whichever witch hid in the woods was a seasoned chronomantic, that much she could tell from the layering of hexes:

One for the Enforcers frozen midstep.

One to hold the area in stasis, cast at a weaker strength, thus the length of time it took for the grackle to pause mid-flight.

One for the witch at the center of their intent. This last hex was the weakest, meant to disorient and distract the poor soul caught in their sigils.

Fortunately for the chronomantic, Milla was about three seconds of linear time away from blacking out.

Unfortunately for the chronomantic, Milla was no poor soul.

She crooked the pinky, forefinger, and thumb of her right hand, dragging through the depths of her Way and summoning intent in the ever-tightening loop of time. A step forward, a lurch back. Forward and back again. Vomit burned the back of her throat, and magick sizzled beneath her skin, growing more intense with each resetting of the loop. The timing of this was precious. She had to cast her intent in the space between a step lest the hex got caught in a twist of time.

Another lurching step, another stomach-churning reset. And another, another, and—

"*Zemřit.*"

Die.

The word left her lips too late, caught in the loop as a useless hex spinning out into the wood. Milla suffered through another round, brows drawn together and bile coating her tongue. She willed her fingers to pinch, to take hold and kill the magick working against her.

"None of that, now." A trio of voices in baritone harmony murmured beside her ear.

The sensation of leather tassels dragged down her spine. She staggered forward as the looping hex dissipated, making it one step. Two.

Her gut cramped, vomit surged, and Milla hunched forward with a groan to empty her stomach on the forest floor. She spat, plumes of green smoke rising as acid burned through the leaves and bracken, and scanned the woods for the source of that voice. Those *voices*.

A blur distorted the narrow space between an ancient oak and the knotted trunk of a bald cypress, vanishing as quickly as she spotted it.

"Oh, Goddess." Her stomach plummeted, bile drying on her tongue and charring the flesh. She held her left hand out in a weak defensive ward. "Three hexes," she slurred. Horned God, had she gotten the count wrong? She was drunker than a skunk and running for her life. Mistakes were common in high-stakes situations like *fleeing for her life*. "One for the Enforcers in the wood." She directed her ward at the still frozen spalování, heart thudding like a bass drum beneath the roar of blood in her ears. "One to hold the surroundings." Her eyes lifted to the grackle, hovering on a phantom wind, talons extended in their reach for a branch. "One to hold the witch at the center."

Milla spun slowly, arm still outstretched, scanning the woods for that tell-tale blur.

"And one for me." The disjointed trio of voices whirred around Milla in stereo. Empty space warbled with heat snakes, smudging her view of the woods beyond like water running down a pane of glass. For the briefest instant, she caught features behind the mirage: a nose, a mouth. Eyes peering at her from behind a chronomantic camouflage. They coalesced into the smudged recollection of a face as the rest of the heat snakes fell away, revealing a witch of medium height, medium build. His fingers twitched and danced at his side while the rest of him remained still, the blurred lines of his face obscuring his identity.

He cocked his head, studying Milla, and she pinched her fingers together.

"*Zem—*"

"*Stasi.*" He clawed his casting hand, sweeping it between them. Color leached from his blurred features and the air around Milla sizzled with magic. The chrono-hex slapped against her bare legs and torso, crawling up her body and suffocating her in a pocket of time, save for the twitch of her left pinky finger. Her eyes bugged, and Milla choked on the scream trapped at the base of her throat.

"Look at you." The witch skittered forward, his movements jerky and disconnected as though someone had edited out every other frame. "Still fighting, even at the last."

The ink splotches that made up his eyes studied the scarred surface of her palm and the twitch of her little finger. He moved along the line of her arm and brought his featureless face close, snatching her sunglasses and tossing them into the woods.

He brought his hand beside Milla's face; fingers splayed as if he intended to cup her cheek. The proximity curdled the bile in her belly, and a tear slipped free, curving around her cheek to dangle from her jaw. The witch held there, two smudges of coal above the rise of a nose trawling her face and settling on her eyes. Every fine hair on her body rose, anticipating the touch of his hand.

A touch that never came.

"Yes, yes. I see now." The reddish-brown slash of his mouth widened into a grin. He curled his hand into a fist and swung out of sight, though Milla could feel his presence lurking in her periphery. Unseen, unknown, but there all the same. A gentle exhalation against her ear had every muscle in her body twisting in dread. "We are going to have such fun together, magissa."

Another tear joined the first, Milla's eyes burning with the need to close. He laughed, a tiny huff that crashed against her neck, and the world resumed its natural spin.

The pressure holding her body peeled away like a thin layer of dried glue stripped from her palm. Pinpricks exploded in her hands and feet, and she gasped, lurching forward as her body caught up with the relentless march of time. The grackle whistled and trilled its displeasure, wings flapping wildly as it gained the branch. Clouds roiled and churned before settling into the spin of the earth, and the witches in the wood moved at once.

"Oh, Goddess." Milla spun, dizziness overtaking sense. She thrust her left arm at the witches in the woods, locking her elbow and calling on her Way. "Where is he?"

"Secure the target!" The meteomantic barked, throwing out an arm and clenching his fist. Again, air siphoned from her lungs, the muscles in her chest seized, and she clasped hands at her throat, clawing at her skin in a futile effort to breathe. All the while spinning in a frantic circle and searching the woods, working her mouth in a silent question: *Where is he? Where did he go?*

"Nicely cast," a deeper voice, rich and rolling like the steppes, boomed. Someone grabbed her arms, jerking them behind her back and manacling her wrists in one meaty hand while the other gripped the back of her neck. Their palm was a coarse, leathery warmth against Milla's clammy sweat, gloved for protection. She half expected them to jerk away at the onset of rot eating through the hide, but the warmth of their hand rose to a tingling burn.

Milla jerked as her neck and wrists began to sizzle, belatedly realizing that they'd coated their gloves in salt. Blisters rose, and she eked out a whimper, cinching her eyes against the pain.

They squeezed her neck, tipping her head forward. "Secured."

The meteomantic released his fist-hold on the air. A whistle of wind ribboned between her teeth and then she was wheezing and gasping, scanning the woods for that *witch*. "Where—where is he?"

"Where is who?" The meteomantic scowled. Deeper in the wood, the witch with the cross-body bag pocketed his tablet, and further away, the spalování pushed to his feet, brushing leaves and pebbles from his chest and legs. Behind them, the green witch tucked her pods away and turned in the direction of the parking lot. She patted the obnubilari on the shoulder as she passed by, circling a finger in a gesture for him to wrap it up. Five. Five witches plus the one at her back, easily twice the size of the chronomantic, so where?

Where did he go.

She fixated on the missing chronomantic, ignoring the pain of salt-burned skin to cling to what she thought to be true. Because he'd been there, holding Milla in a pocket of time while he examined her scars and eyes, and now he was nowhere.

Where is he? Where did he go? Where is he?

"Down you go." The Enforcer at her back nudged her legs with his boot. Her knees all but buckled, the grip on her wrists the only thing keeping Milla from crumpling as he guided her down. "Easy, now."

"Where did he go?" She pleaded, tongue thick and head growing foggier by the minute. She craned her neck, needing to see his face. Needing to be *sure*. Tall and broad, the Enforcer had the distinctive look of the Eastern Plains. With his accent, cropped dark hair, and hooded hazel eyes, sober Milla would have placed him as a witch from the Caucasus. Or maybe the Urals.

All drunk Milla knew was: *this fucker is huuuuuge.*

"Why do they always run?" The spalování strode into the clearing. Wavy blonde hair fell loose over his forehead, tousled from their brief scuffle. He stopped several feet away, eyeing Milla as he brushed sand off with one hand, dousing his flames with the other.

"Desperation makes fools of us all." The witch with the cross-body bag shoved his tablet in Milla's face, sneering at her as the device screeched its alarm. "Would you look at that? Her signature is identical to the one from St. Augustine." He punched the screen with a finger, narrowing his wide brown eyes, and slid the device into his pocket. "That makes it easier, at least. You good, Donmar?"

The witch behind her grunted in reply, adjusting the grip on Milla's wrists to ease the pressure on newly risen salt blisters. "Until she gets here, Cyrus, thank you."

"The sooner we're through with this business, the better." Cyrus shielded his eyes, scanning the woods. He scuffed the ground with a boot, kicking dust, grit, and dead leaves into Milla's face. She sneezed and coughed, silently cursing the witch.

"Have somewhere to be?" Donmar rumbled in his rich accent.

"Yes, actually. I would very much like to be anywhere *he* is not," Cyrus muttered, adjusting his cross-body bag. Donmar chuckled, earning a scowl from the hippocromantic. "Oh, like you are not scared of him when he gets all"— he rolled his eyes and waved a hand in front of his face, fingers splayed —"you know."

"Better than most."

"Are y'all talkin' 'bout the chronoman-*hic*-tic?" Milla asked, straining to catch any extra footstep or stilted, shuttered breath. Anything to tell her where the creepy witch had gone.

Cyrus stared blankly down at her, then shared a look with Donmar. "Is she drunk?"

"Drunk?" A tanned face dropped next to Milla's, assessing her state. She pasted on a watery grin, wincing as his movement aggravated her wrists. "*Oh sheshesin.*" A smile twitched, and Donmar straightened out of view. Clearing his throat to hide laughter, he eased the manacle of his fingers. "Hang on, little witch, any minute now, and this will all be—"

A burst of light like a camera flash silenced the large witch. Shadows stretched long, thinning and burning out altogether as the light grew brighter and brighter. Milla slammed her eyelids closed before the caustic white burned her blind. A beat of silence followed, the heart of the world bottoming out and thrumming with a low *wummmm* as it swelled back into being.

"—over." Donmar finished. "Ah, my wife is here." A smile entered his tone. "It took you long enough."

"The entire park is warded; my E.R.I.E. could barely get a fix on your location." A lilting, musical voice rose over the ringing in Milla's ears. "You should get going, Agent Sterne. He was in a temper when I left, and there's no telling how quickly he'll get here."

"Oh, Goddess." Milla knew that voice and that practiced calm as well as she knew Darkly's pained expression whenever he heard it.

"Of course." The spalování, Agent Sterne, cast one last inscrutable look at Milla before vanishing from her limited field of vision.

"She lobbed a blood blade hex," Cyrus supplied.

"It didn't hit him," Milla protested.

"Horned God, witch, keep your mouth shut." The new witch snapped at her, then exhaled. "Right, then. Let's get this going, the sooner we can get her out of here, the better." Clearing her throat, she pivoted, steel-toed boots landing directly in front of Milla. "Ludmilla Saxana Probuditna, by the authority granted to me, Luminescence Fiona Simmons, Senior Aural Insurance Investigator, Enforcers Division—" Milla snorted. All panic and fright forgotten for utter disbelief.

Luminescence Fiona Simmons was arresting her.

Lou.

Darkly's *sister*.

Four

"OH. MY. HORNED. GOD." A drunken laugh bubbled up from her belly. "Of course, it's you."

"You are hereby—" Lou blinked down at Milla. "Sorry, did you just laugh at me?"

"Still am," she managed between snorts. It was too rich. Too unbelievable to be *anything* but reality. "Holy shit, my life really sucks."

"Is she laughing at you?" Cyrus stepped beside Lou.

"I have never seen one of them laugh at you before," Donmar added, his rich voice steeped in mirth.

"Yes, well." Lou swept a hand over her head, skimming white blonde hair pulled into a perfect bun. "I suppose there is a first time for everything, even if the initial impression is lacking." Bright blue-green eyes fixed on Milla. A snort escaped, earning her a glower. "As I was saying, you are hereby placed under arrest and Waybound for the gross misuse of magicks both Forbidden and Foule."

Lou motioned to Donmar. He re-adjusted his grip, and she brushed a finger along the inside of Milla's wrists. A cold so deep it burned followed her touch, worming into and around bones and tendons to strangle her Way.

She grunted as her magick was stifled, refusing Lou the pleasure of hearing her cry. The tingle in her hands muted and snuffed out, and a shiver racked her body in the absence of the ever-present heat in her veins. A heat she had taken for granted. That boiling, painful energy she fought so hard to control, now dammed and restrained by an Enforcer of C.R.O.W.

"You have the right to remain silent; any hexes, allures, maledictions, or glamours you use can and will be used against you." Lou crooked her fingers, and Donmar released Milla's wrists, gripping her by the shoulders and lifting her from the ground. Blisters rose beneath his palms, and he muttered an apology at her pained hiss, releasing her arms to pull off his gloves. He tucked them into a pocket and set a palm at the center of her back, nudging her forward with a gentle press.

"In light of the serious charges against you," Lou continued, "all rights to consult with your jezibaba are hereby waived by the power of the Tribunal."

"Wait, are you serious?" Milla stumbled. Donmar grabbed her upper arm to keep her from faceplanting, and finally, *finally*, she struggled against him, twisting to jerk free. Revoking a witch's right to speak to their jezibaba, their mentor, their *protector* was unheard of. Even for the Forbidden and Foule, it was not *done.*

"Careful," Donmar murmured in a tone almost too low to hear. But Milla heard it, the subtle edge of care within the warning, startling enough to stop her from struggling. Lou, on the other hand, continued to read Milla her rights with the single-minded focus of a woman in a position of power who felt constantly threatened.

"If you cannot afford an advoccultant, one will be appointed for you before any questioning if you so desire. Should you decide to answer questions now without an advoccultant present, you have the right to stop answering at any time. We retain the right to pursue your confession to a full degree of satisfaction." Lou brought her mouth close to Milla's ear, hissing in a low voice, "So I suggest you play along."

"I don't—"

"Feigning ignorance is fine." Lou dragged her forward. Loose sand, pebbles, and twigs thinned and leveled to the packed dirt of a parking lot crowded with Enforcers, a dozen official C.R.O.W. vehicles, and a silver Land Rover. Cyrus led them through the maze of vehicles and witches to an ambulance at the far edge of the lot, yanking the door open. Donmar lifted Milla from the ground and stepped inside, setting her gently on the gurney.

She barely had time to process the weirdness before a device buzzed somewhere in the ambulance. Donmar slid a beeping phone from his pocket.

"What is it?" Lou arched a brow as the screen lit up his frown.

"Incoming."

"Shit." She whirled around, seething at Cyrus. "Why didn't you catch him?"

"I cannot isolate his signature." He tapped his tablet, brows cinching together as he scanned the screen. "There is too much social distortion."

"Life goes by so fast," Milla offered, then broke into a peal of giggles.

"Come again?" Lou asked.

"Social Distortion.'" Milla swayed on the gurney, grinning like an idiot. "Like, the *band*."

"No." A muscle ticked in Lou's jaw, and the gleam in her eyes cooled. "As in those wankers outside have clogged the air with too much magick. The E.R.I.E. cannot pick him out"—she shot a glare at Cyrus's tablet—"and we never got a warning."

"About what?"

"There he is," Cyrus said. "Ninety meters."

Lou grabbed Milla's upper arm, hauling her off the gurney. "We need to get you—"

The ambulance rocked, metal groaning under an onslaught of wind. Donmar's phone beeped again and again, faster and faster, and Cyrus clamored inside, struggling to close the heavy door against a cold, arctic gale.

"Right on time," he grunted. "Are we ready?"

Lou jerked her chin at Milla. "Are you ready?"

"Ready for *what*?"

Another fist of wind pommeled the door, ripping it out of Cyrus's hand. Milla only caught a glimpse of the parking lot—Enforcers running in every direction, hands held out in defensive wards—before the sun blotted out. A blink-and-miss-it eclipse that had every Enforcer stopping in their tracks and scanning the lot.

Every Enforcer, except for Lou, who pursed her lips, the whites of her eyes glowing from within. "To play along."

She hauled Milla from the ambulance, dragging her through the lot. Trees bowed and whipped, and all around them, E.R.I.E.s screeched in alarm over the howling wind. Stones jabbed the soles of Milla's feet while more fine-grain bullets of sand blasted her bare skin. She stumbled, struggling to match Lou's pace. Even Waybound, she suffered the effects of her magick, the world spinning and warping, her legs heavy and disjointed like she was darting across the deck of a ship in a storm.

"What's happening?" Milla yelled over the gale.

"My brother," Lou hollered back.

At her words, an arctic wind burst from the trees, tearing around the parking lot, battering against the witches and pommeling the vehicles. Palm trees thrashed, and cypress groaned while the Enforcers teetered off balance, lowering their arms to brace against the gale.

Milla shielded her eyes from the curtain of grit, sand, and leaves flying from the woods. Shadows followed, slithering out from between the trees and across the parking lot, aimed directly at Lou and Milla. Silken cold braced her ankles and coiled up her shins, steadying her against another punch of wind and then—a blanket of starless black sped across the sky, obliterating the midday sun.

The trees stopped thrashing, and the winds died away. As quickly as the storm rose, it vanished, and the darkened world fell still. Milla strained to hear leaves rustling in the wind, the muffled warning cry of a grackle, the scuffle of a boot, or a whispered curse, but there was nothing.

Nothing but the faintest whisper of a name singing through the trees.

"*Luminescence.*"

"Shite." Lou glanced over her shoulder, jerking her chin to someone behind them both. "I didn't get a shield up in time. Hold her."

A thick hand came down on Milla's shoulder, and Lou let go, bracing her feet a shoulder's width apart and facing the trees. Tiny orbs of light danced across her fingertips, the lines in her palm glowing pink. Milla watched, enthralled, as the memory of a chagrined, shirtless Darkly in a tiny hotel room surfaced.

"Fiona," Darkly had explained using his sister's alias, "she's a Light Witch."

Between his confession and everything that followed, Milla had forgotten. It made sense then, just as it made sense now. A Light Witch as a handler for a Dark Witch, as his *sister*. Two sides of the same coin; though where Darkly's Way dealt with Shades and emotion, Lou's dealt with the Soul and the truth of things.

"*Luminescence*," Darkly sang her name from the wood, his voice deep and resonant. Entirely his and something else. Something Other. Milla shivered as his *voice* ribboned into her ears and danced along her bones. "*Let her go, Luminescence.*"

"Ready wards and defenses!" Lou thrust her right arm to the sky, casting hand glowing like an LED. Static crackled and danced up Milla's arms, raising the fine hairs as the shadows tightened their clutch on her legs. "Hex to hinder only. If any one of you hurts him, it'll be the Tribunal you answer to."

The Enforcers around them settled into defensive stances, arms held out in a vast array of wards and ready hexes. Spalování conjured their flames, illuminating the parking lot in a rainbow of varying hues. A trio of obnubilari ran to separate points, spinning their illusions to hide the witches from the world. Further out, the Green Witch threw down a handful of pods to conjure up ivy, kudzu, and thornbush, weaving them together in a formidable hedge.

A bank of fog rose around Milla and Lou, purling across the parking lot to hide the witches at its center. She dragged her gaze away from the treeline to Donmar, circling his free arm in a fluid motion. He twisted his wrist and curled his fingers, pulling condensation from the air.

"How in the nine rings did he find us so quickly?" Lou cursed.

"As you said, zhanym," Donmar replied, "you did not get the shield up in time."

She muttered under her breath, pulling light to hand and swooping her arm in a familiar motion, scooping and pulling at nothing until light coalesced into a gleaming ball. "One of these days, light of my life, you are going to learn what a rhetorical question is."

"Not today, I am afraid," Donmar chuckled, the fog thickened.

"*I'll nae ask again,*" Darkly threatened from the shadows. A warning wind followed, teasing Milla's hair and leaving a heavy silence in its wake.

The ball in Lou's hand brightened and condensed into a blistering white. She muttered a rapid run of Irish, and the ball shot from her palm, bursting over the trees. Static crackled, and the ball stretched and thinned, curving over the parking lot like a film of glitter-imbued plastic wrap.

Black clouds billowed from the trees, pushed by Darkly's winds. Indiscernible shapes writhed and whorled in the roiling fog, and Milla gasped, pressing against Donmar as she realized what she was seeing. It was not wind pushing a deep fog; it was—

"Shades," she exhaled, caught somewhere between fear and wonder.

"I think we may have gone too far this time, Lou," Donmar said in a low voice.

"Not yet," she grunted, layering more of her Way onto the ward, thickening it to an opaque, sparkly mucous membrane reaching for the ground.

The Shades swallowed the Enforcers on the perimeter, dulling their cries. Lou's arm shook. A bead of sweat escaped her hairline, trailing down her jaw. She let out something like a sob, gripping her elbow and widening her stance. Lean fingers trembled, and tendons strained along the back of her casting hand as the shimmering ward dribbled faster and faster down, racing the churning black.

A wisp of shadow slithered for Milla as the barrier connected, and the rest of Darkly's Shades crashed uselessly against the near-invisible wall, sweeping up and over the rounded dome. The membrane bowed beneath his Way. Lou hissed, teeth bared and forehead dotted with sweat, but her ward held.

Thickening roils of black smoke, charcoal fog, and living Shade churned against the barrier, and through the teeming dark, a sliver of deeper black swelled to form shoulders, a trim waist, and the outline of the witch who held shadows in the palm of his hand. Clad in his Enforcer gear, Darkly's black eyes glimmered, his hair glinting gold and scarlet in the multi-hued spalování firelight. Dancing flames cast long shadows beneath high cheekbones, sharpening the already cut line of his jaw. Milla's heart did a little flip at the sight of him in all his wicked glory, stalking through the dark for her.

"This has gone too far, Luminescence."

Donmar made a choked sound. "See?"

"Quiet," Lou barked over her shoulder, eyes on Darkly.

Left hand working tirelessly to dispell Lou's magick, he parted the gloom with his right, fog and shadow swirling into a dense curtain and swallowing the space behind him as he advanced.

"Bloody idiot." Lou shook her head, following the path of the one Shade to breach her barrier. It wound up Milla's leg and looped around her waist, tightening in a possessive, weirdly comforting manner, and a drunken giggle escaped.

"Bloody *idiots*," the Light Witch amended, wrenching her arm down and conjuring another caustic ball of light. "Stand down,

Keir, Tribunal orders." She aimed her hex at Darkly. "You don't want to draw attention to yourself, now do you?"

"*Dinnae care, Luminescence.*"

"Oh, Goddess," Donmar exhaled, shooting a worried look at Lou. Milla cocked her head. Why was he so worried? Darkly *obviously* didn't care if he drew attention to himself. Why else would he wear rip-stop pants a size too small if not to show off his finer assets?

"Horned God-dammit." The light in Lou's hand winked out. She made a series of quick gestures to the Enforcers on the other side of the barrier. Two of them—the other weather witch and a spalování with flame gloving his hands—crept closer to Darkly.

He narrowed his eyes to onyx black slits and pinned his elbows to his waist, turning out his arms, hands palm up. A cruel grin slashed across his face, and he curled his fingers.

The Enforcers jerked ramrod straight, a gasp rattling from both. Their chests swelled toward Darkly as he closed his hands into fists, and then, as quickly as it began, he ended it.

The Dark Witch tugged.

Wisps of shadow drifted toward Darkly, and their bodies relaxed into a slump-shouldered posture, eyes dim and jaws hanging slack.

The witches within Lou's barrier cried out, magick crackling and spitting, ready to be released, and Lou whispered, "No."

One simple word crackling with a desperation not meant to be heard. But Milla heard it. She snapped her attention to Lou, taking in her wide, panicked eyes as the caustic ball in her hand sputtered out. "No, no, no, are you mad?"

"*Beyond.*" Darkly paced the perimeter, black eyes locked on his sister. He traced a finger on her ward in a lazy whorl, testing the intent behind the Way. Shadow trailed his touch, a charcoal effluvium tainting Lou's magick. She hissed through clenched teeth, and if Milla didn't know any better, she'd think the witch was scared of her own brother. *"Give me back Ludmilla, Lou."*

"You're being a fool." She jerked her chin at the Enforcers held in her brother's grip.

"Lou," Donmar warned in a low rumble. She ignored him.

"Look at the mess you've caused, Keir. Look at how far you've stepped. Go home, get yourself under control, or I will do it for you." She clawed her casting hand and leveled it at him. "I say the word, and you are *done*."

Something in the threat registered with Darkly. He winced, a slight twitch of the eye and tic of his mouth, but Milla saw it all the same. It was the same face he made when she laid out her plan to take down the Loa and again when they faced Marie Laveau in her foyer. The same tic Milla had noted when Belie Belcan possessed his body.

It was fear. But of what? He was a Horned God-damned Dark Witch. *The* Dark Witch. Outside of Milla, Darkly was the scariest thing in this parking lot.

She scanned the Enforcers, swaying where they stood and awaiting his command. She read Darkly with his black eyes and rich, resonant *voice*. Saw how Donmar tensed and glanced between Lou and her brother and felt the rise of power electrifying the air as every witch called on their Ways.

What in the nine rings was she missing?

"Go home, Keir," Lou repeated, "I will meet you there, and we will talk."

He stopped pacing, studying Lou for a beat before switching to Milla. A hand pressed against the barrier, long fingers stretched wide. Sinuous arcs of charcoal vapor spiraled out from his palm, poking and prodding the defensive ward. Habit had Milla reading the lines on his palm. Will ruled by logic, level-headed, and, above all else, emotionally driven as only a Dark Witch could be.

"Go home," Lou stated for the third time, a plea from sister to brother. The tips of her fingers began to glow, stealing Darkly's attention away from Milla. "Leave, Keir, before it's too late."

Darkly blinked, green flaring beneath the black of his eyes. He glanced at the enthralled Enforcers as if noticing them for the first time, and an anguished sound tore from his throat. Throwing his arms wide, he released their Shades, and their bodies fell like lifeless sacks of meat. "Horned God, Lou." Darkly scrubbed his hands down his face, backing away from the ward. "I—"

"I know, wee yin," Lou said. "I know you didn't, but you need to leave."

Figures formed in the deep fog, the remaining Enforcers surrounding Darkly, and at that, Milla knew.

"Oh, Goddess." Her hands flew to her mouth as she understood. "They didn't know."

"No one knows," Lou said, her eyes never leaving Darkly.

Goddess, he had stormed the arrest every inch a Dark Witch, seizing Shades and bending the will of two Enforcers to his own, and they *did not know.*

Milla searched the Enforcers trapped within the barrier, reading the fear, hate, and unease on every face. She saw flame rising and poisonous plants seething, and she knew. Horned Goddammit, she knew that Darkly would not stop until he had Milla safely away.

Tears blurred her drunken gaze, a lump rising in her throat as she was weighed down by dread.

A Dark Witch and a Death Witch, Forbidden and Foule.

"Oh, no, Darkly, no."

He heard her. He must have heard her or felt her or assumed what she would realize because he turned that miserable gaze on her. She cowered back, wanting to yell at the fool of a witch, to scream at him to run, get as far away as he possibly could, knowing with one hundred percent certainty that he would not.

"It's not too late, Keir." Lou edged closer to the barrier. "Cyrus can still fix this; it's not too late."

"Milla." Darkly pressed both palms against the barrier, nails digging in as if he would tear through the ward with his bare hands. "Milla, please."

"Let me take her in, let the Tribunal handle this and you'll get everything you wanted."

"Everything he ..." Milla angled her face at Lou.

"*Leannán*," he begged in the *voice*. Smoke drifted over his eyes, and Milla knew even more. "*Believe me, Milla. I didnae mean for this to happen.*"

He said he needed her. Weeks ago, in a hideous flower-and-seashell office, with that stupid beanbag filling the corner, he said he needed her.

"Milla, I'm so sorry."

Every long day he spent in St. Augustine and not with her, hiding in the swamp.

"Please, believe me."

It had been too easy—she'd made sure it was easy. From the moment he knew what she was and asked her, "What do you need?" Milla had fallen for the lie.

From the *instant* she had shown her hand and let down her guard, this witch, this Enforcer, had kept close. Too close, seeing Milla as the Forbidden and Foule thing she was. Witnessing firsthand the desecration and decay she was capable of. Running his E.R.I.E. and taking calls from his sister. Disappearing to

St. Augustine for hours and hours and hours, claiming he was keeping C.R.O.W. distracted and busy and *Goddess* she was a fool.

A tremble built in her arms, and her shoulders, dread gripping her throat tight even as she forced her words free. "What did he want?"

"He wanted out," Lou said. "He struck a deal to earn himself freedom from the job."

Her heart was a bass drum, thudding heavily in her chest. "What—" she croaked, eyes darting from Lou to Darkly and back. "What was the deal?"

"He didn't tell you?" She tutted, shaking her head in mock dismay. "To surrender a Death Witch to C.R.O.W."

"Milla, no." He beat a fist against the barrier. The shimmering film rippled, casting a nauseating light on the witches within. "Dinnae listen to her, *leannán.* I promise I will fix this."

"Fix this," she repeated, twitching a startled gaze from brother to sister as the last pieces of the puzzle clicked into place. Still, she needed to hear it spoken aloud to be absolutely certain she understood because so much of this made no sense.

Stepping out from behind Lou, she stared down the Dark Witch, watching his face closely. "How did you find me?"

Her wards in the swamp were sound. Ezra's wards on the hut were sound. Only a witch who knew it was there could find it. Only a witch with knowledge of the where, the how, and the who could have led these Enforcers here and Darkly …

He opened his mouth, but no excuse or denial came. The shadow around her waist tightened, an answer all its own. Bile pooled on her tongue, her stomach heaving as tiny white lights pulsed at the corners of her vision.

"How do you think?" Lou frowned at the errant Shade. With a slash of her fingernail, she sliced it clean through. Deep, gray smoke curled free, dissipating to nothing. "We got your location from Keir."

Five

THE WORLD BOTTOMED OUT, crumbling beneath Milla's feet and dragging her down with it. She heard Darkly shouting her name. Heard him ranting and cursing in unintelligible Scottish, pleading with Milla to believe him, to trust him. Even now, trying to walk her back from the razor's edge of panic.

She couldn't stand, couldn't breathe. Lou was gripping both of her arms now, struggling to keep Milla from curling into a ball on the ground in her fucking *bathing suit*, which was so beyond unfair at this point.

"Milla, listen to me, Milla. Five things!" And Darkly, Horned God damn him, even now, despite all of his bullshit, was trying to help her. "Five things you can see, *leannán*, three you can touch, Milla. Lou, please! Dinnae do this!"

None of it made sense. None of it and all of it. The world was a sinking black pit, and she drunkenly teetered on the edge, ready to swan dive into that abyss.

Lou hoisted her up, which was ridiculous, considering the Simmons siblings were stupidly tall and Milla was barefoot. She let herself be dragged along, sand and grit shredding her soles, fitting, considering what was happening internally.

She didn't want to believe it; didn't want to think for a fraction of an iota of a second that Darkly had told C.R.O.W. where she was. It was too much, too fast, and she had to pack it down, down, down if she was going to survive what came next.

Lou propped her against a silver Land Rover, shouting in her face as Milla stared across the lot, seeing and not seeing, her reactions slow in a world muted by a funereal clanging in her ears.

Five things you can see, Darkly advised, weeks ago in the foyer of a suburban home. *Five things, Milla.*

One: Darkly pounded against the barrier. Shades clawed, scraped, and heaved as a living mass of midnight, seeking entry through the barrier to reach the Death Witch.

Two: an Enforcer appeared from the dense wall of cloud, hand raised in a hex aimed at Darkly.

Someone shrieked his name, the sound tearing over the soft tissue of her throat like razor blades. At the same time, the Enforcer barked something in a language Milla did not know. Darkly whipped around, deflecting whatever hex had been thrown with a flurry of shadows.

Three: The Enforcer staggered back, clawing at the shadows swallowing his face. He crashed into another Enforcer, who tripped into another, creating a toppling line of woolly-pully-clad dominoes.

Four: Lou's eyes, wide and bright as she screamed in Milla's face. Her perfect features were twisted into a panicked mask, and the explosive slap of her palm against Milla's cheek ripped her from her Waydrunk haze.

"—just like you, Ludmilla," she hissed. "Forbidden and Foule, they cannot see—"

"Keir, no!" Donmar dropped the fog he had raised and grabbed Lou's arm. "Stop him, zhanym."

She snapped her head around, face falling as Darkly tipped headlong into his Way. Churning black clouds frothed around him, his eyes darkening to pitch black as his features harshened. He seemed to swell with the Shades, larger than life, terrifying, and *Other* as he held his arms out wide, fingers working graceful sigils Milla had never seen. All around him, the Enforcers groaned, clutching their chests and staggering to a halt. Those pitch-black eyes found Milla, his face a cold, unfeeling mask, and Lou said, "Please, Ludmilla."

Five: Darkly didn't deserve this.

Milla stared back at the Dark Witch, letting him see her anger and her hurt. Shades pressed in on Lou's barrier, the bubbled dome groaning against the weight of his magick, and Milla knew.

This would never end. If she somehow made it out of this, if she let Darkly plummet into his Way, let him damn himself to save her, this would never end. C.R.O.W. would keep coming, sending their Enforcers to chase them to the furthest reaches of the earth, and Milla was so tired of running. Of hiding. She'd spent so much of the last few years doing just that, and for what? To end up arrested and taking another witch down with her?

Darkly didn't deserve that, despite the lies and the betrayal. He didn't deserve to fall with her when he'd been navigating his own way as a Forbidden and Foule witch. She saw the truth of that as clearly as if Lou had cast it.

Darkly didn't deserve her fate. Liar, he may be, but he was a good witch. And Milla?

Milla was wicked.

"Darkly." She stepped forward, holding that stygian gaze. "No."

He staggered back as though her words had been a direct hit. The Shades receded, sucked into the Dark Witch like the man was a living vacuum, and the black winked out, revealing an over-wide, horrified green gaze.

Late winter sun painted the parking lot beyond the barrier ward in warm yellows, and Milla sank to the ground, one elbow gripped at a painful angle by Lou. On the other side of the shimmering opaque shield, three Enforcers tackled Darkly to the ground. Milla lowered her gaze, unable to watch what happened next or process anything beyond how utterly fucked she was.

She was done fighting, done running, done *hiding* and if this was her end, hadn't she earned it?

"Which coven will try me?"

If the Panhandle Coven still held her in their jurisdiction, she would be tried locally. If they chose to defer to the rulings of the American Oversight Coven, she would be extradited to New Bedford. That might be best, she supposed. The Panhandle wasn't fond of Milla and her history, but the Whaler's Wives were a fair coven, one of the oldest existing stateside. They had seen their fair share of shit.

"No coven," Lou announced, and Milla's heart blackened further. "Not for a witch like you."

Tires rumbled over the worn brickwork of the Old Dixie Highway, bouncing Milla in her seat every time they hit a patch of sand. She sat back and watched the blur of palmetto green and shrub brown rush by, her Waydrunk eyes unable to bring the world into full focus. Only when they passed the historical marker did she realize how weird their route was.

The freeway was a straight shot to Jacksonville, where she would be shoved onto an airplane and shipped off to Český-Krumlov. Even Highway 1 and Highway 17 made more sense than taking the Old Dixie Highway. The road was unkempt, un-trafficked, and paved with thousands of bricks cast from southern red clay. Even Waybound, she could feel the energy radiating from the century-old road, the history of the witches who had tended this specific demesne, casting their Ways and performing rituals to charge the earth.

"Why this way?" Milla asked, nudging the back of Lou's chair with a foot.

She glanced in the rearview mirror and frowned, perfect brows dropping low. "You didn't think I was daft enough to drive the Witch of the Demesne through the heart of her *actual* demesne, did you?" When Milla didn't answer, she glanced in the mirror again, gaze falling to her wrists. "How is the binding?"

"Good." She turned her hands over, scanning the scars on her palms as she reached for her Way. It was there, a faint warmth in her veins like the heat of sore muscles after a workout. "Weird."

"Let us know if it begins to chafe. Keir mentioned you use tea to manage things. We can arrange to have some brought to you if the burn gets too much."

Milla jerked her face up, startled by the plain way Lou stated such intimate knowledge. No one knew the purpose of her tea beyond herself, Diego, and Ezra. No one but Darkly, who apparently couldn't keep his ginger mouth shut. "He told you?"

"There isn't much Keir keeps from me." Lou turned up the volume, blasting twangy country music throughout the Land Rover and ending their conversation. The sun warming the window and the rumble of the brick road sent a weariness crawling through Milla's limbs, dragging her back into the seat and anchoring her eyelids. She dropped her forehead against the glass, her Waydrunk mind lulled into something like sleep, only to half topple out of the car when Lou yanked the door open.

"Only you could fall asleep on the way to your own arrest."

"I thought I was already arrested," Milla mumbled. Sunlight glinted off the windows of a tall building to the east, making her squint. She scanned the parking lot and surrounding structures, recognizing the charming white brick antebellum manse on the corner of West Duval and Hogan in the heart of Jacksonville. The Confluence of the Panhandle Coven was situated as most coven headquarters were: in a bustling downtown sandwiched between government buildings. Surrounded by the US District Court Clerks, City Hall, and a charming downtown greenspace, the coven headquarters was absolutely riddled with wards, sigils, and look-away hexes applied to any scrap of organic matter that could tolerate the magick.

Milla frowned.

"I also thought you'd be taking me to the airport."

"In your bathing suit?" Lou sniffed again. "The Panhandle Coven will process you as a Witch of a Demesne within their jurisdiction. At which point I will file for extradition to Český-Krumlov as is within my rights as a Tribunal-sanctioned Enforcer."

"Lotta paperwork for little ol' me."

"You haven't the slightest." Lou gripped her by the elbow, escorting Milla barefoot across the asphalt.

♣

"How long is this going to take?" Milla asked again. She adjusted her seat, peeling bare legs off of sickly green plastic as she scanned the rows of identical desks and uncomfortable chairs.

Around them, Enforcers worked on laptops and chatted in low voices, going about their day while ignoring Milla to an intentional degree. She had imagined, being a Death Witch and all, that her eventual arrest would come with some fanfare. Perhaps an escort into the coven headquarters under the cover of darkness with a bag over her head. Anything other than this indifference.

Lou kept her eyes on her laptop, punching a few keys before replying, "Have somewhere to be?"

"A cell?" Milla prompted. "A scouring?"

"All in due time."

"What will happen to Darkly?"

That earned a glance. Lou's fingers stilled, and the stoic expression slipped as her lower lip pinched between perfect white teeth. "None of your concern."

"Beg to differ," Milla retorted, "considering he gave you my location."

Lou danced her eyes over Milla's face before returning to plucking out her report. Milla waited, attention drifting from Lou to the witches coming and going from the large room.

A pair of Enforcers escorted a rangy-looking youth through a pair of double doors. Dirt smudged his cheeks and forehead, and the tips of his fingers were stained the deep, rich earthen brown of a Green Witch while red eyes and a hazy expression announced the cause for his arrest. Further down the row of desks, an Ink Witch was being questioned by a female Enforcer, pointing at a stack of photographs and nodding fervently. It was so mundane and *dull* that Milla was tempted to drop her head on the desk and fall asleep.

More than tempted, truthfully. She was *exhausted*. It was almost a relief to be sitting in this room with her magick bound, unable to fight, to run, to hide. Almost a relief to have all choices, all options taken from her hands, leaving Milla free for the first time in years to do *nothing*.

Almost.

She was still arrested. She would be taken before the Tribunal in Český-Krumlov and found guilty of being a Death Witch, likely to be cleaved—

Lou's phone chirped—a sharp, staccato alarm that had the Light Witch jerking her attention away from the laptop to read the screen. It chirped again, and a line formed between her brows. Further down the row of desks, another phone pinged an alarm.

And another and another. The room filled with a discordant medley of chirps, whistles, and rings. Enforcers pulled their phones free from pockets and pouches, all activity stopping as they read an alert that had the entirety of the Panhandle Coven screeching to a silent, bewildered halt.

"Whatever that is"—Milla raised her hands in mock surrender—"at least you know it isn't me."

Lou ignored her, grabbing her phone and jumping to her feet. The silence in the room burst at the sudden movement, exploding into a flurry of activity. Magick crackled as fingers worked in rapid sigils, forming wards of protection and defense. Sparks danced from the hands of svítilna lamplighters, technomantics shoved cylinders of conductive metal into their pockets, and hippocromantics rushed from desk to desk, handing out tubes and flasks of vinefica made potions, while the chatter rose to an alarmed roar.

"Another one?"

"Who keeps summoning these things?"

"Wait, what's going on?" Milla sat up, calling after Lou as she stalked down the row of desks. She stopped behind a technomantic hunched in front of a computer, her eyes narrowed behind thick-lensed glasses. Lou gripped the back of her chair, bending low to read the screen. "Where is it?"

"Calibrating." The witch's fingers flew over the keys. "Just give me one second—"

"We need a heading."

"I know."

"Now, Agent," Lou barked. "Give us a heading, we can redirect en route."

"I just … I need … it's not—"

Milla scooted to the edge of her seat. "What in the nine rings is happening?"

"*Agent.*" Lou's eyes began to glow with a foglamp brightness as the witch tapped into her Way. "What are we looking at?"

"A Dullahan." The technomantic slammed the device closed and whisked it away, twisting around Lou as she rose and shouted directions at the Enforcers. "Flagler Estates. All teams south on I-95, head east on county road two-oh-four."

"Whose demesne is that?" Another witch asked.

"St. Augustine," the technomantic answered. "Someone inform the Witch of the Demesne, there's an old cemetery—"

"Pellicer Creek." Milla jumped up, immediately sandwiched between two overly large witches. "It's me! I'm the Witch of the Demesne; the cemetery is Pellicer Creek."

"Sit down." A meaty hand shoved her into the chair. "The steward will take care of it."

"The what? No. It's my *demesne*," she argued, scanning the room and seeking out Lou. "You have to let me help; that's my demesne."

"Not a chance." Lou scanned the tablet in her hand, nodding as she handed it off to a witch. "C.R.O.W. already has a steward in place; he'll handle it."

"Who—what is a steward?" Milla shrieked, wincing at her shrill panic. But seriously, it was her demesne, her home, her responsibility. Just because she was arrested didn't mean they could cut her off from doing her job. She had done so much, given so much of herself. They could not just hand her demesne over to a steward. "St. Augustine is mine. Whatever a Dullahan is, Lou, you have to let me help."

"I don't have to let you do anything," the witch replied. "You are a witch guilty of the Forbidden and Foule. What guarantee do we have that this isn't part of some ploy?"

"It's not, I promise, it's not." She twisted in her seat, clocking the Enforcers gearing up to fight whatever a Dullahan was. "Let me help, Lou. It's my demesne; I've fed it with my Way, please!" Another hand came down on her shoulder, leather-soft fingers digging into her skin. She looked down at the gloved hand, following the long line of an arm up to the face of an all-too-familiar witch. "You."

Agent Sterne, the witch from the beach, glared down at her, all high cheekbones and a cold, blue-eyed stare. He'd changed out of the swim trunks she had last seen him in, donning C.R.O.W.

issued Enforcer blacks fitted to his frame. The fabric clung to his torso and arms, cutting his musculature into sharp relief and making him seem three times larger than he was. He worked his jaw, his frown deepening. "Come."

And for the first time, Milla was afraid.

Six

CHRONOMANTIC Witches with the ability to manipulate time; House of Aragon

THE MARBLE HALL STRETCHED before them, impossibly long and vanishing to a dark point meters or miles away. Milla squinted and rubbed an eye with her knuckle, hissing as the abraded skin sizzled in pain.

"I can request a lotion," Agent Sterne said. Milla glanced at him, dropping her eyes quickly to the floor. It was bad enough that he'd chased her through the woods and tried to set her on fire, but did he have to be her appointed guard?

"No, thanks." She dropped her arm, skin tight and tender from the scouring she had undergone, and stepped into the hallway.

Iridescent specks in the checkered flooring winked and strobed beneath humming fluorescent lights, and odd, angular shadows peeled from the puce-green doors dotting the walls. Sinuous gray veins crawled in the marble, up the walls, and across the ceiling, pulsing in the flickering light and turning Milla's already upset stomach.

She closed her eyes, took a long, strained breath, and exhaled through her teeth. The scouring left her shaky and disoriented—salt had that effect on a witch—and whatever fight she still had was scrubbed away in a sterile room. Agent Sterne pressed his hand between her shoulder blades, half steadying Milla and half urging her onward.

One shaking step, two, keeping her head down and counting. Ten, twelve, fifteen.

Agent Sterne grabbed her shoulder, stopping Milla inches away from running into a nondescript iron door. She jerked her head up and around, jaw falling open at the dingy hallway. Brown carpet, brown walls, flickering fluorescents. Three doors lining the walls on either side.

"What?" she croaked.

"Obfuscari illusion," he said.

"I didn't notice any illusion."

"You would not." He flicked two fingers at her wrists. "You are Waybound."

A chill swept down Milla's spine at how defenseless and trapped she was. Arrested for Actes Forbidden and Foule, she had no magick to call on. She couldn't even sense an illusion that should have been as obvious as a neon sign at midnight.

"They increase in strength the further we go," he added.

Milla didn't say anything. What was there to say? She was in the heart of the Panhandle Coven being escorted to Horned God knew where. Why even bother explaining the layers of defenses C.R.O.W. used when she would never leave this place? No coven meant no trial, which meant Milla was going to be tucked away and forgotten—or cleaved.

The iron door opened with a groan and he led her down a winding stair, through another pulsing, stretching hall, and down again. Milla lost count of the floors and hallways. Her head spun from the winding descent, and a cold sweat broke out over her skin, made sticky by the muffled heat deep in her arms and chest.

Even Agent Sterne was affected by the hexes and illusions. He grunted in the third hallway, and muttered a curse under his breath in one of the stairwells, finally hissing out a sigh as they entered a hallway identical to the illusion above, save for the lights.

No fluorescents flickered or hummed in this hallway. Instead, it was illuminated by softly glowing orbs floating in glass sconces; each hung on the wall beside a door with a narrow window set near the top.

Milla trailed one of the orbs with her eyes as they passed, recognizing the svítilna cast light. Like spalování flame witches, svítilna could conjure energy from nothing, but where a flame witch like her Enforcer dealt in combustion, a svítilna dealt in light across the spectrum. Fun for birthday parties and holidays, but as far as C.R.O.W. was concerned, they were as useful as a stitch witch in a nudist colony.

As in the hallways, iridescent specks on the walls shimmered in the magick light, begging Milla to touch them.

So she did, sweeping her fingers over the marble. They came away wet, and she had just processed that the walls were coated with a thin sheen of water when the singe of a saltburn had her shaking her hand and cursing.

"Estuary salts?" she asked, though she knew the answer: salt water disrupts magick, and marble deflects it.

"We are deep beneath the St. John's River." He nodded. "Preventative measures, should any witch feel like taking a long walk through enchanted hallways."

"Noted." Milla dried her fingers on her thigh. Maybe she hated herself or felt like spitting in the face of fate because she said, "Building a basement this deep in Jacksonville feels a bit excessive."

"The cells at Český-Krumlov are carved into an ancient salt mine," he replied. "Would that suit you?"

"I'm just saying"—she shrugged—"there's a witch queen in New Orleans with a basement like this."

"Then perhaps you would prefer her hospitality."

He cocked his head, and Milla could have sworn she saw a tiny smile flicker at the corner of his mouth, there and gone again. Or maybe it was a trick of the low light because his face was a stern, cold mask as he pressed his palm beside the darkened window near the top of the door. Metal churned and ground, heavy clanking rumbled within the marble, and the door swung open, revealing a tiny cell half-lit by the svítilna-cast light.

An iron bed frame with a pillow and a sagging mattress was shoved against the far wall, and a sink, a warped, beat metal mirror, and a toilet hugged the corner to the left of the door. She should probably be grateful there was a toilet. It was better than having a bucket, and considering the spotty history between witches and buckets, a crapper on full display was an infinitely better option.

"In here."

With another gentle press between her shoulders, Milla stepped in, ignoring the shadowed half of the cell to turn and glimpse Agent Sterne's frown as he pushed the door closed. The river of light that had bled in from the hallway shrank to a slanted rectangle on the floor, dropping the cell into darkness as a loud metallic clang echoed throughout her cell.

It felt final. Damning.

A faint crackle of magick skittered around the walls, and she shivered as the hairs along the back of her neck rose. She approached the door, and the stern-faced witch watching her through the window.

"So what happens next?"

He did not respond, not that she expected him to. Agent Sterne was her personal guard. Befriending Milla was obviously not part of the job description. Still, a witch had to *try*.

"Fine, then at least tell me what's happening in my demesne."

He did not move, did not blink. Only stared back at Milla with blue eyes made bright by the burn of his Way. She slammed her fist against the glass, seeking a reaction, but he remained unnaturally still. Not a twitch, not a flutter of muscle in his clenched jaw. Even the spalování flame licking his eyes remained still.

The crackle of magick in her cell rose, the only warning before a sickening swoop in her belly had Milla staggering back from the door. She bent forward, arms wrapped around her waist as she hissed through her teeth to stem the sudden rise of nausea. Another static wave rolled over her back and shoulders, and Milla jerked her face up, meeting Agent Sterne's unseeing blue eyes. A scream swelled in her throat, surging up from the deepest parts of her only to be caught in the static hold.

"No," she strangled out, the rest of her protest frozen as a thought. *No, no, no, not again.*

From the darkest corner of her cell came a whisper of fabric and the release of a quiet sigh. "Did you forget about me, magissa?"

Another static wave rushed from the shadows, enveloping Milla and gripping her entirely. As in the woods at the state park, she was held, suffocating beneath the weight of a magick she couldn't dispell. Bent at the waist, hands gripping her knees, and her panicked gaze stuck on Agent Sterne looming in the window. The furthest edges of her vision went hazy, blurring as the chronomantic stepped out of the shadows. His vague shape was briefly visible before the empty air warbled and blurred, erasing the witch from view.

Gone and not gone. Lurking in the periphery and standing directly beside her. Goosebumps rose, Milla's body reacting to his nearness. Every nerve screamed in anticipation of his touch, and when he spoke again, his breath puffed against her ear.

"I did not forget about you."

Seven

MARBLE A natural magickal deflector, marble is commonly used in barrier wards, shields, and the construction of C.R.O.W. occupied buildings.

*W*AKE UP, *M*ILLAPET.

There is a specific torture to the not knowing. To the wondering and the waiting and the anticipating. A torture in being held on a precipice, dangling on the edge of release or pain or a fall and never knowing when, or if, the consequences of whatever choice had led to that moment of *waiting* would come to pass.

He held her there. For minutes. Hours. Days. Milla had no way of knowing, no way of accounting for the time she lost when he was in her cell and that was the true terror because he wasn't always there.

She never saw him enter, never saw him leave, so she watched Agent Sterne through the window in her door, attempting to pinpoint the exact moment the chronomantic's Way gripped him, pinning his bright blue gaze on Milla, but she never could. So she frantically searched her cell, sweeping her hands over the walls and launching herself at the darkest corners. Her fingers curled around nothing, her nails scratched at the empty air.

This was a puzzle—a test—one she ought to be able to solve. Morgen had pitted her against chronomantics time and time again, teaching Milla how to recognize the crackle of their magick and the faint blur of their hexes.

"Your Ways are not dissimilar," she had lectured. "You advance rot; a chronomantic advances time. You both hold the key to eternity in your hands."

"Then why are they Fine and Faire, and I'm not?" she had asked. Morgen shrugged, one shoulder rising and falling in apathy. "It's not fair."

"No, it is not," Morgen stated. And then she gestured to the chronomantic on the field.

Milla had evaded their hex and the next, seizing the magick and twisting it into something of her own.

But now, she had no magick. She was a Waybound witch, and there was a chronomantic in her cell, so she raged and shrieked, tearing over the marble walls and tossing her bed until he arrived, entering without a word and going to work.

You'll drive yourself crazy like this Milla. Wake. Up.

He never touched her, never stepped into her line of sight, but he was *there*. If she could only turn her head and catch the brush of his fingers in her hair, but no—he held her still and kept his distance. Torturing Milla without touch, whispering in a voice almost too low to hear, and leaving her a trembling mess of nerves dragged to the very limits of her endurance only to release his Way and send her sprawling over the salt and marble floor.

And when she looked up, Agent Sterne was at the door.

You're doing it again.

Her gaze slid away from the warped reflection in the mirror to study the empty space over her shoulder.

It's going to scar, Millapet.

She glanced at the scar running from wrist to elbow on her right arm, now raw and red from the scrape of jagged nails over sensitive skin.

"It already has."

More.

She spun away from her reflection, barely visible in the low light. For once, Agent Sterne wasn't at his post, and the light filtering through the window was a warm orange-yellow. "I told you to stop calling me that."

Calling you what, Millapet?

"Yes." She whirled and addressed the nothing. "Stop."

No, I don't think I will.

The door clanked. Iron gears groaned as they churned through the fine salt dust fitted into the grooves and tumblers. Milla whipped around, muscles bunching, and pressed her back against the wall, scanning the cell for any shift in the air or hint of static.

He isn't here, Millapet.

"Shut up." She settled her face into a carefully blank expression as Agent Sterne dragged the door open. Light filled the cell and he peered in, frowning when he saw her pressed against the wall. With a shake of his head, he disappeared from view. Milla held her breath. If *he* were going to appear, it would be now, when her guard was distracted and the door left open.

Instead, Agent Sterne returned with a tray in his hands. "Special delivery."

Steam rose from a large bowl, carrying the scent to Milla's nose. Her stomach rumbled, saliva pooling on her tongue. Ginger and garlic, a hint of anise—*Oh, Goddess, is that pho?*

He set the tray down on the edge of her bed and backed away, bright eyes on Milla the entire time. The door groaned shut, and she darted over, sweeping the tray off the mattress and settling on the floor with it in her lap. It *was* pho. Mushrooms and fat squares of tofu were nestled among the noodles in a piping hot, fatty broth, and a pile of sprouts, onion, jalapenos, and herbs filled a plate beside the bowl. She could have cried.

Instead, she jabbed the plastic spork at the tofu and mushrooms, catching noodles and raising the delicious mess to her mouth.

"Tray," Agent Sterne stated. Milla froze, spork hovering an inch from her mouth. He stood just inside the door, hand outstretched.

"You just delivered this." She lowered the spork. "I have fifteen minutes."

"Correct." He nodded, gesturing for the tray. "You had fifteen minutes to eat. Whether or not you choose to do so is up to you."

"But I haven't—"

Flame licked his eyes in warning, and the air tingled. She shoved the sporkful into her mouth, flavor bursting on her tongue and gone all too quickly. She dropped the utensil into the bowl, splashing tepid broth on her knee. It crawled rapidly across the fabric, drowning it in cold.

"Now, Probuditna," Agent Sterne barked.

She grabbed the tray and burst to her feet, rushing across the room on jittery legs and thrusting it into his hands. More broth spilled over the bowl's rim, and Agent Sterne whisked away, the door shutting in a blink.

It was all so fast—too fast. Why was everything so fast? And the broth—it had been hot, steam rising and filling the cell with its delicious scent, but then it was cold, and that made no sense unless …

Milla straightened, holding her body tight. Still. The jitteriness in her legs had not subsided, and only now did she notice the rapid beat of her heart. The short, staccato breaths.

She inched toward a corner of the room, or at least, she thought she did, but time was not moving the way it should and she slammed into the salt and marble, biting her tongue to keep from crying out. Faint orange light glowed through the window, lighting a singular patch in the center of her cell.

He could be anywhere, and she'd never see him. She would never know for certain if he was actually there until it was too late.

But didn't she already know?

You look as though you've seen a ghost.

The voice filled Milla's head, bouncing off the curves of her skull and forcing her down into a crouch. She closed her eyes and covered her face in her hands.

"You're not a ghost," she whispered, her voice weak and thin. "You're Gone."

Do you hear that?

Milla swung her legs off the mattress and cocked her head, straining to hear what he had. A footstep?

Goddess, she was exhausted. She was probably hearing things, but if he heard it too, then it had to be real.

Didn't it?

There, hear it?

And she did—the faint tock of a bootheel against marble. And another, drawing closer. Her fingers prickled, pins and needles climbing into her palms. She would only have one shot at this. Goddess knew he'd never let her try a second time. Gears groaned in the door, and she tensed her muscles, ignoring the spread of pins and needles to her toes. Tumblers clicked and whirred, the door cracked open, and Milla launched from the mattress, sprinting across the cell.

The tingling in her fingers and toes shot up her limbs. The walls stretched around her as the door grew further away without moving at all. Her arms slowed and stilled, and glue encased her legs.

Milla pressed against the hex, muscles screaming as she fought against the witch she could not see. She was faster than this, better than this. Even tired and hungry and half out of her mind, Milla was better than this. She was trained by the Morgenhexe. She had been broken down piece-by-piece and rebuilt by Ezra, made into the witch she was, and *she could do this*.

Every muscle in her body snapped, the tingling fell from her arms and legs, and the walls rushed forward. Milla crashed into Agent Sterne. He spun her around, one hand gripping her skull, turning her head, and pressing her face into the salt on the walls. The burn was immediate, crawling into her jaw and up to her temple. She whimpered and wriggled against him, but Agent Sterne was stronger. Bigger.

"*Verdammt noch mal,*" he cursed under his breath. *For fuck's sake.* She knew that one. Horned God knew Morgen had uttered it enough. With a booted foot, he kicked out her heels, forcing Milla flush against the wall.

"This is your position," Agent Sterne snarled. He pressed hard against her head and then released, heels scuffling over the floor as he backed away, breathing heavily. He cursed again, pacing around the cell.

From the corner of her eye, Milla watched him sweep both hands through his hair, dropping his head back and staring at the ceiling as he panted. His eyes closed, his shoulders went tight, and he let out a long, slow breath. The space over his shoulder shimmered like a heat snake on a summer horizon. Half a heartbeat later the tingling resumed in her fingers and toes, crawling into her belly and holding Milla in place, one eye on Agent Sterne and the witch hiding behind what faint light eked in from the hallway.

Heels clacked against marble, echoing sharply down the hall and growing louder as they approached. Not boots. Heels.

A visitor?

Milla shambled to the wall, biting her lips as she placed her palms against crusted salt. Tiny grains crunched under her scars, driving into the narrow channels of her skin. The tingling numbed most of the saltburn. That, or she had grown so used to the sizzle that it didn't bother her as much anymore.

Neither prospect was comforting, but taking her position was far better than the alternative.

The gears in the door commenced their groan and churn. She closed her eyes, no longer caring if the air blurred or time stopped. What did it matter? Time did not exist in her cell. It was only Milla, four walls, and the ghosts she could not see.

Is my company that bad?

"More like uninvited."

Beg to differ.

"Hello, Ludmilla." Lou's lilting accent rose above the clack of heels on marble. She stepped close enough that Milla could smell her perfume, a faint vanilla spice that made her think of cookies, blondies, pie, and cozy blankets. It was terrible. "I see they've managed to break you."

"I would like to speak with an advoccultant."

"They tell me you aren't eating." Lou leaned closer, bringing her face in view. "They say you've been rejecting meals, eating only the barest portions required to stay alive."

"I'm eating what they give me the time to eat." Her stomach growled, and Lou arched an eyebrow. "I would like to speak with an advoccultant," Milla repeated.

Lou moved out of sight. A moment later, the bedframe creaked under her weight.

"Non-compliance will lead to force on our end."

Milla fisted her hands against the wall, shoulders bunching tight. She wanted to argue, to yell that she wanted to eat, that she was starving and exhausted, and if they only gave her enough time to eat the meals they brought, and to sleep, then maybe these threats would not be necessary.

But she knew better. She was the foster daughter of the Morgenhexe, after all.

"We have a highly trained corpomantic on staff—"

"I would like to speak to an advoccultant."

Lou's teeth clacked together. Milla could practically feel her glare. "You will have one."

"When."

"Soon," Lou snipped out. "The Coven Aural Review Board has finished reviewing the evidence and alerted your advoccultant that the time has come to make arrangements."

"I thought wasn't getting a trial."

"Whatever gave you that idea?" The *scritch scritch scritch* of Lou's nails as she picked the mattress made Milla's eye twitch. She'd gotten used to the silence in her cell, relishing in the emptiness between visits from her tormentor. "No one lies to an agent of C.R.O.W., Ludmilla."

Milla bit her lips.

"Not even Keir." Lou waited for a reaction and Milla continued failing to meet her expectations. "I thought it would interest you to know that he is on judiciary probation until a full and exhaustive investigation has been conducted."

"Good."

Lou sighed, and the bedframe creaked. Her heels clacked across the floor, and her vanilla cookie perfume tickled Milla's nose. "You'll need to start working with us. After that performance at your arrest, I hoped you would."

Milla finally dragged her gaze away from the wall to look Lou in the eye. Her white blonde hair was impeccable as always and worn in a low bun, the severity of the hairstyle making her blue-green eyes larger and more intense. Her lips were a perfectly blushed pink, and her cheeks glowed beneath the skilled application of bronzer and from the force of her Way.

"My performance?"

"You told Keir to stand down." Her lips pursed, the corners turning down into a slight frown. "Just as I asked."

In that frown, Milla noted the first of many resemblances between the Simmons Siblings. Darkly frowned in the same way, as though it slipped free from behind a carefully curated mask.

And their mouths formed words in a similar manner, though Lou held on to an Irish accent, whereas Darkly spoke with a whiskey-thick brogue that rolled over Milla's bones.

"I didn't do it for you," she said. "I did it because, despite what *he* did, he doesn't deserve to be put in a cell."

Lou studied Milla, scanning her cheeks and lingering on her eyes before rising to her bony wrists and, finally, her left hand flat against the wall.

"That's healed nicely," Lou changed the subject. Milla turned her hand over, showing Lou the riddle of scars on her palm. The Light Witch studied the mess for a moment and then chuckled. Another bit of family resemblance. The dry chuckle that Milla loved in Darkly's throat and hated in his sister's. "I thought he might have been exaggerating, but Horned God, it is really difficult to get a straight answer out of you."

When Milla kept silent, Lou huffed.

"All of this can go away, Milla." She snapped her fingers, and a shimmer of light sparkled from the tips. "Quick as a flash, but only if you agree. Don't you want to leave this cell? Return to St. Augustine and Keir?"

Goddess, why did she keep bringing up Darkly? The witch had lied to her and given C.R.O.W. her location. He'd strung Milla along only to throw her under the witch-filled bus. Who in their right mind would think Milla wanted to return to *that*?

You do have a history.

She bit her lips to keep from responding, and Lou stepped closer. The sickly sweet scent of her perfume turned Milla's stomach.

"Work with us," she said.

"No."

"Why ever not?"

"I'm a loner, Dottie." Milla leveled a tired gaze at the Light Witch. "A rebel."

"Come again?"

She clapped her hands four times, the sharp sound bouncing off the walls. "Deep in the heart of Texas!"

She paced her cell after Lou left, and when exhaustion and hunger won out, she lay back on her bed. Metal springs prodded into her spine and shoulder, making it impossible to find a comfortable position, which meant sleep was difficult to find.

Which was good because no matter how hard she tried, she could not get Darkly out of her head. She had avoided thinking about him for so long, and all it took was a little prodding from Lou to haul the witch back to the forefront of her mind. His sharp smile and the gold flecks deep in his eyes. His patience in helping Milla work through her Way, day after day, never once showing if he was frustrated with her inability to control her magick. His refusal to stop touching her, even when she pointed out how it was hurting him.

How he left her in the swamp only to return and lie to her face, pretending everything was fine when it wasn't.

She trailed her eyes along salt veins in the marble ceiling, idly scratching her scars as if they were the Darkly-shaped itch she couldn't get rid of.

Stop that, Millapet.

"How long?"

Pardon?

"How long have I been down here?"

The silence in her head stretched long enough that she turned her head to scan the darkened cell, looking for the witch she couldn't see.

You don't know?

Eight

OBFUSCARI A designation of mind witch with an affinity
for visual illusion; House of Aragon

"TOUCH ME." MILLA STRETCHED out her arm, reaching for the witch at the edge of the bed. "Please."

"I am touching you." A shade wisped free from Darkly, winding around her wrist and swirling up her arm. She shivered at the silken cold, her skin burning beneath his gaze. Gembright eyes flitted up from her chest and her fingers, and he flashed a quick smile. More Shades stretched across the bed, up her calves, cradling Milla's thighs. His gaze darkened, and one Shade wafted up her exposed front, circling a breast and pooling in the hollow of her collarbone before cradling her cheek.

She flinched.

It was an instinct, a reflex to having her fevered flesh caressed by something cold—something intangible. The tiniest flinch, but he saw it. The Shade wafted away, and Darkly eased off the bed, his jaw clenched and hurt, dragging his mouth into a frown. The Shades retreated, disappearing into him and darkening his eyes further.

"I'm sorry." Milla sat up, adjusting her bra and covering her breasts before reaching again for Darkly.

"Dinnae." He leaned away and ran a hand through his hair. Loose strands fell over his brow and he shook his head, looking at Milla with an expression that was as hungry as it was sad. "It will get better."

"When?" She hopped off the bed and grabbed her shirt from the floor, yanking it over her head. "It's been three days."

He raised his index finger, cheek dimpling with a slick smile. "It's *only* been three days."

Milla crossed her arms over her chest and glared at him. "Don't be cute right now."

Darkly puffed out his chest, half-heartedly preening and deflating when Milla's glare failed to soften. He cleared his throat and rubbed his hand over his heart. "I ken this is hard for you—"

"How could you possibly 'ken'?"

"Because I *know* what was in that shite tea, Milla, and why you drank it. You were poisoning yourself, and now you can barely tolerate your Way. It's gonnae take time."

"I don't have time," she spat. "I have a demesne to run."

"A demesne that is overrun with Enforcers," he countered. "You need to be here, where it's safe."

"I need to be cleaning up my mess."

"I'm happy to—"

"It's *my* demesne, Darkly. It's my *job*. I can't lose it again, not after I—" A lump in her throat choked off the rest of the sentence. Her fingers trembled, and the next breath she took was thin and weak. "After she—"

"I ken." He sat on the edge of the bed, hands dangling from his knees. Silence bled from the Dark Witch, drowning the room as deeply as his Shades.

Wake up, Milla.

It stretched and stretched, longer than Milla remembered it lasting, until every thread connecting her to Darkly went taut and snapped, save for one.

A jarring, tinny, electric song ripped through the hut. Milla whirled around as Darkly's phone began buzzing along the makeshift table, the name Luminescence flashing across the screen.

"Bollocks timing," he grumbled, grabbing Milla's shoulder with a cool, slick hand and giving a little shake as he passed by. She tensed at the touch, staring at her shoulder. "Aye?"

She did not remember that happening, nor did she remember him touching her or when his hands had ever had that texture—like worn, supple leather.

Wake up.

"Another one?" He ran a hand over his face and glanced at Milla. "Aye, an hour." Lou's voice rose, and he winced. "I'm tired, Lou, and it's nae as if the body is going anywhere, just—aye, yes. I understand, but—" His brows pinched, and Darkly turned his back on Milla, dropping his voice to just above a whisper. "Gies an hour, please? I cannae risk getting lost." A long beat passed where neither Simmons sibling spoke. Lou's voice hummed over the line, and Darkly sighed. "See you soon."

He ended the call and dropped his arm, phone clutched tight. Veins popped along the back of his hand. Milla followed the taut line of his arm to his shoulders, and his neck, spotting the muscle working in his jaw. "I need tae—"

Horned God, Probuditna, wake up.

"Just go." She sat on the edge of the bed, counting specks in the worn blanket as he pulled on his Enforcer blacks, hesitating in front of Milla on his way out the door. When she didn't look up, he sighed and left.

The door clacked against the crooked wooden frame, and only then did she lie down, jolting upright with a startled gasp. Heat flared down her arms, butting against her wrists and curling over on itself. Every inch of her skin crawled as tingling receded from the tips of her fingers and toes. She sucked in a harsh breath through her mouth and nose, choking on the acrid stench of harsh vanilla and burnt sugar, sweet rot, and a clean, almost astringent aether. The stink of it all churning her stomach. She clamped a hand over her mouth to keep from heaving, squinting in the dark until her eyes adjusted to the dim light bleeding in through the open door; only then did she notice the darkened silhouette of Agent Sterne.

"You are awake."

She nodded, afraid that if she spoke, she'd vomit on her bed. Not that it would be a tragedy.

"Good." He gave a terse dip of his chin, his accent cutting the word off with a crisp snap. "You have a visitor. Come."

He led her through a twisting warren of tunnels burrowed deep within what Milla thought might be a mountain, which made no damn sense. On the walk to the cells, the hallways were long and nauseating, their walls pulsing under layers of illusions and terrible mid-century fluorescent lighting.

Hadn't they?

Water dribbled down coarse white stone walls hewn to follow the earth's curve. More glass orbs filled with conjured light hung high on the dry side of the passageways, brighter than the lamps outside her cell. She squinted and kept her eyes lowered, hyper-aware of the space she occupied.

How long had she been in that cell?

Long enough to become so used to her own four walls that the stretch of the hallway felt too big and foreign. This space was too open, there was too much light, and *he* could be anywhere. She clenched her fists against the urge to cling to Agent Sterne and the rising desire to turn back and run to her cell, focusing instead on the pain of nails digging into her palms.

The floor shifted, rising higher. Her thighs began to burn, and her breathing grew raspy and uneven from the climb, but she pressed on, only stopping when they passed a narrow window and she caught sight of the landscape beyond her prison.

"No." Milla rushed the wall, pressing her cheeks against the stone on either side of the window. The sear of salt was immediate, but every speck of her awareness in her body was on the view: a narrow valley, the bend of a river fat with winter run-off, and the red-tiled rooftops of a quaint, medieval town. "No, nonono."

She reeled away from the window and saw the hallway with clear eyes for the first time. Tunnels burrowed in the heart of a mountain, glass orbs filled with conjured light, and the dribbles of water—a measure taken to disrupt the Ways of the witches housed in the salt and marble cells of Český-Krumlov.

"Keep moving, Ludmilla." Agent Sterne moved to grab her arm, and Milla twitched away from his touch. Her panic was an animal, thrashing madly in her chest and strangling the air in her lungs.

This was impossible. She was in Florida, in the holding cells beneath Jacksonville, not in the salt and marble. Not in Český-Krumlov. Not … home.

"I can't be here," she whispered, flattening her back against the rough-hewn stone and shaking her head. "This can't be happening."

"They get stronger the deeper we go," Agent Sterne replied. He gripped her wrist, peeling Milla from the wall and dragging her through another bend in the hall. She caught glimpses of Český-Krumlov through more narrow windows. Light glinted off the surface of the Vltava. A flock of birds burst from the dark green spire of St. Vitus, and a cluster of students ran across the footbridge into the old town.

She faltered at the fourth window, tracking the birds as they flocked around the spire, resettling along the rooftop and steep eaves of the church. Agent Sterne released her wrist, stepping away. When Milla looked at him, he wore the same stern expression as always, but he tipped his head toward the window behind them. "Do you see?"

She backed up a step. Another. And when he did not move, she retreated to the window, staring at the same scene.

The birds burst from the spire in a thick, undulating cloud of feathers. The students ran across the bridge, and a bright flash glinted off the river's surface. Milla squinted and stepped closer, reading the scene as Ezra had taught her. She searched for consistent inconsistencies and found them in the students huddled together at the end of the bridge when they should have been disappearing into the warren of cobbled streets that made up her hometown.

"It's an illusion."

Agent Sterne nodded. "Obfuscari."

"No." She moved to the next window and the scene reset. The children rushed across the bridge, and she forced herself not to squint at the bright flash of light off the river. "Those illusions are in the mind. This is obnubilari."

"Are you so sure?"

"You see it too, don't you?" She looked at him then, noting the intensity of his gaze, searing through Milla as if looking for something. He had to know she'd been trained by the Morgenhexe, a master illusionist, and mentored by Ezra, C.R.O.W.'s darling obnubilari, before Milla left him in the dark. Agent Sterne nodded. "Then yeah, I'd say I'm pretty positive on that point."

The deep cut lines at the corners of his mouth softened, and blue flame danced across his fingertips. He snapped, and the illusion in the window vanished, revealing blank marble. Milla's mouth fell open, shock and awe competing for space, and before she could form a word, he tipped his head down the hallway. "Come along."

Approaching a heavy oak and iron door, he pressed his hand against the wood and muttered under his breath.

Pressure built in her skull, forcing Milla to work her jaw as if they had gained altitude. A heavy bolt thudded into place, and the door swung open. Her guard guided her through, and bubbles popped behind her eardrums, the torpid, drunken feeling from the cells vanishing.

Wards, she realized with a start, stumbling at the giddy, unbearable lightness. Crossing into a warded space normally felt like walking through a wall of static but, Waybound as she was, this felt like layers of sodden cloth being ripped away from her body.

"Where are we going?"

Agent Sterne slowed his pace from a march to a stroll. "You have a visitor."

"I'm allowed visitation?"

"You are imprisoned, Ludmilla, not interred."

She cast a leery eye at the hewn marble walls and ceiling, then lifted her eyebrows. "Are you sure about that?"

In lieu of an answer, she received a quiet snort. He turned them once again, revealing a brightly lit hallway. The floor became checkered tile, the Way-infused orbs switched to LED track lighting, and through the open door at the end of the hallway, sitting in a metal folding chair with her fingers laced on a metal table, was the Nachthexe.

Nine

ADVOCCULTANT

Natje Tage.

The Nachthexe.

She was the spitting image of her twin sister Morgen, minus the perfectly coiffed blonde hair. Natje wore hers in a blunt brunette bob that skimmed her jaw with bangs running in a straight line just above her eyebrows. Where the Morgen was daylight and warmth strapped beneath lace collars and pressed slacks, Natje was midnight and cool, gripped in black leggings and boots.

Milla had idolized Natje from the moment she laid eyes on her. From the calf-height boots to the sway of her hips and arrogant hold of her shoulders, Natje was every inch the witch Milla wished she was. Though her face was the wrong shape to wear a bob with such glamorous austerity, Milla's bangs were proof enough of her adoration.

"Of course, my hourly rate is non-negotiable." Natje rose from her chair and swept toward Milla, bringing a fresh midnight breeze. "A very interested third party handled the retainer, so we

will not need to discuss that at any great length." She nodded
to Agent Sterne, ignoring how her client gawked at her like a
codfish. "That will be all, Agent, and, for Horned God's sake,
Sterne, try to smile once in a while."

Impossibly, the creases at the corner of his mouth deepened,
and he stepped through the open door, leaving Milla with a living
legend.

At least, a legend in her mind.

"Did Morgen send you?"

"No." Natje slid into her seat, gesturing to the empty chair on
Milla's side of the table, and set a large, black, patent leather tote
beside her. She withdrew a folio, tap-tap-tapping deep magenta
fingernails on the edge.

Milla eased into her chair, sat on her hands, and eyed the folio.
"So what do we do?"

"*We* do nothing, girl. Horned God, you have done enough on
your own. Walking them back from a cleaving will be the battle
of a lifetime. I cannot wait to get started."

"A cleaving?" Milla slammed back in her seat, stunned. "They
haven't cleaved anyone since McCarthyism ended."

"Indeed." Natje's grin was a knife slash, her eyes flashing cold
with starlight and far too amused by the prospect of a cleaving.

Killing a witch was no small thing, and cleaving was the
highest corporal punishment allowed by C.R.O.W. One that had
not occurred since Joseph McCarthy started up his nonsense in
the middle of the twentieth century.

Yes, a witch could suffer a hanging or a burning at the stake.
She could be tied in chains and tossed into a river, or buried alive,
or flayed, or drawn and quartered. Bones could be salted, familiars
could be stewed, but a witch could be resurrected from hanging
and reborne from bone dust. Diego was proof enough of that.

A cleaving was final. The ultimate punishment in which the three separate pieces that made up a witch were torn apart—the Body, the Shade, and the Soul—leaving behind nothing but an empty husk for time to turn to mulch and dust.

She gripped the edge of her chair, focusing on a jagged mote lacquered into the table to keep from screaming. Of course, they would push for a cleaving. She was a Death Witch, Forbidden and Foule. She'd flung a blood-blade hex at Agent Sterne in front of an audience of Enforcers. She'd reduced a Loa to a pile of dust and banished Ezra beyond the reaches of even the strongest witches of C.R.O.W. She was anathema to all the coven stood for, kept hidden from the moment her Way reared its rotting head. Like that jagged mote on the table's surface, Milla was a flaw, a taint ruining the otherwise glossy sheen of C.R.O.W.

Blood thrummed in her ears, drowning out whatever Natje was saying. She tapped her nails on the table, Milla's name leaving her lips as a shout underwater. She blinked, biting her tongue to take her mind away from the horror of a cleaving.

"What?"

"I asked, 'Have they allowed you a candle'?" Natje tapped the folio, sky-blue eyes intent on Milla. She shook her head. "Bell or book?" Another head shake. Natje flipped open the folio and summoned a Montblanc roller pen to hand, taking down Milla's answers in a looping script. "Visitation?"

"Other than you?" Natje held Milla's eye until she relented. "Agent Simmons," she said. Natje straightened, and Milla felt a momentary rush of victory that she'd managed to surprise the Nachthexe. "Not that one."

She nodded and flipped through the folio, stopping at the beginning of Milla's charges. "As you can see, C.R.O.W. was more than willing to supply me with the discovery, cocky witches that they are."

Milla caught hints and suggestions as to how incredibly fucked she was as Natje skimmed the file. A photo of herself and Diego taken through the front window of Southern Gothic, a grainy shot of her running through the Colonial Quarter, knees bleeding and the fingertips of one hand blackened and cradled against her chest. A pile of white dust on the ground and a report from Agent Simmons, though which one she could not tell.

There were a few photos taken by city security cameras showing Milla running with Darkly, the two of them grinning at each other at a stoplight, or Milla paces ahead of the Dark Witch as she flew across the bridge. One of Milla pacing in Toques Place with a phone to her ear as Diego and Darkly looked on.

Notes in a familiar hand peppered the file, and though Darkly's handwriting was neat and concise, it was nearly impossible to read at a glance and upside down.

Natje picked up a form, and Milla caught the word "Incomplete" typed across the page. "The report from your arrest," Natje explained, flipping the page over to scan the back before returning it to the file. "Considering the lack of scrutiny given to your arrest and processing, I might consider pursuing a line of Enforcer incompetence."

"How so?"

"None of your aural scans are conclusive, and you were neither processed at the site of the arrest nor seen to by a hippocromantic in good standing. Without medical assessments to support A.I.I. claims, what aural readings and E.R.I.E.s Agent Simmons and her team did manage in that swamp are inadmissible." Natje pressed the tip of her finger to her lips and winked. "A convenient coincidence."

Milla lowered her gaze to the file, the half-completed form, and the empty medical form beside it, an idea percolating in the back of her head that she had no wish to acknowledge.

But how could she not? Lou had managed her arrest, and the Light Witch did not strike Milla as negligent. Beyond that, witches did not believe in coincidences. She looked up from the forms to find Natje watching her closely and nodded once to show she understood. The implications, at least. Horned God knew she had no idea what the rhyme or reason was for her botched arrest.

Natje smiled and sat back in her chair, adopting a more casual posture. Her magenta-tipped fingers folded together on the table, and her elbows rested on the edge. "The charges levied against you are severe, Ludmilla."

"How bad are they?"

An eyebrow disappeared beneath the line of Natje's bangs. "Apparently, someone performed an act of magick Forbidden and Foule involving a desecrant creature in your demesne, witnessed by two Aural Insurance Investigators."

Milla shrank in her chair, uncertain to *which* act of magick Natje referred. There'd been the raw-head, whom she had reduced to a pile of dust, the summoning of a Shade into Darkly and the following exorcism, and then the whole thing with the Loa, more summoned Shades, and a banishment that had left Milla drunker than a skunk and her Way jacked-up on Dark Witch juice.

At least the Aural Insurance Investigators in question were obvious. Darkly had had a front-row seat for all of it and confirmed his sister was with him when Milla dusted the raw-head.

"Anything you care to add?' Natje prompted.

"I'm an idiot?"

Natje smirked, cold blue eyes warming as she snorted quietly. "Anything useful?"

"I wouldn't have dusted that raw-head if those two idiots hadn't used me as bait."

"Yes, well, the odds of that accusation sticking to C.R.O.W.'s darling Light Witch and her pet are slim to none." Natje flipped the folio closed. "And that is the last time I want to hear anything resembling an admission of the Forbidden and Foule from you."

"Aren't you my advoccultant?" Milla asked, swallowing the rise of sudden dread. She thought back through their conversation, seeking out the moment Natje stated as such. She had asked after Milla's care in the cells, and shown her the evidence gathered against her, but she could just as easily be here to prosecute Milla, and she, idiot that she was, had just admitted to using magick Forbidden and Foule.

"Milla, du musst die Kirche im Dorf lassen." Natje tutted. "I can hear your mind running in circles."

She startled, the rapid-fire German breaking her out of the doom spiral. "I must … what am I doing with the church?"

"Leaving it in the village," said Natje. "You have always overthought things, even as a little girl. Getting so carried away that you forgot to pay attention to the little things." She leaned forward and reached across the table, frowning when Milla flinched and pressed harder against her chair. Those cold eyes flitted over her face and body, and Natje straightened. "So I will speak plainly: I have been retained by a third party who wishes to remain anonymous to represent you before the Tribunal representative being sent to hear your case. As such, the knowledge you share with me must echo your behavior as a Fine and Faire Witch of the Demesne."

It helped. Hearing Natje state she was here to represent her *helped*, but it did little to unravel the festering dread in her belly.

"I thought … I thought I was supposed to talk to my lawyer."

"Yes, of course. Tell me how you tend the demesne and reign in the local desecrants. Tell me how the raw-head was a threat to the mortal populace but, Horned God, girl, do not tell me anything that can be used against you."

"That doesn't make any sense, you're my advoccultant. I'm not supposed to lie to you."

"Then do not." Natje threw her hands up in defeat and sat back in the chair. "Paint for me a rosy picture of a Fine and Faire witch in good standing and omit the nasty details. Nobody lies to an agent of C.R.O.W., Ludmilla, least of all me."

"But that doesn't make any sense."

"The Tribunal does not make sense. By the Triple Goddess, you are the daughter of the Advoccultant General. A witch suspected of the Forbidden and Foule is guilty until proven innocent. How do you not know how this works?"

Milla opened her mouth to argue, closed it, and picked at the dark mote on the table's surface. "Your sister didn't include witchy legal process in her lessons," she said.

Natje scoffed, disgust flickering across her face. "Morgen's idea of child-rearing and mine are vastly different."

That earned Milla's full attention. She had always sensed tension between Morgen and Natje. On those few visits, always around a lunar or solar eclipse, the sisters would bicker and argue over the tiniest things before retreating to opposite ends of Morgen's tower or Big Torch Key. She had thought it odd that even when the sisters resided in the same place, she rarely ever saw them at the same time. "And what would the Nachthexe have taught me?"

Again, that cold, clear gaze pierced her from across the table, taking in the ragged line of Milla's bangs to the hunched slope of her shoulders.

"How to use your Way, rather than hide from it."

The weight of the accusation further compressed the already heavy dread in her stomach. She swallowed, her throat tight, and bit her lips even though no reply rose to her tongue.

Natje sighed, releasing Milla from the intensity of her gaze, and when she blinked, she was no longer the Nachthexe and every inch an advoccultant.

"Being a Witch of a Demesne earns you the right of expedition. As such, things will progress quickly from here. My arguments for a closed hearing with the Elder Witch of the Panhandle Coven were denied. However, the appeal for judgment by Tribunal Rite was successful. The old biddies agreed quite readily, considering the PR disaster you have created."

"I'll be sure to send them my condolences," Milla muttered, trying to catch up to Natje's train of thought. "So I won't be tried by a jury of my peers?"

"How depressing it is that you were instructed in the ways of our prisons but not our legal system." She sighed, shaking her head. "The Tribunal is sending one of their Heads to hear the charges against you, review the evidence, and make a ruling."

It was not the worst outcome, all things considered. Prejudices, like gossip, ran deep among witches. Even if the Panhandle Coven could source a jury of Milla's "peers," the likelihood of them not bringing preconceived notions about a Death Witch was slim to none. A Tribunal Head was a different story altogether.

Founded after the Hundred Years' War, the Tribunal consisted of three elder witches voted into position by the covens under

C.R.O.W. jurisdiction. Morgen had served as the Second Head of the Tribunal for close to a century before retiring to run the Enforcer training base on Big Torch Key. Her replacement as the Second Head had been the only witch voted into the position in Milla's lifetime. The seats were lifelong until the witch retired or left this earth to pass through the Gates, which, considering what Milla had done two years prior, was not something she wanted to devote much thought to.

"As their pet Light Witch is still skulking about your swamp," Natje continued, "I imagine they will obtain the services of a svítilna to aid her in performing a Soul Projection."

Milla replied with a flat stare.

"This is where you say 'thank you'."

"For *what?*" she balked. "I'm not getting a fair trial, and my fate is subject to the whims of one old witch hearing a biased accusation? What is there to be thankful for?"

"That you have me." Natje rose and glided around the table, stopping beside Milla's shoulder. The cold of a starless sky embraced her, raising goosebumps along her arms and making her shiver. "That you are the foster daughter of the Morgenhexe and a problem the Tribunal would prefer was dealt with quietly."

"Cleaved, you mean."

Natje shrugged one shoulder, the corner of her mouth lifting as she did. "Who is to say?"

"That's not helping." The door at her back clanked and groaned before Natje could answer. She resumed her seat, gaze leveled on Agent Sterne as he entered the room.

"Nobody lies to an agent of C.R.O.W., Milla. It would be a pity to start now." A cryptic smile joined her words, and Natje tipped her head in Agent Sterne's direction. "Be careful with this one, Agent." He glanced at her, face still and impassive as ever. One eyebrow twitched, and Natje's smile became a smirk. "Patience, Milla," she addressed her. "Now that the Tribunal Head has been summoned, it is only a matter of time."

Ten

 C.R.O.W. managed Aural Insurance Investigator training installation in the Florida Keys. One of four such installations in the Americas.

See: AOC Facilities; Tage, Morgen

LOOK AT ME, MILLAPET.

Milla entered her cell alone. She sat on the edge of her bed as the door was closed and barred. Alone.

No voices in her head, no ghostly whispers. Only Milla alone for the first time in ages.

Only at me, understand?

And then a meal came—vegetable biryani topped with crisped onions that tasted like the biryani from her favorite Indian restaurant in St. Augustine, albeit reheated.

Right?

And what next?

She did yoga and jogged in place, bathed in the sink, and changed into fresh scrubs. Then she slept. Alone.

And then, Milla? Keep going.

Her back ached. Her eyes burned. Every finger and every toe prickled, her limbs full of static, and she was alone.

She had to be because if she was not alone, he had been here the entire time. Her eyes focused on the space in front of her face. The empty, blurred air. She sucked in a staccato breath, her heart pounding wildly.

But she had entered the cell *alone*.

Look at me, not at him, he demanded, panic straining each word.

"What are you thinking about?"

Don't think about him, don't look at him.

He was close. If she could reach out, she could touch him, but she could not move, could not blink and he was *right there*.

I'm what's here, Millapet. I'm real and I'm right where you left me. LOOK AT ME.

It was only a matter of time. Natje was here, and it was only a matter of time. She just had to hold on.

Just a little bit longer. It was only a matter of—

"You're doing so well, magissa," the witch whispered. Warm breath caught in the curve of her ear and filled the air with the stale reek of garlic and lemon. "Better than we expected." The edge of the mattress dipped beside her hip and again on the other side. A scream lodged itself in her throat, straining against the tendons she could not move, the muscles she could not flex. Another dip in the mattress beside her head. She wanted to blink, to cry, to bury her head and hide from the blurred air in front of her face. Three points on the mattress. Two knees, a hand, oh Goddess, he was right over her. Leering down at Milla with a face she could not see.

"Perhaps we misjudged you."

It was not supposed to be like this. Milla had been raised on stories of C.R.O.W.'s cells. Tales of thumb screws and witch prickers, repeated drownings, and scalding iron shoes. Obnubilari would cast hallucinations and figments of an imagined hellscape while chronomantics messed with time. Meteomantics would attack with a blinding cold until her toes were frostbitten, the hippocromantics would be called in to heal the damage, and the witch trials would begin again.

Every Enforcer endured time in the cells as part of their training. They trained on Big Torch Key or Grim Ness or any of the Enforcer bases until deemed ready for the field, and then they were entombed in the salt and marble until they broke.

One of the instructors, a meteomantic, had told her about his time in the salt and marble. Waybound and forced to endure blizzards, sand storms, drownings, and gale-force winds. The witch had nine fingers, claiming he lost one to frostbite in the cells.

An audiomantic once told her about the two weeks they spent in a soundless chamber, unable to manipulate their voice after being rendered mute by a corpomantic hex. Upon their release, they gave themselves tinnitus for the sole purpose of never again being left in silence.

Even Morgen had shared her own experience in the cells, lulling Milla to sleep by telling her of the witches slipping their intent into the mundane, altering tiny facets of each day until Morgen doubted any change had occurred at all, trapping her in one grand obscuration of reality. She theorized no less than three obnubilari and five obfuscari went to work on her, along with a mixed coven of audiomantics and chronomantics weaving their Ways in a mass ritual with the sole intent of breaking the mind of the Morgenhexe.

"They succeeded, of course," she told Milla over a breakfast of black coffee, a semolina pudding called griessbrei, and fresh fruit. "But that is the purpose of the witch trials: to break the witches and make them confess to their weaknesses so they may build themselves back up again."

"What could they possibly do to me?" Milla had scoffed, scooping a spoonful of brown sugar from a bowl and dumping it onto her griessbrei. "Put me in a room full of living things?"

Morgen had narrowed eyes at her foster daughter. "That is something you must ask yourself, Millamäuschen."

Milla scowled, hating the nickname. Darling Little Milla Mouse. It made her sound like the weeping eight-year-old girl Morgen had escorted across the ocean.

"The mass illusion worked because I could not manipulate the scene. It was untouchable and, therefore, untenable to my mind. You must consider what makes *you* you. What is it the trials could use, with their knowledge of Ludmilla Probuditna and her supposed Way, to strip away the very essence of self?" Derision dripped from her words, souring the clipped accent. "What confession could they steal to leave you a quivering mass of clay ready to be molded by the Senior Enforcers of C.R.O.W.?"

Milla stirred her griessbrei, fishing out a strawberry and chewing it before pointing her spoon at the Morgenhexe. "It sounds like you don't think too much of the witch trials."

"I do not." Morgen closed her eyes. Sniffed. "Though I recognize the utility of the exercise. An Enforcer must be unwavering. They must be tested and tried and unable to be swayed by a witch that has strayed towards the wicked and weird."

"Not the Forbidden and Foule?"

Morgen smiled, a tight-lipped, patient thing. "To be faced with that which you cannot control, that which you cannot manipulate or beat in the usual traveling of your Way, Millamäuschen, is to be defenseless in the face of true adversity.

The exercise comes in stretching beyond your known ability, in overcoming that which should make you fall but instead forces you to rise higher."

"If Enforcers need to rise higher, why doesn't C.R.O.W. issue them brooms?" Milla had snickered.

"Do not be absurd." She crossed the kitchen and flicked on the electric kettle. "You are correct, however. I do not approve of the weight C.R.O.W. places on breaking their witches before promoting them to the role of Enforcer. I find it needless torment bordering on torture. If the exercise were coupled with proper care for the surviving witches rather than throwing them right into the field, I might find the trials less distasteful. Consider yourself lucky you will never have to endure said abuse."

"But what if I wanted to? Be an Enforcer, I mean."

Morgen pursed her lips, her stern features softening just a little. Just enough. "You know that is impossible, Ludmilla, being what you are."

As always, whenever this topic arose, she slumped down in her chair, dropping her head back to stare at the ceiling. "I know. I just—is this what I'm supposed to do for the rest of my life? Haunt Big Torch and watch other witches come and go?"

"Your father placed his trust in me, Ludmilla. To keep you safe. Alive. C.R.O.W. must not know the truth of your Way."

"So I only use the vesticism from my mom. Or present as a chronomantic, a green witch, nine rings, I could even be passable as a vinefica. Actually"—Milla straightened and smiled—"I think I'd make a damn fine poison witch." Morgen clicked her tongue. "Ugh, then what is the *point?* Why teach me how to siphon and use other witches' Ways against them if not to become an Enforcer?"

"Millamäuschen, always asking too many questions," Morgen muttered, more to herself than Milla. "Sehr dramatisch, even knowing you are leaving for Flagler in the fall."

"Yeah, where I'll just have a new babysitter."

"Your new mentor is skilled in the deception of the Ways. He will improve upon the groundwork I've laid in ensuring your survival and secrecy from C.R.O.W."

Milla? Where did you go?

The memory shattered, edges falling away like glass to reveal the dark hell of her cell. The weight near her head moved, and a low, gravelly chuckle echoed off the walls of her cell.

"Almost done, magissa. Only a few more moments."

A whimper wheezed free from Milla's lips. Goddess, it was not supposed to be like this. The cells were supposed to be torture and pain and all the things Milla had spent a lifetime conjuring up ways to resist and survive. But it wasn't supposed to be like *this.*

Eleven

"HE'S GOING TO KILL me when he sees you."

Something snapped over Milla's skin. She lurched forward, hauled off of her bed and onto her knees by a sharp pull at the center of her belly. She threw her arms out, catching herself on hands and knees to keep from crashing to the floor.

Each breath came too quick, too shallow, her heartbeat one continuous thrum, buzzing in her chest like the drone of hummingbird wings and prickling in her hands and feet. Spots bloomed at the corners of her vision. She fought to fill her lungs, and then a breath caught. And another, pants slowing to gasps. Her heartbeat tripped into quick pulses, longer now, dropping into a steady thub-dub. Her vision cleared—or slowed? until the veins in the marble were no longer smudges but fine and separate details.

"I-I'm in the cell," she panted.

Millapet?

"I'm in Jacksonville."

"What are you going on about?" Heels clacked against the floor, stopping just out of MIlla's line of sight.

"I'm in the cells, in Jacksonville. I'm a Death Witch, my demesne is St. Augustine, and" —she raised her head, scowling at the pointed shiny-leather toe of an expensive high heel—"those are the stupidest shoes to wear in a prison."

"Charming," Lou drawled. Milla followed the stitched line on her Ponte pants up to a tailored blouse and blazer combo. A Dara Knot hung low against Lou's breastbone from a thin gold chain, the twisted metal gleaming in the orange-yellow light.

For all the care put into her outfit, Lou's expression was strained. A tightness pulled at her mouth, and her makeup barely hid the faint shadows beneath her eyes. Hair that had been meticulously styled every time Milla saw the witch was pulled now into a bun at the nape of her neck, the fly-aways and uneven coil suggesting she'd tied it back while rushing out the door.

Lou glanced back at the door, eyeing the empty hallway for a moment before returning her blue-green gaze to Milla.

"You look tired," Milla stated, still on her hands and knees. Lou frowned, nudged her fingertips with the toe of one heel, and stepped back. A long moment passed before she tossed a tan folder on the bed and crossed her arms.

"You look wretched," she replied. "I know regular showers are out of the question, but would it kill you to eat?"

Who is that, Milla?

"No one." She rose slowly, closing her eyes as a wave of dizziness surged in her head.

"What was that?"

"No." Milla faced Lou, fists clenched at her sides. "No, it wouldn't kill me to eat. Any chance I'll ever get more than thirty seconds to do so?"

Lou narrowed her eyes. She swept the folder from the bed and tossed it at Milla's feet. "We need your expertise."

"My expertise?" Her entire body twitched in shock. "With what?"

"An affair for which you are uniquely qualified to offer insight." Lou gestured to the folder, waiting as Milla stooped and took it from the floor.

It was unlabeled, the edges crisp, suggesting whatever was inside had been assembled moments before Lou headed to the cells. She perched on the edge of the mattress, her crisp appearance at odds with the dingy, worn bedding, waiting as Milla opened the folder and immediately wished she had not.

The first page was a graph of multi-colored wavy lines, some arcing high, others a warble of tight curves. Reds, blues, purples, and yellows woven together almost in synchrony, while an anomalous line arced and fell so tightly, it was almost a blur.

The next page was the same, so Milla flipped back, frowning at the location listed in tiny point font beneath the graph. "Daytona?"

"From the day of your arrest," Lou said. "We've pulled the E.R.I.E. records to use as a baseline."

"For what?" She scrunched her brows together and turned to the second page, frowning as she read the exact words she expected to see.

St. Augustine.

"With this, the readings from Daytona, and help from my brother, we isolated the signature of a Death Witch." Paper crinkled between Milla's fingers, and she forced herself to remain still. "At first, this report could be explained away as coming from your demesne. The residual echoes of your magick are imbued into every tree and stone."

"If you know all that, why do you need my expertise?" Lou's face was just visible out of the corner of her eye, watching her closely. "Why tell me any of this?"

Lou plucked the St. Augustine paper from her hand and held it beside a third printout of an identical graph. Milla bit the inside of her cheek, scanning the graph and squinting at the tiny font.

"This signature surge is from an unsanctioned ritual in Savannah three days ago." Lou pointed to the yellow line. "Hippocromantic, chronomantic, vinefica." And traced the different warbles and arcs before finally flicking the topmost peak of the black line. "And this blur here is a Death Witch."

"That's impossible." Milla flipped the page over and back again, glancing between it, the St. Augustine graph, and Daytona. "I've been in here for …"

How long, Millapet?

"Which is precisely why we require your expertise." Lou took the folder, replaced the sheets, and tucked it under her arm. "We identified a commonality between the instances. A member of my team is running the data on a third recorded instance in Hattiesburg."

Milla sank to the floor, leaning against the wall and propping her forearms on her knees. Waiting. Lou stared back at her as calmly as if waiting for a bus. When she offered nothing else, Milla drawled, "Please, the anticipation is killing me."

"Missing witches," she said. "In each of these events, a witch has been reported missing by their home coven. Your arrest is the outlier, and I want to know why."

"Why what?"

"Why your signature appears in unsanctioned rituals resulting in the disappearance of witches."

A harsh bark of a laugh shoved out of Milla's throat, rushing past her lips before she could stop it. "How in the nine rings would I know? I've been *here*." She threw her arm out, gesturing to the cell.

"You have, yes." Lou stepped closer, looming over Milla, serene and tall. "But what of another Death Witch?"

"Don't be ridiculous."

"Then tell me what you know."

Milla dropped her head back against the marble, closing her eyes and relishing the dull pop of pain. "I don't know anything. I'm not even supposed to exist; isn't that why you put me down here?"

"I did not put you down here, Ludmilla," Lou answered. "You put yourself here."

Maybe it was the cool, calm way she delivered the words. Or maybe it was the way she looked down at Milla—perfect, put-together Luminescence Simmons, with her tailored Ponte pants, flawless bone structure, and tilt to her mouth that was all too much like Darkly's. Whatever it was, it snapped the last of Milla's restraint.

She popped to her feet, rising on her tiptoes and still falling short of being anything close to threatening to the tall witch. "Your *brother* is the reason I'm down here. He used me as bait for that raw-head. *You* used me as bait. All I did was defend my demesne from a desecrant and a Horned God-damned Voodoo spirit. All I *did* was my job, and then *your brother* gave C.R.O.W. my location."

"Is that what you think happened?"

"It's what I know happened!" She ducked around Lou, putting space between herself and the witch before she did something truly stupid. "Goddess, if you need to talk to missing witches so badly, why don't you ask him? Maybe they're dead. Isn't talking to ghosts, like, his whole deal?"

She lobbed that last bit over her shoulder, which was the only reason she saw it—the crack in Lou's veneer. Her upper lip twitched, and she blinked. It was tiny. Subtle and so brief anyone who wasn't looking never would have noticed.

But Milla did. She had spent weeks learning Darkly's tics and tells. Running beside and behind the witch, sitting across from him at tables, and studying him from that asinine bean bag.

And it had only taken a week for Milla to recognize when she managed to land an insult.

She faced Lou and crossed her arms, biding her time with this tiny triumph. Something had earned that reaction, and if she could determine what it was, she could—what, exactly? Insulting Lou was not going to get her out of the cells.

She exhaled, stuck between wanting to stay silent and feeling a weirdly displaced need to apologize, when Lou sighed and swept a hand over her hair.

"You need to work with us," she said. "I have seen the evidence, Ludmilla. I have read the case C.R.O.W. has built against you—"

"No fucking shit, you were there for most of it."

Lou's eyes flashed a brilliant teal. "This does not have to be so hard on you, Ludmilla. Work with us. Explain away this supposed Death Witch. Help us so I can help you."

"Help me with *what*, Luminescence?"

Wait. Is that Lou?

Milla swatted the empty air, brushing away that voice as one would brush away a fly. Lou tracked the movement. Her mouth softened, and, dare it be suggested, she smiled.

"The Third Head is a dear family friend," she said.

"I—" Milla blinked and backed away. "What?"

"It will take some finessing, but it is within the realm of possibility." She raised one finger, eyes gleaming. "If you agree, that is."

"Agree to what?"

Don't listen to her, Milla, the voice in her head urged. Louder, now, and more frantic than ever. *You can't trust a thing that witch says.*

"Work with us." Lou's voice was calm, her posture easy and confident. "The team of Enforcers I lead is unique, but for all my witches bring to the cauldron, we're operating at a loss." She tossed the folder onto the mattress and crossed her arms, but Milla was not fooled. A tendon stood out tight against her neck, and her shoulders were held tight, their line too straight. It was all too staged, too perfect. Goddess, even the glowing light from the hallway caught perfectly along Lou's cheekbones, making her look like some otherworldly fae creature. "We need you, and you need out of this cell."

What is she saying, Millapet?

"Are you implying that you can get me out of here?"

It was ludicrous. Deranged and unfathomable. Milla was a Death Witch accused of the Forbidden and Foule, and the very witch who witnessed her dust a raw-head was offering her freedom?

Not freedom.

What had Darkly said? He had been benched for something. He had needed Milla to—no. He wanted out, and the price of his freedom was delivering her to C.R.O.W. Darkly had traded Milla for himself, and now Lou wanted to get her out of the cells.

Think! For once in your life, think, that voice hissed.

Milla pressed her fists against her temples when Lou did not answer and turned her back to escape that piercing, needling gaze. She wanted to sit, curl into a tiny ball on her awful mattress, and block out the world so she could think.

What else did she know? What else had Darkly let slip that could not be discounted as a lie?

Lou was his handler. A Light Witch for a Dark Witch, two sides of the same coin. She had been his guardian and his *jezibaba*, caring for a Dark Witch just stumbling into his Ways. A Dark Witch who had been allowed to become an Enforcer while Milla was hidden away in the Keys, kept under C.R.O.W.'s nose by one of their own. Forced to ignore her Way while Darkly was allowed to thrive.

Something noxious churned in her chest, tightening as a pressure around her lungs. He had been allowed to *live*, but at what cost?

Natje's offhand comment crept along the edges of Milla's mind, slipping in under the anger and stretching tall.

C.R.O.W.'s darling Light Witch and her pet.

Yes, he had been allowed to live, but Lou—his guardian, his *jezibaba*—clearly held a tight leash.

Milla had been handled before. She'd been kept on a similar leash by Morgen and again by Ezra, only tasting a semblance of freedom for the year and a half she was back in St. Augustine before that Horned God-damned Loa and Darkly arrived.

But what sort of freedom was that? Drowning her Way, ducking her head, and keeping out of notice, out of sight. If she said yes—if she agreed to work with Lou, agreed to be handled by her; if any witch could convince C.R.O.W. that Milla was worth using rather than cleaving, it had to be Lou, the Light Witch who had raised a witch forbidden and foul.

"There will be training with the core team," Lou stated. "As Keir explains it, your tolerance for your Way is abysmal—"

"Lovely," Milla bit out, crossing her arms. Ezra's voice sang in her head, the tone soft and patient as it always was in those early days. *Test the scene*, he would advise, guiding Milla by the hand through the grand illusions he had cast just for her. *Prod the edges, and seek out the inconsistencies.*

"—and I cannot have you endangering the rest of my coven," Lou finished and narrowed her eyes. "You'll have to get over whatever that is." One finger flicked in Milla's direction. "You don't have to like everyone on the team, but trust among us is necessary."

Apply pressure and see what gives.

"Trust?" She barked a harsh laugh. "How can I trust the witch who turned me in?"

"Is that what you think happened?"

"He said it himself." Milla leaned against the wall, assuming as casual a pose as she could while her attention never strayed from Lou's face. If there were going to be a tell or a tic, it would be now. Another twitch of the lip. The flicker of an eyelid. "He needed a win to get unbenched."

Lou's stupidly perfect face remained serene. "I suppose he did."

Okay, not that, then.

"What's in it for me?" Milla tried.

"Beyond living?" One heel tocked against the floor as Lou took a step. And another, the sharp sound bouncing off the walls. The light within Lou, the force of her Way that made her skin glow, brightened, the blue-green of her eyes heating to a painfully bright teal. Milla pressed against the wall. Every cell in her body screamed for her to drop her gaze, close her eyes, look away, but Milla had stared down worse and survived. "What else could a Death Witch want?"

"I want …" The words died on her tongue, even as she screamed them in her mind.

Out of these cells. My demesne and Diego. My store and Julie, and the occult boards. Freedom. A life.

If she could just get her mouth to work, get her tongue to form the words, she could answer the question and Lou would relent. Instead, her fingers and toes tingled. Searing pain cut into the inside of her wrist, scraping up her arm. Milla ripped her gaze away from Lou, down to where her nails dug into the crook of her right elbow. Angry, jagged lines crawled up her inner arm, trailing the stretch of her scar, and beads of crimson red welled in a dotted line.

When did I do that?

"One last chance, Ludmilla." Lou backed away, her bright gaze still on Milla but absent the caustic gleam. "Work with us."

In the end, the decision was easy. Milla supposed it always had been, and why wouldn't it?

Hadn't she made the same choice time and time again? Hadn't she sacrificed bits of her Shade and Soul for years? Chaining herself to Ezra, agreeing to perform the ritual on Lake Pontchartrain, dusting the raw-head, and sending Anaisa back to the Gates—hadn't she done all of that for a chance to live?

Millapet, no.

"Yes."

Lou's shoulders hitched, her eyes widening momentarily in surprise before her entire posture relaxed. "Oh, thank the Goddess." She spun and knocked on the door. The tumblers groaned, gears clacking, and the door opened to reveal Agent Sterne on the other side. Lou nodded to the Enforcer and crossed the threshold without looking back.

"Wait." Milla rushed across the cell and skidded to a halt as Agent Sterne held his palm out in warning. She popped onto her toes, barely able to see Lou over his shoulder. "How are you going to convince C.R.O.W. not to cleave me?"

Lou slowed and spun, regarding Milla with the same cold calm she had during her arrest. After a long beat, she nodded, and something like a smile curled her lips. "Same as I did last time."

Twelve

VESTIC Diviners and soothsayers. Includes alomancy, astrogalomancy, favomancy, geomancy, tasseomancy, pecthimancy.

Nae bones, entrails, blood, or teeth.

hahahah okay

LOU'S PRESENCE LINGERED LONG after the witch left, her vanilla and sugar, cookies-fresh-from-the-oven scent clogging the cell and turning Milla's stomach. She lay on her mattress, frowning at the folder Lou had left behind and wondering how royally she had just fucked up.

If the silence in her head were anything to judge by, it was pretty royal. The voice had snapped at her, just once, after she had agreed, and then nothing. No more snide remarks, no pleas for Milla to focus on the voice and the voice alone. No more utterances of the nickname she hated that had become a comfort in the horror of the cells.

But worse than the silence was that every time she closed her eyes, she saw Darkly.

Black-eyed and furious, his hair tousled and windblown. Panicked and broken, surrounded by the whirling mass of his Shades. Reaching for her and begging desperately, "Milla, please."

"I'm so sorry."

"Believe me."

She bolted upright, hauled from her captive sleep by that lurching feeling at the center of her chest. The tingling was back in her fingers and toes. Her heart hammering in her chest. She pressed a hand against her sternum, focusing on every tiny, panting breath. In time, her heart settled. In time, she lay on her side and stared across the cell, focusing on the dim glow of the svítilna light until her eyelids grew heavy and sleep pulled her back into its arms.

Black-eyed.

Broken.

"Milla, please."

And again, lurching from the bed as if someone had woven a rope through her ribs and hauled with all their might, leaving Milla gasping for air that was too thin to fill her lungs.

"I'm so sorry."

And again and again and again and again.

"I promise." He beat his fist against the barrier, begging her to look him in the eye. To believe him even as he lied. "I will fix this."

"Horned God knows why you couldn't agree to work with us earlier." Lou tugged on the belt, jerking Milla forward by the hips. She fed the tail through the buckle, frowning at the excess leather and lack of grommets. "It's hard enough getting my brother to dress appropriately." She leaned back and flitted her gaze over Milla, frowning deeply. "You look like a child wearing her mother's clothes as fancy dress."

Milla flicked the belt and pinched the billowing fabric of her dusty rose blouse. "Why is this even necessary?"

"Appearances matter, Ludmilla." Lou tutted and stooped, hooking her fore and middle fingers into a pair of pointed-toe heels and presenting them to Milla. "You can at least walk in these, yes?"

"No?"

Lou sighed and tossed the shoes on the mattress. "Sit." She pointed. "And put those on. We don't want to keep them waiting."

Them. The Elder Witch of the Panhandle Coven and the Third Head of the Tribunal.

Milla followed Lou and Agent Sterne through the halls, teetering in her borrowed heels. As before, the illusions on the walls made her dizzy. True to Agent Sterne's claim, they grew weaker the higher the trio rose within the building. Pulsing walls and hellish landscapes became never-ending corridors and utilitarian, mid-century office building nightmares. Only after climbing yet another flight of metal stairs in a beige stairwell and exiting into a densely populated cube farm did Milla realize they had left the hexed hallways behind.

Witches in office-casual attire bustled down the narrow rows between cubicles, glancing at Milla and rushing away. Whispers rose at her back, and she caught "Daytona" and "St. Augustine" from multiple mouths. Neck prickling and chest heating, she crossed her arms and shrank into the too-large blouse as they passed through the large room and into the front lobby of the Panhandle Coven.

Harlequin tiles stretched across the floor, the bold black and white offset by sage green scalloped pillars topped by gilded Corinthian caps. A row of mid-century leather chairs hugged the walls on either side of large oak and iron doors, and a desk nearly as tall as Milla filled the opposite wall. Behind it was a mural she had only ever been able to think of as "Soviet chic."

Three witches stood together, one facing forward and the others caught in a profile. La Voison with her deck of cards on the left, Margarete von Leipzig with her astrolabe on the right, and Catherine of Aragon in the center with her bible, bell, and candle. The original Tribunal of C.R.O.W.

Lou strode across the hall, heels clicking steadily against the marble floor. She bypassed the front desk altogether, aiming for another, smaller set of doors.

"Ma'am." A young witch looked up from her computer as they crossed the hall. "Ma'am, do you have an appointment?"

"Yes." Lou grasped the handle without glancing at the receptionist. She fluttered a half-hearted wave over her shoulder as she yanked the door open to reveal a dark, wood-paneled hallway Milla had not traversed in years. She hesitated and glanced back at Agent Sterne, who peeled off toward the desk.

"With me, Probuditna," Lou said.

"Don't we need to …" She pointed at the desk.

"*We* need to keep moving." Lou grabbed her arm and tugged. "Come along."

Compared to the bright, echoing lobby, the hallway was quiet as a tomb. Tall windows lined the wall to Milla's right, the world beyond the Panhandle Coven obscured by cream-colored curtains. What light bled into the hallway was a sickly yellow swallowed by stained oak panels on the interior wall and the rich reds, browns, and blues of the carpet.

A young witch waited for them halfway down, arms crossed behind his back and his expression patient. Like the witches in the cube farm, he wore business attire: pressed pale blue seersucker pants with a faint off-white pinstripe, a tailored button-down, paisley bow tie, and tan suspenders. The rounded tortoiseshell glasses and styled mop of chestnut brown curls completed the image of a witch who cared deeply for appearances, and, against all odds, the jaundice-yellow light only flattered his bright hazel eyes and golden beige complexion.

As Lou and Milla approached, his attention jumped to somewhere over their heads, and a step later, she felt the tell-tale crackle and pressure of magick.

"Triple warded," the witch said with a smile as they passed through. "Can never be too careful." He stepped forward, extending a hand to Lou. "Rhett Marchand, *polednice* to the Elder Witch."

"I didn't know she had an apprentice," Milla said. Rhett cocked his head, eyes darting briefly her way before returning to Lou.

"Agent Simmons." She took his hand, shaking once and frowning when he did not immediately let go. Still smiling, Rhett's hazel eyes flashed a bright copper. Quick and barely noticeable, it marked a vestic stepping into their Way. Lou scoffed, jerking her hand free. "Do you mind?"

"As I said," he smiled, unbothered by her disdain. "One can never be too careful. The ward is against illusions, ensuring that all who meet with the Elder Witch are who they claim to be."

"And the vestic doorman is to assess intent?" Milla asked. The witch looked at her in full, and his smile washed away. With one steady bob of his throat, he extended his hand for Milla to take.

So she did, setting the tips of her fingers against his palm in the most limp-wristed, cold fish handshake she could muster and slipping away before he could get a read.

"I—" Rhett started.

"My mother's a vestic," Milla finished with a sharp smile. It was tacky and probably stupid, but she had been a prisoner in the cells beneath this building for Horned God knew how long. If he did not know who she was by now, why should Milla help him out?

Rhett coughed into a fist, narrowing his eyes at Milla before turning swiftly, crooking his fingers in the air for them to follow. "This way, you've kept them waiting long enough."

Another set of large oak doors filled the end of the hall, and Milla mentally steeled herself for what waited on the other side. Nothing changed in the salt and marble, and nothing changed here. The overly plush carpet and the eye-stinging scents of wood polish and mothballs. The sick light bleeding through the curtains no matter what time of day it was. Once upon a time, in the floral pastel comfort of Key West, she thought that she'd dreamt of this place or had a particularly awful nightmare about Gilded Age mansions multiplying in the Reconstruction Era South.

But standing here now, once again on the outside of these foreboding doors and pondering the fate awaiting her within, Milla felt every inch the little witchling who had cast this place into the darkest corners of her mind.

How long had it been since that first visit? Eighteen years? And still, nothing had changed. Not the carpet or the smell or the fear fluttering in her belly like an eclipse of moths.

The door opened without even the slightest whisper against the carpet, and Rhett ushered them in. As she had feared, the room was exactly the same. Windows filled the wall behind a broad mahogany desk, covered by the same gauzy curtains from the hallway. Behind the desk, twin Tiffany lamps glowed a warm, welcoming greenish-gold, casting a cozy ambiance over the parts of the office the light could reach and leaving the furthest corners cast in deep shadow.

Floor-to-ceiling bookcases lined the walls to Milla's left and right, the shelves stuffed with leather-bound grimoires, shadow books, and tomes delving into the intricacies of the Ways. Wherever there weren't books, there were bell jars full of bones and bundles of twigs tied with twine and hair, innocent-looking trinkets that Milla knew housed curses and allures, and vases filled with flowers in perpetual bloom. A small silver tray full of graffiti-covered rocks was tucked high on a shelf to her left, and a bronze sextant held the attention of the only other witch in the room.

Natje flicked a knob at the base of the sextant, frowning as she ran a finger along the telescope affixed to the frame. As ever, her tall figure was draped in midnight. A deep black tuxedo jacket with silk lapels offered glimpses of an intricate lace bodysuit and a series of gleaming silver necklaces of varying lengths. Sleek leather leggings dripped down her legs, and as Milla and Lou entered, she strode across the room in a pair of studded leather heels as easily as if she were barefoot.

She crooked two fingers at Milla, gesturing for her to sit in one of two plump leather chairs facing the desk, and nodded at Lou.

"Thank you, Agent Simmons."

Lou replied with a terse nod of her own and retreated to the corner of the room opposite Natje, standing out as a prim and proper pastel harpy against the gloom clawing up the walls.

Milla slipped into a chair, settling against the plush leather and stabbing the carpet with her heels to keep from slipping off the sleek cushion. She gripped the armrest, pushing herself back into the chair.

Natje clicked her tongue. "Everything alright?"

"Peachy," Milla said through clenched teeth. "What's going on?"

Natje flitted her gaze over Milla, a crease forming between her brows. "Remember what I told you, Ludmilla: no one lies to C.R.O.W."

Before she could reply, a door tucked between the bookcase and the window swung open. A door that had absolutely not been there a moment prior. Milla's breath hitched, and she gripped the armrests tighter as Constance Abernathy, Elder Witch of the Panhandle Coven, swept in.

Thirteen

"Natje!" Constance's booming, lyrical voice ricocheted off the bookshelves.

A stout woman, she was barely more than a whisper over five feet tall, but her personality filled the room. Her curly dark hair was cropped close to her skull, and though she favored loose black skirts and tunic-style tops, her jewelry and glasses matched the vivacity of her voice. Ruby-red winged glasses inlaid with diamonds perched on her nose, a massive green gem in a buttery yellow-gold setting swallowed her right index finger, and the baubles, beads, and crystals she wore, tinkling merrily together with every sweep and step, had Milla checking the room for vampires.

"It's been an age and a day!" She swung her arms wide, and Natje stepped into the embrace. Air kisses were shared, and then Constance Abernathy, lauded Ink Witch, advoccultant, and Elder Witch of the Panhandle Coven, addressed Milla directly. "Look what the broom swept in."

"Hi, Connie." Milla sent her a faint wave. "It's been a while."

"It's Aunt Connie or nothing, girl." Constance swept past Lou and wrapped her sturdy arms around Milla before she had fully risen from the chair. Though short, the Elder Witch was strong, and Milla's spine cracked in her hug. She held Milla at arm's length, bright brown eyes taking her in. "Did you hit yourself with a wasting hex? What's happened to you?"

"I—"

"Ludmilla ran afoul of a rogue loa a few weeks ago," Lou interrupted, startling Milla.

Weeks?

She knew she had lost time in the cells, knew she had been down there for longer than she could track, but how many weeks was *weeks*?

Lou's eyes glinted cruelly at her, and she pointed between Milla and Constance. "You know each other?"

"Constance and my sister are close," Natje said. She settled in the chair, one leg crossed over the other, her face impassive.

"I've known our little Milla Mouse since she was a tiny thing in pigtails." Constance let go of Milla's shoulders, waving her hands as she doddered behind her desk and plopped into the wicker-backed rolling chair. "Did you ever manage to get on top of the tower?" she asked Milla, smiling broadly. Before she could answer, Constance told the room, "She was determined to free-climb Morgen's tower. I thought the witch was going to have a heart attack the first time Milla fell. How did I not know you took down the loa?"

"If it is all the same," said Natje, "I would like to adhere to formalities."

"Alright, fine." Connie leaned back in the chair, swiveling side to side. "Dina should be here any minute."

"Dina." Natje straightened, uncrossing her legs to place both feet on the floor. "Of course, it would be Dina."

"What's wrong with Dina?" Milla whisper-hissed. Natje brushed her question off with a flick of her wrist.

"The Third Head takes accusations of the Forbidden and Foule quite seriously," Constance said. "Her sympathetic nature has kept more than one witchling out of trouble." Her eyes lifted to the back of the room where Lou hovered in the corner. Milla fought the urge to twist in her seat and put eyes on the Light Witch. She could practically feel her gleaming gaze boring into the back of her head, and the hairs along her neck prickled with an uneasy chill. "Better her than Em. You'd think she would have calmed down after twenty-six years as the Second Head, but she's cleaved more witches in the last decade than any Tribunal member before her."

A tight, quiet cough came from the back of the room, and Milla gave in, glancing over her shoulder at Lou, who stared calmly back at her, a fist pressed to her mouth.

"Are we besmirching the good reputation of my colleague?" A bright, lilting voice punched into the room, followed a moment later by a middle-aged presenting witch in a forest green power suit charging through the door. Coppery hair pulled into a clean French twist drew attention to the sharp line of her cheekbones and slope of her nose. Though not quite pinched, her face had a fox-like appearance, the features all pointing inward to the tight button of her lips and crowned by keen brown eyes. She swept behind Constance and summoned a tufted leather wingbacked chair to sit in. "At least wait until I'm situated; I love a good gab at Em's expense."

"As fun as that would be, we have a more pressing matter to attend to." Constance tipped her head toward Milla. "Morgen's girl has gotten herself into a bit of hot water."

"Ah, yes." Dina leaned forward in her chair, propping her elbows on the edge of the desk and resting her chin on top of her laced fingers. "Took out a raw-head, did we?"

"I—" Milla started. Natje swatted her thigh and hissed sharply. "Ow." She glared at Natje, rubbing her thigh with the heel of her palm.

"You understand the risk this poses to C.R.O.W., yes?" Dina looked pointedly at Milla. "A caretaker of a demesne utilizing magick Forbidden and Foule without consequence threatens the very foundation of our ideals. Regardless of her status as a daughter of the Morgenhexe."

"Foster daughter," Milla corrected. Natje swatted her again, and Dina cocked her head.

"Did you or did you not utilize magick Forbidden and Foule to rid your demesne of a raw-head?"

"Objection," Natje barked.

"This is not a trial, Advoccultant Tage," Constance stated.

"Then kindly cease badgering my client into an admission," she said. "There is no evidence of magick Forbidden and Foule having been performed in the demesne of St. Augustine on the date in question."

"And yet two Enforcers in good standing bore witness," Dina replied. "Their report states—" The lights flickered, surprise cutting off her tirade. Constance swiveled in her chair to put her eyes on one of the lamps. Something brushed against Milla's ankle, and she stiffened, the hair along her arms and scalp prickling with unease.

"The Elder Agent Simmons filed the report in question." Natje dismissively flicked two fingers over her shoulder at Lou. "Her report declares that the E.R.I.E. signature retrieved at the scene of this supposed crime was inconclusive."

"Social distortion," Lou confirmed.

Dina's eyes narrowed in her direction, and for a brief instant, her gaze slipped to the side. A frown pulled at her pinched lips, the slightest furrow appeared between her brows, and then the coolly disinterested mask slipped back into place. "How so?" she asked Lou.

"The good intent of the holiday obstructed our readings."

Dina blinked, straightened, and snapped her fingers. A manila folder identical to the one Natje had shared with Milla appeared in her hands and she set it down, flipping through the pages. "Valentine's Day?"

"It was impossible to get a clear read with the obstruction from vinefica, obnubilari, and augury magick."

"Then why did you suggest that the guilty in question performed an acte of magick Forbidden and Foule?"

The question hung in the air, unanswered. At Milla's back, the slight ruffle of clothing suggested Lou was adjusting her weight from foot to foot, and Natje's warning—everyone's warning—came roaring to life in her head.

No one lies to C.R.O.W.

Dina dropped her gaze to the file, eyes darting from side to side as she waited out the silence, and then—she laughed.

"Inconclusive signature suggests the potential for magick Forbidden and Foule," she read aloud. "Request approval to deploy a team of Enforcers to join singular officer in an evidence-gathering mission." She flipped the file closed and smiled beatifically at Lou. "Clever clog."

"Without a clear reading upon which to accuse the guilty of magick Forbidden and Foule, there is no reason my client should continue to be detained by C.R.O.W.," Natje stated.

"You are forgetting that this report is based upon the eyewitness accounts of two Enforcers," Dina replied. "The Elder and Younger Agent Simmons have been a great boon to C.R.O.W.; at the end of the day, it is a matter of their word against hers." She tipped her head at Milla. Again, something soft lapped at her ankle. She shuffled her feet, rubbing the exposed skin against the hem of her pants. "If Agent Simmons suspects magick Forbidden and Foule, then C.R.O.W. is inclined to investigate the matter to the full extent of their capabilities."

"Investigate, but there is no precedence for elongated detention," Natje argued.

"And what about her dues?" Constance asked. "Milla is several years in arrears, not to mention outstanding fines and fees associated with summons, dealings, transactions, and transgressions, all of them unsanctioned." Her eyes bored into Milla as she spoke, voice laced with maternal disappointment.

"No." Milla sat up. "That's not right, Morgen has been paying my dues—"

"To the Biscayne Coven, dear." Connie frowned slightly. "But you have been a practicing witch in a Panhandle demesne for several years." She clicked her tongue and shook her head. "Not only did you never come to visit your Aunt Connie, but you failed to update your affiliation when you moved to St. Augustine."

"She's also unregistered," Rhett added from the back of the room. "And uninsured."

Milla twisted in her seat to glare at him, and Natje flicked her arm.

"Now, I know things have been a little"—Constance tapped her bejeweled finger against the desk—"chaotic, but a Witch of the Demesne must remain in good standing, which means paying their dues, continuing to register with their regional oversight coven, and maintaining insurance equivalent to the risk their Way presents the Staid populace. Any witch who fails to do so is subject to fines, and if they do *not* pay and adhere to the regulations set forth by C.R.O.W., it is within my right as Elder Witch of your regional coven to detain you."

"But I'm registered with the Biscayne Coven," Milla argued. "And my dues have been paid there. Can't we just transfer the paperwork?"

"And what of the ritual dues?" Constance countered.

Milla bit her cheek. It was not that she'd forgotten about paying her ritual dues, or hadn't wanted to, it was just—*how* was she supposed to pay them? The Witch of a Demesne was expected to tend their city and charge the magick coursing through the earth. She paid her dues to the demesne, and the demesne supported her in return. It was a conversation between Witch and Earth. A give and take to ensure both were made stronger by the other. And Milla paid her dues to St. Augustine. Or, at least, she had. Running daily, treating with the desecrants, performing small, untraceable magicks disguised as hippocromancy or chronomancy to feed the demesne and fill the well of magick waiting at her fingertips.

The magick Anaisa had stolen.

But how was she supposed to pay her ritual dues to the Panhandle Coven when she wasn't supposed to exist?

"We can't transfer those between covens, and even if it were possible, Biscayne reports you have not attended a single ritual with their coven in close to a decade." Constance tipped her head at Milla, peering at her over the bright red frames. "It is within my right to hold you in custody until the monetary and ritual debt is paid."

Milla sank lower in her chair. Beside her, Natje grumbled under her breath, casting a sidelong glance her way. "How much does my client owe?"

Constance summoned a pen to hand and scribbled on a notepad, tearing the paper free and sliding it across the polished mahogany. Milla leaned over as Natje plucked it from the desk, trying to gauge just how fucked she was, but the witch turned the paper away before she could see. Face blank, Natje folded the paper between her fingers and it vanished to wherever the Nachtehexe stored her secrets.

"How much?" Milla asked.

"More than you make in a year."

"How do you know how much I make in a year?"

Natje sent her a droll look, giving all the effect of slowly rolled eyes. To Constance, she said, "I will require a full report of all lapsed dues, fines, fees, and an account of ritual dues owed, of course."

"Of course." Constance nodded. "My assistant will be happy to put that together for you. Rhett?"

"Yes, ma'am." The vestic answered from behind Milla, nodding to the room and slipping through the office doors.

"Well." Dina picked up a stack of papers from the folder, tapping the edges against the desk to straighten them. "As intriguing as local bureaucracy is, I did not fly all this way to discuss lapsed dues." She pointed her pen at Natje, then Constance. "The Tribunal is only concerned in this matter as far as the allegations of magick Forbidden and Foule are concerned. With the eyewitness accounts of two witches in good standing, and without a reliable E.R.I.E. scan to disprove their claims, it is my opinion that she remain under coven custody until extradition to Český Krumlov can be arranged."

The light winked out as briefly as if Milla had blinked, so fast that she would have happily believed that she'd imagined it if not for Lou's angry hiss at her back and Constance's tiny yelp of surprise. She swiveled around to stare at the window, frowning at the glowing lamps.

Lou cleared her throat, stepping beside Milla's chair. "There is one way," she said. "Or rather, one *Way*, I suppose."

"Oh?" Dina lifted one brow, waiting.

"I do not mean to impose, but if it would aid the Third Head in her review of the events, I am happy to offer my services." Lou looked around the room, eyes bright and face the picture of innocence. "If there is a svítilna, on hand, of course."

"You don't mean to suggest …" Constance craned her head around to gape at Lou, her body slowly following as she spun her chair. "A Soul Projection, Agent Simmons?"

Milla sucked in a breath, holding herself as still as she could. A Soul Projection was a specialty of Light Witches. Soul was the memory, the truth of things as seen and lived without personal biases and feelings distorting fact, and a Soul Projection put all of that on display. With their Way, a Light Witch could summon any specific memory to hand and, with the aid of a svítilna, project it for all to see. It was an infallible means of discerning truth in given testimony and only called upon when the need was dire. Veritas potions could be worked around by a clever mind, and allures could be dispelled, but Soul-bound memories were fact writ in stone.

"The tribunal wouldn't dream of asking you to perform such an invasive ritual for a trivial matter."

"A witch's life lies beneath the cleaving blade, Dina," Natje said. "This is hardly trivial."

For the third time, something tickled Milla's foot, slipping around her ankle and staying there. It was a soft possessive touch that had her clenching her teeth and staring at the corner of Constance's desk to keep from whirling around and glaring at the gloom in the corner.

"I agree." Lou's fingers drummed the back of Milla's chair. "As the younger Agent Simmons was the witch assigned to St. Augustine, this matter is anything but trivial"—leather creaked under her nails as she gripped tight—"to me."

Dina's eyes narrowed, and she regarded Lou for a long moment. "I was unaware that your brother was the agent in question," she paced out. "One would think I would have been alerted."

"An oversight," Lou said.

Dina pursed her lips, nodding as she weighed the matter silently. Without warning, she slapped both hands down on the desk, the sharp sound making Milla flinch. "Very well," she waved the back of a hand at Lou. "Get thee to a svítilna."

"We have one or two on hand," Constance said, reaching for a phone at the edge of the desk. The doors at the rear of the office opened, and Rhett stepped in, accompanied by a youngish witch carrying a Bankers Box. Hair styled into a neon-pink faux-hawk clashed wonderfully with their burgundy and tan suit, and the teal pocket square on their suitcoat called the eye to finer, lusher threads in the weave. "Ah, Rhett," Constance smiled at the witch. "Well done, as ever." He nodded his thanks and Constance gestured to the witch carrying the box. "You can place that over there, Maddox." She pointed at Milla, who barely had the time to react before a hefty box full of what had to be rocks dropped on her lap. The witch, Maddox, turned to leave, and Constance asked, "If you have a moment?"

Maddox's shoulders hitched, and they froze midstep, creaking around to face the Elder Witch. "Yes?"

"You are a svítilna, correct?"

Their eyes widened, darting from witch to witch in the room, lingering on Lou before returning to Constance. "Yeah?"

"Excellent." Constance clapped her hands. "We require your Way. Agent Simmons has offered to perform a Soul Projection."

"A Soul …?" Maddox shook their head, backing away from Lou. "I've never—"

"I have." Lou took in the witch from head to toe, looking unimpressed. "It requires little effort on your part; all we need is a mirror."

"I can go get one." Maddox pointed at the door, already leaning into the step

"No need." Constance waved her hand, and a large red velvet drape that had absolutely *not* been hanging on the wall a moment earlier pulled aside, winding in on itself and disappearing to reveal a gilded framed mirror nestled among the bookcases. "Let's get this over with, hm?"

Fourteen

SVÍTILNA Witches with an affinity for light. As opposed to a Light Witch (see: Celtic Practice), a svítilna bends and refracts light to project illusions and imagery against solid surfaces. House of Český Krumlov.

"I'll retrieve the memory of the event in question." Lou's blue-green eyes faded to a hazy white fog, glowing from a light within. The effect was eerie but not unfamiliar. Darkly's eyes did the same thing—almost. Where Lou's gleamed with that ethereal warmth, his would smoke and cloud with a wickedness that called to Milla's Way. "And play it in its entirety. You project the image onto the mirror for the room to witness."

"Like a camera obscura?" Maddox asked, shifting their weight from foot to foot. Sparks danced across their fingers, the only show of any nerves. Lou nodded, a tiny smile easing her expression. "I think I can do that."

"Excellent." Lou shook out her hands and settled on the corner of Constance's desk, one leg crossed over the other, her back impressively straight. "Give me a moment to recall the memory." She flexed her right hand and pressed the tips to the side of her head, brows bunching as that fog lamp gleam in her eyes burned brighter. Her other hand she held flat in the air, palm up like she was balancing a tray.

The room held its breath as Lou stepped into her Way. Intent left her lips as a whisper, the same soft sing-song Irish that Darkly used, and a faint glow appeared at the tips of her fingers. The corners of her eyes tightened, and she slowly pulled her fingers away from her head. Shimmering gold strands followed, thin as spider silk, stemming from each finger and weaving into a singular gleaming thread. Lou straightened her arm, curling and straightening her fingers to gather the summoned memory in her hand. As gently as separating egg whites, she dripped it into her waiting palm.

"Press the base of your palm to mine," she advised in a tight voice. "Form a wall behind the memory."

Maddox did as she asked, gasping with surprise as the memory flared brighter. The teal and magenta sparks that had danced across their fingers fizzed and spurt, the color glowing brighter and brighter until it matched the gold of Lou's memory. "I think I get it."

"Good, now project as you normally would."

Maddox took a deep breath and, in a low, rasping voice, joined their intent with Lou's. Breathy consonants danced a subtle harmony with crisp Irish. Light bent around their hands, the svítilna manipulating the physical manifestation of memory into something tangible to their Way. It fanned out from Lou's palm as light arcs from a film projector, striking against the propped mirror and bouncing back to the opposite wall where it appeared right-side up, Lou's memory now successfully transformed into a living camera obscura.

The memory began, showing them all a view through a windshield. Mid-century storefronts rolled by, and Milla recognized one of the breweries on Anastasia Island as the car turned.

"She's running to the bridge." Darkly's voice flooded the office. Lou must have turned her head because there he was, dressed in his Enforcer blacks and gripping a tablet. His throat bobbed, and he closed his eyes, looking for all the world like he was about to be sick. "There's a raw-head that lives underneath." A beat of silence. "She forgot to feed it today. I can bait it with the Shades, and you'll see. Even if she's a—" The screech of tires cut him off. He lurched forward as Lou slammed on the brakes, catching himself against the dash with a locked arm. Whipping his head to the side, he glared at his sister with coal-black simmering eyes. "She's nae wicked."

"But to use her as bait…"

"You'll see." He worked his jaw, squinting through the windshield. The camera of Lou's eyeline followed his gaze, fixed on the bobbing black ponytail of the witch in question. "We shouldnae be here."

"Keir." Lou's voice held a warning note. She looked at her hands, gripping the wheel, glanced at her brother, and then back to the road. "You'll be vulnerable as well."

He huffed a bitter laugh. "Like you'd let anything happen to me."

"That's not the point!" Lou slammed her palm against the wheel. "It's a needless risk."

"Aye, but if it's the only way to prove to you, definitively, that she isnae responsible for that swell we tracked—"

"Baiting a raw-head with a witch suspected of the Forbidden and Foule on Valentine's Day? Nine rings, Keir, that's cold—even for you."

"She's a clever witch with a terrifying paranoid streak. She'll be fine."

"And if the raw-head turns her, what then?"

It was silent for a moment. Darkly stared out the windshield, his eyes darting left, right, left and landing on the same slight figure running on the sidewalk, her ponytail bouncing with each footfall.

"You can bubble the bridge, and I'll cleave the raw-head," he finally replied in a voice gone distant and cold. "Both of them."

The memory played on. Milla watched herself through Lou's eyes stagger onto the green, pinching her side and bending at the waist to catch her breath. She watched herself run onto the bridge. Watched herself stumble and fall. She saw Darkly send his Shades to trip her, saw them turn her head, saw herself bleeding and terrified, caught in the headlights of an SUV as Darkly yelled out, "Turn the wheel! Turn the fucking wheel!"

In a silence so heavy Milla could hear the blood rushing in her ears, the Elder Witch of the Panhandle Coven and the Third Head witnessed Darkly catching her in his shadows as the raw-head ran past. She saw Lou summoning a shimmering dome and Darkly running at the shield with twin blades of midnight in his hands. He beat against his sister's shield, yelling for Milla. Yelling for Lou to drop the ward while his Shades crashed against and clawed at the barrier, just as they'd done during her arrest; all the while, the E.R.I.E. app on his phone shrieked at the swell of energy Milla had manipulated into her necro-hex.

At the swells of magick Forbidden and Foule that *he* was pumping into her demesne.

She watched it all, letting her anger build and bubble. All she could focus on, all she could think was, "*He* sent a Horned God-damned raw-head after *me*."

He knew.

Just as he'd known what she was from their fourth meeting, he knew she had forgotten to feed the raw-head. He set her up, stacking the deck against Milla, knowing there was no chance in all the hells she'd stay put when her demesne needed tending, and Milla was a gentle tug away from unraveling.

Stay in tonight, aye? He'd asked her. Like he cared.

He baited the damn thing and was willing to let Milla get flayed alive. Willing to take out the raw-head and the progeny it would have made of the Death Witch.

What a Horned God-damned asshole.

A long, silent beat passed. And another, before Dina blew out a breath and chuckled. "Well, that's rather inconclusive."

"How so?" Natje challenged. "My client was clearly attacked by C.R.O.W. agents and utilized her Way in self-defense."

"The Elder and Younger Simmons acted within their rights as Aural Insurance Adjusters. It is their charge to secure the Staid world from witches with Ways Forbidden and Foule, but the question remains, what is her Way?" Dina steepled her fingers, blinking wide innocent eyes at Natje. "As it appears to me, neither you nor the eyewitness account has concluded whether or not the guilty in question is indeed a wicked witch. Until the question is answered, she must remain under coven custody until extradition can be arranged."

Milla's heart lurched. She jerked toward Natje, who was half-risen in her seat, cheeks uncharacteristically flushed.

"Given testimony via Soul Projection," she stated, cold as a German winter, "a Soul-bound memory from a Light Witch no less, cannot be considered faulty or misleading."

"I am not arguing that point," Dina returned. "But the angle from which Agent Simmons viewed the events and the clouding of her own efforts to seclude the Staid from these acts obscure the truth of the intent."

"Then call the other witness." Natje waved a hand over her shoulder, a flippant gesture considering Milla's life was on the line. "Subpoena a mortal, or whoever you deem capable of giving testimony. There is no precedent in C.R.O.W. regulation for detaining a witch on suspicion alone."

"And yet clear and undeniable innocence is required to cleanse the guilty of her accusations." Dina shuffled the papers and shook her head, the dismissal was obvious, the disregard. Natje was arguing a failed point. C.R.O.W. had already decided her fate, just as they had decided that she was Forbidden and Foule, a witch not worth investing time or effort into. She was wicked, her Way was weird, and she was a thing to be scrubbed out and forgotten.

It was only a matter of time, she supposed. Two borrowed years after the ritual at Lake Pontchartrain. That she'd made it this long without bringing down the hammer of C.R.O.W. ought to be considered a miracle.

The only truly confusing part of this was that she'd been caught out by the *raw-head* and not all the wildly wicked magick she'd used at the Fountain of Youth.

"This is not the only matter of importance to the Tribunal, Mistress Tage. Neither I nor the First and Second Heads have the time to waste waiting for a witch to answer our summons. Despite Agent Simmons' illuminative testimony, the fact remains that she was too far away for a conclusive ruling to be made with the evidence provided."

"We do have a secondary witness," Lou said, drawing the room's attention. She spread her hands, and her head tipped toward the shadows occupying a corner of the room. "Willing to give his testimony immediately."

She gestured toward the gloom, and in the stretch of her arm, Milla knew what lurked in those shadows. She stiffened, clenching her jaw and fighting to keep her expression blank. Natje gently squeezed her knee, half in support, half keeping her in the chair as shadows peeled from the walls to puddle on the floor, and Darkly stepped into the room.

He looked like shit.

Haggard and pale, in a three-piece suit that had no business fitting him so well. His cheeks held a hollowness beneath their stubble, and his jaw cut sharper than she remembered. Or maybe it was the ill-advised haircut. The thick auburn waves she had run her fingers through were gone, and his clean-shaven scalp only drew attention to his lowered brows and dark glower.

But even this wraith-like appearance could not diminish the presence that was Darkly. Instead, it lent the witch a dangerous air. The dimple was traded for a hard jaw, his easy slouch replaced by a straight, determined stance.

Rhett gasped at the sudden arrival of a Dark Witch, and Maddox slapped a hand over their mouth to stifle a scream. Lou only rolled her eyes and muttered, "So dramatic."

Darkly ignored them all, dropping the weight of his gaze on Milla and Milla alone. His lips parted, but no sound came out. A shadow peeled away from the swirling mass at his feet, stretching across the floor toward her chair. She hugged the Banker's Box to her chest to keep from throwing it at his face and kicked out, shooing the shadow away before it could wrap around her ankle.

What right did he have to touch her with his Shades? To attempt to soothe her, or comfort or claim her when the whole reason she was in this mess was his fault?

His glower darkened, and Darkly redirected his attention to Dina and Constance. The Elder Witch watched him with a shrewd smile, her quick eyes taking in the brief exchange with Milla. Or rather, his reaching out and her shutting him down. Something like amusement sparkled behind her glasses, and she shook her head, covering her smile with a hand.

"Agent Simmons," Dina greeted him brightly. "What a treat to see the two of you at once."

"Third Head." He nodded curtly.

"I understand you were the agent assigned to the St. Augustine case. Is there anything you wish to share before we begin?" Darkly worked his jaw and flexed his fingers before crossing his arms at his back, both hands tightly fisted. "I see." Dina flipped open the file, making a show of sorting through the reports. "And what is the nature of the guilty's Way?"

"Vestic," he stated.

Dina looked up at him without raising her head, patiently waiting for Darkly to continue. When he did not, she chuckled and turned to another page. "I would like to revisit the conversation in the car before the events on the bridge if that is alright." Darkly nodded. "I'm sure you saw what your sister shared while haunting us from the shadows. Do you need any priming to recall the day?" He shook his head. Dina finally looked up, frowning at him as if his silence was a personal insult. "Very well, let us begin."

"Objection!"

All eyes whipped toward Natje, seated in her chair with crossed arms. She pointed at Rhett, seething beside the door. His eyes were wide, nostrils flared, and bowtie dancing as his chest heaved. He pointed a trembling finger at Darkly.

"Are you really going to believe the testimony of that—that—"

"Careful," Milla warned.

"*Witch?*"

Darkly scoffed, sliding his hands into his pockets and regarding Rhett down the line of his nose. "Is that the best you could come up with?"

"He should be cleaved!" Rhett charged between the chairs and slapped his hands on the desk. "He shouldn't be allowed to live, and you're going to let him testify?"

Constance drew her lips into a line. Her nails scraped across the desk, but Dina spoke first.

"I do love the younger generation." She smiled dotingly at Rhett, but it was a serpent's smile. Close-lipped and narrowed-eyed, hiding the fangs and venom behind a sleek, slippery exterior. "Warriors for truth and sticklers for the law."

"C.R.O.W. regulation states that a Dark Witch shall be cleaved upon identification." Spittle flew from the young witch's lips. He jabbed the desk with a finger. "For all we know, he's seized Agent Simmons' Shade and forced her to—"

Lou burst out in tinkling laughter. "Oh, good Goddess, that's rich." She grinned at her brother, who dropped his eyes to the floor. Her smile faded, and what was left more resembled a predator baring its teeth in warning than an amused witch. She stepped close to Rhett, looming over him in her heels, and hissed in a low voice, "Do you honestly think C.R.O.W. would allow a Dark Witch to work within their ranks untended?"

Milla hugged her box tighter, wondering over her choice of words. She knew Lou was his handler, but what did "untended" mean? He said he'd needed Milla to get back to his life. Lou had said he'd needed to deliver a Death Witch, which he'd done, so what was this all about?

"I—" Rhett darted his gaze between the Simmons siblings. He licked his lips, taking a breath to argue.

"For Horned Gods' sake, witchling, sit down before you hurt yourself," Constance snapped at her assistant. "And next time, deploy one-eighth of that brain of yours before you speak." Her bangles and beads clacked and jangled as she spun to face Dina. "If word gets out that the Panhandle Coven hosted a Dark Witch, there will be nine rings of hell to pay. Will you accept his testimony?"

"I assure you, his Way is well-tempered and under control," Lou added with a glare at Rhett. Darkly cleared his throat and slid a hand free to adjust his tie. Milla zeroed in on the movement, her mind running through the implications of that gesture and Lou's words.

How often had she seen him react like that whenever she came too close to the truth? She'd lost count over those weeks in St. Augustine. Had lost count during their week in Daytona because he'd done it whenever she asked about her demesne or when she could go home. Whenever he was uncomfortable.

So why now? He'd delivered a Death Witch to C.R.O.W. and was still waltzing his stupidly tall body freely around while Milla rotted in a cell. What in the nine rings did he have to be *uncomfortable* about?

"I do not doubt that, Agent Simmons," said Dina. "Let's get to it. The sooner we're through this farce of a trial, the better."

"Objection," said Natje.

"Triple Goddess's tits." Dina rolled her eyes. "We've been over this already, advoccultant. What on earth are you objecting to?"

"Is this, or is this not, a trial?" Natje cocked her head, the sharp line of her hair bobbing.

"This is most assuredly not a trial."

The Nachthexe smiled and pointed a finger at Dina. "Then I object to your use of the word 'trial'."

"Oh, for—" Dina whipped around in her chair, all but hollering in Constance's face. "Yes! The tribunal will accept the testimony of a Dark Witch if only to get this circus over with." She glared at the Elder Witch, then Darkly, then Lou. "Now get on with it."

Fifteen

NATJE CEDED HER CHAIR to Darkly, rising gracefully to lean against the bookshelf, arms crossed in an impossibly casual pose. Milla hugged her Banker's Box, leaning away from Darkly as he sat beside her.

"From the car, I think," Dina instructed. "I'd like to revisit your conversation without the sound obstruction."

Lou took her position behind Darkly, squeezing his shoulder in a show of sibling support as Maddox cast a longing look at the door before sighing and stepping between the chairs. Milla was grateful for the wall of their body, whippet-thin as they were. She didn't trust herself not to tear off the lid of her box and start lobbing wads of paper at the asshole Dark Witch as he prepared to tell the Third Head of the Tribunal that, yes, Milla was a Death Witch, and *yes,* she had worked magick Forbidden and Foule as easily as breathing.

A lie.

It hadn't been easy, but how would they know that? She had been desperate and terrified and *hurt*. She had fed that raw-head every day for two years, keeping the mortals safe and the desecrant alive. Dusting the awful thing had taken all Milla had, and no Soul-bound memory would show the pain it caused her to take a life. No Soul Projection could offer the color of emotion and depths of regret. How she had hated herself in the moment and how she had drawn from the very dregs of her Soul and Shade because she wanted to *live*.

No. All they would see is a witch dusting a desecrant in full view of the human population of St. Augustine, and Milla would be cleaved.

"Do you need any help recalling the day?" Lou asked her brother. He shook his head, eyes firmly pinned on the mirror across the room. Gripping both armrests, he closed his eyes and breathed deeply. Lou pressed the tips of her fingers to his head. He tensed, shoulders hitching, and almost immediately, the faint glow of a Soul-bound memory pulsed beneath her touch.

She pulled her hand away, and the gleaming strands danced along her fingers and palm like static electricity in a plasma ball. Unlike before, where she gathered the memory into a palm, this time, she plucked and pinched the strands with her other hand like a harpist playing their instrument. When the bulk of the glowing strands had been gathered, she again pressed her fingers to Darkly's scalp and lowered her hand, laying it flat in the air, palm up, for Maddox to project the memory.

The image bled across the mirror, revealing the tablet in Darkly's hands and the rising and falling arcs of the signatures dancing across his E.R.I.E.

"She's running the bridge." His voice held the same slight echo Lou's had in her memory. The image winked out, and Milla remembered that he'd closed his eyes. "There's a raw-head that lives underneath."

"Ah yes, this is the part." Dina sat back in her chair and summoned a bag of candy to hand. She tossed a few brightly colored pieces into her mouth, chewing loudly.

"I can bait it with the Shades, and you'll see." His attention slid from the tablet to the car floor between his booted feet. "Even if she's a—"

Tires screeched, and the dashboard rushed toward his face. Darkly whipped his head to the side, revealing a wide-eyed, startled Lou pressed back against her seat. She gripped the wheel, staring back at Darkly as if he'd just sprouted wings.

"She's nae wicked," he growled.

"But to use her as bait…"

"Wait." The image dimmed and slowed. Maddox flexed their fingers and massaged their wrist, brows drawn together in confusion. "Sorry, I think I messed it up."

"Perhaps." Dina tossed another handful of candy into her mouth. Hard sugar cracked beneath her teeth as she chewed. "Hard to hear over those tires."

"But what did he say?" Rhett stepped into view beside Milla. "He knows what she is; what did he say?"

"You heard him as well as we did," said Constance. "She's not wicked."

"No, no, before that." He jogged a finger at the wall, then twisted around to look at the reverse image in the mirror. "Even if she's a what?" He appealed to the Elder Witch; his voice tight and frantic. "Ask him what he said."

"I thought you said we should not hear the testimony of a Dark Witch." Dina smiled back at him, the expression pasted on. "At least, that is what *I* heard. Connie?" She rolled her head along her neck to look at Constance, tossing another handful of candy in her mouth.

"I heard the same." Constance pressed both hands on the desk, leaning forward to seethe at her assistant. "Any more of these outbursts, Rhett, and I'll be submitting a requisition for a new assistant. Am I understood?"

The blood rushed from his cheeks, leaving Rhett's complexion sallow and pale. "Y-yes, ma'am." He nodded tersely and backed away.

"Maddox?" Constance gestured to the svítilna. "If you're good to continue?"

"I am." Maddox rolled their wrist. Bones crackled and popped; they shook out their hand and pressed it again to Lou's palm.

Darkly's memory shot onto the mirror and resumed. Every witch watched them bait Milla. Watched her run, watched his Shade catch her, watched her fall and wrestle with the raw-head. But Milla watched Darkly, searching his face for any show of remorse or regret. Anything resembling the pain she'd heard in his voice when he admitted his involvement to her in that Tallahassee motel. When he'd told Milla he was trying to save her and she'd thrown herself at him like a sad, desperate witchling.

He sat straight and tall in the chair, hands gripping the armrests, jaw clenched, without an ounce of emotion playing out over a face she had once thought to be cartoonishly expressive. He was a stranger to her, in his suit with his ill-advised haircut. An Enforcer, and not her Dark Witch.

Never her Dark Witch.

He was a lie.

"Hold that." Dina stood.

Constance let out a heavy breath, sagging into her chair as the image froze. "Goddess, it's worse the second time."

Milla frowned at the mirror and the image of Darkly's fisted hand frozen mid-pound against Lou's barrier. Beyond him and slightly out-of-focus, she saw herself on her back, fingers clawed into the raw-head's side. Her face was turned away, her neck arched as the raw-head scraped jagged nails down her throat.

"Reverse, please," Dina said, intent on the memory.

"How far?" Lou asked. Her voice trembled, and she swayed in her heels, cheeks an ashen gray. A fine sweat dotted her brow, and the foglamp gleam in her eyes dimmed.

"Two or three—no, I'll do it." Dina shook out her arms and pinched the air, twisting her fingers like a radio technician adjusting dials. The projection on the wall wobbled and reversed, and every hair on Milla's arms rose.

Chronomantic.

She flexed her fingers, wiggled her toes, and fought against the scream rising in her throat as the Third Head of the Tribunal reversed an isolated pocket of time *within a memory* as easily as she'd breezed into the room.

"Can you zoom in?" Dina asked Maddox. The svítilna nodded, bringing their thumb and ring finger together in a pinch and then spreading them. The image zoomed in, a little blurry. "On her hand, if you please."

Maddox repeated the motion, this time turning their wrist slightly, adjusting the position of the Soul Bound memory. Darkly's fist blurred at the edge of the screen, and all eyes were guided to Milla pinned beneath the raw-head, her left hand forming a weak chronomantic return.

"Did you know she did this?" Dina asked Lou.

"During my brother's interrogation of the accused the following day, it was assessed that she had been instructed in the formation of chronomantic hexes by the Morgenhexe."

"Why was this not in the report?"

"Must have slipped my mind," said Darkly.

Milla couldn't believe what she was hearing. No one lied to an agent of C.R.O.W., and here was Darkly omitting scraps of memory in front of an Elder Witch and a Head of the Tribunal.

What is happening?

"Well." Dina relaxed into her chair, her expression close to relief. "It looks to me as though the guilty deployed a standard chronomantic hex. Continue the Projection, please." Lou nodded and flicked her fingers.

On the wall, Milla watched herself wrap her legs around the raw-head and roll the desecrant onto its back. The shield Lou had thrown distorted the image, a little piece of luck Milla hadn't considered—it hid the ash spewing from her lips as she cursed the creature.

Her left hand never left the raw-head's side. It writhed beneath her, pawing at her arms, her legs. Clawing at her wrist and tearing the skin. Its movements grew sluggish, and then it stopped altogether, crumbling like sand as it succumbed to a necrotic hex disguised by years of careful training and lies.

The office was silent as the final images of the memory played out. Darkly approached the pile of marlstone dust, scooping the remains of the raw-head into his hand. He jerked his face up, briefly catching sight of Milla as she stumbled into the Colonial Quarter and disappeared. The image jogged, Lou yelled his name, and the wall went blank.

After a long, stressful moment, Dina exhaled and leaned back in her chair, releasing every witch from the chokehold of Darkly's memory.

Lou sagged forward, catching herself on the back of Darkly's chair, making him jump in his seat. He twisted around, grabbing her elbow and peering worriedly up at his sister. She murmured something too low to hear, and he nodded, the worry easing, but he did not let go of her arm until Dina spoke.

"Well," said the Third Head. She took in the Simmons siblings, scanning Milla with a pensive look before letting her gaze drift to the empty air over her head. "Well," she said again, "while we do not have an answer as to what the guilty's Way is, we can at least determine that the desecrant in question was hexed with a textbook chronomantic reversal, which rules out the use of magick Forbidden and Foule. It's the readings I can't figure."

"As this is not a trial, and I cannot be accused of conjecture," Natje called from where she still leaned against the bookcase, "it might bear considering the amount of magick deployed by the younger Agent Simmons during my client's run-in with the desecrant."

"My team's technical witch posited a similar theory," Lou added. "Keir's Way, paired with the intent of the evening, would test the reporting capabilities of our devices. According to Cyrus, the E.R.I.E. has rarely been attuned to a Dark Witch, and certainly never a Dark Witch operating under the magick of Valentine's Day."

Dina tapped her lips, eyes slitting as she considered the suggestion. She shook her head and covered her face, dragging at the skin under her eyes as she pulled her hands away and peered at her over her fingertips. "I am sorry, dear girl."

"I—" Milla glanced over her shoulder, then back to Dina. "Me?"

"I can argue the use of a chronomantic hex, we all saw it and your rearing by Morgen's hand, but the E.R.I.E. readings are going to be a point of contention."

"I don't—"

"She's a vestic," Rhett grumbled in a low voice that was absolutely meant to be heard. "No vestic has ever been capable of working chronomancy."

"Rhett," Constance snarled, rising from her chair and thrusting her arm at the door, finger pointed. "Out."

"Goddess, this generation. Let him stay." Dina waved her hand, dismissing both Constance's demand and Rhett's outburst. "Tell me, witchling, what is vesticism if not the magick of glimpsing the future and reading the intent of the past? Soothsayers cast their bones and favomancers their beans, but each is traveling through time to gain answers. To read history and predict the future." The vague amusement softening her features vanished, and Dina hit Rhett dead-on with a cold, imperious stare. "Better you learn this lesson now than several more years into what will assuredly amount to a failed career in C.R.O.W.: the Ways are not as disparate as your textbooks would have you believe. Magick comes from one of two sources. As a vestic, yours is a gift from the Triple Goddess, and the Mother, Maiden, and Crone contain multitudes. Am I clear?"

Rhett swallowed and rasped, "Yes, ma'am."

"Good. Now kindly shut up and let the adults work." She pursed her lips, clearly about to say something else when Maddox blurted:

"But it was her left hand."

"Oh for—" Constance drooped forward, thudding her forehead against the desk.

Dina slowly faced Maddox, a disbelieving little smile displaying the top row of her teeth. "And what might that have to do with anything?" she said, her lips barely moving, eyes unblinking.

"I prepared her file." Their eyes darted to Milla, then the floor. "Her record states she's right-handed, but that chronomantic hex was worked with her left."

"You were watching the mirror, Maddox," said Constance. "An easy mistake."

"I'm sorry, Elder Witch, but this is *my* Way," they argued. "I know my Way better than I know myself most days, and she used her left hand."

"*Fine*," Dina snapped in an arctic voice. "Agent Simmons, again."

And Lou went again, withdrawing the memory from a tense and pale Darkly. Maddox held the projection on Milla's hand, an argument broke out between Natje, Dina, and Constance, and Maddox played it again, and again.

Rhett's glare bored into her back, and the Banker's Box was heavy on her thighs. Milla shrank into herself, wishing she could disappear from the room, from the Horned God-awful memory being played for a sixth time and the pained little grunts of the Dark Witch who supplied it.

When the scene had played out, and Milla had once again disappeared into the heart of the Colonial Quarter, Lou released the memory with a gasp, staggering back and bumping into the desk. Darkly slid lower in the chair, chin dropped against his chest and panting as if he'd just sprinted a mile. Even Maddox sagged where they stood, running a shaking hand through their neon pink pompadour.

"Are we satisfied with the guilty's ambidexterity?" Constance finally asked. "Or shall we call another svítilna?"

"And draw out this charade further?" Dina retorted. "Horned God forbid."

"If any question remains," Darkly suggested. He pushed himself from the chair and loomed over the desk. "Project her memory. I'm finished."

"Finished," Dina repeated.

"You've seen all I can offer and nearly burnt my sister out. Grant the guilty her testimony," he said. "See the events of the day from her own eyes if you're still nae convinced, or order me to cleave her here and now. You'll get no more from me."

"Oh." The sound left Milla unwanted, but Horned God, she really ought to have known. Of course, Lou would be involved with this. *Of course*, Darkly would be summoned to attend and show up wearing his funeral best. A cleaving was the final severing of a witch's body from her Soul and Shade, and of all the known Ways, only two were known to be capable of the task without requiring a full coven casting their support. "That is fucked up."

"Ludmilla," warned Natje.

Dina twerked her gaze to Milla, and the corner of her mouth gave the tiniest, amused little twitch. She flitted a shrewd gaze over Darkly and nodded in agreement. "Natje," she said, not bothering to seek out the advoccultant. "Any objection to your client giving her testimony?"

Natje shrugged one shoulder. "I was under the impression this was not a trial."

Dina rolled her eyes and wagged a finger. "Consider my petard hoisted. You, witchling." She snapped at Milla. "Call up the day."

Sixteen

"Just a little longer," Lou mumbled as she positioned herself behind Milla, so low she almost missed it. "This next bit is up to you."

"What—" Nails pinched her shoulder. Milla hissed, eyes darting to where Natje leaned against the bookshelf and landing on Darkly instead. He stood beside the advoccultant, hands in his pockets and back against the shelf, his body too stiff for the pose to be casual. The green eyes were back, his face a storm cloud as he glared over Milla's head. At Lou.

"Not that any of us expect the answer to be 'no,' Ludmilla, but do you require assistance recalling the events of the day?" Dina asked, already bored. Milla shook her head. "Blessed be." She gestured to Lou. "Ready when you are, Agent Simmons."

Lou pressed her fingertips against Milla's head and dropped into her Way, the faint Irish of her allure trickling into Milla's ears like cold honey. There was a rush of warmth across her scalp; her skin tingled, and then that warmth bled deeper, dribbling around

Milla's mind in a suffocating embrace. Her presence felt like the brush of a feather against her thoughts, a tickling, aggravatingly soft sensation deep in the recesses of her mind where no nails could scratch.

Heat flared in her veins as the intruding magick itched beneath her skull. Milla sat on her hands to keep from scratching her arms and closed her eyes to avoid looking at Darkly, hating how he had tolerated this with a detached calm, as if he didn't feel his sister's creeping presence like a testing poison in his mind.

She gritted her teeth and pressed her tongue against the roof of her mouth to keep from crying out. Lou grunted, a tiny sound, almost a whimper, and then her presence retreated.

"Are you alright?" Maddox asked.

"I can't—" Lou started, then drifted back among Milla's memories. Searching and searching and searching and unable to grab hold of any of it. "How are you—"

Milla felt the Lou's Way slip and fumble. Her touch grew more aggressive, more demanding, and the tell-tale prickles of a migraine began behind Milla's eyes. She hissed, pressing her palms against the pain in her temples. Lou's presence grew weighted, the warmth rising to boiling in Milla's head. Someone panted, tight, pitched breaths that had to be doing more to raise their panic than calm them down. Lou pressed harder, and whoever was panting gave a low, pained groan.

"Objection!" yelled Natje.

"For Horned God's sake, this is not a trial," Dina clapped back. "Are you *really* objecting to your own client's testimony?"

"This isn't a testimony; this is torture."

And that's when Milla realized *she* was the someone groaning, held to the chair by Lou's clawing grip on her head, in her mind. Her migraine throbbed, one wicked pulse, and bile rose in her throat. She hiccuped and slammed a hand over her mouth, frantically searching the room for a trash can. Arctic cold crashed against her chest and neck, crawling up Milla's cheeks and into her hair. The room went pitch-black even as the ache in her skull was soothed by the chill of a shadowblind.

"No." Milla hunched over her knees and buried her face in her hands. She didn't want his help, didn't want to need his help, didn't want to be cut off from the room and the witches in it, drowned in the dark. But here he was, throwing his Shades at Milla as easily as he threw her under the bus. "Please," she gasped.

"*Five things, Milla,*" a voice whispered, and the dark receded, revealing the room and a furious Darkly, his face parchment pale except for two angry red blotches on his cheeks and black eyes raging at Lou. Shadow swirled and curled in on itself, settling in Milla's lap like a cat.

Her shoulders shook, every muscle in her body taut to the point of trembling. She fixed her eyes on her knees to keep from seeking out that voice, gripping the seat of her chair and digging her fingernails into the wood until they threatened to bend back. She couldn't catch her breath, couldn't gain control of herself, and oh *Goddess*, it was still there. Puddled in her lap without touching her at all, and that *voice.*

"*Five things you can see.*"

"She's—" Lou rushed around the chair, filling the space in front of Milla. There, right there. A real witch. One she could reach out and touch with a face she could see. It took every ounce of effort to raise her head, to see Lou and register that her eyes were wide and terrified. Her mouth opened and closed, trying to form coherent words.

"Agent Simmons?" Constance called out. "What's happened?"

Lou looked at the Elder Witch, ran a trembling hand over her perfectly smooth hair, and spoke. "I am unable to pull a Projection from the guilty."

"And why is that?" Dina demanded.

"Because"—she cocked her head at Milla, mystified—"she's already been cleaved."

Maddox jumped away from Milla, joining Natje and Darkly against the bookshelf, and Dina dropped her head, massaging her temples.

"Horned God, this is a bloody PR nightmare."

"What does that mean?" Rhett stormed up to the desk. From where she sat, Milla had a fine vantage of the sweat sticking his shirt to his back.

"It means that all Soul-bound memory of the witch in question is inadmissible as testimony," Natje answered.

"B-but—" he sputtered. "She dusted that desecrant, and we don't have any answers!"

"This is ridiculous." Dina pointed at Milla. "You, witchling, when were you cleaved?"

"How in the nine rings would I know?" Milla answered.

"I don't think any witch would know when they'd been cleaved," said Constance. "No one has ever survived a cleaving, much less been able to answer the question as to how."

"So ask her and find out," Rhett pressed. "You're the Third Head of the Tribunal. Call a vinefica up with some veritas brew and make her talk."

"And what would that resolve?" Lou asked. "Her Soul-bound memory is irretrievable, and even if I could grab hold, her apparent cleaving renders it inadmissible. Short of gathering the shorn pieces of her, we are treading into the unknown, the

Forbidden, and the Foule." Rhett blanched, leaning away from Lou. "Interested in a cleaving of your own?"

"N-no, ma'am." He scurried away, whisking the pocket square free to pat his brow.

"How do we proceed?" Constance laced her fingers under her chin, regarding Milla sharply.

"You could acquit her," Natje suggested.

"Not a trial," muttered Maddox.

Natje smiled dotingly at them and continued. "The testimony of several witnesses shows that the guilty acted in self-defense, utilizing a Fine and Faire application of a chronomatic hex. Ms. Probuditna is guilty under suspicion of utilizing magick Forbidden and Foule in the destruction of a desecrant creature, and the evidence shows that my client is innocent of the charges levied against her. By Rite of Invocation and Manipulation of the Ways, my client is entitled to an acquittal."

"So it's clear," said Constance, "no cleaving."

"It's not as though we can exact a punishment the witch in question has already suffered." Dina mused. "Proven innocent by dint of not drowning. Just like the old days." She hit Milla with a hard stare, eyes flitting over her form. A frown pursed her lips, her eyes narrowed in thought, and then she slapped the desk. "C.R.O.W. is satisfied. The witch did not perform magick outside of regulation, and she has already suffered a cleaving. The problem now is the optics of it all."

Lou cleared her throat, drawing the attention of the room. "If the Tribunal is willing, I believe I have a solution that would satisfy C.R.O.W."

"Oh?"

"As you know, Third Head, my field partner, the younger Agent Simmons, is a Dark Witch." Darkly surged from the wall with a snarl, halting midstep when Lou threw out her hand. Across the room, Rhett whimpered, earning a glare from Constance. "His record in the field is sterling, and, barring the events in St. Augustine, he has yet to fail an assignment."

"Lou, no," Darkly snapped. She shot him a quick look, lips pursing in response, and Dina cut her off.

"What about the Harlingen Incident?" Her shrewd gaze leveled on Darkly, and she poked the air as she asked, "Weren't you benched after a run-in with a lorelei?"

Milla whipped her head around, along with half the room, to see Darkly's already gloomy expression darken further. He dropped his eyes to the floor, his lip twitched, and when he looked up, the cold, stony mask was firmly back in place. "The desecrant I hunted was destroyed."

"But weren't you benched?"

"Hospitalized," he answered through clenched teeth. When his lip twitched again, the mask cracked, and Milla saw the tic for what it truly was: pain. "And placed on probation."

He had never told her what landed him in the hospital, only that he'd been placed into a coma, which explained why he wasn't managing the Shades when Milla and Ezra attempted their ritual. But he had mentioned an incident in the Netherlands and that when he'd woken, the Shades warned him there was someone at the Gates.

Someone Milla had left there.

This additional knowledge added a piece to the puzzle Milla had been trying to assemble for years, sending a chill racing down her spine. Darkly had been injured in the field and placed into a coma. At the same time, Milla and Ezra had been told everything was ready, which begged the question: was Darkly's injury truly an accident? Or had he been caught in the same manipulative web as Milla?

She scanned the room and the witches in it, seeking the weaknesses in the facade. Lou, Dina, Constance, Natje. Powerful witches at the top of their respective fields, and none of them had been surprised to learn Darkly was a Dark Witch.

Images of that night in New Orleans flickered through her mind. Masked witches in a decadent hall embracing and welcoming Milla as one of their own, their identities hidden behind masks and a drunken haze from the alcohol continually placed in her hand.

She couldn't trust the memory. So much had happened so fast, and Milla had run, hiding away in that apartment, in Czechia, and finally in St. Augustine, where Darkly had found her. Darkly, who had lied to her and betrayed her and was somehow the only witch in this room she knew without a doubt had not been there that night.

And his absence had made it all possible.

She bit the inside of her cheek, silently willing him to say more. To help her understand *why* he'd betrayed her and turned her in to C.R.O.W. because none of this made sense. Not his memories with its curious blanks, not her cleaving, not this mockery of a trial that wasn't a trial.

"My brother suffered a fall in executing his task," Lou cut in. "Injuries in the field cannot be held against the agent, especially when sustained in completing an assignment."

"Too true." Dina clicked her tongue and shook her head. "Dreadful injury it was. The First Head and I were rooting for you, Keir."

"Thank you, Third Head." His reply was quiet. Restrained and unsettling. Perhaps it was the familiarity between Lou and the

Third Head; more likely, it was that she'd just admitted another member of the Tribunal was aware of Darkly, his role, and his Way.

But then there was that twitch of his lip. The tiny little tic she recognized as a wince he was trying to hide.

Natje clapped her hand on Milla's shoulder, jarring her from her thoughts. Her grip was tight, a warning as if the Nachthexe were aware of the direction her mind had run. A crescent of moonlight glowed in her eyes, and she tipped her head forward with a whispered, "Shh."

At that, Milla saw the room for what it was: an elaborate performance in which only half the actors knew the script. Her attention swerved to Dina at ease in her chair, nudging this not-trial in her desired direction, and then her eyes found Darkly.

His lip twitched, one eye half winking closed in a tiny wince. A flutter of confusion danced across his face and he looked away.

Which—what in the nine rings did *he* have to be confused about? All of this was his fault, and it wasn't like he was on trial. *He'd* been allowed to live and practice his Way. Been allowed to become an Enforcer while Milla had been hidden like a dirty secret and manipulated by witches using her Way to achieve their aims when all she had wanted, all she had *dreamt* of being was an Enforcer like him.

Heat flared again in her arms and spread across her breastbone. A noxious mixture of Waybound magick and rage. The unfairness of it all, the hypocrisy. Raise a Dark Witch and use him as a tool while condemning a Death Witch for merely existing.

"I will fix this," he had promised, but he was a liar—he had been from that very first day. Darkly couldn't fix this, not when the system was inherently broken and biased against her. He could make all the promises he wanted, but in the end, he was a conniving, controlling little witch. Even if he managed the unthinkable by lying to C.R.O.W. to get her out of the mess he had caused, she refused to bend in her anger.

"I think I see where Agent Simmons is going with this," said Dina. She leaned closer to Constance. "Keir was initially mentored by his sister," she told the Elder Witch. "It was at her pestering—"

"Requesting," said Lou.

"Pestering," Dina smiled at her fondly, "that we agreed to the initial trial run."

"A trial run that has run for what?" Constance eyed Darkly. "Twenty years?"

"Nothing so egregious," said Dina. "Agent Simmons trained as an Enforcer with the coven at Grim Ness, and has served as an Enforcer for, what has it been, love? Eight years? Nine?"

"Ten," Darkly rasped. "Ten years."

"There, you see?" Dina wagged her finger at him. "A decade we've had a witch with a Way Forbidden and Foule serving as an Enforcer. And not just any Enforcer, one of the highest rated and regarded in his field." She pursed her lips and frowned at Darkly the way someone frowns at a dog who just shat the carpet. "Minus the Harlingen Incident, of course."

"Horned God, Dina." Constance looked from the Third Head to Milla, to Lou, and back. "Are you suggesting that we—"

"I'm only offering backstory. Agent Simmons is the one making the suggestion."

"It's unheard of!"

"Quite the contrary," Natje replied, "and the living proof is haunting the corner of this office."

At that, every witch's attention landed on Darkly. Shadow seethed from his shoulders and billowed at his feet, and a very angry, very black-eyed glare shot over Milla's head.

A heavy beat of silence followed before Constance exhaled and addressed Lou. "What exactly are you proposing, Agent Simmons?"

"I—"

"Lou," Darkly barked, his voice a thunderclap. In an instant, Milla was back beneath the barrier ward, barefoot in her bathing suit, as the Dark Witch and the Light Witch argued. Only this time, Lou did not beg her brother to stand down. She simply threw up two fingers, gesturing for her brother to remain quiet while the grown-ups talked.

"I propose that you assign Ludmilla Probuditna to my team as a Junior Enforcer, call it probationary if you must. It would be a similar arrangement to the one we made so long ago with my brother and a responsibility for which I have proven myself more than capable."

"Luminescence," he warned again. "We talked about this." Milla felt a tendril of night circling her leg like a manacle waiting to be snapped closed. She lifted her feet from the floor and hooked them around the legs of her chair. Darkly let out a soft, broken sigh, and she glanced back, immediately wishing she hadn't.

His mask cracked, black eyes lightening enough for her to catch the rim of his iris. Enough for the hurt to show, and then it was gone again, buried beneath the anger of the Shade.

"The way I see it, this solves your PR problem," Lou continued. "Harlingen and St. Augustine aside, my brother is a testament to not only the firm hand of C.R.O.W. but the importance of regulation among our ranks."

"The proposition has merit," Dina mused.

Rhett scoffed and spat bitterly, "I can't believe you're even considering—"

"*Master Marchand.*" Constance boomed, slapping her hand against the desk. The sharp sound ricocheted off the walls along with her voice. Milla jumped, and the Banker's Box slid out of her lap, papers scattering across the floor. "Leave."

"Elder Witch," he protested, "I—"

"You heard me," Constance hollered. "Leave, or I will have you removed from this room and your post."

The younger witch huffed, but a moment later the door of Constance's office slammed closed. She dropped her head into the crook of her hand, taking a few deep breaths, and then added, "You as well, Maddox."

"Ma'am?"

Constance raised her head, looking closer to her true age than the vague fifty-something Milla had known for nearly two decades. "Thank you for your assistance; I know you must be exhausted, so please, take a break. Nine rings, take the rest of the day off." Maddox edged away from the desk, hesitating behind Milla's chair. "Grab something to eat before you leave, hm?" Constance added. "Tell the kitchen witches in the commissary to charge it to my account."

"Yes, ma'am." Maddox rushed away, closing the door far quieter than Rhett had.

Another tense silence spread over the remaining witches, broken by Dina's chuckle.

"Well played, Connie." She patted Constance on the shoulder, a slick smile brightening her expression. "I wondered when you'd send them off."

"Goddess, with any luck, Rhett is already fuming in the secretary pit." She rubbed her temple and grinned at Milla. "I hope you're ready, girl."

"Ready for what?"

"For the big leagues," Constance answered. "We're trying to soft launch a Death Witch, a certain amount of finesse is required."

Milla's mouth fell open, the anger and rage that had been simmering beneath her skin cooling by an uneasy degree, and she said the only thing she could.

"What."

Seventeen

TRISKELION A sigil common in Celtic practice representing the cycle of birth, life and death

Light witch binding *you DO know how fucked up this is, right?*

well aware, thanks

"WHAT?" DARKLY'S VOICE ECHOED Milla's, and she damn near snapped her neck as she whipped around to catch him gawking at her. "She's a … *what.*"

"Oh, Horned God." Lou rolled her eyes and approached her brother carefully, hands out and voice soft. "Not now, Keir."

Darkly pressed against the wall, wide green eyes bouncing from Milla to Lou and back, looking as if someone had just told him the sky was purple. He winced again, hissing and pressing the heel of his palm to his temple. "I dinnae—"

"I'll explain later, wee yin." She gently gripped his shoulders, getting close to Darkly's face and whispering in his ear. His cheeks blanched, smoke wafted over his eyes, and after a long moment, he pressed his lips together, gaining control of whatever had frightened him and wrangling it into submission. "Just a little longer, alright?"

"I dinnae understand…" Even as he whispered, Milla heard the quiet plea in his words. He looked at her over his sister's shoulder, winced, and closed his eyes, face tight with pain. "Why can't I—"

He went still as Lou cupped his cheek, forcing her brother to meet her eye. "Later, Keir."

"Poor dear," Dina tutted. She leaned over and whispered to Constance, "Would it help if we put the boy out of his misery?"

The shift in the room was palpable, reflected by the mischief vanishing from Constance's face. She sent a sympathetic smile in Darkly's direction and shook her head. "I'd rather not have to explain why an unconscious Dark Witch is being carried from my office."

As much as she hated liars who betrayed their pseudo-girlfriends to save their own skin, Milla hated the games C.R.O.W. played even more. She shouldered her anger, hooking her thumb at Darkly. "What's his problem?"

Natje settled in the chair beside her, leaning over the armrest to brush her arm. "Nothing for you to worry about."

"All offense meant, but that's bullshit"—she jerked her head at the Simmons siblings—"that's fucking *weird*, and what do you mean 'soft launch a Death Witch'?" She spat out this last bit directly at Constance. Aunt Connie. A witch she had known for close to twenty years and was just now realizing she didn't know at all.

"Why do you think I was always down in Key West?" Constance replied.

"I—but—*what*." She whipped around to Natje, who nodded slowly, which did nothing to help Milla settle this new knowledge with the life she had known. "How many witches *knew?*"

"You resurrected a dog in the middle of Český Krumlov, Ludmilla." Dina pushed back from the desk and rose. "Not even the Advoccultant General could hide that from C.R.O.W."

"Perhaps if he had called me first," Natje muttered under her breath.

"It was a new moon, and you know it." Dina rolled her eyes and strode around the desk, settling on the edge in front of Milla. "No one lies to C.R.O.W., dear." Dina patted her head. "But a small amount of obfuscation goes a long way."

"And some clever social engineering even further." Constance grinned mischievously at Milla as if she were in on their joke. Considering she wasn't laughing, Milla decidedly was not.

"I don't—"

"Gossips, girl." Dina cackled in Milla's face. "Witches are terrible gossips. Put the right witnesses in a room together, one prejudiced and one sympathetic, and you can spin whatever story you desire."

"By now, Rhett has likely commandeered a secretary's computer to pull up Keir's record, which will corroborate everything he heard in this office." Constance eased back in her chair, bangles jangling as she crossed her arms. Her smug expression lit up her eyes, and her full lips split to place brilliant white teeth on display. "He'll see, with an audience of onlookers, that our Keir is a witch in good standing with a decade of stellar work as an Enforcer under his belt."

Something about the way she said his name, the possessiveness in her tone, rankled Milla. Goddess knew why. She pushed her lips together as Constance spoke, pouting instead of giving in to the overwhelming urge to demand Darkly answer to the one damn question she had: *Why.*

Because *none of this made sense.*

He knew her Way, had suffered and learned her Way, and sought to help her control it. Yes, he was a liar, but nobody lied to C.R.O.W.

That he had managed it—along with a life as a Dark Witch and a career as an Enforcer—that he knew the Third Head and was conspicuously absent the one night the Neitherworld needed it… at all of *that*, some nasty little voice in her head began yelling that he was being played as much as she was, and it felt *terrible*.

"Maddox, dear witch that they are, will confirm the Soul Projections and that the Elder Agent Simmons was unable to pull your memory. Everyone will be so distracted by the witch who survived a cleaving that the reality of your Way will either fall by the wayside or act as an explanation rather than a reason for blame."

"Can't cleave the Death Witch," Dina sang. "And can't blame the Death Witch for being uncleavable." She tapped her nose, pointed at Milla, and winked. "Especially if she works for the very agency desiring her cleaving."

"…what," croaked Milla.

"It's nothing you haven't already agreed to, Ludmilla." This came from Lou, still haunting the wall with her brother. Something slammed against the bookshelf, a fist, or a foot, and Lou hissed, "Not now."

"We should have a decent enough handle on the optics when it comes time for you to pay your ritual dues at Beltane," Constance spoke over the tussle by the shelves, "and from then on out, the Death Witch of the Demesne will be a management issue and not a—"

"I'm not going to Beltane," stated Milla. "I never go to Beltane."

"You owe the coven, Milla Mouse." Constance clicked her tongue.

"And it's a crowd of *thousands*, Aunt Connie," she argued. "You want me to come out as a Death Witch in front of a mass of Waydrunk witches?"

"It's nothing as dramatic as all that." Dina swished her hand again, and Milla's eye twitched. If she saw one more dismissive gesture from that witch, she was going to steal the athame from Constance's cupholder and solve the problem for good. "Every Witch of a Demesne gives a brief display of their magick for a gathering of coven Elder Witches. Feed some of your magick into the greater ritual and be on your way."

"Every witch?" Lou asked. Four sets of eyes landed on her, and Milla zeroed in on the bob in her throat.

"Every witch with a demesne, yes," Dina confirmed. "The American Covens handle the regional maintenance of power differently than those on the Continent."

"Archaically," Natje coughed into a fist, earning a smirk from the Third Head.

"You're years overdue, Milla," Constance continued, "and aside from Dina's motives, it is the most efficient way to pay and prove to C.R.O.W. that you are not a witch to be feared."

"Disagree."

"With which point?"

"Both of them." Milla narrowed her eyes at the Elder Witch, who ought to know better. "But mostly the last one."

"Ludmilla." Natje leaned over. "Consider what they are offering: a chance to return to your demesne and walk without the sword of Damocles dangling over your head."

Milla tucked her chin, sending her advoccultant a highly skeptical look. "Doesn't that refer to those in power laboring under the specter of anxiety and death?" Darkly snorted, which she just hated. "How is this *any* different?"

Natje clenched her jaw, and a strange look crossed her face. A fleeting admiration marked by mirth. Before she could reply, Lou stepped away from the bookshelf, her arms at her sides, palms facing Milla in a subtle plea.

"You'd be allowed to step into your Way," she said. "Under close surveillance, of course." She took another step and another, the room seeming to darken until it was only Lou. She loomed over the back of the chair, a shining light amidst the gloom, forcing Milla to twist at a weird angle and crane her neck to look at her. The position was awkward. Supplicative in a way she hated. "All of this, everything that has happened in the last hour, was put into motion by your agreement. Work with us, and agree to be placed in my custody. Consent to the Soul Binding, and all of this ends. Today."

Millapet.

She jerked her head around, searching for that voice, and only then did she notice how dark the room had gone. Shadows teemed and roiled, climbing up Milla's legs as easily as they were repelled by the warm, glowing light emanating from Lou.

This wasn't right. This was miles from right; this was coercion. Her fingers tingled in fright, and she squinted into the shadows. Why wasn't Natje saying anything? How in the nine rings were an Elder Witch and the Third Head *okay* with this? And why wasn't—

"*Lou.*"

Ah, there it is, she thought.

"*This isnae what we agreed.*" Darkly's voice boomed through the darkness, far beyond warning and now outright menacing.

Lou huffed, rolled her eyes, and threw her arm back, fingers curved and clawed as they were in Daytona. Her eyes did the creepy fog-lamp thing and without any ado whatsoever, she stated, "Done."

Milla had only a second to register the word and the action. A second to blink and react to the familiarity of the scene and the pose of the witches before the shadows withdrew into Darkly in a rush of wind, fast enough to send him staggering off balance. Light returned to the office, and his back hit the bookcase, jostling the trinkets and vases. The lunar sextant wobbled, tipping off the shelf and landing on the floor beside Natje with an ominous thud.

"Young man!" Dina pounded the desk, and the rest of the room came to life.

"Horned God," cursed Constance. "Now I'll have to explain that to the technomantics."

"That is *quite* enough, Keir," Lou spat each word with a caustic bite. Darkly slumped, gripping the edge of the bookshelf to keep from joining the sextant on the floor. He raised his head, shaking it once before glaring murderously at his sister.

"What is a Soul Binding?" Milla asked when the tension was thick enough to smear over toast. Darkly's attention snapped to her, and Lou slowly turned, wearing a soft smile that Milla didn't like at *all*.

"Think of it as a version of the Waybinding you already wear." Two fingers on her casting hand flicked toward Milla's wrist. "But unlike the Waybinding, a Soul Binding can be controlled, like the lock of a dam maintaining the water flow."

"Controlled by who?"

"By me." The smile spread, softening her features. Milla looked down at her palms, eyes trailing the web of scars. Beneath the thick, marbled tissue, beneath the lifelines she had tried to erase, her Way simmered, surging against the Waybinding with a desperate need to be released into the world. Were this any other day, under any other circumstances, she would be running herself to exhaustion, feeding her demesne until the world grew hazy and her body too heavy for her weary legs to carry. Were this the years before Lake Pontchartrain, she would be throwing herself at Ezra, begging him to help her burn off the worst of the boiling heat until she could think and focus while he slept sated in their bed.

Were this that week in Daytona, hidden in a swamp, she would want nothing more than a way to touch Darkly without hurting him.

Funny how things changed.

She curled her fingers over her palms, ragged nails digging into the scars. "It will control my Way?"

"Until I deem your control and tolerance satisfactory, yes." Lou moved around the chair, standing beside the desk where Constance and Dina watched the exchange with rapt attention. "This is an opportunity, Ludmilla."

"It's a leash." Darkly pushed from the wall, teetering as he stood. "And I dinnae want her on the team."

"Well, fuck me then, I guess."

"Tried that." He shot a heated look her way, his face harder and colder than she'd ever seen it. Milla opened her mouth, but only a shocked squeak came out.

"I fail to see how you have a say in the matter, Keir," said Dina. "This is the settlement proposed by your sister and agreed upon by Mistress Tage." At that, Milla gaped at her advoccultant, who stared at the lunar sextant on the floor by her feet. "We leverage the reputation of the Simmons siblings against that of Ludmilla

Probuditna. She agrees to a Soul Binding and undergoes strict training in her Way until she is no longer perceived as a threat."

"And she returns to St. Augustine where I can keep an eye on her," Constance said with a firm look at Milla.

"The choice, ultimately, is up to Ludmilla, not you." Dina pointed at Darkly. "She cannot be cleaved, so she'll either rot in the salt and marble cells of Český Krumlov, or she can work for C.R.O.W."

"I'll do it," Milla blurted. Goddess, anything was better than those cells, even selling what was left of her cleaved Soul to C.R.O.W.

St. Augustine, her store, Diego. A semblance of a life, and one not spent ducking and hiding? Fuck yes, she was going to take their offer.

"Milla," Darkly croaked.

She jumped from the chair, spinning around to hiss at him, "Milla, *what*, Darkly? Is a Death Witch not good enough? Don't I deserve the same deal you got?"

"No, Milla, that isnae—"

"All of this is your fault." She threw her arm out, gesturing to the office, the witches in it, and then herself. "You put me here; what did you think I would do? Roll over and die?"

His cheeks blanched, what color was left bleeding right down into the collar of his suit until he was ghostly pale. So different from the freckle-dusted, sunburned witch she had known. The room fell so silent she heard the creak of floorboards under Darkly's feet as he straightened and stood tall. Then he shook his head once, eyes boring into his sister, turned, and left.

Milla flinched as the door snicked shut, staring at the stained wood as she tried to settle his reaction to her words. It was the blankness that bothered her. The Darkly she knew, or thought she knew, was an expressive disaster of a witch unable to hide his emotions. He wore them like that suit: fitted to his frame and tailored to perfection. To see him so detached was … jarring.

"Well." Dina clapped her hands together. The sound bounced off the walls, battering Milla back into her chair. She exhaled and sank low, her head aching and fingers trembling. "Let's get to it, shall we?"

"Yes, let's." Lou snagged Milla's wrists, locking them in a far stronger grip than expected. She jerked her forward in the chair until Milla was flat over her knees, arms stretched out in front of her. "Hold still," Lou murmured and ran her thumbs over Milla's pale, blue-veined skin.

A burning ache rose in the path of her thumbs, and she squirmed, tugging against Lou's grip. "What are you doing?"

"Removing the Waybinding." Lou lifted gleaming eyes to Milla's, unleashing a whispered intent that was little more than a cool, vanilla-grass breath.

"Wait, what?" She tugged again, and Lou held tight. "No, nonono." Her Way flared to life in a rush of furious heat, the backlog of magick searing a path up her arms, demanding to be used and burning in its fury. Milla yelped. Panic had her breaths coming in short, gasping pants, and—

"Breathe," Lou ordered, tightening her hold.

"Oh, Goddess," Milla gritted out. "Oh fuck, oh fuck, it burns."

"Is this normal?" Dina appeared over Lou's shoulder, wearing a gleeful smile.

"Not really," Lou grunted. "But she's been Waybound for weeks."

"Weeks." Milla echoed, looking to Natje. She knew time had gone funny in the cells, but so much of this was not adding up.

How long had Lou been devising this plan? How long had the Third Head been a part of the plot? How many weeks was weeks?

Natje frowned, intent on Lou's fingers manacling her wrists. She reached out and gripped Milla's arm. Whether it was in assurance or apology, she had no idea. All she knew was that this fucking *hurt,* and she hadn't had her tea, and any second now, she was going to start rotting C.R.O.W.'s darling Light Witch through no fault of her own.

A hot sweat bubbled across her brow, followed by a sticky, prickling flush down her back and around her ribs. She groaned and pressed her mouth to her shoulder, gnashing her teeth as she tried to hold back her magick. Weeks of magick. Weeks of her Way, oh, Goddess, how long had she been away from her demesne? Diego? The store?

A sob tore free before she could bite it off. Her shoulders heaved, and Lou adjusted her grip, damn near hauling Milla out of the chair. Irish flew from her lips in a steady stream, her thumbs pressing down at the base of Milla's wrists hard enough to curl her fingers.

She clenched every muscle, weak as they were, to restrain the heat coursing through her body, involuntarily tugging against Lou's grip. Her sweat-slicked wrist slipped, slid free, and before Lou could react, Milla dug her nails into her arm, scratching and tearing at the skin to alleviate the sensation of a thousand fire ants chomping down on her arteries.

"Let go," she begged. "I can't hold this much longer, Lou. Let go!"

Dina seized her arm, jerking it down so Lou could regain her grip, and Constance filled the empty space behind her. Delight lit up her face, and a heartbeat later, Milla felt the shift in the intent, a new heat battling the burn of her Way. A bone-searing, marrow-boiling heat that had her eyes tearing up and a tiny whimper escaping before she could clench her teeth. Threads of shimmering light blossomed from under Lou's fingers, bleeding into Milla's veins and searing a path up into her very Soul.

She panted, unable to catch her breath enough to scream. Goddess, it *burned,* and no one cared. Not her advoccultant, not the Elder Witch she called an aunt.

And right when the pain was too much to bear, when white spots danced in the field of her vision, and her lungs ached for air—the heat snuffed out. Lou rocked back, catching herself against the edge of the desk. A bubbling giggle escaped and she smothered it with a hand, tittering between gasps for air.

Dina and Constance huddled over Milla's wrists, pointing as the threads sank deeper into her arms and an empty, bracing cold replaced the searing heat. With it came a weight, a heaviness to her hands that had not been there before. She blinked, clearing the tears from her eyes, and stared at the mark of the Light Witch gleaming against her skin.

Twin triskelions, one on each wrist, in a shimmering, minty moss green. A sigil only a witch could see. A sigil that did not appear in any grimoire she knew, but one that Milla had traced on the skin of a Dark Witch.

She lifted her head and the room tilted on its side, muted browns and golds swirling into a putrid swathe of dull colors. A wild tremor overtook her fingers, exhaustion barreling down on Milla like a freight train.

"Oh, Goddess." Natje lurched from the chair, cursing under her breath as she made for the door and bellowed down the hallway, "Agent Sterne!"

"Are you alright, Milla?" Constance crouched in front of her, a tender hand on Milla's knee, but she only had eyes for the Light Witch braced against the desk with a drunken smile.

"This yours?" She raised her wrists to show the twin sigils to Lou, grunting against the unfamiliar weight.

"Soul Sigil," Lou nodded, dropping her head back to blink at the ceiling.

Black spots joined the white; Milla's vision went dark at the edges, and before she passed out, she slurred, "Li'l early for matchin' tattoos, dontcha think?"

Part II
Demesne

Eighteen

"Do you have to go?"

He dropped his chin, peering at Milla under heavy eyelids. "One of us has to be there." A lazy smile toyed at his mouth, and he cupped her head in his hand. "We both know it cannae be you."

Milla bit her lip. This was dangerous, she was too close to him, and the towel separating their skin would only last so long. But for now, she would enjoy it. The heat of his long body beneath her, the press of his fingers against her waist.

"I have to go home eventually," she said. "You remember what happened the last time I left St. Augustine."

"There are no Loa left to steal the demesne, Milla."

"No, but there's plenty of witches."

"Nothing is gonnae happen to St. Augustine." He grinned and wound a lock of her hair around one finger, tugging just this side of too hard. "Believe me."

Another tug, this one from her center, hauled Milla upright, her stomach swooping and lurching like she was on a rollercoaster.

Faint voices carried into the room from elsewhere, an argument or at least an unfriendly conversation. A door slammed, and in the ensuing silence, Milla's groggy brain finally comprehended that she was in a bed, in a room, in a house, and not her cell.

Bracing her hands against the sheets, she counted to three as she inhaled, exhaling with a hiss between her teeth. And again until the nausea settled and the tingling numbness receded from her fingers and toes. Only then did she raise her head and take in the room.

Black silk sheets under a gunmetal grey comforter, a mountain of pillows, and a deep maroon throw blanket covered the king-size bed. The bedside table, holding a lamp, charging cable, and a neatly folded pile of clothes, matched the mahogany bookshelf on the opposite wall. A mess of academic journals, trade paperbacks, and leatherbound classics crowded the shelves, and a large grimoire with a black leather binding so dark it seemed to suck the light out of the room was displayed on a stand. An unsettlingly familiar bean bag crowded the window, next to a small table hosting a charcoal grey Le Creuset Dutch Oven on a hotplate, a bone-handled obsidian athame, and a half-melted black candle with thick gobs of wax dripping down the side.

Milla frowned at the bean bag and the candle, an idea forming in the back of her mind that she had no desire to address.

From the running shoes and combat boots tossed haphazardly in a corner and the dark fabric of masculine-cut clothes visible through the open closet door, the room belonged to a man. Hints and suggestions of personality were tucked among the dark hues

and decadent bedding: a turntable atop a narrow set of drawers
and a vinyl collection in a plastic crate, boxing gloves discarded
on a gym bag, and two lengths of black elastic stretched over
the back of a plush maroon wingback in the corner. A worn,
dog-eared copy of *Don Quixote* lay open and facedown on the
armrest, and Milla barely suppressed an eye-roll.

On the dresser parallel to the bed was a framed photograph of
a family in front of an RV: a father, mother, and two children,
one a red-headed boy who looked to be nine or ten, the other
a blonde teenage girl. Milla eased from the bed, reaching out to
catch herself on the furniture when the floor tipped beneath her
feet. Once the world stopped spinning, she grabbed the frame
and studied the photo.

The boy was the spitting image of his father, the pair of them
grinning broadly for the camera in matching soccer jerseys, while
the girl stood a bit to the side, arms tightly crossed over her front.
A sweet-faced woman, already dwarfed by her daughter's height,
stood between the girl and the father, her mousy-brown hair
pulled into a high, teased ponytail that drew attention to the fine
sweep of the cheekbones she shared with her children.

Milla's eyes burned at the familial likenesses she found among
the literally picture-perfect family. She sniffed and looked away,
taking in the contents of the dresser instead.

A warped glass fish bowl filled with weathered stones and bones
sat beside a tray holding hawthorn twigs bound in a pentagram;
there was a black tin mug stuffed full of smudge sticks and a pile of
green, yellow, and purple beads. None of it was troubling. These
were the trappings of a witch. Wards and fetish, items intended
for ritual use, but it was the odds and ends speckled among them
that raised quiet alarm.

Hair ties and a pile of bobby pins. A slick, leather makeup bag, a tube of deep magenta lipstick, and a hairbrush tangled with long, dark hairs.

If Milla was where she thought she was, and if this room belonged to the witch she very much suspected it did, then all signs pointed toward Darkly sharing it with someone else.

A female someone else.

It was obvious, now that she knew to look. A pair of heels were placed neatly by the door, and a glossy, hard-sided suitcase was visible in the closet. Milla nudged the door open and scanned the clothing on the rail. Dark flannels, sweaters, and a leather jacket gave way to knit dresses, silk blouses, and a trio of identical blazers in rich jewel tones.

Something uncomfortable settled in her belly, though Milla couldn't say whether it was the feminine presence in this room or the total and utter lack of pastels and polo shirts.

She whirled around, regretting the sudden movement as her brain flipped ass-over-tea kettle. Bile rose in her throat, and she lurched for a trashcan beside the dresser, spitting up a grey-green acidic mess.

Wiping tears away, Milla rose on shaking legs and took a deep, steady breath.

She wasn't going to cry about this. He wasn't worth crying over.

"He turned you in," she told her reflection. "He lied to you for weeks, let you rot in that cell for *weeks*."

Her reflection looked unconvinced. And *haunted*.

Gaunt and pale, the evidence of the cells and her fight with the Loa were impossible to ignore. Her cheeks had hollowed, and her skin was papery and thin. Scraggly bangs hung limp, dusting her cheekbones, and behind them, Milla's dark brown eyes were heavily shadowed and speckled with flecks of tombstone grey.

She leaned closer, widening her eyes and then squinting, squeezing them shut and widening them again as if she could clear the flecks away. But they stayed, bright against the deep brown and impossible to ignore.

"Huh." Leaning back, Milla chewed the inside of her cheek and tried to decide what to do. There were people outside of this room. Or, at least, there had been. It had been quiet since she woke up, but that didn't mean she was here alone.

Wherever *here* was.

"Problem for later." She grabbed the clothes from the bedside table, revealing a maroon booklet embossed with a gold harp. She read the name of the country on the passport, read it again, then tossed her clothes onto the bed and picked it up, opening the booklet to the identity page. A younger, just as bald Darkly stared back at her. His face was thinner, shoulders less muscled, and he glared at the camera in challenge. "How the fuck are you *Irish*." She flipped the passport front to back and returned to the photo. "At least the haircut isn't new."

The date placed the passport as having been issued two years prior. Milla flipped through the pages, all of them blank. Again, she scanned the identity page and shrugged, tossing the passport onto the bedside table.

"What's one more lie?" She muttered as she stripped out of the trousers and blouse Lou had dressed her in. "I mean, seriously, this is absurd."

No more absurd than talking to herself in Darkly's weird-ass room, but everything about this was absurd. Elder Witches of Covens and Tribunal Heads pulling the wool over C.R.O.W's eyes? Milla selling her Soul to Lou? Multiple witches knowing her Way and colluding to get her back to her demesne? None of this made any sense; might as well join the madness.

Dumping the borrowed clothes into the trash can, she eyed the pentagram-printed underwear she found folded inside black yoga pants and shrugged. Far stranger things were happening than finding a set of her workout clothes waiting on a bedside table.

Dressed and feeling somewhat less scraggly after borrowing the mystery hairbrush and a hair tie, Milla tiptoed out of the room onto a small landing that curved around the top of a narrow stairwell. She gripped the banister as a dizzying sense of deja vu rushed over her. There was a familiarity to the space. It was in the way golden light filtered through the stained glass window on the landing. In the creak of the floorboards underneath her feet. A prickling sense of *knowing* when Milla had no idea where she was.

Noise from the floor below dragged her down the stairs. She gave one fleeting look to the fogged glass panel in the front door before the front room snagged her attention. Moving boxes filled the space, some broken down and piled against the wall, others sealed with tape and labeled with their destinations: LAUNDRY, KITCHEN, and GARAGE.

The only furniture in the front room was a worn corduroy couch, half covered in blankets, pillows, and a Black Watch tartan flannel, facing a widescreen television mounted on the wall. A talk show played on mute. The slick host grinned and gesticulated wildly as a man in an expensive-looking grey suit smiled, showing off bright white veneers. Milla watched their exchange for a moment, listening for any sound. She had heard voices; she was sure of it: one deep and masculine voice, the other higher-pitched and feminine.

The quietest *tink* of glassware had Milla spinning around, and in the kitchen, on the other side of a rolling island, was a lithe, stunningly gorgeous woman.

Long dark hair parted down the middle framed a heart-shaped face. A dewy complexion and peach undertone to her skin gave the impression she wore a walking soft filter. The contrast was striking and glamorous, polished, where Milla's dark hair and pro-SPF combo looked more at home in a Hot Topic.

Deep, dark eyes lined in a perfect cat-eye stared back at her, and the woman's plump lips parted in surprise. One look at the magenta lipstick and emerald shift dress told Milla all she needed to know.

"It's not what you think," the woman blurted, throwing out a hand with her fingers splayed. Milla's vision blurred, and for half a second, a faint green aura pulsed from the woman. She staggered in surprise, back hitting the column support of the entry to the living room.

"Oh, Goddess." The woman rushed out of the kitchen with her hands out, rambling in a posh English accent. "Are you alright? I didn't mean to give you a fright. Honestly, we thought you'd sleep longer. Toby stepped out to grab some food. He's not eating again, which always puts him in a foul temper, which means the rest of us are dragged right down with him."

"What," Milla croaked, pressing harder against the column.

"It's the bottling," the woman explained. "He knows something is wrong, but he cannot for the life of him figure out what it is. And then they went and disclosed your Way—Lou was *livid.* I haven't seen her that angry since the Netherlands when he—"

"What bottling? And what are you doing here?"

She pressed her lips together, eyes dancing over Milla's face before they widened slightly. She backed away, fingertips pressed to her mouth. "They didn't tell you," she murmured, then splayed her hand at Milla. "Why didn't they tell you? There's so much you've yet to learn, and they did not see fit to start with *that?*"

"Must have slipped their mind." Milla shoved off the wall and skirted around the woman, needing to put a broad distance between them. "What are you doing here?" she asked again.

"Making your tea." The woman glanced warily over her shoulder at the window above the kitchen sink. "I'm the team vinefica," she added in a low voice.

At that, Milla wide stepped further out of the woman's reach. A vinefica was a potions witch. Or poison witch, depending on who you asked and how you'd interacted with one. Though not considered Forbidden and Foule, along with corpomantics and mind witches, they were certainly given the side-eye.

The most commonly given advice was to only accept something to eat or drink from a vinefica if you were willing to bet your life.

With little more than a touch and muttered intent, they could alter the makeup of a glass of water. And while most people would notice they were drinking hydrogen peroxide, a vinefica only needed to wait until the water had been absorbed into their bloodstream. Then, a simple brush against a bare arm on their way out the door could kick off the transformative intent.

And not that Milla had any experience, but she assumed adding a two to the O in H2O would be the opposite of fun.

The front door creaked open, keys jangling in the lock, and the worry straining the vinefica's features vanished in a blink. Shoulders straight and face calm, she said in a loud voice, "You'll have to drink it twice a day for the first week to help you acclimate to the Soul Binding."

"Oh, fantastic." Lou entered the room, dressed in the same pants-and-blouse combination from Milla's not-trial. "You're awake. Is it done then?"

Milla slid along the wall, shoving herself into a corner to keep an eye on both witches. "Is what done?"

"The un*bottling*," Lou stressed the word and leveled a droll look on the vinefica. "You didn't tell her?"

"*I* didn't want to be involved." She put up both hands and whirled away in a cloud of soft, floral perfumes.

Lou scoffed, facing Milla. "He's been unbearable for weeks, but the last few days have been downright abysmal."

"That's not fair, Lou," the vinefica called from the kitchen. "You know how keenly he feels."

"As well as you do, Rai," she shot back.

The vinefica froze, tea kettle in one hand, empty mug in the other. Her eyes narrowed further, and she set both down sharply against the counter. "Twice daily," she told Milla. "For a week, and then we'll discuss next steps." To Lou, she offered the barest nod and slipped out the rear of the kitchen. Music flooded the house, a driving double-kick and power chords, and cut off as a door slammed.

"Well, I hope you're ready to work." Lou pressed her index finger against her temple, looking aggrieved. "She's likely gone to tell him you're awake, and if there's one witch my brother never questions, it's Rai."

"I literally just woke up." Milla put up both hands, shoulders hunched to her ears. "I have no idea what you want me to do."

Lou sighed the sigh of the heavily put-upon, crossing her arms and waiting. When Milla didn't magically understand what was happening, Lou sighed again. "Honestly, the two of you are the most egotistical pair of witches I've ever—"

"Hey, why don't we pretend for a second that I've been in prison for Horned God knows how long and explain this to me like I have no idea what's going on, which I don't."

"Seven weeks," she said. Milla went still, not sure she'd heard Lou correctly. "And my brother has been walking around with holes in his memory for the last two, making the rest of our lives miserable, so if you would be so kind as to think outside yourself for a moment, it would be greatly appreciated."

"Seven …" Milla sat on the arm of the couch, too startled to argue further. Seven weeks. How had it been seven weeks? Time had gone funny, but this felt aggressive. "I don't …"

"Have you not thought at all about how he pulled off that little stunt during your trial?" Lou snapped.

"That wasn't a trial, and *I* just woke up!"

"Use that brain Lightner supposedly trained, Ludmilla." Lou dropped her arms with a slap against her thighs. "Nobody lies to C.R.O.W., so my damn fool of a brother had himself bottled to omit the damning memories."

Milla gripped the back of the couch to keep from tipping over. A bottling required surgical precision and was horribly invasive. Like, a thousand nicks of a razor blade, followed by salt in the open wounds invasive.

To start, it involved a deep scouring to erase all echoes of the source of the memory. A hot lye bath and coarse exfoliation of the skin. Hair removal, gargling with bleach and Listerine, and internal fluids release—all to remove the physical memory before you could begin bottling the memories in the mind.

The ritual itself was straightforward and no less painful: identify the memories to be suppressed, or bottled, separate them from the Soul, and tuck them away where not even a Light Witch could reach them.

Ezra had served as the obnubilari for bottlings in the past, along with an obfuscari, a vinefica, and a hippocromantic, the standard assortment for the task when a Light Witch could not be had. He had come home in a foul temper after each one, his black mood lasting for days until he and his Way recovered from the casting.

But for all the work a bottling demanded, undoing one was absurdly simple: a single touch from the source of the memory.

Milla swallowed thickly, mentally charting the specific omissions in Darkly's testimony. She didn't know how much had been bottled, could not know for sure, but he had been singularly surprised to learn she was a Death Witch, which meant she was the one witch capable of unbottling him.

"Uhh…"

"Understood?" Lou asked.

"Hardly." It made sense on the surface, but more than a bottling had occurred to get Milla out of the cells. Multiple layers of subterfuge from multiple witches. An amount of effort she didn't think she deserved. "Why did you leave so much? Why not have him forget me altogether?"

"Keir does not tolerate bottling well," Lou stated, resigned. "I can remove the memory of the thing and tuck it away where he cannot access it, but the emotion tied to the memory is a different story. With any other witch, it could be attributed to misplaced nostalgia or deja vu, but to a Dark Witch … if I removed you entirely, there would be a mass emotion caught in a void. Sense memory and heartache he cannot account for, and believe me when I say that is a nightmare to manage."

That last bit hung in the air between them. Lou waited expectantly as Milla mulled what she'd been told against what she knew.

"Speaking from experience, I assume," she said after a moment.

Lou remained unfathomably still, save for the slight narrowing of her eyes. "Yes. Of course." The rear door slammed, and she whipped around, a bright smile on her face. "Ah, Keir. I was just looking for you."

Nineteen

Darkly stepped forward, glaring at his sister. "Get out."

"Well." Lou met Milla's gaze. She tipped her head in Darkly's direction with a small, conspiratorial smile conveying a sense of *You see what I have to deal with?* before addressing her brother. "You're in a mood."

"Wonder why that is, Lou." He brushed past her, whipping the towel from around his neck and dropping it on the back of a chair. Bare-chested, flushed, and sweating, every muscle in his torso and arms was flexed. Beneath the waistband of grey joggers, the Adonis belt at his hips was even more pronounced than Milla remembered, and not in the "he's been working out" sort of way, but more a "the vinefica said he hadn't been eating and *wow* isn't that obvious" sort of way.

Still, his movement was smooth, almost liquid, as he opened a cupboard and reached for a glass. Milla couldn't look away from the flex and roll of muscles in his back. Mad as she was at the witch, it wasn't worth denying how Horned God-damned attractive he was.

He filled his glass from a pitcher, turned, and dropped against the counter. Every bit of Milla's attention went to the bobbing of his throat as he drank. The bead of sweat rolling from his temple and catching along the sharp cut of his jaw. The tiny little pant he let out when the glass was empty.

When he was finished, Darkly raised an eyebrow at his sister. "You're still here?"

Lou pressed her lips together, nostrils flaring. After a long, awkward moment, she said, "Well," again and strode into the living room. "Ludmilla, I assume you know what to do?"

Milla jerked her attention away from Darkly, but not before catching the smirk dimpling his cheek. A sarcastic snort carried into the living room, and her skin flushed.

"Unfortunately," she mumbled. One touch was all it would take. Maybe she could smack him. "How much of me did you take?"

"Just your Way," Darkly rumbled. "Unless Lou's been withholding?"

"And ruin the surprise?" she sassed him over her shoulder, then addressed Milla. "I'll leave you to it. Training begins tomorrow. We only have a few weeks to prepare you for Beltane, and there are the mystery rituals to contend with, so the sooner you get this over with, the better." Lou patted her on the shoulder and strode away.

The door closed, and a butter-thick silence filled the room. Milla turned slowly, tensing when she met Darkly's intent stare.

He had not moved from the counter, gripping the glass in one hand and drumming the fingers of the other along the edge. Milla swallowed, too angry to speak first, too nervous to move. He had bottled himself for her. He had undergone a seriously invasive scouring and ritual to get her out of the cells, to get her here, and Milla did not know how to navigate this.

It did not erase his lies, and it did not come close to making up for giving her location to C.R.O.W., but it was still the single most romantic thing anyone had ever done for her.

She scrubbed her face with her hands and groaned. "Something is so wrong with me."

"Beg to differ," said Darkly.

She slid her hands lower, peering at him over her fingers, and again, that thick, heavy silence condensed between them. It was less a tension and more a suffocation of words and accusations unsaid. Apologies unspoken and the one big question that would capture every tumultuous thought and feeling in her tired body.

Why?

As if she'd said it aloud, Darkly flinched. The glass *tinked* against the counter, and he took two quick, long strides out of the kitchen. Closer to her.

Milla threw her hands out, teetering off balance. She landed on the couch cushions and rolled to the side, popping to her feet and backing away. "Wait."

She needn't have said it. The instant she toppled backward, Darkly had stopped, half-reaching for her. He slowly fisted his hand and lowered it to his side. A muscle ticked in his jaw. "How bad is this about to be?"

"How—how bad?" Milla huffed in disbelief. "You used me as bait for a raw-head." He pressed his lips together. "You turned me in! How bad do you think this is going to be?"

"Milla, I—"

"I don't want to hear it, Keir." He flinched, and she threw her hands up, stomping in an angry circle. It was easier to give over to the fury burbling in her blood than admit that his bottling and his body threw her. Goddess, that body. Long and lean and sweaty. She wanted to hex him to desecration as much as she wanted to feel his weight crushing her against the wall, if only just to *feel* him. To touch his skin and know the thrum of his heartbeat beneath her hands.

Her eyes burned, and her chest felt tight. How could she be so *angry* with someone she wanted so *badly?*

"Goddess, there is something so wrong with me." She whirled around, appealing to him instead of trying to figure this out alone. He was the bottled one, after all, and well overdue in answering some questions. "I don't know what I'm supposed to do here. I mean, I know what I'm supposed to do, but I don't understand why you did it." She threw her hand out, accusing or pleading, silently begging him to take it while holding him off all at once.

He took an uneasy step forward, longing written over every line of his body. "Is that not obvious?"

"Nothing about this is obvious!" She rolled her shoulders, trying to get her suddenly uncomfortable sports bra to sit right. To let her breathe. "Your closet is stuffed with flannels and skinny jeans. Your bed is covered in silk, there's this whole metro-goth aesthetic to your room that makes no sense, and you're *Irish?*" Why that was the direction her brain went, the Horned God only knew. Milla could hardly think in a straight line, much less decipher why she'd latched onto the nonsense of his bedroom. But whatever it was, it was where she'd landed, so that was where she would focus. "What happened to all the Chinos?"

Something about that made him smile, and the appearance of that infuriating dimple made her rage.

"You *lied* to me," she accused through clenched teeth.

"That right, Ludmilla Lightner?" The smile fled, and his face settled into cold anger. "Seems you lied to me first."

"Technically," she mumbled.

"And more often."

"Debatable."

Darkly scowled, the twist of his lips more rueful than anything else. He took another step closer. And another, crowding Milla against the wall while staying out of reach.

Her heart raced, pounding out a thousand beats per minute. She pressed her palms flat against the wall, holding his eyes when all she wanted to do was curl into a ball and wait for this all to blow over. "I don't know what you *want*," she managed. "I don't even know you! I've never known—"

"Ken you're gonnae learn a lot about me in the coming days, but know this first: I want you." He stated it clear and sure as fact, as if it should have been obvious when it was anything but. "All of you."

"Keir." His name came out at the tail end of a breath, weak and desperate, the fight sucked out of her by the overwhelming desire to smack him, kiss him, hold him.

He frowned. "Please, dinnae call me that."

"It's your name, right?" She didn't know why it mattered, only that it did. If she was supposed to trust someone, shouldn't she at least know their real name?

"Aye, that it is," he conceded. "Turns out I enjoy being Darkly more than I ever liked being Keir."

Goddess, who could argue with that?

"Keir doesnae know what Marie said to you in New Orleans, or what you told Darkly in the back of that minivan, or did to him in that woman's bedroom. I want to know, Milla. I want to think of you without it hurting." He pressed the base of his palm against his shorn skull, brows cinched together. "Knowing your Way isnae enough when I know something's gone, and I want it back. I want you back, and Darkly had *you*."

Somehow, he'd gotten closer without her noticing. The angst and the need in those words tilted her head back until she looked up into bright green eyes limned in red.

"Please."

And that was it. No longwinded explanations, no groveling, no arguing. Just one little word uttered from that gorgeous mouth, and every bit of Milla's anger crumbled away.

"Darkly…"

He swallowed, eyes dancing over her face, and raised his hand, ready to cup Milla's cheek. "I never meant for any of this to happen."

Aaaaaand nevermind.

"You never *meant?*" She batted his hand away, ducking under his arm and darting across the room. "Never *meaning* implies intent, you asshole."

Milla spun around, ready to continue reading the damn fool witch his rights, and froze.

He hadn't moved. He just stood there, staring at the space where she had been.

"Darkly?"

His head whipped toward her, he blinked, and then six-feet-and-change of lanky Dark Witch crumpled to the ground.

"Darkly, get up." Milla toed him in the side. When he didn't move, she did it again. Harder. A tiny grunt left his mouth, but whether it was from her prodding or the result of the awkward angle at which he'd fallen, she had no idea. She crouched low and shook his shoulder. "Dude, come on."

Nothing.

Not even a sleepy grumble.

Milla rose, puffing scraggly, overgrown bangs out of her face, and chewed her lower lip as she mulled over what to do.

One touch was all it took to unbottle someone, and apparently, for once, C.R.O.W. hadn't been lying. She'd barely touched him, just swept his arm away, and his brain had shorted out, resulting in … this.

"Well, shit."

Backing away, Milla scanned the living room and peered into the kitchen.

No phone. Of course there was no phone. She hadn't seen one in his room, and Horned God only knew where her phone had ended up. How in the nine rings was she supposed to call for help?

Her eyes landed on Darkly, crumpled in the narrow space between the wall and the couch. He'd gone down like a Southern Belle with a fainting spell, landing with the side of his face smushed against the carpet, torso twisted, and knees bent. An odd, bulky outline was visible in what she assumed to be the pocket of his joggers. It was just the right size to be a phone and one hundred percent too close to his groin.

"Double shit."

The last thing she needed was for him to wake up with her hand down his pants. Knowing Darkly, he'd get ideas, and Milla would have another lapse in restraint, and where would that get them?

Somewhere fun.

"Shut up, brain."

She stomped into the kitchen, making a half-assed attempt to wake him up by slamming cupboards, clanging pots and pans, filling his glass, and flicking his face with water.

Nothing.

Not a flinch or a flutter of eyelids, though he had started drooling.

She downed the glass and set it beside the sink, gripping the counter's edge as she thought. Someone had to come back, eventually. The vinefica, Rai, was staying here; that much was obvious, and also, *what the fuck, Darkly*. And hadn't she mentioned someone was coming back with food?

Wait.

"The vinefica." Maybe she was still here. She'd gone out through a backdoor; maybe she was biding her time until Darkly was unbottled and Milla had left so they could—*no. Nope. Not going there.*

She skidded into the hallway, only half-tracking how familiar the layout of this house was: the bedroom at the top of the stairs, the landing, and the narrow stairwell. The glass pane in the front door. Even the open concept flow from the living room into the kitchen through an arch.

Like a mosquito bite she'd forgotten about, the itch came roaring back a half second before she stepped out into a humid Floridian sunset. Pale green petals burst from the limbs of a witch hazel tree in the corner of the shared yard, and the setting sun illuminated the deep purple sheen of out-of-season lilies.

Milla rushed to the edge of the porch, catching herself on the railing as a cry rose in her throat. This was impossible. It was insane. It couldn't be *real,* and yet it was. From the cockle-bell blooms of the Solomon's Seal beneath a bay window to the little bundle of hay rustling through the shrubs.

"No, nonono." She hopped down the stairs, her knee buckling and ankle twisting as her foot hit the ground. Threads of power shot up from the earth, latching onto Milla and winding in among her bones. She gasped, tears bursting in a mixture of relief, pain, and horror. No obnubilari was this good, no illusionist this skilled, but she had to know. Had to see for certain.

They get stronger the deeper we go. Wasn't that what her guard had said?

Grass poked and prickled her bare feet, and every step across the yard sent a warble of pain up her leg. But she kept on, scraping nails along the woodgrain in the porch rail, gripping the worn steel handle on the gate, and hissing as splinters cut into her palm.

Because the gate always stuck. The wood was warped from years of humidity and sunshine, and it stuck, so you had to brace the fence and yank to open it.

They couldn't know that. There was no way C.R.O.W. could know that; no witch was so thorough unless they'd lived here for as long as Milla had, which meant this was real.

She sobbed, confusion and anger warring for space in her body, and yanked open the gate, nearly colliding with a motorcycle as she launched herself into the gravel side yard. Pebbles bit into the soles of her feet, and she darted around the classic bike, down to the sidewalk, and into the middle of the street.

A white SUV screeched to a halt, and someone called her name, but Milla only had eyes for the butter-yellow slats and faded trim of the Victorian duplex before her. The left half was dark, electric candles flickering in the front window as a beacon for the wandering and the lost, while the right half glowed merrily, the muted talk show still visible on the television screen.

She took it in, clasping her hands on top of her head and taking one deep breath before yelling, "What the *fuck*."

Twenty

made those hideous leggings even worse

GLAMOUR Illusory casting. Forbidden and Foule manifestations not only disguise but allure, making the hexed item irresistible to mortals. Glamours cast by desecrants (see: Huldufólkr; Fair Folk) hold no sway over travelers of the Ways.

IT WAS REAL. THIS was real. It was too big to be an illusion, and she ran without thinking, following the path she had walked day after day for years. Asphalt turned to cobbles, streetlamps turned to gas, and Milla burst into a store before she realized where she was.

Bells jangled, and the witch behind the glass counter jerked his head up, dropping his phone and blinking at Milla before a distraught cry tore from his throat.

"¡Pequeña bruja!" Diego tackled her in a hug, arms wrapping around Milla like pistons. At his voice, at his touch, his smell, at *him,* the last bits of her restraint fell away. He was just as she remembered, his deep brown hair pulled in a loose bun, wearing a bright floral shirt and tailored khakis cuffed at the ankles.

She fisted her hands in his shirt and sobbed into the crook of his neck. It was all too much, and she was so *tired*. Darkly, her house, the bottling, the cells, her arrest, the betrayal.

"Diego," Milla managed between sobs, dragging them both to the ground. "Everything happened so fast, and I couldn't—" she gasped, unable to stop panicking long enough to string together a sentence.

"Shh, shh, Milla, I know." He stroked her hair, gently swaying them both side to side. "I know; Darkly told me everything."

"He lied," she blubbered. "He lied, and he—"

"Not now." Diego cupped the back of Milla's head, his breath warm against her ear. He held her impossibly tighter, and his voice broke as he spoke. "Not now, sobrina, you're home. You're home."

It was not lost on Milla that this was the second time she had run into her store a bleeding, crying mess. Diego made short work of cleaning off her feet and, once the bandages were applied, sat her on his rococo throne while he braided her hair and lectured her in the loving way only Diego could.

"First thing we will do is a mask." He held up the braid, frowning at the dry, frazzled ends. "When was the last time you had a deep condition, bruja? Your hair is pésimo."

"I can barely remember the last time I had a shower, much less hair product other than a bar of soap."

He shuddered and dropped her braid, swinging around to the front of the chair. Crouching, he gripped Milla's knees and studied her face. "And the eyes?" he asked softly. "Those little flecks are new."

She pulled her lips between her teeth and shook her head. "I don't know. I think it's from the Loa? I'd never used that much magick before, not without multiple covens helping me channel it; it was bound to leave a mark." She trailed the corner of an eye with her finger as if she could feel the discoloration. "Didn't even notice it until I woke up in … in Darkly's bed."

Diego cocked his head, interest lighting up his face. "Oh?"

"Don't get excited." She brushed his hands off her knees and tentatively stood, setting her weight gently on her feet. The pain was dull but bearable. Diego had pulled her checkered slip-ons from his sewing room for the walk home, so there was that to look forward to. "Also, why aren't you surprised he's living next door to us?"

"He has been there for weeks." He shrugged and rose, pulling out his phone and glancing at the screen. "I have had time to get used to it. Mierda, where is our OverEats?"

"Weeks." Milla waited for Diego to explain. He tapped on his phone, smiling at whatever was on the screen. It was a different sort of smile than she was used to seeing on him. Softer, almost blushing. Despite being born in the sixteenth century, Diego wasn't old. He had been in his late twenties when he died and was barely thirty now, but that smile made him look younger. More carefree. Milla knew her next question would wipe it away, and she hated herself for it, but she had to know. "What day is it?"

Diego ripped his face from the phone, that beautiful smile vanishing and leaving him looking stricken. "¿Qué?"

Her brow bunched, and she took a moment, dreading the answer. "I don't know what day it is."

Diego gently gripped Milla's elbows, looking her in the eye. How he understood how alarming this was, how disorienting, Milla couldn't fathom. Maybe it was from the years he had spent at sea, telling time by the sun and relying on a captain or first mate to tell the passage of time. Or maybe it was just Diego, reborn into modernity with the strongest thread of empathy Milla had ever known. But he knew, and he broke the news to her as plainly and gently as possible.

"April 18th." His grip tightened, refusing to let Milla back away. "Today is April 18th, you were arrested on February 29th."

"Goddess." She blinked rapidly, staving off the immediate burn of tears. Seven weeks was an idea, an intangible concept of time. Hearing the date made it concrete. "I missed my birthday."

Diego worked his jaw, releasing one of Milla's elbows to adjust his glasses, and then burst out laughing. "*That* is what you are worried about, pequeña bruja?" He swept his thumb under an eye, grinning at Milla. "You had me worried. Here." With a twist of his wrist, Diego handed Milla a box. "Feliz cumpleaños."

"You got me a phone?" She turned the box over in her hand, ten kinds of confused.

"To be fair, C.R.O.W. got you the phone, Cyrus set up the phone, and I am handing you the phone." He brushed imaginary dust off his shoulder. "So yes, through a very strange sense of logic, I am giving you a phone."

"Why is C.R.O.W. giving me a phone?" Milla balked. "And who the hell is Cyrus?"

"We just assessed that *I* am receiving the credit for your gift, muchas gracias." Diego glanced at the door as someone rapped sharply on the glass. His face lit up, and he hurried over to grab their dinner from the OverEats driver, thanking them and locking the door. "Cyrus is one of the witches, he runs the E.R.I.E. for Lou's team. Look, he put the app on your phone."

"And you know this how?"

Diego side-eyed her as he set out cartons of food. The salty-sweet aroma of fried plantains wafted to Milla's nose, and her stomach growled. "Darkly called me after your arrest." He set the carton in front of Milla, along with a fork. "Morgen and I were on the road within the hour, and, by the way, what did you do to Julie?"

She froze with a plantain halfway to her mouth. "Julie?"

"Redhead, nurse, your only other friend beside me?"

"No, I know who Julie is; I just..." Realization struck, and she slowly lowered the plantain. "Ooohhh. Oh, no."

"Milla."

She pulled her mouth wide in a grimace, voice rising with each word, along with her shoulders. "I may have stolen her ICYMI badge to get into the convention?"

"Milla!"

"What?" She put up her hands. "It was either that or use a Jericho Stone to rot through the walls, and you know how hard it is to desecrate coquina." Diego hit her with a stern glare. She rolled her eyes. "It wasn't anything damaging. She just"—Milla waved her fork in a circle—"took a nap, and I took her badges and saved St. Augustine from being taken over by a life-force-sucking Voodoo spirit bent on revenge. Honestly, I thought you'd be more upset about Ana."

"I have had over a month to come to terms with what Ana did." He pulled another carton out of the bag and opened the lid. The mouth-watering scent of roasted vegetables, yucca fries, Cuban-style beans, and grilled meat accosted Milla. Her fork was halfway to spearing a yucca fry when Diego slammed the lid closed. "You owe her an apology."

"She's *dust*," Milla whined, prodding the compostable box with her fork. "Whatever's left of her is at the Gates."

"To Julie," he clarified, moving his dinner out of reach. "She refuses to work in the store alone, and even when I am here, she insists I do my sewing up front. Do you know how difficult it is to top stitch a pleat without a dedicated workspace?"

Though she was pretty sure Diego meant to lighten the mood and soften the blow of his reprimand, Milla felt the sting. Goddess, she had been reckless, and not just when dealing with Ana. She had been reckless for years, and it was finally catching up to her. First with Kayleigh and the review-bombing, then with Anaisa and her demesne. She had possessed Darkly on a whim, hexed someone she considered a friend, and she had been careless with Diego's *life*, taking him for granted and thinking he wanted to hide away from the world as much as she did.

One glance at the witch told her that was anything but true. He had been engrossed in something on his phone, something that made him smile. He had set up his own bespoke tailoring business and had run the store without her. From the looks of it, he was far more successful in the endeavor than Milla was.

New items stocked the shelves: pristine vintage turntables, haunted records, a vestic's scrying bowl, and a row of obviously enchanted conch shells. Even her old items held an inviting luster, practically begging customers to take them off the shelves and bring them home. The ICYMI display in the front window looked less garish and migraine-inducing than Milla remembered, and it was all due to Diego, who she had taken for granted from that very first day.

"I'm sorry," Milla said, forcing herself not to blink. If she blinked, the burn in her eyes would turn into tears, and then she'd be sobbing again. Making her problems Diego's problems, and how fair was that? "I never meant for—"

The words died on her tongue, and the image of Darkly crumpled on the floor flickered through her mind's eye as she echoed his own words. Tears welled up, and the fork clattered to the glass countertop as Milla covered her face in her hands.

"I'm so s-sorry," she sobbed.

"Oh, Diosa." Diego swept around the counter, wrapping an arm around Milla. "I know you did not mean for any of this to happen, but it did." He cupped the side of her head, forcing Milla to rest against his shoulder. "So now it is time to do what you do best: fix it."

"I don't even know where to begin." Milla swept the back of her hand under her nose, clearing away snot.

"Asquerosa. " Diego gagged and summoned a handkerchief into his hand, forcing it on Milla. She blew her nose, letting out a watery laugh at his look of revulsion when she offered the handkerchief back to him. "No, gracias." He let go and shooed her away. Sidling around the counter, he grabbed a notepad and pen and swept their dinner to the side. "We will make a list and start with the easiest. ¿Sí?"

"Okay," she said, all too willing to have Diego take control. Horned God knew she had only made a mess of things, and his Stitch Witch mind had probably identified all the trailing threads around her and determined what needed to be tackled first to disentangle her life.

"Number one, apologize to Julie." He scribbled the instruction down in a flowing script, looking at Milla over the top of his glasses. "Inmediatamente. And remove the glamour from the leggings."

"Yes," she agreed. "First thing tomorrow. After I run my demesne."

Diego hesitated, and then he wrote as he said, "Talk to Darkly."

"Absolutely not." She tapped the notepad. "Cross that out."

"No, bruja, you need to talk to him."

"Why?" She grabbed her fork and the carton of plantains. "He lied to me."

"You lied to him." He pointed the pen at her.

"Oh, Horned God, not you too." Milla glared at him, speared a plantain, and shoved it in her mouth, chewing before speaking around the bite. "Yes, I lied to him to keep *us* out of trouble."

"And how well has that turned out?" When Milla shoved another plantain into her mouth, Diego continued. "I understand why you made the choices you did, Milla, but you need to talk to him."

"He turned me in."

Diego went still, pen hovering over the paper, and exhaled with an expression she had never seen him wear. It was not cold, but it was distant as if he had mentally taken a giant step to the side to get out of her way.

"Talk to Darkly," he repeated and wrote a new line as he continued. "And work with Cyrus, get him to teach you how to use the E.R.I.E."

"I don't have an E.R.I.E.," she mumbled.

"Sí, tu puedes." Diego snorted and poked the phone box with his pen. "What do you think this is?"

"A birthday present?" She tried on a half-smile, attempting to lighten the mood. Everything had become so heavy. Once she had calmed down, grounding herself in Diego and the store, she only wanted to eat her dinner and exist. Not make lists of all the things she had to tackle. The cost of her so-called freedom would come due soon enough; couldn't she have one night to *be* before the shitstorm began anew?

"When has C.R.O.W. ever given you a gift?"

"Did you know in German, 'gift' means 'poison'?"

"Sí." He sighed and set down the pen, pinching the bridge of his nose under his glasses. "It is impossible to spend more than a day with Morgen without learning some German, and I was her houseguest for weeks."

"Oh, Horned God, I forgot to ask." Milla leapt at the weak opening, wanting nothing more than to change the subject away from all the shitty things she had to do. "How was Key West?"

Diego's brows twitched, and a tiny smile flitted over his lips, easing the stern lines. "It was … different."

"Different good?"

"Sí." The smile widened, and a faint blush darkened his cheeks. "I met a few cultists—"

"Oh, Goddess, those idiots?" Milla cackled, beyond happy with the diversion. "I used to run into them all the time, passed out on Higgs Beach or chasing after whatever magick they could." She shook her head and chuckled, reaching for a cylindrical carton she hoped was Cuban-style black beans. "Pathetic."

Diego cleared his throat and scanned the four items on the list, a sour twist erasing that faint smile. "When I returned, Darkly explained what had happened—"

"When he turned me in."

"—and Julie brought the mail by." He bent to the side and straightened, dropping a stack of mail on the counter. "You should start with these."

The topmost envelope was a bill. She flicked it aside and the next, sorting the pile with all the attention it warranted. Bills, business license renewal reminders, a letter from their landlord, junk mail from a real estate company, a bill—

"Wait." She grabbed the letter and scanned it, pressing a hand on her head as what she was reading sank in. "What is this?"

"The landlord revoked our right of first refusal," said Diego. "And sold the property to a company from San Francisco."

"He can't do that!" Milla re-read the contract, starting with the letterhead announcing the buyer as Homestead Commercial Real Estate. "We have a forty-five-day window; it's in the lease agreement." She flipped the page over, scowling when she saw it was blank, then re-read it a third time for good measure, picking out the key terms and dates. "This puts him in breach or something. Right?"

Diego shrugged and pulled another envelope from the bottom of the stack. "Julie had to explain it to me, but apparently, there are a few clauses in place that would allow the property owner to terminate. She said it had to do with the value assessment or something. I could not follow, but her ex-husband works in real estate. If anyone we know would know, it would be her." He pulled out another stack of papers. "And this came two days ago. The new lease."

She took it unwillingly. It was hard to ignore a stack of papers being thrust under your nose. Diego ate while she read the lease, her appetite dimming with each clause and dying an unremarkable death when she saw the new annual rate.

"This is almost double what we're paying now." She looked up and found Diego watching her intently. "Can we afford this?"

"¿Tal vez?" He waved his fork at the ICYMI table near the window. "The leggings have given us a little wiggle room, but you are going to remove the glamour, ¿no?" Milla opened her mouth. Closed it. "What?"

"I can't."

"What do you mean, 'I can't'?"

She turned her arms, showing Diego the inside of her wrists, and smiled weakly. "I might have had to do a thing to get out of jail."

"Pequeña bruja." He cupped the backs of her hands, staring in horror at the twin triskelions. "This is … I have seen this."

"In a grimoire?" she asked, hopeful. If anyone had seen this sigil before, it would have been Diego in his first life.

"On Darkly." He trailed the arcs of the sigil on her right wrist. "What is it?"

"How have you seen this on Darkly?" She took her hand back, holding it against her chest.

"He has been living next door for weeks." Diego shrugged. Then, a sly little smile pinched his lips. "It was not hard to memorize his exercise schedule."

"Diego, ew!"

"What?" He raised his hands in mock surrender. "It is not my fault he prefers to punch that bag without a shirt on."

"Are you stalking him?"

"I am taking my tea," he replied plainly, "on the back porch, which is my right."

"Oh, my Goddess." Milla covered her face with her hands. "You are absurd." But she laughed, and the laughter made her feel lighter. After a moment, she smiled softly. "Thank you."

He closed his eyes with a smile and a shrug, then re-opened them and pointed at the sigil. "Do you want to tell me what that is?"

"A binding," she said. "Lou put it there; it will allow her to control my Way. I think."

"¿Crees que sí?"

"There wasn't really a lot of time to ask questions. Everything happened so fast. One minute, they were talking about cleaving me, but it turns out I'm already cleaved, and it was a setup, anyway. Lou, Constance"—Diego mouthed "Abernathy," and she nodded—"Even the Tribunal Head that came in from Czechia. They knew my Way, and they had these two young witches in the room to witness, and Darkly bottled himself so they wouldn't—"

"¿Él hizo qué?" Diego reared back, searching Milla's face as though looking for a lie. When all she did was nod, he let out a low whistle. "I wondered about the haircut."

"And now I have to work with him and Lou." And once she'd started talking about *that* aspect of her so-called freedom, there was no holding back. She had unloaded it all: the absurdity of her not-trial, the raw-head, how she'd felt corralled into agreeing, and how they had used Darkly's years as an Enforcer to support Lou's suggestion. "They want me to pay into the ritual at Beltane," she sniffled, wiping her nose with the back of a hand. "In front of Elder Witches of every coven in the Southeast." She took a shuddering breath and let out the hardest part. "I'm scared, Diego."

"Por supuesto," he said, gathering Milla in his arms. "Of course you are, which is why you must apologize to Julie and get over yourself enough to talk to Darkly."

"Diego—"

"Milla." He hit her with a stern look. "I am right, and you know I am right. You need to talk to him and clear the air between you. I do not know what happened on that beach—"

"He turned me in."

"—but whatever happened *happened*, and I am certain you both have your reasons. What I do know is that when I returned, our home was safe, our store intact, and Darkly made it so."

"Probably driven by guilt."

"Whatever it was, he has earned five minutes of your time to shut up and listen," Diego snapped. Milla tucked her chin, leaning away. "Do you even want to work for Lou?"

"No."

"Then you have common ground; start there." He poked her shoulder. "The sooner you and Darkly learn to work together, the sooner Lou might undo whatever this is, and you can undo the glamour." His finger swept over the triskelion on her right wrist, and he frowned. "I suppose this is a bad time to mention the desecrant."

"Oh, Goddess, what is it now?"

"Something new," he said. "A water horse, under the Usina Bridge."

"All the way up there?" The Usina Bridge connected St. Augustine to Vilano Beach, crossing the mouth of the Tolomato River. "When did it get here?"

Diego adjusted his glasses and tipped his head. "I am not sure, exactly. It was here when I returned from Key West. Darkly called it something I cannot pronounce."

"If he knew about it, why didn't he handle it?"

"Again, you will need to talk to Darkly, as I refuse to get in the middle of this." Another narrow-eyed glare was sent her way. "But he implied it might have had something to do with whatever magick you performed in Vilano Beach."

Milla swallowed, none too happy with how thick the lump in her throat had become. "Possessed him with a dead woman."

"¿Qué fue eso?"

"I *said*, 'I possessed him with a dead woman.'"

Diego's face went blank. He took in a quick breath, more of a sip than anything else, held it, and then said, "And you wonder why he felt the need to surrender you to C.R.O.W."

"Shut up."

Twenty-One

DAWN WAS A LONG time coming and not due to any time-fuckery.

Milla tossed in her bed, unable to get comfortable among the over-stuffed pillows and thick, too-soft comforter.

She'd kicked the comforter away hours ago and pulled out a hand-stitched quilt, tugging it tight around her body. And then she'd tossed the pillows across the room, staring at the ceiling and willing her mind to quiet and her eyes to close, but she couldn't escape the creeping absence in the back of her mind.

When was the last time she had been left alone? For weeks, that voice had taunted her while the witch teased, and now she was alone and ill at ease without either of them there.

"This is ridiculous." Milla rolled over, staring across the empty space. After reviewing the ICYMI inventory and Southern Gothic's sales reports from the last seven weeks, Diego had forced her to walk home, practically shoving Milla into the shower and chatting about merchandise displays, the food at El Siboney, and the charming architecture of Key West while waiting out the threatened hair mask and following deep conditioning.

And now she was alone in her bedroom with a yellow candle burning. No chronomantic, no guard at the door, no whispers from a witch who wasn't there. Just Milla in her bed, unable to sleep because she was afraid to be alone, and her mind was running a million miles a minute in every direction.

"Start at the beginning," Diego had advised, tapping the first item on the list and shoving it into her hands before wishing her goodnight.

Start at the beginning. Apologize to Julie.

It was easy enough if Milla ignored the suffocating guilt that came along with it. If she were being honest with herself, which was becoming more difficult with every passing day, she had not given a single moment's thought to Julie since she'd left her in the back office of Southern Gothic. It had been the least of her concerns, and the guilt at recognizing how easily she'd shoved all thoughts of her friend to the back of her mind was nauseating.

She had spent a week in that swamp focused on her Way, on wrangling her magick back under control, and for what?

To be able to touch Darkly.

Goddess, even thinking it made her sick. She had lied to herself for days, saying it was to return to St. Augustine, to tend her demesne, to get back to her abnormal life, and in the same breath, she'd desecrated a towel just to lie next to him.

Had she really been so driven by her hormones that she'd shoved all else aside?

Yes.

"Shut up." She rolled onto her other side, facing the closed closet door and her dim reflection in the mirror. A pale face haloed in dark hair in a dark room. Her eyes were little more than black pits, wide in the low light and reminding her all too much of the witch on the other side of the wall.

When she and Diego got home, the lights were on in Darkly's half, but the television was turned off, meaning either the vinefica, Rai, had returned or Darkly had woken up. Neither option left Milla feeling good about the situation, and her mood only worsened the longer she lay in her bed, wide awake.

Was he still awake? Or was he upstairs in that massive bed, cuddled in the silk sheets with Rai?

An uncomfortable twinge of muscle in Milla's chest had her backing away from that thought, turning over again to put her back to the wall. Then she crept off the side of the bed, taking the thin quilt with her, and lay on the floor, falling into a light doze until the shrill bleating of an alarm had her bolting upright.

"HolyHornedGod." She slapped the surface of her bedside table, searching for her new phone and knocking it off the side. Rolling onto her hands and knees, she hissed at the tingling in her fingers and reached under the bed. The shrill, jaunty alarm blared, and she cursed under her breath, fumbling with the device.

The alarm finally quieted with a sweep of a still-asleep finger. Milla slumped against the edge of her bed, her heart slamming in her chest, and the quilt pooled around her waist.

Sunlight crept through the seams in the drapes, reaching across the floor in a quiet summons of demesne to witch. With it came a subtle tug at her middle and a drag at her legs. A not-so-gentle reminder that she was well overdue.

"Yeah, yeah." Milla kicked out of the quilt and dropped it on the bed on her way to the closet.

Less than five minutes later, she slipped out the front door and shouldered into a heavy-legged jog down Cedar Street. The demesne swelled to greet her, clinging to her calves and dragging her steps like she was running through molasses. But unlike her return from New Orleans when the demesne attempted to suck every last bit of magick from her to refill the reservoir Anaisa had been draining, this was the embrace of a clingy toddler.

Gripping her legs and refusing to let go. Needy in the intensity of missing her.

Yet, for all the neediness, there was a hesitance. With every step she took, the clinginess lessened to a fierce handhold, one that felt … shared, stretched between two points until thin enough to snap.

That had Milla drawing up short as she approached the San Sebastian River. A prickling crawled up her neck like a phantom breeze teasing the fine hairs and loose strands that had fallen from her ponytail. Sun beat against the stucco facade of the St. Augustine Distillery, and she squinted, shielding her eyes and scanning the empty road behind her.

"You're being stupid." She shook off the feeling and darted across the road, falling back into the same struggling gait. Not even a mile in, and her legs were heavy, the weak muscles struggling to move starving bones. Where she had flown down this same road only weeks before, now she fought for each breath, wrestling against the urge to give up.

This was *her* demesne. Hers. And even if Lou's sigil dammed her Way, she was going to tend it, dammit.

A cluster of palms tucked between twin Key West cottages offered a brief respite from the sun, already bearing down only an hour after dawn. She slowed, shuffling along the edge of the sidewalk to make room for a runner approaching at her back, their footfalls steady and strong. Bending at the waist, she gripped her knees, sipping in long, measured breaths as she waited for the runner to pass.

No one did.

She angled her head back the way she'd run. The road was empty and quiet, save for red-faced, gasping like a fish out of water, Milla in shorts that barely stayed on her hips and a Pork 'n' Butts BBQ shirt she'd modified into a tank top.

Again, the hairs along her neck prickled. She straightened and spun around, squinting into the shadows cast by the palm trees. Nothing moved, and the stillness was so intentional that Milla saw red.

"*What*," she spat.

Another long moment passed before Darkly stepped out of the shadows, looking every inch as wrecked as she felt. Pale, wan, his hollow cheeks flushed, and that idiotic haircut covered by a blue baseball cap with MAGIC embroidered across the front. His tech shirt clung to his torso, and Milla hated that she noticed. She glared at him, crossing her arms. "What do you want?"

He put his hands up and had the good grace to back away. "Cannae go for a run without any ulterior motive?"

"No." She fought against the desire to stomp her foot and pout. "Yes. I mean—don't run with me."

"Wasnae."

"Yes, you were," Milla argued. "This is my route. You know that."

"Own the road, do you?" His tone was short, but he maintained the same hang-dog expression he'd worn in Constance's office and again in his half of the duplex.

His half.

Goddess, remembering that was enough to have Milla raging all over again.

"No, but you know damn well I designed this route to best tend *my* demesne." She thrust her finger at the ground and treated herself to that little foot stomp. A spark of interest flared in his eyes, and his brows twitched upward. "Soulbound or not, I think it's safe to say that, yes, in a way, I do own these roads."

Whatever humor he'd found in Milla's little display faded at the mention of her binding. Darkly's gaze fell to her hand, still pointing at the ground. He frowned deeply, working his jaw side to side, but said nothing.

"Ugh, fine." Milla threw her hands up in frustration. "Just—either run ahead of me or far, *far* behind me."

"Milla…"

"No, Darkly," she snapped. Horned God, he had the worst timing. Cornering her in a living room and stalking her on a run. Not that anyone could call what she was doing *running*, but it was the point of the thing. The intent! He was a witch; he ought to know better than to try to have an emotional scouring in the middle of the street on a hot-ass April morning. "I don't want to hear it."

His brows dropped, nostrils flaring as he pressed his lips together. A look she knew well. A protest was coming, a demand, and she just *couldn't.*

"Not now," she said before he could get the words out. 'Talk to Darkly' was on her list, but Goddess, not like this—when she was exhausted and could barely think straight, when he looked like he hadn't slept in weeks. Not in public. "I just want to run my demesne. Can you at least allow me that?"

Darkly blinked, his shoulders dropping and posture relaxing. His throat bobbed once, and he nodded, but he didn't take off running in the opposite direction or even move, for that matter.

Milla rolled her eyes, grumbling as she put her back to him and took off jogging at her halted pace. A few strides later, his footfalls echoed hers, keeping a distance as he followed her the length of

Bridge Street. She was wheezing when they hit the waterfront, and a cramp pinched her side, but she pressed through the pain, fueled by her anger at the fact he wasn't even breathing hard.

He kept his pace, running six feet behind Milla, and followed her lead. Just as he'd done on that first run, after the raw head, and when she confronted a Loa, he shadowed Milla as she attempted to reclaim the witch she was.

♣

Lou waited for them on the front steps of the duplex, an e-grim in one hand and a sour expression on her face.

So, really, it was just her face.

"Where were you last night?" She stormed down the stairs, stopping short of barreling into Milla. "Both of you, for that matter."

"Why?"

"You ken where I was," said Darkly. Lou lifted her gaze over Milla's head as a cool shadow draped over her back. "And Milla was with Diego."

"Yeah." Milla nodded. "Wait." She twisted to ask him, "How did you know I was with Diego?"

"Had a message when I woke up," he explained as if it should have been obvious, "letting me know where you were."

Milla's neck heated. She whipped her head around, glaring at the weeds growing through cracks in her front path, not at all comfortable with the idea of Darkly and Diego texting about her.

"What is this about, Lou?" Darkly edged around her, his body a wall between Milla and his sister.

"There's been another one." She handed him the e-grim, waiting as he scanned the screen, a deep line pinched between his brows. "Near Lake City."

"Where's that?" He tapped the screen and squinted, then extended his arm halfway, blinking as he read what Milla assumed to be an E.R.I.E.

"About halfway to Tallahassee," Milla said. "Is this about that ritual?"

Lou stared at her as if just remembering she was there and then nodded. "It is, good memory."

"How could I forget." She moved beside Darkly to read the screen. "You left the readout in my cell; it gave me something to think about until my guard took it away."

"And what did you learn?"

Milla scanned the graph on the tablet, tracking the rise and fall of the multicolored lines and the blurred signature behind them. Darkly swept the graph forward, and the lines converged into one thick black line, arcing and falling in harsher peaks and valleys. A detail that had not been part of the printout Lou had left. "That you only gave me part of the picture."

Darkly tensed, the tablet trembling slightly as his arm went taut. He jerked his head up, and from the hot huff of breath that hit her head, she knew he was glaring at his sister.

"Goddess, get over yourself." Milla grabbed the e-grim and climbed the stairs onto the shaded porch. On a hunch, she pressed her finger to the screen and swept to the right. The graph moved with her gesture, traveling back along the X-axis. The lines de-converged and separated into multi-colored strands. She studied that, chewing her lower lip in thought, and then held out the e-grim to Lou. "This reading is from last night?"

"That's what I said."

"Then you have a problem." Milla turned toward her door, gripping the handle and freezing as Lou said, "*We* have a problem."

She looked back over her shoulder, eyes hopping from one Simmons sibling to the next. Darkly stood beside and just behind his sister, a dark scowl twisting his face as he bore holes into the side of Lou's head while she remained straight and tall, waiting for Milla to challenge her.

And who was Milla to disappoint?

"I have to get to work." She depressed the handle, and the glass pane rattled as she pushed the door open.

"Congratulations." Lou mounted the stairs, approaching Darkly's doorway. "You're here. Now grab your Stitch Witch and come next door."

With that, she stepped inside, followed a moment later by Darkly.

Twenty-Two

SABBAT Any one of eight annual festivals of seasonal celebration and ritual observance, including the solstices, equinoxes, and other days. Rituals performed on a sabbat wield inherently more power.

AN HOUR LATER, MILLA re-entered the bizarro-world version of her home. The same hardwood flooring and soft off-white paint with its faint greenish tint. The same arcing entryways and open-concept flow from the kitchen to the living room, where a coven of witches huddled around a coffee table that had not been there the night before.

Darkly jerked his head up as she and Diego entered and burst to his feet, the sudden movement and his outfit startling Milla to a halt. Though she had seen the clothing hanging in his closet, seeing the witch in a tight black V-neck, a slouchy heather gray beanie, and low-slung faded black denim jeans was a different experience altogether.

She trawled her gaze from the arresting green eyes staring at her from behind tortoiseshell glasses down to the cuffed hem of his jeans brushing the top of black matte leather boots. The overall effect was, for lack of a better word, mouthwatering. She licked her lips and made the mistake of meeting his gaze.

"Please." He gestured to his vacant seat, and the rasp in his voice broke Milla from her thirsty shock. She glanced at his vacant seat and the witch beside it.

Icy blue eyes, white blonde hair, broad shoulders, and a cold, stoic expression.

Her back hit the wall, pulse thundering as Agent Sterne tipped his head in a tight nod.

"Milla?" Diego's face hovered into view, but she couldn't look away. The tips of her fingers tingled, and she pressed harder against the wall, every muscle in her body taut. If she was fast enough, she could make it out the door before Agent Sterne tackled her. This was her neighborhood, her city. With luck and adrenaline, she could make it across the Flagler campus and lose him in the Colonial Quarter.

The tingling spread into her hands, and white static bled from her toes into her feet. She bit her lower lip, the flash of pain not enough to distract her from the fright of seeing Agent Sterne here because wherever he was, the other witch wasn't far away.

"I know what you are thinking." Milla twitched her head to the side, startled by the presence of a witch she had not noticed. A hair taller than Diego, slight and entirely nondescript, he had wedged himself into the corner of the room. Leaning closer, he lowered his voice to a conspiratorial whisper. "They are all so tall."

"But now Milla is here." Diego brushed fingers against her arm, settling her in the here and now. The tingling receded, bit by bit, and after an odd lurch in her belly, she took a long, slow breath. "Our numbers are growing."

The other witch laughed and nudged Milla with his shoulder. "Cyrus," he said. "It is nice to see you again."

"Again?" She stared at him, unable to place his face, but who could? No remarkable features, no birthmarks or blemishes to recall. He was the most normal, boring-looking person she had ever seen and yet, something about *that* struck her as familiar. "I'm sorry, I don't recall—"

"No one does." He shook his head sadly and gestured to his face. His voice was rich and thickly accented, perhaps the most distinguishing feature about him. "Features only a mother could love. If she could remember what I looked like."

"Your utter forgetfulness has served us well on more than one mission," Lou called from across the room. "And now that we are all here, *finally*, we can get started."

"Lou, you have already met," Cyrus told Milla. He smiled dotingly at Lou, a feat she didn't think was possible. "And that is Rai Zhou." He pointed to the vinefica, who waggled fingers at her. "But I believe you know her as well?"

"Yeah." Milla nodded.

"Good. The stern-looking German is Tobias Sterne." He pointed to Agent Sterne. "We were fortunate to have him in the cells to look after you." Darkly snorted, drawing attention to himself as he took a seat. "Keir, of course, who we are glad to have back in fighting form, which brings us to me, who you do not remember from your arrest."

Milla stared at him, running through the faces of the witches she recalled. Agent Sterne in his bathing suit, the large meteomantic, Lou, a Green Witch, and—"The hippocromantic."

"The what?" Cyrus looked affronted.

"In the trees. You had the medical bag," she explained. "And in the ambulance, I thought …"

"Cyrus does not like to get his hands dirty," a new voice said.

"And that," Cyrus smiled and pointed at the large witch entering the room, "is Donmar Bolatov."

Donmar gently squeezed Darkly's shoulder as he made his way to Lou. Milla immediately recognized him as the meteomantic who had so gently handled her during the arrest. Just as she remembered, he was a towering mass of muscle and padding. Crow's feet sprung from the corners of his eyes, and his deeply tanned, wind-worn skin, warm against a cream henley, belied his Way as a weather witch.

"He prefers to fiddle with technology." Donmar winked at Milla with a tip of his head toward Cyrus.

"It is how we got your location off of Keir," Tobias stated, his intense gaze leveled directly at Milla.

"Wait." She found Darkly on the edge of his seat, fingers digging into the armrest. "What?"

He opened his mouth to say … something, but Lou cut him off. "Not now, Toby."

"It is best to get that out of the way," Toby said, each word clipped and precise. "How else are we going to work together as a team?"

"I agree," said Rai. "If Milla cannot trust us, what is the point of having her here at all?"

"Now is not the time." Lou gestured to the coffee table, covered in tablets and reports. Graphs identical to the one she had shared with Milla in the cell were repeated over and over again, along with photographs of abandoned ritual sites, C.R.O.W. identification profiles, and city maps. "We have a coven of rogue witches to hunt down and a new recruit to train up."

"If you intend on keeping her in the dark, then toss her back into that dank cell," Rai sassed back. A silence that could only be described as pre-explosive filled the air.

"No one is putting Milla anywhere," Darkly rumbled after a moment. "Cyrus, explain; she willnae hear it from me."

"Rude," Milla said, more on instinct than anything else. Who was he to decide what she would or would not hear?

"Factual," Darkly retorted, which, *fair.*

"Oh!" Cyrus clapped his hands, glee lighting up the plain features of his face into something almost memorable. "You will love this." He summoned a tablet and huddled close to Milla. "The update is being pushed to all C.R.O.W. issued e-grims at the end of the month, but here, let me show you."

His fingers flew across the screen, sorting through a file, pulling up a report, and fiddling with settings. "We first noticed your signature in the reading from the Fountain of Youth, see?" He angled the screen and pointed to multiple spikes and lines on a graph. "When I isolated Keir's signature and removed it, it left us with the desecrant and an anomaly." More taps and one of the lines, wavering at what Milla interpreted as a lower resonance, or whatever the technomantic term would be, vanished. "The desecrant's signature matched the readings another team pulled from Hattiesburg, but the anomaly stumped us."

"Until I left my E.R.I.E. running during lunch with Keir," Donmar said.

"Exactly!" He tapped the screen again, showing Milla yet another chart with two disparate waveforms over a faint gray blur.

She nodded, even though she had no idea what he was showing her. Lou had explained that each line was a different magickal signature, a different Way, but she hadn't considered that the E.R.I.E. would also register desecrants.

"This is Donmar, see?" He traced a series of slow ramping lines climbing the y-axis, driving his finger down when they reached their apex and plummeted into a brief flatline, only to begin climbing again. "And here is Keir." He traced a typical-looking wave, the basic sort she remembered from her pre-calc textbook in high school. "And here is our anomaly."

Instead of tracing a third line, he tapped the screen twice. The image increased, and what Milla had at first taken as a blur or a smudge became a rapid waveform, the peaks and valleys so tight they were practically on top of one another.

"The E.R.I.E. syncs with my e-grim every hour," Cyrus continued. "I had a ping set to alert me whenever another anomaly occurred, and it did—when Donmar had lunch with Keir." Milla glanced at the witch in question, who stared at the table's edge, his mouth a firm, thin line. "From there, I cross-referenced the anomaly with the Fountain of Youth and your home, which is lovely, by the way, and then widened the field to see if I could determine your location."

"Wait." Milla straightened as all of the lingo clicked into place. "You're saying that you," she pointed at Cyrus, "got my location off of Darkly."

Cyrus nodded fervently, showing her yet another readout on his e-grim. This one was a map of the greater Jacksonville area, all the way down to Daytona. St. Augustine was all but obscured by a black circle, set to a low enough transparency that she could still make out the major roads and waterways, as was Jacksonville, and just north of Daytona, where the Halifax and Tomoka rivers met, was another.

"All rituals and Ways leave an echo," he said, "a social distortion and yours is no different. The magick you used to confront the Loa is still registering on the E.R.I.E. scans taken from the Fountain of Youth. Whatever else you did, it lingers on Keir as well."

Again, her attention drifted to Darkly, who had slunk down on the couch, spinning a glossy vape pen in his hands and looking everywhere but at her. Had he told them how her Way had gone weird? How his magick had affected hers, and she rotted him with every little touch?

Diego leaned over the table to better see the map. "But Darkly was with her in Daytona. Would it not have been easier to set the E.R.I.E. to search for his signature?"

"Isnae how the Soul Sigil works," Darkly answered in a toneless voice, pressing the vape to his mouth. A chill prickled Milla's skin. Darkly was a clown, with his dimply smirk and bad flirting. She had never heard him sound so defeated, so dead.

"After finishing his work with the Shades, Keir is close to burnout. His Way is not strong enough to register elsewhere." Lou stepped forward and seized command of the room. "Which brings us to the matter at hand."

"Not quite," Rai said. "I, for one, will not be able to concentrate until the mystery of the hour has been solved."

"Mysterious rituals and missing witches aren't enough for you?" Milla asked, brow proudly furrowed.

Rai shrugged. "I'm from Hong Kong," she said as if that explained it. "What I would love to know is—is it true she's cleaved?" This, she asked Darkly, who dropped his head back and blew a vapor stream at the ceiling.

"Wouldnae be here if she wasnae."

"But *how?*" Donmar asked.

Darky raised his head, staring blankly at his brother-in-law for a moment. He sighed and gestured to Diego. "He's got it."

"I'm sorry." Milla pressed a hand in the air, glancing at Diego, who was clutching the terrarium pendant around his neck. "*What?*"

"Noticed it that first day," he explained, speaking around more wintry-scented vapor. "Diego's got a wee sliver, and you're missing about that."

"Is that what that was about?" Milla asked. She vividly recalled how terrified Diego had been to see Darkly in their living room, and Darkly—his Shades had stretched long across her walls, and he had looked like he'd seen a ghost. Which, she had to admit, wasn't that far off the mark.

"Again," Donmar said. "How."

"Am nae up on my resurrections, but I ken it's safe to assume Milla gave a bit of herself to Diego when she raised him."

That landed like a lead balloon. Lou's coven glanced at each other while Darkly stared at Milla as if waiting for her to argue.

When she did not, and how could she when her thoughts had shot almost twenty years into the past to dwell on the *other* resurrection she had performed, Darkly shook his head and looked away, pen already at his mouth.

"Now that that's handled," Lou said, "let's focus on the important things."

She launched into a description of the charts and readouts on the table, detailing the *how* beyond the readings rather than what they were looking at. Milla zoned out. She knew well enough how the program worked and had been married to the witch who helped train the technology to recognize an obnubilari.

Even if Milla wanted to listen, she couldn't. Not when everything she thought she knew, the anger that had fueled her time in the cells, had turned out to be little more than a willful omission of the truth, manipulating Milla's thoughts and actions a certain way.

Lou said she got Milla's location off of Darkly, and when Milla had repeated as such in the cell, she had not argued. She had let

Milla continue to believe it while claiming she needed to trust everyone on the team.

She glanced at Lou now, her arms crossed, head tipped to the side as she listened to Cyrus.

On the couch directly across from her, Darkly dropped his head back. To the untrained eye, he was a witch in repose, bored by the technomantic discussion, but Milla could see each tight, tense breath. She did not miss how his fingers dug into the armrest nor the glances Tobias and Rai kept sending him.

"The job," Lou's commanding voice jerked Milla out of her thoughts, "is threat assessment and containment." Around the room, every witch straightened and leaned in, fully intent on Lou. Even Diego, who at one point had perched along the armrest beside Darkly, straightened, his expression more serious than Milla had ever seen.

For not the first time since getting out of jail, Horned God, *yesterday*, she felt every one of those seven weeks and the impassable distance time had put between her and the outside world. Looking at Diego, it was obvious he had fitted himself into the cogs and found a purpose among this coven. It was in Cyrus's excited answer to his question and how Lou had not brushed him off but offered something useful for once. In how she had demanded Milla bring him along, yet Diego had led her through the backdoor.

In how he left her leaning against the wall to sit with the cool kids.

She crossed her arms tight over her chest, wishing she'd opted for leggings and a hoodie instead of a black keyhole halter and skinny jeans. It was hard to pout when her vibe was so on point.

"In a joint effort with the Gulf and Low Country covens," said Lou, "Cyrus and I have been assessing the disappearances of registered witches in good standing and matching their specific locations to those where the surges occurred."

Cyrus grabbed an e-grim from the table and fiddled with the screen. A moment later, a map of the Gulf appeared on Darkly's television. "Casting," he snickered. "Never gets old."

Seven red circles, not unlike the transparent black radius representing Milla, were speckled across the territory. Corpus Christi, Texas, a small dot on the San Antonio Bay, and another near Houston. They skipped Louisiana entirely, resuming in Hattiesburg, Valdosta and Savannah in Georgia, and Lake City just under two hours away.

"The Texas rituals occurred last year on Mabon, Samhain, and Yule." Lou named the three major sabbats at the end of the year, aligning with the autumn equinox, Halloween, and the winter solstice. Times when the veil, as humans called it, was thin. Or, as Milla thought of it, days when the world was prime for witchy shit. "Where the latter three occurred seven weeks ago"—Lou pointed to Hattiesburg—"four and three weeks ago"—Savannah and Valdosta—"and last night in Lake City."

"And you are certain these rituals are being cast by the same witches?" Diego asked.

"Positive." Cyrus tapped on his tablet, and an E.R.I.E. scan appeared. As on the printout she had been shown, the location was listed in the lower right: Matagorda. "At first, the Gulf Coast and Pine Curtain Covens disregarded the anomaly in the readings. Off-shore drilling and C.R.O.W. environmental efforts have resulted in false readings before, and the Gulf itself is a basin for magick." As he spoke, two more E.R.I.E. scans appeared on the screen: A small town outside of Corpus Christi, and one near Houston. With a swipe of his finger, Cyrus layered the three. "See? Identical."

"When the ritual was not repeated at Imbolc, the covens were happy to dismiss it as irregular readings and assumed the anomaly to be typical of the region," said Lou. "And then, seven weeks ago, it repeated in Hattiesburg."

Milla looked to Darkly. They had been in Hattiesburg right before this ritual, dealing with the glamoured leggings, and of course, this could be a coincidence, but witches didn't believe in coincidences. A Dark Witch and a Death Witch in Hattiesburg, all the chaos Anaisa had caused with ICYMI and her downline. There would have been echoes, remnants of magick left behind for any witch to use.

Darkly met her eyes and gave a slow nod, confirming her fear as if he could hear her thoughts.

She wanted to sit. Wanted to curl up in a tiny ball on the floor and tuck herself away until all of this blew over. But if she was right, and Milla was getting *really* tired of being right, it would be a long while before she got to do so. The timing was too much of a coincidence, and witches didn't believe in—"Wait." She jerked straight as a thought occurred. "Then what happened when I was arrested?"

The room looked at her, each witch wearing the same question on their face.

"When you were arrested?" Lou asked, for once thrown off her consummate cool. "How is that relevant?"

"There's was this whole thing." She fluttered her hand in the air and stepped forward to insert herself into the conversation. "When all those Enforcers rushed out, the chatter said it was something in St. Augustine, but my demesne isn't on this list."

"It was a Dullahan," Lou said. "The steward handled it."

"And that would be?"

"The one C.R.O.W. assigned to manage the demesne in your absence." Her gaze turned haughty, as if Milla ought to have known all of this, which … now that she thought about it, she probably should have. Constance had mentioned a steward when they were in her office, but Milla had been too distracted by Darkly's outburst and her not-trial to catch the reference.

"Then I want to meet with this *steward*," she demanded, spitting the word like it tasted foul, "and find out what happened."

"A Dullahan is an Irish desecrant," Darkly said, calling Milla's attention to him. He picked at a line in the corduroy upholstery, pointedly not looking at her. "Summoned by the Witch of the Demesne."

"Oh, Goddess." Rai gripped his shoulder. "Is that the headless horseman we caught outside on Connemara?"

"That would be the one."

"But I didn't summon anything." Milla knocked her wrists together. "I was Waybound and in the middle of being arrested. And my desecrants tend to be Slavic."

"Or Spanish," Diego added.

Darkly raised his brows slightly, lifting his chin in moderate challenge as if daring her to keep arguing. For the first time since seeing him in Constance's office, he looked like himself. "Perhaps the demesne meant to protect its witch."

"I—" she squeaked, staring across the room at Darkly. For a brief, fleeting instant, the dimple appeared as his mouth curved, only to vanish when Cyrus cleared his throat.

"As I was saying, once I identified your signature on the E.R.I.E., I recognized it as the anomaly we saw in the Texas rituals and again in Valdosta. We tested the theory with the Valdosta and Savannah readings, and this morning, I applied the calculations live for Lake City." Cyrus beamed at the room, eyes sparkling.

Two taps on his e-grim revealed more E.R.I.E. scans on the screen. He hard swept his finger to the left, and the multitude of lines oscillated in what Milla's decade-old pre-calc knowledge interpreted as speed or an increasing frequency. The patterns became sharper, closer. The peaks steeper, the valleys plunging lower until—

"Tah-dah!" Cyrus threw his arm out, fingers splayed wide at the screen as he bounced his joyous expression from witch to witch.

"Tah-what?" Donmar asked.

"Tah-what?" Cyrus shook his arm at the E.R.I.E. scan, now one gray blur of mathematically impossible waveform. "Tah-Death Witch!"

Twenty-Three

MILLA LAUGHED. ONE HARD, sharp bark of scornful humor. "Impossible."

"Improbable," Cyrus replied.

"No, Spock, *impossible*," she doubled down.

"The data does not lie," he replied. "That is a Death Witch. It matches your signature on a mathematical level. We are dealing with a rogue coven of witches performing magick Forbidden and Foule under the command of a Death Witch."

"And sometimes two plus two equals five." She snatched the tablet, ignoring his flustered protest, and swiped to the right until the supposed Death Witch became a blur behind the disparate Ways and then nothing at all. Pinching the screen, she spread her fingers wide to zoom in. And again. "Lou showed me some of the graphs when I was in the cells. Printed out on *paper*." She sent Lou a withering look. "Seriously? Paper?" Lou rolled her eyes, and one of the witches on the couch snorted. "It was only a snippet of each ritual telling this same story, but look." She zoomed in again, right on the point where the disparate signatures converged, and the anomalous blur began. "Can't do that on paper."

"Do what?" Donmar asked.

"Examine the finer details," Diego answered. He moved closer, adjusting his glasses and squinting at the television. "Oh por Diosa." He whipped around, blood rushing from his cheeks as he said to Milla, "It is a constellation."

"A what?" Lou asked.

"A constellation." Milla tossed the e-grim on the table and crossed her arms. "A coven of witches stepping into their Ways in a joint ritual to mimic the Way of another witch."

"An old term," Rai added. "I have not heard it since leaving Kowloon." She rose gracefully and approached the screen. "C.R.O.W. did away with the categorization several decades ago."

"The older generations still use it on the steppes," said Donmar, tension deepening the crow's feet around his eyes. "They called the stryzga—"

"This is not the stryzga." Lou set her hand on his shoulder. "Not here."

"I know." Donmar closed his eyes, leaning into her touch, and nodded.

"In my first life," Diego said softly, "my sister and I would cast with a vinefica to mimic corpomancy."

"Good Goddess." Rai pressed a hand to her chest. "To what end?"

"Someone had to keep our patients still." Diego shrugged, unbothered by the look of disgust that washed over Rai's face. "Magick was regarded differently then," he said. "C.R.O.W. was in its infancy, and not many could afford the services of a corpomantic. With a potion to induce sleep and a Stitch Witch to keep the patient from bleeding out, a hippocromantic could work their cure."

"As fascinating as this history is," said Lou, "it is a practice no longer deployed by C.R.O.W."

"Is it not?" asked Toby. "C.R.O.W. bottles witches more often than you are available."

"Yes, well—"

"Ezra was called in for bottlings like six times while we were together," Milla added. "What makes a coven of witches doing the work of one Light Witch any different than this?"

"The suggestion holds merit, Lou," Rai gently added.

"It would change the scope of our investigation." Cyrus frowned at the e-grim Milla had tossed on the table, a thoughtful line pinched between his thick eyebrows. "All of my projections are based on the assumption that a Death Witch is commanding the ritual, but if they are not …"

"Then it could be anyone attempting to do anything," finished Darkly.

"Hardly anything," Lou scoffed. "What all can a Death Witch do? Rot and revive?"

"Revive the dead, command the dead, mass summons and possession"—Milla counted off on her fingers—"phylactery transference, astral projection, enthrallations, Soul and Shade tethering, Shade summons, corporeal divination, willful malediction—"

"Alright, yes, we get it. There are many Death Witch rituals."

"Death Witchuals," Milla corrected.

Lou gave her a droll look, and Rai hid a smile behind her hand.

"I do not get it." Cyrus glanced from witch to witch, and Tobias took pity on him.

"It is a pun." He frowned at Milla, but his voice was absent the harsh seriousness she remembered from the cells. "A terrible one."

"So where do we start?" Darkly sat forward, propping his elbows on his knees.

"I will need to re-run my projections," Cyrus began, "and base them around the coven itself. Then I will need to cross-reference the Ways against registered witches in the affected demesne—"

"And the missing witches," Milla added. "What were their Ways? You could work the problem backward, narrowing down which Ways are in high demand for the ritual or, um …"

"Burning out," Tobias supplied.

"You think this is a matter of burnout?" Lou angled her face at him, lips pressed together as she considered the suggestion. "It would make sense, I suppose. A ritual with a signature of this magnitude would require the casting witches to step deeply into their Ways."

"And I've nae come across their Shades," Darkly added.

"If it is burnout," said Milla, "and you can figure out which Ways are being exhausted, it would narrow down the potential Death Witchuals."

Lou tucked her chin, lip curling. "I am absolutely not calling them that."

"Yeah, you are, Big Yin." Darkly's eyes shone behind his glasses, and a genuine grin lit up his face. "It's too good not tae."

"Goddess, you clown," Lou muttered, some of her tension easing at his smile. "Right, so we have a heading, which is more than we had yesterday. Anything else?"

"I will need to borrow Milla's grimoire," Cyrus added.

"Why do you need my grimoire?"

"To review the Death Witchuals," he said. Lou muttered under her breath and left the room.

"Good luck finding them." Milla shrugged. "My grimoire was a gift from my dad when I turned sixteen. I've read that thing from front to back; there's no Death Witchuals in there."

Cyrus' cheeks blanched. He looked down at his e-grim, the table littered with tech and data, then back to Milla. "So how do we—"

"Casting range." Tobias rose and stepped over Darkly's legs. "I need to prepare her for Beltane. We will run Milla through exercises and have her cast the rituals she knows. Would that suffice?"

"It would help, but I—"

"Tomorrow." Tobias hit Milla with a bright blue stare. She backed up a step, crowding against Cyrus. He put a hand on her shoulder to steady them both. "First thing."

"I have to run my demesne in the morning," she said. It was a weak excuse, but Horned God, anything to get out of special forces alone time with Agent Sterne. "I have to tend it."

"I fail to see how that is possible when you are Soulbound." Lou re-entered the room with a cup of tea in her hands. She held it out to Milla, huffing when she did not immediately take it.

"But it's my routine," she argued, "my demesne. I can't just let it—"

"Then run it in the evenings if the mileage is so important."

Milla lurched back, hot tea spilling over the cup's rim and splashing on her hand. Vaguely, she was aware of Rai and Donmar leaving the room. Of Diego grabbing Cyrus by the arm and hauling him away from his tablets and charts. But they were on the periphery, and Lou's commandeering, belittling tone was right in front of her. "So I'm just supposed to let this mystery steward continue tending my demesne?"

"I'm sure it will be fine." She flipped a dismissive hand in the air.

"And I'm sure it's my demesne; I think I understand it better than any of you."

"St. Augustine doesnae care when you tend to her." Darkly filled the space behind Lou, and a wave of red washed over Milla's vision in seeing him there. What was it Natje had called them? *C.R.O.W.'s darling Light Witch and her pet.* "So long as you—"

"Horned God, would you stop mansplaining my demesne to me?" Pure silence filled the room. Milla glared at Lou and Darkly. "No? Nothing?"

"The casting range is within city limits," Tobias spoke from the couch, where he had settled with a tablet. "And Lou will have to release your Way for you to cast. That will suffice."

Milla's jaw dropped at the sheer audacity, *again*, of this witch, but no words or argument formed.

"There we have it." Lou clapped her hands and stepped away, leaving Darkly standing far too close for Milla's comfort. "First thing in the morning, we head to the casting range. Keir, will you be joining us at the cottage for dinner?"

Her question, so flippant compared to the rest of their conversation, left Milla reeling for solid ground. She sat in the metal folding chair, gripping the teacup in both hands and willing its warmth into her chilled bones, only half hearing Darkly's reply.

"Nae tonight," he rumbled. "Gonnae run with the cultists."

"Right." Lou sighed and swept a hand over her hair, looking at Milla in a way she did not like at all. "Best take Ludmilla with you, then. It's time she met them properly."

"Goddess, seriously?" she groaned.

"Are you not the Witch of the Demesne?" Lou arched an eyebrow. "I seem to remember you saying something to that effect."

"I am, obviously, but that's not how my demesne works. I tend to St. Augustine and keep far away from the cultists."

"It is in your best interests to—"

"Horned God, we *just* went over this. My demesne. Mine. Not yours, not his." She pointed at Darkly, who flinched. "Mine. I ran it fine before any of you got here."

"And then you lost the demesne to a Loa and regained it in an act of magick St. Augustine has never before witnessed or felt," Darkly countered. "But the cultists did, and they have questions." He stepped close enough that Milla caught a whiff of his clove and spice scent. Close enough that the heat of him warmed her more than the tea could manage. "The steward has done what he can, but Lou is right. It is time you meet with the cultists and get to know them."

Though he lowered his voice and softened the edges, the demand was there, lacing through each word and granting his speech an air of know-it-all-ness she hated.

"You're not a secret anymore, Milla," he continued. "Come Beltane, you'll need all the support you can get before revealing your Way to the Elder Witches."

Darkly trailed a knuckle down the outside of her upper arm, lingering at her elbow. She bit her lips, willing her body to remain still as the desire to lean in and seek out more of his touch became overwhelming. His eyes dropped to where he touched her bare skin, and then he reversed the path, brushing hair over her shoulder and slipping his hand away.

Again, she saw a hint of the Darkly she had come to know over six weeks and not the lying Enforcer she knew him as now.

It was heartbreaking.

"You need to foster a relationship with the people who can best support you in your demesne," he said sadly, "and that begins with the cultists."

She exhaled, not breaking away from his gaze. Because once she saw that Darkly, the one she knew, the one she trusted, the one who only ever asked, "What do you need?" she was a lost cause.

"Okay," she whispered, low enough only he could hear. Darkly's eyes bounced from one of hers to the other, asking that silent question. When he gave the tiniest little dip of his chin, she knew without words that he'd heard her answer.

"I'll pick you up."

Twenty-Four

SUMMONS To call or heed a physical item to hand. To summon, one must know the exact location of the item being called. Many summoners choose to store items in an organized cupboard to ensure what they require is always at hand.

"¿NADA?" DIEGO ASKED, LOOKING at her over the top of his glasses.

"Nothing." The greasy fabric slipped through her fingers, pooling in a neon floral puddle on the counter. Milla shoved the leggings off the counter with a grunt. "Goddess, I'm fucking *useless* like this."

"Would she let you take a few boxes to the casting range? Removing glamour has to use enough magick to fuel the demesne."

"I don't know." Milla set her elbows on the counter. Diego had whisked her away from Darkly after that confusing moment in his living room, and they came straight to the store, where her every attempt at seizing normalcy failed. She propped her forehead on her fingers, and her bangs fell forward, tickling her nose. She puffed them out of the way. "I can ask. It's a simple casting, but it's got to count for something Cyrus needs. Right?"

"No sé." Diego shrugged and pushed away from the counter, picking up the leggings by pinching the fabric between two fingers. "I will go take care of this." He wrinkled his nose in disgust and walked them down the hall with his arm stretched out as far as it would go.

She spent the next few hours helping the occasional customer and sorting through her inventory. Diego had done well in her absence, just as she had gleaned the night before. Even the leggings were organized by color, season, and size, meaning Milla could only wander around poking her curios and antiques for so long before even that grew old. So she turned to the new lease, re-reading the clauses and glaring at the price.

"What kind of asshole raises rates this much?" she asked the lease. Lacking a reply, Milla pulled out her phone and entertained herself by researching the company, making what amounted to, in her mind, a case against them.

Homestead Commercial Real Estate, the new owners of the building, was one of many companies owned by Erlich Industries, headquartered in San Francisco. It took a bit of hunting, but she eventually found an organizational chart showing everything Erlich Industries owned. Multiple food brands, clothing brands, an electric vehicle company, utility companies, makeup manufacturers, commercial and private real estate firms, and textile companies. For each big brand name listed, at least ten more brands sat beneath those.

"Horned God, this dude owns everything." She swiped the phone screen, scanning the never-ending list of businesses.

"Who?" Diego asked from his throne, burrito in one hand, phone in the other.

"Stefan Holfstaedter." Milla tapped back and turned her phone around to show him the CEO of Erlich Industries—a silver fox of a middle-aged white man with salt and pepper hair that looked too meticulous to be real. Everything about him was manufactured. His eyes held the perfect amount of crow's feet, his teeth were finely veneered, and his suit looked—

"Por la Diosa, is that a cashmere herringbone *Kiton*?" Diego stole her phone and zoomed in on the suit jacket. "Notched lapels, a welt pocket, look at that top-stitching." He blew a low whistle before shrinking the image to normal size. "And why are we stalking billionaires?"

"He owns the building." She took her phone back. "Well, one of his companies does. Homestead is a subsidiary of a larger real estate arm."

"And?"

"And," she raised her voice over the ringing of bells, tucking her phone in a pocket as she turned to greet their customer. "I want to know why a billionaire who owns half the businesses on the planet needs to raise our rent so much."

"Because he can?" Julie halted halfway to the counter, clapping her hands as a giant smile lit up her face. "Welcome home, Milla! How was Key West? Is your mom okay? Hi, Diego!"

"Hola, Julie." He waved, distracted as his phone buzzed with a notification.

"My … mom?" Milla glanced at Diego for clarification and, a half second later, was tackled into a big Julie hug. "Oof."

"Oh, Mylanta, it's so good to see you!" Julie muttered into her shoulder, squeezing Milla tight. She let go and leaned back, bright blue eyes dancing over Milla's face. "Diego told me everything; I hope that's okay. It was so sweet of you to put your life on hold like that."

"I—"

"It was fortunate I could head down early until Milla had someone to cover the store," said Diego.

"Gosh, it's been a madhouse." Julie dropped her shoulder bag on the counter. Her eyes lost their excited luster, and she glanced around the store. "First, there was the explosion at the Fountain of Youth, and then the gas leak shut down the Colonial Quarter for a week and—"

"Gas leak?" asked Milla.

"Carbon monoxide poisoning," Julie said. "Same thing that put all those women in the hospital. They sent a whole team down to look into the mess and found a load of corrosion in the city pipes; oh!" She snapped her fingers and held out a key. "Here, you probably want this back. Darkly had a set made so we could open without y'all."

Milla stared at the key pinched in Julie's fingers, which had definitely not been there a moment before. "Uhh…"

"Or actually, I should probably hold onto it since I'm closing tonight?"

"Closing?" Milla hesitantly took her eyes off the key and glanced toward Diego for help.

"You have your run club," he replied without looking up from his phone. "I need someone to work the front while I catch up on my tailoring."

"You're not coming?"

He pocketed his phone and stared back at Milla. "I do not run."

"B-but, you—" she stammered as Diego slipped out from behind the counter.

"I'm happy to help," Julie said with a smile. "Honestly, it beats sitting at home and watching Gilmore Girls re-runs." Her face fell, and she eyed Milla warily. "It is alright, isn't it? I just thought … since I worked while you were gone that I could still help out and—"

"No, Julie, it's fine." Milla tucked Julie's shoulder bag on a shelf beneath the counter and hauled her in for a hug. Julie let out a tiny "eep" that had Milla holding her even closer. She had never been a hugger, and people had never really hugged Milla. Except Ezra, who ran so hot her naturally clammy cold self didn't bother him. And Darkly, in the few days that she let him before all hell broke loose. "It's really, really fine."

"Yeah?" Julie hugged her back and laughed quietly. "When did you become a hugger?"

"I'm not." Milla sniffled and held her tighter as Diego's list burned behind her closed eyes.

Apologize to Julie.

"I'm so sorry."

Julie's arms twitched, and she crushed Milla against her. "No. No no, Milla. None of that."

"I stole your badges, and I went to that convention without you, and I—"

"Inadvertently saved my life?" Julie wriggled free enough to lean back and look her in the eye. "There were so many people there, and Ana." She looked away and blinked to keep tears from falling. "I'm not mad about you stealing my badges, Milla. I can't be, though, why you, of all people, went to that ICYMI cult gathering is beyond me." She shook her head with a mystified look. "Maybe we should have the store checked for another le—" Her words cut off as Milla hauled her into another hug. Julie rubbed her back and chuckled. "Okay, now I'm starting to get concerned."

Milla let go and put space between them, tugging her shirt into place and smoothing her jeans. "I just missed you, is all."

Julie pinched her lips, eyes bright and wide, and she stifled a smile. "Mhm." She nodded exaggeratedly. "Got it."

"Shut up." Milla jabbed the screen of the store's tablet, entering the passcode.

"Sure thing, boss." She gave a saucy little salute.

"And about that key. You said Darkly made it?"

"Oh." Julie looked at the key, still pinched between her thumb and forefinger. Confusion flashed over her face, and she held it up, turning it side to side. "Yeah. When the city re-opened the Colonial Quarter, he helped me run the store, but we could only find one key, so he made a duplicate. I guess he still has the other key because Diego got back, and *he* had a key. Wow, we should probably keep better track of these, shouldn't we?" She frowned and unpinched her fingers.

The key vanished in a blink. Or Milla blinked because one second it was there, and then it was gone, and she was nine whole rings of confused.

"Uh, Julie—"

The rumble of a motorcycle cut her off, and Julie bounced on her feet. "Oh good, he's here early; we can ask him about it."

"Who?"

"Darkly." Julie tipped her head to the door. Milla followed the gesture, mouth falling open in shock as the motorcycle she had nearly toppled in her driveway parked across the narrow street. A tall man, suspiciously tall, now that Milla thought about it, swung his leg over the saddle, drawing attention to the faded black denim cuffed over black matte leather boots.

"No fucking way," she exhaled.

"I know." Julie fanned herself. "You should have seen Diego the first time he pulled up on that thing."

"A Triumph," Milla said.

"Down girl." Julie swatted her arm and laughed. "Though I guess that's one way of putting it."

"No, the bike. It's a Triumph. What the hell is he doing on a Triumph? Where's the hybrid?" When Julie didn't answer, Milla glanced at her and found the nurse gazing dreamily out the window. "Jules?"

"This is the best part, Milla." She propped an elbow on the counter and her chin in her hand. "Don't ruin it."

Milla followed her gaze and, Horned God damn her, the nurse was right.

Darkly set his helmet on the bike saddle and gazed down the narrow road toward St. George Street, catching the late afternoon light *just* so. It carved sharp shadows along his jaw and drew the eye to the days of stubble. He unzipped the leather jacket, shrugging it off and setting it beside his helmet, and ran a hand over his shorn head. The move exposed a bare swathe of skin above the waist of his jeans, and Milla must have audibly swallowed because Julie giggled.

"Down, girl."

"I'm not—"

"Mhm."

She had no time to reply. Darkly sauntered across the street, walking into the store as if he had done so every afternoon for as long as it had been open. He strode up to Julie and Milla, smiling and greeting the nurse before looking at her.

"Ready to go?" he asked.

"What the *shit*, Darkly," Milla answered.

"I'll, um." Julie pointed over her shoulder. "I'll go see if Diego needs help." She scurried away, barely concealing a smile. Milla waited until the door to Diego's sewing room snicked closed, then glared at Darkly.

He raised an eyebrow, waiting for her to speak, and she threw an angry hand toward the Triumph in all its black satin and shiny chrome glory. With a twist at the waist to glance at his bike, Darkly turned a dimply-smirk on her.

"Fancy my motorbike?"

"I'd fancy a freaking explanation," she spat. "That thing is yours?"

"Aye."

"The Bonneville T100 I almost toppled in my driveway belongs to you, Mr. Not-An-Aural-Adjuster."

He blinked several times slowly and inhaled, the patient settling motion he had done so many times in the first weeks she had known him. "Would be why I parked it there, yes."

It was too much. The clothing she could handle. The lies that weren't lies she could handle. If given enough time to work through her feelings at the fact he'd been used and hadn't lied to her, that he hadn't betrayed her, that he now lived next door to her for some abysmal reason she could *handle*. But him driving the world's sexiest motorcycle and looking like a Horned God-damned dream doing so?

"I can't handle this." She stomped around him, needing to put distance between herself and the witch who, for some reason, got under her skin more than even Ezra had managed. "What are you doing here?"

"Came to pick you up for the cult. Like we discussed."

"Yeah, but like, on a motorcycle?" She gaped at him. "I don't even have my running clothes."

"I brought you some."

"Ew, did you dig through my clothes?"

"It's the set from your bag in Daytona."

Milla slammed her mouth closed, jarred by the knowledge he'd kept her things. It didn't feel … wrong. It felt considerate, and she didn't know how she felt about that. "And what am I supposed to do, then? Ride that thing in shorts and a tank top? No, thank you."

He huffed, eyes crinkling with a smile he wouldn't release. "You can change when we get there."

Both brows shot up her forehead, and she scoffed. "In front of *people?*"

"Would you rather I called Toby to give you a lift?"

She didn't like the challenge in his tone, the way he made the offer as if knowing with certainty she would refuse. But he wasn't wrong. It was bad enough she'd be spending her morning with Agent Sterne, but having to ride with him in a car? Alone?

"I'll call an OverAuto, thanks."

"Milla." Darkly scrubbed a hand down his face and let his arm drop. "Could you at least try to let me help you?"

Milla startled back as if the words were a physical blow. A hundred half-formed retorts rushed to mind. How dare he— who was he to— what right did he have—

On and on and on without resolution. Without the thoughts manifesting on her tongue.

The silence in her store was pea-soup thick, coating her skin and choking her throat. She swallowed thickly, frozen in place by her inability to speak.

Darkly let out a frustrated growl, running a hand over his head in an identical gesture to his sister. He pinched the back of his neck, regarding Milla before saying, "I dinnae ken how to navigate this, *leannán.*"

"Don't call me that," she snapped. "I'm not your … whatever that word means." She had an idea. He had uttered the nickname enough during their week in the swamp and had only started using it after New Orleans when they—when he—

Her body flashed hot. She pressed her thighs together at the memory of New Orleans. And Tallahassee. And those endless days in the swamp where they couldn't touch.

"Aye," he said in a rasp. "I ken." He shot her a look so full of misery that she almost launched herself across the distance, arms itching to wrap around him and ease all of that strain from his face.

Talk to Darkly.

It was the second item on her list, and how hard could it be? She'd blown right through the first with ease and more than a little guilt.

"Give me something here, Milla," he begged. "I've been working my Way to the dregs for weeks to keep your store out of C.R.O.W.'s sigils. I bottled myself for you, I—"

"I never asked you to. I never asked for any of this." She threw her arms out to encompass him, C.R.O.W., his sister, everything. "I wanted to keep my head down and live my life in peace, and then your stupid handsome face waltzed in here, and I—why are you smiling?"

"No reason." Darkly ducked his head, hiding the smile. Milla glared at him, running back through what she'd just said and failing to find what was so funny.

"I'm supposed to talk to you; it's number two on my list, but I don't even know how to start because I don't know who you are, Darkly." A pained grimace replaced the smile, Darkly immediately sobering. "Not really."

He let the accusation ripen, swelling with the weight she put behind the words. And then he straightened and reached for Milla. A helmet appeared in his hand, whisps of dark smoke wafting from the visor. "Then let me show you."

She stared at her warped reflection in the glaze, then up to Darkly, zero percent interested in further unpacking all of *that*. "You seriously want me to ride that thing?"

"Aye, I do. Call it a trust exercise." Milla narrowed her eyes. "Poor choice of words, but we're gonnae be late. So either call your OverAuto, or take the helmet." He shook it at her, and when she didn't move, a teasing grin eased the tension on his face. "Scared?"

"No."

"It's alright if you've nae ridden before; I'll be safe."

"Please." Milla rolled her eyes, gathering her hair into a low ponytail. She snatched the helmet from his hand and tugged it on, brushing against his arm as she headed to the door. "My college girlfriend rode a Springer Softail."

"I'm sorry, your *what?*"

"Girlfriend." She spun around and flipped up the visor, loving every bit of shock on his face. Darkly's mouth hung open in an incredulous half-smile, half-gape, and a tiny squeak escaped. It was all Milla could do not to laugh outright. Surprising him felt like winning a piece of herself back, and then a keen interest lit those green eyes. "Ugh, gross. It's not a plot point."

She put her back to him, flipping the visor closed to hide her smile, and walked out of her store to the sound of his quiet chuckle.

Twenty-Five

WITH A HAND ON Darkly's shoulder, Milla stepped onto the passenger footrest and swung her leg over the saddle, dropping behind him and scooting close in a smooth, practiced motion. She wrapped her arms around his waist and balanced her weight along the centerline, earning a quiet hum of approval she didn't hate.

"Hold on tight." Darkly gripped her thigh, right above the knee, and gave a firm squeeze.

She scooched closer, lacing her fingers together, and they were off. He maneuvered the bike around clusters of tourists on Hypolita, taking the turn onto Cordova and then King Street, where he opened the throttle. She could sense his elation as they sped west across the bridge. It was in how he held his shoulders and tilted his head back, the controlled line of his body on the turns, and the utter confidence with which he drove the bike.

Every minute she spent on that motorcycle erased more of the chambray and khaki lies, and she found it harder and harder to convince herself she didn't like the witch revealed by their absence.

Darkly turned them off the main road onto a tree-lined street, and Milla's stomach sank. The trees grew thicker, dripping with Spanish moss and choked by Kudzu. Through the thick trunks, she caught flashes of a worn wrought-iron fence. Long grasses bristled through the bars and clung to the stone bases of statuary speckling a green field.

Milla tightened her arms around Darkly, wishing with every atom of her being that he would drive past. Instead, he slowed the motorcycle and pulled over to the side of the road, parking behind a white SUV. Two dozen people in running clothes gathered near the open gate, chatting and sipping from red plastic cups, a handful of them glancing over and raising their hands in greeting as Darkly pulled off his helmet.

"I can't be here," she said once hers was off. "Seriously, Darkly, this is a bad idea."

"It'll be fine." He tossed his jacket on the saddle. "The cemetery runs along the border of St. Augustine, so we're technically nae in the demesne.

"It's not the demesne I'm worried about." She nervously glanced around, then popped onto her tiptoes to whisper, "It's the dead people."

Darkly's eyes widened. He jerked his head up, scanning the cultists and the cemetery. "Do you see dead people?" he asked in all seriousness.

"Shut up." Milla swatted his arm. "You know what I mean. I'm a Death Witch." She pointed to herself, then to the open gates and lawn. "*That's* a massive cemetery."

"It'll be alright, Milla." He grabbed her hand and squeezed, not letting go. "The pack is excited to meet you; they wouldnae chase a trail that puts you, or anyone else, in danger."

"And how do you know?"

"Trust me." He dug in the saddlebags, withdrawing her running clothes and shoes. She took them, and he circled a finger in the air over her head. "May I?"

"May you what?"

"Offer some privacy?" Smoke clouded his eyes, and shadow bloomed in his palm. Milla nodded, and he grinned widely. Thick wafts of smoke spilled from his palm, crashing against the ground at her feet and curling in over itself. Higher and higher until Milla was hidden behind a roiling wall of shade.

Though shut off from the cultists, she heard their muffled chatter, and the space within Darkly's casting remained evening bright. Swirls and whorls of dense fog twisted and rolled on a phantom breeze, and she caught the faintest whiff of clove and smoke. It reminded her of incense burned in censers. Of warm tea and flannel blankets. And him.

Milla ran her fingers through the smoke, and a shiver of what she could only define as pleasure ran up her arm.

"You can't see me, can you?"

A moment of silence followed, and then that *voice*.

"*No.*"

"Why don't I believe you?" She tugged off her boots and shimmied out of her jeans. Darkly did not respond, but she could feel his presence all around her like the Shades were an extension of himself and not summoned from the Neitherworld, the space between the living and the dead from which he called his Way. The thought had her dressing more quickly, and when her clothes were wadded in her arms and laces tied, she cleared her throat. "I'm done."

The wall of shadow smoke crashed down, revealing Darkly in his running gear and a beaded necklace matching those the cultists wore. He held out a hand for her clothes.

"Thank you," she said, handing them over.

"Dinnae fash." He stashed them in the saddlebags and faced Milla. "You ready?"

"Nervous," she admitted, which wasn't a lie but was far from the full truth. Milla avoided the magick-addicted cultists as a rule. Morgen had always explained it as a side effect of being exposed to large amounts of the Ways. As mortals, the Staid, their bodies were not equipped to process magick, and it altered their chemistry, causing an addiction that had them obsessively seeking out more for the high it gave.

Cultists were rampant in Key West. Milla and Morgen had worked hard to keep them from noticing her Way, and for good reason. The Ways were many and spread across the globe. Chronomantics and meteomantics, stitch and green witchery, technomancy. Most cultists gained their first hit of magick from one of the common Ways, building tolerance and, with time and care, remaining functional citizens of wherever they lived. But death magick?

To Morgen's knowledge, no cultist had ever been exposed to her Way, and to do so risked not only Milla's discovery but catastrophic results.

What would happen when a horde of drunks addicted to her Way were unleashed on the unsuspecting mortal world?

"I've never spent much time around them." Every horror story Morgen had spun ran through her head. She shivered and raised her hands, wrists up, catching the light in the shimmering swirl of Lou's Soul Sigil. "Guess it's good I have this then."

"Yeah." Darkly said, hard and cold enough that Milla jerked her face up. He stared over her head at the cultists, eyes distant and jaw tight. The bob of his throat had her eyes dropping to the beaded necklace. She read it the name it bore. Then, read it again.

"Hold on." Milla hooked the necklace with her finger and pulled it away from his throat. She'd known about this particular quirk of the cultists. Many of them were lawyers or physicians, teachers, and law enforcement. Respected members of their communities holding positions of power and influence. Because of this, they kept their day-to-day identities separate from the cult, adopting nicknames to protect their real lives from the life affected by the Ways. It was only—she had never expected a witch to also earn a nickname. "Peter Pansexual?"

Darkly's cheeks flushed pink. He raised his hand, sliding his fingers beneath Milla's and gently pulling them away. "Earned it in Glasgow," he said, not letting go. "Working a job for Lou."

With one brief squeeze of her fingers, he sauntered away. The cult greeted him by name, cheering Darkly's arrival and welcoming him with high fives and pats on the back.

Her cult, by rights. Members of her demesne greeting him like an old friend.

Milla staggered at the unexpected hurt—the pain at seeing how easily he had inserted himself among the mortals she had so carefully avoided. She slipped into the cemetery, perching on the nearest tombstone to gather herself. A swell of magick surged to greet her, reaching for the exposed skin and stopping shy of latching on.

Her wrists felt heavy. Her entire body felt heavy. Unwanted and out of place in the city she had called home for eight years. A thickness developed in her throat, and her eyes prickled. She pressed the heel of a palm beneath her eye. Crying in front of the cultists wasn't an option. Milla was their Witch of the Demesne, and while she might have been acting in absentia for close to two months, this was still hers, and she was theirs. She had tended the demesne daily, treated with the desecrants, and fed enough of herself into the land that they should know her Way, even if they didn't know her.

But they knew him.

A cool breeze wafted over the ground, wrapping around Milla's bare ankles and grounding her in the moment, the place. She inhaled deeply, taking in the loam and moss, the sticky-sweet scent of late spring. Her body relaxed into the comforting cold and she exhaled, examining the gathered crowd and picking out faces she recognized.

The bartender from Drake's Fire. Paul, an audiomantic she knew from attending concerts with Ezra. The meteomantic from the yacht club, and, to her shock, Agatha the Augurist seated in the open sliding door of a minivan with a beer in hand. Witches she knew and didn't know at all, laughing with Darkly like they'd known him for years while Milla clung to the outskirts of her own city.

"He is good with them," Tobias said.

"Holy Horned God." Milla jumped off the tombstone. She pressed a hand to her chest, half afraid her heart would burst through her ribcage. "What in the Goddess' name are you doing here?"

"Keir asked me to come."

"And you just," she wheezed, "do what he says?"

"I sometimes do as he asks," Tobias answered. "Generally, that is what friends do."

Milla crossed her arms and cocked a hip. "Friends."

"Yes." He mimicked her pose, gaze darting to the cult as a whistle blew. "Time to go."

And with that, he was off. The front runners tore through the cemetery like greyhounds in a race, led by Darkly in his white technical shirt, their bobbing forms disappearing among the tombstones. Milla held back, watching the chaos unfold and sort itself into something resembling order.

A second wave of cultists followed, holding a steadier, more maintainable pace. They seemed to know the route without a map, choosing the correct turn at an intersection between mausoleums and down a narrow path worn into the grass. It left Milla with the uneasy knowledge that either they ran the cemetery often, or she was more out of touch with her demesne than she had ever considered. The former was unsettling for a number of reasons—she and Ezra had trained her Way here, practicing for their failed ritual, and no small amount of her power would have seeped into the ground, fueling the outskirts of St. Augustine with her magick.

Far easier to deal with than the latter, which was a whole other box of thoughts and big feelings she had no interest in unpacking.

She shouldered her worries, packing them down, down, down as she fell in with the third wave of cultists. Their speed settled somewhere between a jog and a speedwalk, and she followed a bobbing brown ponytail and a woman with a pixie cut for close to a quarter mile before realizing the cultists did not magically know which way to run—they were following a trail.

A handful of white powder had been thrown down every five or so strides, leading the pack, but it was more than that. There was an energy, a humming in her ears she could not quite place. A sound that was not a sound but present all the same, turning Milla left, then right, then left again.

The pair she followed stopped at an intersection, kicking a pile of flour dropped in the center of a crudely drawn chalk circle. The ponytail pointed down the road, and the pixie cut shook her head.

"We could wait for the walkers," she said. "One of them has a map."

"There's a map?" Milla asked as she jogged up.

"More of a vague idea," Ponytail said with a smile warmer than Milla felt she deserved. Friendly, as if she knew who Milla was, even though she could not place the woman at all. "Paul isn't the best at sticking to the plan."

"Paul." Milla looked from one woman to the other. "The audiomantic?"

"Yeah." Pixie Cut tapped her temple. "You feel it in your head?" When Milla nodded, she grinned. "Smells like a fog machine and weed to me."

"And sweat," Ponytail added. "But the other witches describe it as a dull tone they can't quite hear. Or, like, tinnitus."

At the mention, Milla widened her jaw, attempting to pop her ears, and both cultists smiled.

"Told you," Pixie Cut said.

"I didn't disagree; I just said I didn't know what she was." Ponytail scanned Milla head to toe, then leaned closer and sniffed. "Can't place it, but definitely witch."

Milla stepped back, not liking how the cultists were eyeing her hungrily. "How did you know I was a witch?"

Pixie Cut snorted and broke into an easy jog, following a barely visible arrow on the ground pointing to the left. Ponytail tapped Milla on the arm and gestured for her to follow.

"You reek of it," she said, tapping her nose. "It's what your Way is, I can't figure." She angled her head at Milla and inhaled. "You're earthy, kind of? But not like a Green Witch, and there's a mineral-y note, crisp like a meteomantic."

"And loamy," Pixie Cut added. "Like the water. My money's on vinefica. All those potions."

"Not a potion witch," Milla said.

"Well, whatever you are, it's familiar," she replied. "Smells like home, in a way. Like it's a part of the city."

They slowed at another intersection, Ponytail jogging ahead to look for more flour. Further ahead, whistles shrilled, and distant cries filled the night. A handful of cultists joined them at the intersection, and Pixie Cut held out her hand.

"Daddy's Leather Girl, by the way."

"Come again?" Milla coughed, unsure she'd heard correctly.

"My cult name, Daddy's Leather Girl. And that"—she pointed to Ponytail, who was jogging back their way, pointing at the road to their right—"is Whorelando. She's newer, but her first hit must have been strong. I've never seen a cultist take to the lifestyle so quickly."

"Really?"

"Yeah." They took off together, the other cultists falling into stride behind them. "It's impressive; she drives up from the parks every week to run with us."

"Is that usual?" Milla glanced at her newfound running partner, brimming with questions. Though her muscles ached from their misuse in the cells, and her endurance was a joke, the nature of the trail they followed allowed for brief breaks to recoup her energy and maintain a decent pace to the next intersection, or check, as Daddy's Leather Girl had called it.

Beyond that, the company kept Milla moving. The cultists were more welcoming than she'd expected and far more lucid than Morgen had ever painted them to be. Her stories had been full of stumbling addicts begging for a hit, not friendly conversation, and a sense of belonging. Even as a witch, the very thing she'd been told the cultists hunted for their next high, this group of mortals seemed happy to have her there. Yes, their eyes were bright and speech slurring, but there was a lightness to it all. An innocence and exhilaration so different from the anxiety-inducing fear she'd been raised to expect.

"Oh yeah," Daddy's Leather Girl answered. "We travel all over the place. Campouts, cult parties up and down the state, mass rituals."

That got Milla's attention.

"Have you attended any?"

"Oh, dozens." Daddy's Leather Girl grinned, her expression hazy. "Samhain in Orlando, Imbolc in the Villages. Oh! And Beltane. That one's my favorite. Are you going?"

"I think so."

"Awesome, we'll have to meet up for a drink." Daddy's Leather Girl grinned at her, and Horned God be damned, it looked genuine. The smile, the invitation. All of it.

A series of sharp blasts on a whistle pierced the night, closer now, and a cry rose from a block ahead that had their tiny pack of cultists cheering, "Beer near!"

Without warning, they broke into a sprint, almost leaving Milla behind. She grit her teeth, shouldering into a run and swinging her arms like this were the last straight-away of an 800m sprint. Hands like scythes, legs churning over asphalt, a cramp building in her side. She sped past two cultists, eyes pinned on Daddy's Leather Girl and Whorelando just ahead. The weight at her wrists kept her from overtaking the pair; no amount of internal competitive drive was enough to break through the heaviness of Lou's Soulbinding.

Still, she ran into the parking lot of a brewery with a grin on her face and sweat rolling down her back, immediately finding Darkly amid the crowd, grinning like a fool. Shirt tucked into the waistband of his shorts, he led the pack in a bawdy song with a red cup raised above his head. On the far side of the crowd stood Tobias, cup raised to his mouth and eyes pinned on Milla. Still and stern, without a hair out of place, watching her as he had in the cells.

She nearly jumped out of her skin when Whorelando thrust a cup into her hand, beer spilling over the rim, and flinched when Daddy's Leather Girl hollered, "Down, down, down, down!" gesturing for her to drink.

Gasping for a breath when the beer was finished, Milla stepped back from the crowd, signaling she was taking a break. Her head spun from the alcohol and the run and the heady crackle of magick. Darkly's she would recognize anywhere—the cool waft of his Shades and wintry scent. But other Ways choked the humid night air, and finally, she saw what Morgen had warned about.

The cultist's smiles turned manic, their gazes hungry as they surrounded the witches at the center of their circle. A plume of fire burst over their heads, and the rustle of tall grasses and wind through the Spanish moss sang a song only an audiomantic could compose.

She settled on a picnic table, happy to let the festivities play out and be forgotten. To her surprise, Daddy's Leather Girl followed, handing her a fresh beer, and sitting beside her in a quiet understanding of the cult's overwhelming nature.

"You get used to it," she said after a minute. "First time is always the hardest."

"Whatever you say." Milla raised her cup in cheers and took a sip.

"But it's not your first time, is it?" Daddy's Leather Girl tipped her head. "I can't remember you coming around, but your Way … whatever it is, it's really familiar."

Milla kept her expression as blank as she could. "Maybe you've met another witch like me."

"No." She shook her head. "It's not that, but I can't shake the feeling I've had a taste of you before."

"That is a wildly colorful way to put it." Despite her misgivings, Milla liked the cultist. Daddy's Leather Girl was rational and one of the few not participating in the madness of the circle. Even Darkly had extricated himself and stood beside Tobias, scanning the crowd with a worried expression. On a whim, Milla raised a hand and waved, catching his attention.

A broad grin replaced the worry, and he began working through the crowd.

"Maybe it was at my sister's?" Daddy's Leather Girl continued. "I was up there a few weeks back. Couldn't be anyone here; we've had the same witches for ages." She frowned at Milla, eyes going hazy. "Except the new steward, but his Way is like … like Christmas."

Milla straightened as the words registered and were promptly overwritten by something else she had said. An idea prickled in the back of her mind. She gazed over the cultists, singing and dancing, pounding their feet, and clapping their hands; their energy feeding into Paul and the Mix Witch, into Tobias, who sent little fireballs into the air with a small smile.

As if she could see it, Milla scanned the air over their heads, recalling everything she knew about mass rituals. Everything Ezra and Marie had put in place for their own. Witches, hedge witches, and cultists working to support Milla's casting on the lake. Ways upon Ways, muddled together and fueled by the cultists' fervor, feeding power into the witch at the center, supporting her in her attempt to summon the Shades of the Neitherworld and open the Gates.

Her eyes landed again on Darkly, and a puzzle piece snapped into place, connecting her disparate thoughts to his Way and hers—how their magick had worked together against the Loa and Milla had become stronger. Become something wild and more.

Cyrus' E.R.I.E. scan and the weaving of all those Ways into one flickered in her mind's eye.

"You said," she started, stopping to swallow a sudden lump in her throat. "You said you'd felt my Way before? At your sister's?"

"I think?" Daddy's Leather Girl cocked her head. "I went up for a campout a couple of weeks ago, so I could be mistaken."

"Where does she live?" When she did not answer, Milla faced her, gripping the woman's knee and asking again. "Where does she live?"

"In Georgia." Daddy's Leather Girl leaned away from Milla's intense stare. "Outside of Valdosta. Why?"

Twenty-Six

"AND WHAT WERE THEY doing there?" Lou crossed her arms and leaned against Milla's kitchen counter.

"It was a campout," Milla explained for the third time. At Tobias' call, the witches gathered at the duplex to discuss what she had learned, and she had insisted they meet in her half. Being in Darkly's half was too unsettling, and Milla had more chairs. "They do them a couple of times a year."

"They drive from city to city in search of magick?" Lou shook her head. "Unbelievable, even for cultists, and I refuse to believe they stumbled upon the ritual in Valdosta by coincidence."

"Which would imply a degree of collusion," Darkly added, blowing a thick vapor plume from his mouth. "Fits with our rogue witches theory."

"But what would they need with cultists?" Rai asked. She had been mostly quiet, arriving with a teak box under her arm and immediately setting to work grinding herbs and weed together for Darkly before starting on Milla's tea. "There are, what, six signatures on the E.R.I.E.? That's more than enough to perform a ritual."

"Seven," Diego corrected. He hovered behind Cyrus, who had set up his laptop and tablets on Milla's kitchen table, enthralled by the technology and readouts. The pair had been in their technomantic world, tweaking Cyrus' reports and discussing the E.R.I.E. while Lou interrogated Darkly, Tobias, and Milla. "And it is about the power."

"How do you think?" Lou asked.

Diego straightened and studied her, his mouth a tight line and eyes sharp behind his glasses. Milla knew that look well. He was trying to determine if Lou was goading him, teasing the witch out of time, and trying to trap him in a misstep or if she was serious. He had made that same face often in their early days until his growing trust in Milla surpassed suspicion.

And then he laughed, a surprised little chuckle that had her longing to know whatever thoughts had just passed through his mind.

"Ustedes, brujas tontas, estarían perdidas sin nosotros." He shook his head, still laughing. Milla bit her lips to keep from joining in as she mentally translated the rapid muttering.

You dumb witches would be lost without us.

"Care to share?" Lou asked.

"The cultists do more than hunt magick for the high," Diego explained, unable to keep the mirth from his voice. "They can be used to strengthen rituals. It is how Morgen maintains her barrier wards around Key West."

"How in the nine rings do you know that?" Milla blurted. Even she had not been trusted with Morgen's secrets regarding her demesne, and wow, had she asked. Fresh off a resurrection ritual and terrified that C.R.O.W. was going to bust down her door any second, she had begged her foster mother for advice on how to tend the demesne she'd accidented herself into.

Morgen had replied that this was a moment of growth, and trial and error were the only way forward. So Milla had gone for a walk to clear her head. And again the next day and the next until the walks became her morning run—a centering exercise to ground the witch and tend the demesne.

"I have a source," Diego answered.

"Goddess, that's right. I forgot you befriended the drunks." She was being unfair, and worst of all, she knew it, but he was being so damn cagey about Key West, and she had missed so much. Like, when the hell did Diego learn so much about the cultists?

He sent her a cold look and continued. "The cult leader in Key West explained it as … an agitation. Of the molecules."

"Molecular agitation?" Cyrus looked up from his laptop. "How so?"

"Think of the demesne as an empty glass," he answered. "The witch or witches in charge may fill the glass with magick, but without agitation, it does not do much."

"Way to discredit all the work we do." Milla crossed her arms. "Tending a demesne is more than just 'filling a glass.'"

"Sí, of course, but for the purpose of this discussion, let us listen to the witch who actually speaks to the mortals in question." The look he gave her was withering. The same one he'd worn when she sassed the wrong Karen and got their store review bombed. Milla shrank back. Unable to hold his stare, she dropped her gaze to the tile.

"As I was saying, when the cult runs, they are agitating the magick in the demesne." He picked up a half-full cup of water and circled his wrist, spinning the liquid inside. "If the pack were directed to run in a particular area, it would create a funnel."

"A positive feedback loop," Tobias said as he entered the kitchen, stopping beside Milla. "If this is correct, it would explain why they have not yet succeeded in their ritual."

"How so?" Rai looked up from her mortar and pestle.

"The energy needs somewhere to go," Darkly answered. "Otherwise, it will destroy itself."

"¡Exactamente!" Diego nodded fervently, hair getting in his face. He gathered the mass in his hands and tied it back as he spoke. "That is why Josh and Morgen work so closely." A ghost of a smile crossed his lips as though he had just made a clever joke. "She would charge certain wards around the demesne, and Josh would design a trail for the cult to run and double the charge, but always with a disturbance to keep the magick from destroying itself."

"They rarely start and end in the same place," Darkly said. He wore a dazed smile as if a long-standing mystery in his life had just been solved. "The Glasgow cult always warned against doing so, but I never knew the why. And the pack here tends to run on the outskirts."

"St. Augustine is a notoriously powerful demesne," Tobias added. "Even before Milla arrived, this territory has been a magickal hub since it was settled."

Diego shuddered. "Recuerdo."

"Huh." Milla examined her running shoes, still tightly laced from their run. She had never given much thought to the cultists, not after Ezra and Morgen's repeated warnings. Still, she had also never seen evidence of their trails and strange markings in the Colonial Quarter—or anywhere along her normal route, for that matter. Yet even knowing this, it did not answer the question of coincidence. "So it's a chicken-egg problem."

"A what?" Donmar laughed, looking to Lou for clarification.

"Which came first?" Milla raised her hands like she was weighing two separate items. "The cultist campout in Valdosta?" She bounced her right palm, then the other. "Or the ritual?" Donmar frowned, his lower lip thrusting in a slight pout that was charming on the massive witch. "Either the cultists planned their campout and the rogue witches took advantage of their run to use it as a magick boost"—she waggled the fingers on her right hand— "*or* the cultists are working with the rogue witches, and they knew when and where to stage their campout."

"How do they source their information?" Lou bounced her gaze from witch to witch.

"Morgen works directly with hers," Diego said. "Or, at least, with the two in charge."

"Keir?" She looked at her brother.

"Glasgow is blanketed in magick." He fiddled with the vape pen, raised it to his lips, then scowled and vanished it away. "The pack I worked with said they'd nae worries about where to find their next hit. It was how the obfuscari we hunted kept hidden—couldnae get a clean reading with the older E.R.I.E."

"Wouldn't that much magick put the city at risk?" asked Milla.

Darkly shook his head. "They never start and end at the same place, and the Clyde flows east to west. The water acts as a disruptor, so there's nae worry of a feedback loop." He scratched the side of his neck, eyes unfocused as he thought. "And the cultists here run on the outskirts of the demesne to avoid the same issue."

"So none of us know how the cultists gain their information or even find the magick in the first place?" Lou massaged her temples. "This is why I argued for the database a decade ago. If C.R.O.W. had kept better track of the bloody fools, we needn't suffer these issues."

"And what, chip them like animals?" The kettle cracked against the counter, and Rai spun around, her usually calm expression twisted with anger. "Should we dock their ears, too?" Cheeks flushed, she pointed a trembling finger at Lou. "The cultists do not deserve to be treated as second-class citizens."

Lou's eyes widened, the effervescent blush fading from her cheeks. "Yes, of course, you're right." She swept a hand through her hair. "I misspoke."

Rai's expression shuttered. She nodded tersely, spinning around and sweeping up the kettle. Clove and the nauseating medicinal bite of juniper filled the air as she poured Milla's tea, clogging the kitchen and deadening the silence that followed her tiny eruption.

"Rai was a part of the Walled City Coven," Tobias whispered in Milla's ear. She angled her face to catch him in the corner of her eye.

"In Hong Kong?"

He nodded. "She defected to C.R.O.W., seeking asylum, and they placed her on Lou's team. It had something to do with the cultists they kept within the city walls."

Milla eyed Rai's back. The witch held herself straight and poised, her hair a silken black sheet cascading down her shoulders. Darkly had moved beside her, resting his hip on the counter and a hand lightly on her arm, whispering in her ear. Rai nodded once and turned her head to smile at him.

"Thank you," she murmured. Darkly's answering grin made his eyes crinkle, and though she could not see it, Milla knew the dimple would be on display.

"So what next?" Cyrus asked. His hands floated above his laptop, fingers flexing over the keys. "The E.R.I.E. does not account for cult activity; all my reports from Valdosta are useless if we think they hold some sort of answer." He swiveled in the seat, gripping the chairback to direct his next comment at Lou. "I could try to grab a reading, but adjusting the database to account for their signatures will take me weeks."

"Do we have weeks?" Milla asked.

"Maybe," Donmar shrugged. "Maybe not. The rituals recorded at the end of last year coincided with sabbats, but the three recent events have not followed any timeline."

"They are getting closer," Darkly pointed out. "Seven weeks ago, then four."

"Then three, and last night," Lou finished. "So whatever they are doing, they're nearing their objective."

"Or they are growing desperate." Tobias crossed the kitchen and gestured to the teacup. At Rai's nod, he brought it to Milla. "And desperate witches make mistakes."

He held her eye as he said this, pressing the tea into her hands.

"Obviously, someone ought to ask the cult directly," Darkly said after a quiet moment. He looked at Diego. "If anyone here has someone they can trust to answer plainly."

"Sí." Diego swallowed and shifted his weight from foot to foot. "Sí, claro. I could make a few calls to my … acquaintance in Key West. He—" Diego paused, eyes rounding. "He mentioned an event in Tallahassee."

"What?" Lou snapped, voice ricocheting off the ceiling. "When?"

"A month ago, when he was in town. Several cult leaders were meeting to arrange an event." He glanced from witch to witch, landing on Lou. "I do not think it has happened yet."

"Make your calls." She clapped her hands, an annoying habit Milla had noticed the Light Witch performed whenever she was issuing orders. "Find out everything you can: the when, the where, how many are involved. And I want a list of registered witches in Tallahassee." Lou snapped her fingers at Cyrus, already clacking away on the keyboard. "Cross reference the Ways of every missing witch against that list. I want them all accounted for. And you," she said to Milla, jerking her chin at the tea in her hands. "Drink that tea and rest up."

"That necessary?" Darkly called out. "C.R.O.W. kens she's a bloody Death Witch; we can do away with the poison."

"It is a term of her conditional release," Lou answered her brother, though her eyes remained firmly on Milla. "She drinks her tea until she can be trusted with her Way."

"I thought it was about building a tolerance," Milla muttered.

"It is about being ready." She wheeled around and addressed the room. "That goes for everyone. We're at the casting range early; I want this coven in prime shape before we have to deal with the cultists."

"Believe in me, Milla."

His voice, those words warm in her ear. She braced her feet, widening her stance on the ritual platform to fight against the waves now crashing against her legs.

"Just a little longer, and we're through." Lips pressed against her temple, and the heat cloaking her back vanished as Ezra put himself between Milla and the hole she'd torn in the world. Just a little longer, just a little further. Further than they had ever gone before.

Tongues of black smoke lashed at the water, bilious clouds roiling and teeming in the dark. He took a step, the water rising to his knees. And another. An invisible tug at Milla's arm jerked her forward. And again, harder now, pinching down to the viscera in her gut.

"Ezra …"

"No matter what you see, Milla, believe in me."

I will, she promised. Or did she shout it? She was screaming; that much was certain. Her throat was torn raw, the muscles in her abdomen tight and stabbing with cramps. With every step he took, more of Milla unspooled, feeding the tether between them until she was stretched tight enough to snap and fray.

A gust of freezing wind blew from the nothing, pommeling into her. She stepped back to keep her balance, and the tether snapped, a sharp twang that bit into her very Soul and left her gasping for air.

Nononono.

She squinted against the gale, blinking to clear the water spray from her eyes. Her vision blurred; one Ezra became three. The stars multiplied behind a triple moon, and the tear in the world stretched wider, swallowing the lake and Ezra in its gaping maw.

A hundred potentials flashed before her eyes, the flickering montage showing Milla what could be and what would come. Desecrants and domovoi. Sleeping gods and roused goddesses. Every terror, every horror from every culture in the world, and at the center of the maelstrom was a witch, small against their fury and screaming a name.

"Ezra!"

Goddess, she couldn't do this; she couldn't hold on and watch him walk into the dark. With every inch he gained, she lost more of herself, and where would this end?

Would it end?

"Hold tight, Milla!" His voice carried across the distance, ringing with pride. But not of her, never of her. The smile coloring those words, the faith and belief were all for himself, and Milla was merely the tool he would use until all her sharp edges were dull. She saw it now, as clearly as she Saw the horror this ritual would bring to the thousands of witches stretched across the waterfront and the countless stars multiplying again and again until they were brilliant white spots burned at the edges of her vision.

Twenty-seven Ezras stepped into the dark, reaching that impossible place no living witch had crossed, where no living witch could *survive*, and still Milla held on, summoning all of that shadowed wind and teeming dark to herself. Clearing a path because to stop now would be unthinkable.

There was no one to catch her. No witch to pick up whatever pieces might remain. But she held on—just a little longer. Just until he was far enough away, then maybe …

The tether snapped again, whipping into Milla. And again. She threw both arms forward, grasping onto the invisible thread. Horned God, she couldn't even do this. All of that preparation and work, and she was going to fail on multiple fronts.

"Ezra, come back!"

No matter what you see.

His voice rang in her head as clearly as if he still stood beside her, behind her, guiding Milla's movements.

Blood poured from the wound on her arm, and with his next step, her bone shattered, severing the last connection Ezra held to the living. The visions collapsed into one as Milla sagged back and sobbed over her shattered arm. She tore her eyes away from the gore, and her screaming intensified at the sight of what awaited him.

A deep, crimson bloom unfurled in the dark, impossibly far away and all too close. It beat with Milla's own pulse as it grew larger and louder, thrumming deep enough to rattle the chips of bone floating in her arm.

Bile rose and choked in her throat, hot tears streamed from her eyes, and Ezra kept fucking walking. Deeper into the dark, toward the destiny he demanded for himself. An arm formed in the heart of that dread star. A leg, the suggestion of a head and shoulders haloed by prismatic rings as the Baron she summoned stepped through the Gates.

"No." Milla choked on her vomit, spitting a sour mouthful into the lake. She raised her broken arm, supporting the elbow and crying against the pain as she formed a weak sigil.

This couldn't happen. She could not let it. If they succeeded tonight, if he brought that Baron through the Gate, they would destroy everything. But the tether between them was broken. There was no calling Ezra back, not now, so she would destroy herself instead.

"*Zavřete.*"

Close.

She forced the intent through clenched teeth and in that last moment, as her final casting echoed down the corridor of nothing, Ezra finally looked back and saw the witch he had made.

"*Zavřete bránu.*"

Close the gate.

Twenty-Seven

VERVAIN An all-purpose protective herb, it can be placed under the pillow to prevent nightmares, carried to prevent depression, and used in cleansing baths and rituals before working magick.

M ILLA JOLTED AWAKE, CRACKING her skull against the base of her bedside table.

"Ow, what the fuck." She pressed a palm to her head, craning her neck to search the room.

Empty.

No Ezra, no creepy humanoid monster crawling through the dark. No lake.

Sunlight tiptoed through the seam in the curtains, and little by little, the heavy weight that sat on her chest as she slept pulled away, settling on her wrists.

"Holy Horned God," Milla sighed, flexing still-tingling fingers. She glanced at the triskelion and then her palm. *No blood.* A relief, honestly. She might be Soulbound, but at least she didn't have to add a head wound to her troubles.

Goddess knew she had enough to worry about between her tea and apparent sleepwalking. She had no memory of coming into her room and didn't even remember falling asleep. One minute, she'd been sipping her tea and straining to hear Diego's phone call. It was well after midnight; who in the nine rings did he know in Key West well enough to call them so late?

And then she'd been on the shore of Lake Pontchartrain, screaming for Ezra before she abandoned him at the gates.

She swallowed, her tongue thick and throat dry, and thunked her head against the floor, intending to wait for the fog of sleep to retreat.

The thunk echoed down the hall, and this time her weary mind translated it as a fist knocking at the door.

Cracking one eye open, she again noted the morning light behind her curtains and groaned. "Of fucking course."

They were heading to the casting range first thing, and first thing was apparently right now.

Another thunk echoed in the hall, and the floorboard in her hall creaked, followed by three light raps on her door.

"Milla?" Darkly's voice, muffled through the wood, had her rolling onto her head to the side. The floorboard creaked again as he shifted his weight and muttered a low curse before knocking again. Harder this time. "Ludmilla?"

Milla sucked in a quick breath at the unmistakable worry in his voice. Guilt rushed in as she remembered the last time he'd found her on the floor after her tea. How mad he'd been when she admitted what it was for. How frightened. And here she was, back in that same place with a Dark Witch at the door, and no matter how hard she tried, that stupid, thick lump in her throat wouldn't go away.

"Milla?" he called again, the worry heightening to outright panic. "Please, Goddess. *Leannan.*"

"Coming," she croaked, rolling onto her side. The muscles in her legs screamed as she rose, and she gripped the bedside table, legs shaking. "Ow, fuck."

"You alright?" The knob jogged, the door rattling in its frame. "Milla? Please, unlock the door."

"Why is it locked?" She started across the room, stopping to pound her foot against the floor to return blood flow. From the double runs the day before, her thighs felt like someone had gone to work on them with a meat tenderizer, and her calves were matching cramps. She needed coffee, an egg and cheese biscuit, and a bath.

"Or a nap," she muttered. Darkly tried the knob again, and Milla smacked the back of her door. "Stop that." She fumbled at the twist lock with still-numb fingers. "Give me a second."

It took more than a second, and the moment the tumblers clicked, Darkly shouldered in. She jumped back, barely avoiding getting hit by the door.

"I—Milla." His large body filled the frame, and he swept a frantic gaze over her face, eyes beyond wide and pupils blown out. "When you didnae answer …" His throat bobbed, and he let loose a shudder of a breath.

"Hey." Milla set her fingertips over his heart, biting her lips as she felt the racing muscle, which meant her fingers were at least back to normal, because Goddess knew his reaction to this was anything but. "I slept in, no big deal."

"Right." Darkly nodded, swallowing and licking his lips, eyes drifting over her head. He stilled, then dropped his gaze to the floor and frowned. Milla knew what he saw. Darkly was a clever witch, and it wasn't hard to miss the still-made bed she'd obviously not slept in, and the pile of blankets and her pillow on the floor. His breathing slowed, and when he looked back at her, the fright was gone, replaced with a somber pain. "Milla …"

Talk to Darkly.

"It's not a big deal." She dipped around him, darting down the hall and slamming the bathroom door before he could stop her.

♣

"Holy shit, dude." Milla gripped the oh-shit handle, pressing her heels against the floorboard as Tobias zipped between a semi-truck and a minivan with bicycles hitched to the back. "Death wish much?"

Darkly glanced into the backseat, and though he gripped the handle on the door, a wild grin lit up his face. "Dinnae fancy speed?"

"Dinnae fancy *dying*," she replied, squeaking when Tobias slammed on the brakes, shifted gears, and cut off a pale blue Sebring convertible. "Seriously, what's the rush?"

"We are late," Tobias replied, dry as a desert morning. At her huff, the car lurched forward, zooming even faster down Dixie Highway towards Matanzas State Forest.

Lodgepole pine whipped by the windows in a brown blur, and, swear to the Goddess, if he changed lanes one more time, Milla was going to empty her stomach all over the pristine white leather interior of his BMW. And all she'd had for breakfast was a rushed cup of coffee, so her protest vomit would be a delightful revenge.

"Never understood why American witches build the ranges so far out," Darkly commented breezily. "Bonaly's just off the city."

"The choices in Scotland are either 'just off the city' or 'hidden in the Highlands and only accessible by coo or foot,'" Tobias replied. "At least Americans respect a good road."

"Someone has to," she muttered. Tobias's eyes flicked to meet hers in the rearview mirror, and, to her horror, he smiled. The witch was already unrecognizable in denim jeans, work boots, and a band t-shirt, but seeing him grin? That was a bridge too far.

Another quick gesture at the gear shift had Milla clutching the seatbelt to check that it was properly buckled. He jerked on the wheel, and Milla swore the sporty SUV lifted onto two wheels as it skidded into the parking lot of Frizzen, Flint & Locke.

Owned and operated by a trio of retired spalování Enforcers, the casting range was one of many spread around the world. Modern living enabled witches to live in cities rather than hiding in bogs and swamps, and casting ranges began popping up in the middle of the last century when McCarthyism sputtered its last breath. They offered a ready escape for a cranky witch to step into their Way and work out whatever vexed them. In the years since ranges had become a popular hangout to spar without the fear of a wayward hex burning down an apartment building.

Tobias pulled beside Lou's silver Landrover and Darkly hopped out before he'd killed the engine.

"I'll get us a key," he said before setting into an easy jog toward the large, barn-like structure that housed a cafe, shop, and indoor ranges. Milla unbuckled quickly, leaving the car and lingering near the trunk while Tobias did whatever it was a speed-addicted witch did alone in his car. When he finally stepped onto the gravel lot, he walked past Milla without a word and aimed for the row of golf carts flanking a narrow dirt path disappearing into the woods.

Thirteen miles south of St. Augustine, Matanzas State Forest was a reforested chunk of the Florida coast boasting a campground, stables, watersheds, irrigation ditches, retaining ponds, and abandoned farmland. Clocking in at a massive sixteen thousand acres, plots of orderly trees formed an energy-disrupting wall, and tucked among them were two dozen bocce-sized courts and a football field–sized patch of land reserved for extraordinary acts of magick.

Ezra had been a regular member of Frizzen, Flint & Locke, and though Milla had never joined him, she knew he had added her name to his account before he was Gone. At any point, she could have come out here to vent her frustrations on an unfortunate tree, but that would require a) owning a car, b) being able to drive it legally, and c) registering her intended use of magick for review.

C.R.O.W. had a nasty habit of auditing the ranges, searching for magick Forbidden and Foule, and Milla had made a lifestyle out of flying far, far beneath their radar.

Until recently.

Tobias hopped into the driver's seat of the golf cart nearest the trailhead, checking his watch and tapping his fingers on the steering wheel. Milla followed suit, fastening the seat belt on the rear bench as tightly as possible.

Darkly wandered over after a few minutes of awkward silence, laughing at something Rai, walking beside him, had just said. The vinefica was as glamorous as ever, dressed in deep purple yoga pants and an off-the-shoulder white tunic top revealing a multi-strapped sports bra. Her hair, usually loose and glossy as hell, was pulled into a thick, perfect braid draping down one shoulder, and she carried her teak box of ingredients under one arm.

Milla didn't mean to stare, but holy shit. The woman was a walking fitness ad giving Milla all sorts of regrets about wearing torn fishnets, cuffed shorts, and an old My Chemical Romance t-shirt she had hacked into a crop top. She wiggled her toes in her boots, eyeing Rai's pristine, clean training shoes with no small amount of jealousy.

How fair was it that a witch could simultaneously look *that* good and comfortable?

"Good morning!" With a warm smile at Milla, Rai hopped into the cart beside her, ignoring the seatbelt altogether. "Thought I should wait for you at the front; Lou is in a bit of a mood."

"When isnae Lou in a mood?" Darkly asked with a chuckle. He took one look at Tobias in the driver's seat, rolled his eyes, and shooed him away. "Move yer arse."

Tobias grumbled under his breath but did as he asked.

"Wanker." Darkly dropped into the seat and set the skeleton key, a shrunken skull with an M5 magnet on the base, on the dash.

"Wichser," Tobias replied with a smile. He pressed his thumb against the starter button, and the tiny engine puttered to life. Darkly stretched a long arm across the front seat, twisting around as he reversed the cart. "Alright?" he asked Milla.

She crossed her arms, relieved that Tobias was not driving and annoyed that Darkly had correctly assumed she would prefer any other witch behind the wheel. Goddess, she'd suffer a drive home in Lou's car if it meant never getting into Tobias's nightmare SUV again. "M'good."

He lingered on her for a second, fingers drumming the leather seat, then faced forward and drove them onto the narrow trail.

"Did Diego learn anything?" Tobias asked after a moment.

"I haven't spoken to him," Milla said. And how weird was that? Before her arrest, Diego had been the last person she spoke to before bed and the first person she saw when she awoke. But since being home, she'd barely seen the witch. "He was up late on a call with Key West."

"I am sure he will have news for us this afternoon." He nodded at Darkly. "Stopping these rituals would go a long way with your sister."

Darkly tightened his grip on the steering wheel. "Am nae sure how much good it will do me."

"How did you sleep?" Rai asked, distracting Milla from Tobias's response. She shrugged, preferring to watch the trees pass by at a sane speed rather than engage in a conversation. Rai, unfortunately, had other ideas. "I hope the tea wasn't too strong. With the weight you dropped in the cells, I was concerned."

"It was fine." The golf cart hit a dip in the trail, and Milla slammed her hand against the back of Darkly's chair, bracing herself to keep from jostling into Rai. "Knocked me right out."

"Did it?" Rai cocked her head, eyes narrowing slightly. She studied Milla as if she could read the brew's effects on her. Milla did not know enough about vinefica to assume otherwise, and the idea was unsettling.

"Yeah," she said, needing to fill the silence. "Diego must have tucked me in on the couch, and then I sleepwalked to my room, which is new."

"The couch?" She adjusted the box on her lap, running her nails down the front in an agitated gesture like she could not wait to open it up and get to work.

"The sleepwalking. My tea normally has me out cold."

"Dead to the world," Darkly rumbled. Milla glanced over, frowning when she saw his knuckles blanching white against the steering wheel.

"And what makes you think you slept on the couch?" Rai asked.

The golf cart swerved, and Rai slammed her hand against the ceiling to stay seated. She glared at the witches in front.

"Squirrel in the road," Darkly said, slowing their speed. Tobias covered his mouth, blue eyes twinkling with muffled laughter.

"My blanket," Milla answered, looking from witch to witch. "And a pillow. Why?"

Again, Rai scaled her nails across the wood grain on her box, glancing at the front seat. "I might need to adjust the measurements if you're sleepwalking. The tea is intended to induce a restorative sleep, and knowing how hard Tobias is about to push you today, I'll need to be certain the tea reflects my intent."

"I thought we were casting simple hexes." She leaned forward, placing her face between Darkly and Tobias. "Right?"

"To get a sufficient reading for the E.R.I.E., we will need more than simple hexes."

"Didn't she toss a blood–blade at your head?" Rai asked. Tobias's mouth pressed into a line, and she let out a tinkling laugh. "Would have loved to see that."

The golf cart stopped abruptly, jerking every witch forward in their seats. "Sorry," Darkly mumbled. He swept the skeleton key from the dash and was gone down a small trail before anyone had fully recovered.

Rai watched him go, then slowly faced Tobias. "Was it something I said?"

"You drank your tea?" Lou lightly circled Milla's wrists with her fingers. She nodded, too nervous to speak. Any minute now, Lou was going to undo the binding, and her Way would roar to life.

Milla had no idea if Rai's tea had done anything. All she had was the deadened weight on her wrists and a faint pressure in her arms.

Outside of that weird moment when Rai's aura had pulsed green, an echo of vesticism, or some latent magickal impulse, Milla hadn't felt anything resembling her Way. The idea that it was about to be unleashed after so long was terrifying. She had nearly rotted Lou's hands when the Light Witch set the binding, and Horned God knew Darkly had suffered enough during that wretched week in the swamp. Now, there was a team of Enforcers watching her every move. All of this—her freedom from the cells, her demesne, her *life*—hinged on Milla controlling her magick. And since honesty was apparently her new thing, Milla had to admit that she did not think she could.

Not to the degree they needed or expected, at least.

Unable to look Lou in the eye, she stared across the football field-sized ritual space beside them. Fenced by lodgepole pine for cleansing and disruptive shrubs and weeds, she picked out purple ague blossoms for hex-breaking and protective vervain planted at the feet of oak trees, their branches heavy with out-of-season acorns. Rai knelt beneath one, harvesting the vervain while chatting with Donmar and Cyrus.

"Ludmilla?" Lou squeezed her wrists, drawing Milla's attention back to her. "The tea, you drank it?"

"Every drop." Milla flexed her fingers, wishing Lou would get on with it or let her wrists go. The weight of the Soul Binding was heavier under her cool grasp, like the damn witch was pumping more of her Way into Milla with every second they stood there.

Lou hummed in approval and settled her gaze over Milla's head. "You have her?"

"Aye." Gentle and soft hands clasped over her shoulders. She glanced down, jolting at the sight of black leather gloves against her bare skin. Darkly slid his hands to her upper arms, and warmth blanketed her back as he stepped closer.

"Just a precaution," he said, low and quiet in her ear. "It can be a wee bit jarring when she removes the binding. Wouldnae want you to fall."

"And the gloves?" she asked. When he didn't immediately answer, it clicked. He stood too closely for it not to, all but pressed against her back and warming Milla down to her tea-drunk bones. She shivered at the sudden awareness, and a sensation stirred low in her belly, so long gone it might as well be forgotten—some deep, dark response to the witch and his Way. The fluttering of moths his nearness provoked. She slid her eyes to the side, catching the edge of his profile in view. "Another precaution?"

His answering nod brought the scrape of stubble against her cheek, and his lips brushed her ear as he whispered. "Aye."

The moths erupted into an outright flurry. It was barely a brush, barely anything, but at his nearness and touch, every synapse in her body caught fire.

"Too much?" Darkly's breath tickled her lobe, and it was all Milla could do not to press against him.

"No," she gritted out.

"This space is warded." Lou's no-nonsense voice brought her back to earth. Darkly straightened, tightening his grip on her shoulders just-so, but his warmth lingered on Milla's ear and neck as a blush. "If you need to burn anything off once I open this, you can do so without worry." The stern mask warmed, and she winked conspiratorially. "Just let us get to a safe distance first."

Milla let out a bewildered huff. "Never imagined an Enforcer telling me I could use my Way without worry."

"You're one of us now." Lou smiled at her. She ran her thumbs over the triskelions on Milla's wrists. They shimmered beneath her touch, the binding magick responding to its casting witch. Then Lou tightened her grip and muttered, "*Oscailte.*"

Intense heat flashed on the inside of her wrists, and Milla's Way sprang to life. A tingle in her palms whirled into a sizzling burn, speeding up her veins and knocking her off balance. Her back hit Darkly's chest, and he grunted, holding tight to her arms as Milla's head rocketed above the clouds. It was better than any weed, better than any high from ritual smoke or a race well run. She was fucking soaring under the explosion of magick in her body.

"Oh," she gasped. Despite the heat of her Way, goosebumps flashed the length of her arms, and a not-at-all unpleasant shiver raced down her spine.

"Aye," he rasped, tightening his grip. She dropped her head back, gazing drunkenly up at Darkly—and he winced.

"Let go, you idiot." Lou smacked his arm, and Donmar appeared before Milla, prying her off of Darkly and guiding her to a nearby bench. "Horned God, Keir, have you no sense of self-preservation?"

"She was gonnae fall," he said, his voice strained and tight.

The sound of it, so familiar from those days in the swamp, cleared her head. The front of his shirt was in ruins, ashen where before it had been black, and two swathes of rot ran down the front, right where her bare arms had been. Darkly ripped his shirt off and the cotton disintegrated in his hand. Early-stage rot ran down his body, and reddened skin and rising blisters ran from his chest down to the waist of his pants.

"Oh, Goddess." The rush of her Way, of the power of life and death in her veins, cooled and froze, allowing the fear to slide in. "I can't do this."

Darkly whipped his head up, taking a half step to where she huddled on the bench. "Milla—"

He cut himself off with a wince, pressing a gloved hand to his torso, and all of that fear crashed down like an avalanche.

Heat burned a searing path down her arms. Wood sagged and crumbled beneath her hand, and she scrambled off the bench, backing away. The ground dipped, giving away to sand. She staggered, twisting her ankle, but kept moving as far away from the witches as possible. "Seriously, Lou, I can't—"

"You can and you will." Lou marched forward with her finger in a point. "You owe this to me. And to C.R.O.W."

"You can't make me, please." She stopped as another gloved hand gripped her arm, knowing without looking that it was Agent Sterne. How could she not, after all of those weeks being taunted by the witch she couldn't see and guided by the one she could? The soft, supple gloves on her shoulder, her elbow. The only witch willing to touch her, leading Milla down those endless halls and hauling her off the salt and marble floor.

Bile rose, lodging in her throat beneath that Horned God-damned lump she couldn't swallow, choking off both her vomit and a sob.

"Luminescence," Darkly warned. "Knock it off."

Lou raised her casting hand, showing Milla a palm coated in rising blisters. Goddess, next would come the heat and swelling, then her skin would darken as necrosis set in, and then—

"Pull it together, Ludmilla," Lou stated as breezily as if she were hexed by a Death Witch daily. She flitted her gaze to Tobia's hands, then back to Milla's face, unimpressed. "Sparring court, now. Go burn this off with that little flower trick of yours." She turned her back on Milla, hollering, "Rai!"

"Breathe." Tobias squeezed her shoulders, and only then did Milla realize she'd been panting, unable to fill her lungs. The heat in her arms, the jittering energy of her Way—it was all-consuming, and she had to hold it back—hold it down. She had to get away and rot a tree, a trunk, a mound, anything but these witches. "Breathe, Ludmilla," he said again, only this time it was not Tobias speaking.

It was Agent Sterne.

She sipped a thin stream of air through her teeth. And again.

Near the field, Cyrus waved his phone over Darkly's wounds. "Would you look at that?" he asked, showing Lou the screen. "Goddess be damned, it reads as hippocromantic."

"Fascinating," Lou stated. She frowned at her brother and rolled her eyes. "If you are so determined to be an idiot about all of this, then come along. We've got the big field."

"Open me up first." A nasty sneer curled his lip, but he dropped a hand to his side, flashing five fingers at Milla.

Five things you can see.

"Again," Agent Sterne ordered. So she did, hissing in another breath and counting.

Lou, caging her hand over the triskelion on Darkly's chest. Darkly, closing his eyes and widening his stance. Donmar covering his mouth with a hand, unable to hide his disapproval. Darkly flashing three fingers as Lou said, "*Oscailte.*"

"What do you hear?" Tobias whispered in her ear.

Intent. As clear as a bell. Intent and desire and sacrifice wrapped up in one little word.

Darkly blinked, his eyes dripping black, flashing green, then stained with smoke. The muscles in his arms twitched as if he'd just received a slew of electric shocks, and a broad grin stretched across his face. His exhale was one of relief, and as the tension in his shoulders bled away, a ribbon of smoke blossomed across his shoulders, winding a long, wispy tail around the bicep of his left arm.

"Goddess," he sighed.

"You ready?" Lou shook out her right hand, side-eyeing her brother.

"To kick your arse?" His grin widened, and he lobbed a handful of shadows at his sister. She yelped, brushing it off and hitting her brother with a short-lived glare. Her lips quivered, her eyes narrowed, and a bright, bubbling laugh filled the air. Darkly hooked an arm around her shoulders and walked Lou to the field. "Triple Goddesses tits, am I."

Twenty-Eight

DESECRATION Forbidden and Foule hex advancing the state of organic matter to decay and rot.

counter w/ a poultice of eucalyptus, gardenia, Flax + Fennel

"A GAIN," T OBIAS BARKED.

Sweat rolled down Milla's back. Her arm trembled, fingers of her casting hand shaking, and Holy Horned God, was she drunk. She braced her elbow with her left hand and gnashed her teeth, swallowing another cry of frustration and no small amount of nausea.

They had been at this for hours, starting with small returns so Cyrus could tune his E.R.I.E. to her Way, moving up to desecrations, and finally, a complicated hand-to-hex casting that comprised of Tobias flinging fireballs at her, and Milla trying to deflect them before they singed her fishnets.

Or, at least, that's what she thought the exercise was. The world had gotten a little fuzzy in the last hour, and honestly, it was a miracle she was still standing.

"I need a break."

"You may have a break when you cast properly," he replied, pointing to the grass. "Desecrate."

"*Odsv*—hic—*odsvětit.*" When they'd started with this exercise, she'd been happy. Thankful, even, to be working simple decays and returns. Like riding a bike, the desecration hex had rolled off her tongue, crumpling the grass around their sparring court. But after hours of a slow descent into a waking hangover, the warm-up exercise had become Tobias' go-to punishment whenever she whined for a break.

It was the witchy equivalent of burpees, and Milla hated it.

"*Návrat.*" The return, a low-level healing allure, dribbled off her clumsy tongue, bleeding green into the brittle blades until it was as though she'd never cast her hex at all.

Milla scrunched her eyes, closed one and then the other, and cast her desecration again. "*Odsvětit.*"

The grass withered and browned, crumbling to dust. On a nearby bench, Cyrus's thumbs flew over his screen as he adjusted the E.R.I.E.

"This is incredible," he whispered in awe. "Chronomantic, to hippocromantic, and that last one had a sawtooth waveform." His utterly unremarkable eyes peered at her over the tablet. In truth, his entire face was a blur at this point. Ink splots where his eyes should be, a darker smudge for his mouth. The smudge widened in what she took to be a smile. "For a moment, your casting looked meteomantic! Why do you think that is?"

Milla swayed, took a step to keep upright, and teetered in the other direction.

The technomancy behind the E.R.I.E. had always fascinated her. She made a mental note to have Cyrus run her through how to use the one on her phone and then to have Diego explain it to her like she was five. But right now, she was in no shape to wax theoretical on the whys or hows of her Way.

"Iunno." She shrugged and hiccuped again. "Grass is dead, yeah?"

"Incredible," he repeated, "do it again." Though softer than Tobias's, Cyrus's demand was no less firm.

Milla blew her bangs out of her face and shook out her arms, stretching her neck from side to side. She'd long ago pulled her hair into a messy bun, and curling, sweaty tendrils clung to her neck.

A chilled wind rushed from the field like Darkly had heard her silent wish for air conditioning. She looked over in time to see him volley a wall of midnight at his sister, her jaw dropping when Lou reached for the sky, pulled down a beam of sunshine, and sheared the wall in two.

"Holy shit." Milla backstepped, her bootheel catching the wooden beam at the edge of the sparring pit. She tipped off balance and landed hard on her ass, gawking at the shadow and light show on the field.

The Simmons Siblings had started by running laps, which Milla and her little hexes thought was egregious, before moving on to hand-to-hand sparring with Donmar and individual castings on their own, but somewhere along the way, their friendly workout had become a full-on brawl.

"Oh." Cyrus followed her gaze to the field, hopping to his feet with the tablet held out. He circled two fingers at Milla, jerking his chin at the field. "This is wonderful. Do you think you could—"

"Not today," Tobias called from the far side of the pit. "Milla can barely stand; if we add Keir's Way to the mix, she will be even more useless."

"The fuck, man." She glared back at him. "Does he tell you everything?"

Tobias did not humor her with a reply.

On the field, Darkly flung a handful of obsidian blades like a carnival knife thrower. They tore through Lou's rift in quick succession, *one-two-three.*

She deflected the first two with a basic shield, but the third caught her on the elbow, spinning her a quarter turn. She grunted, shaking out her arm as the knife dissipated into a whorl of smoke. From the pained look on her face, Milla was willing to wager that Darkly had done something to the Shade, granting it a weight or force. She made a mental note to ask him about that as well.

"Get your arm in tighter!" Darkly jeered, dropping into an easy lunge and scooping one arm, collecting the remains of his Shades like they were saltwater taffy on a pull.

Lou barked a laugh and flicked her fingers, sending five pinpoints of light across the field. Darkly cursed and spun, reaching for the trees. His fingers curled, and he jerked his arm back. For a heartbeat, nothing happened, and then bright, hot sunlight pounded down on Milla.

She yelped, jumping up fast enough to send the world into a tizzy. Tobias grabbed her elbow, keeping her from toppling over, and she ripped her arm free, staggering on shaking legs and squinting at the field where every shadow from the trees seethed at Darkly's feet.

Beyond him, squinting in the same bright sunlight, Donmar held a ready casting stance, acting as the referee for this sibling showdown. Beside him, Rai clutched her teak box to her chest, watching the match with a bright smile as the shadows rose and stretched into a pillar, a wall, swallowing half the field and reaching for Lou.

She raised her arm, forming a weak shield as she turned in a slow circle, scanning the shadows and the sun-drenched field.

"Focus," Cyrus muttered. Lou's face twitched in his direction, and a stygian ball of Shades heaved from the shadows, colliding with the back of her head.

"Bollocks!" She staggered forward and Darkly darted out of the shadows.

"Focus, Lou," he taunted. She whirled around, and he sent a dictionary-sized Shade to her face. It wrapped around her head, and a cumulative "Oooooh" left every witch on the sidelines.

"A shadowblind?" Milla asked.

"Ja," Tobias chuckled and released her arm, stepping away. "She hates those."

Lou clawed at her face, her shriek of fury muffled by the Shade. Pinpricks of light appeared at her fingertips, glowing brighter and brighter as she dispelled Darkly's magick.

But he wasn't done. Keeping at a distance, he felled his wall with a sweep of his arm and whipped a ribbon of midnight at Lou's legs. It wrapped around her ankles, and when she tried to take a step—he tugged.

Lou landed on her ass, shadowblind and furious. The whip vanished in a puff of smoke as her dispellation took hold, revealing a Light Witch madder than a cat in a bathtub.

"Called!" Donmar shouted, throwing an arm up. In a wink, the Shades vanished. Shadow shot across the field and tucked into the trees as Darkly stalked forward, offering his sister a hand. She accepted, and he hauled a laughing Lou to her feet.

"Good match, wee yin." She clapped her hand against Darkly's shoulder and lightly cuffed him on the arm. "I haven't seen you work that hard in weeks! Fair play."

"Aye." He scanned the edge of the field, frowning when he spotted Milla wavering where she stood with a drunken smile on her face. "Are we done?" he asked Lou.

"For now, yes." She freed her hair, working her fingers through the shimmery mass before re-tying it into a tail. "I could bloody well use a shower."

"Good." Darkly leaned into a long-legged stride, making it one step before he froze, black eyes darting to the ground, then to Milla. His mouth opened in surprise, and at that exact moment, Milla felt the tiniest, almost infinitesimal tug.

"Wait." She stepped back, eyes dropping to the ground. And again, a tug, a pull, a tipping of scales. "What the fu—"

"Ludmilla," Tobias barked. She ripped her head up, and he lobbed a caustic blue ball of flame at her face. "Catch."

"*Udusit se!*" The hex flew from her lips without thought, her fingers forming the sigil from sheer muscle memory. *Suffocate.* A snuffing, killing hex that would read as hippocromantic, trained into her year after year on Big Torch Key.

Harmless sparks burst and sizzled in the air, falling away to reveal a second sputtering ball of flame flying at her face.

She crooked and bent the fingers of her left hand, weakly drawing the sigil for a ward and ducking to the side when the casting failed. A cold so deep it burned seared across her shoulder. Milla cried out, whipping her head up as fury overtook surprise.

"What the fuck, Tobias!"

"Dispell it, Ludmilla." Face blank, Tobias lobbed a third fireball at her—but it wasn't quite fire, was it? Crystalline blue, the same color as his eyes, sparking as it flew across the distance.

"Hells no." She caught it at the last second, the muscle memory of a lifetime again coming to her aid. "*Převzít.*" *Take hold.* Trapped in the web of her Way, the cold fire burned over her palm, the energy from Tobias' hex wanting to be used and unable to escape. Growing in intensity and beyond cold.

Milla blinked at the caustic fireball, recognizing that this was no simple spalování flame.

Her father was a spalování. Milla had seen the deep orange fire he wielded in the winters of her youth, lighting the hearth and birthday candles, burning mulch in the fall. Her father's Way manifested as heat and warmth, evoking thoughts of hot chocolate and hugs.

Tobias's flame was cold fury.

"Dispell it," he demanded.

"And be useless?" Milla thrust out her right hand, fingers dancing in a blur as she drew a rapid sigil in the air. "No, thank you." Her head swam, the cost of her Way taking more and more and more, but she would be Horned God-damned before she gave in to another one of his demands. Better to be functionally drunk than dysfunctional altogether.

She dropped the take-hold hex and slammed her left hand against the back of her right in one fluid movement, hissing a new intent.

"*Strašný oheň.*" Clenching her teeth against the burn, Milla ruined the brilliance of that blue fireball, twisting Tobias's magick into something of her own—a seething ball of pure necrotic energy Ezra had once referred to as "dreadfire."

It fizzed and popped, deepening in color until the core blackened, and a gray cloud of ash spun in a dervish around the heart of the flame. She felt the void of it in her palm, the weight of the nothing. It thrilled her deep in her bones, this utter decay and destruction—desecration on the atomic level—a facet of her Way so long ignored.

Cold wind teased her hair, wrapping around Milla and feeding her Way. The tips of her fingers darkened, stars burst in her eyes, and the blackened flame deepened to a void. Tobias stepped back, raising his hand in alarm with delicious fear in his eyes.

"By the Goddess," Cyrus gasped beside her, tap-tap-tapping away. She paid him no heed. What did a Death Witch need with E.R.I.E.'s and reports when she was the beginning and the end of magick incarnate?

At that thought, something like certainty stretched and yawned deep in her chest, a reawakening thing ready to be unleashed. Power flooded her body from the feet up, strengthening her stance and Way.

Horned God, it would be so easy to end him. To end them all and walk away without looking back at the destruction. To leave this entire range a charnel field and spread her rot across the land.

Not yet.

Milla blinked, hauled from the depths of her Way by a new, unknown voice booming in her mind. The blackened void in her hand wobbled and listed to the side. "Oh, fuck!" She grasped at her failing intent, tossing the ball of magick from hand to hand. Racking her brain for what to spin it into, how to snuff it out, and flinging it away from herself with a cry of, "*Na popel!*"

To ash!

"Scheisse." Tobias leapt to the side as the smoldering ball hurled in his direction.

A cloud of ash exploded against his shoulder, masking half of his face in charcoal black powder. Milla had one brief second to revel in the hit before he snarled in guttural German. Flame burned in his eyes and his hand, the blue so bright and intense that Milla knew at a glance it would be more painful than anything he'd thrown at her. He reared back, she raised both hands in ready wards, and shock stole the rage from his face.

"Verdammt!" Tobias snuffed out the flame and raised his hand in warning, eyes dropping to her feet. "Ludmilla, give it back."

"Give what—" She followed where his gaze fell. "Oh, Goddess."

Shadow teemed at her feet, frothing and roiling like a heavy fog. She swallowed and followed the faded path of the Shades, twisting around and clapping both hands over her mouth to keep from crying out. Darkly stood less than six feet away, his face pale and eyes a deep, insidious black.

"Give it back, Ludmilla," Tobias repeated. "Do not let Lou see."

"I don't—" She edged away from the Shades, and they followed, slithering through her legs and around her ankles like needy cats. "I don't know how."

"Now," Cyrus hissed. The urgency in his tone jarred Milla enough to look up and see Lou charging to their sparring pit. Light gleamed in both her hands and her eyes burned almost as bright as Tobias's flame.

"Knock it off, Keir," she ordered in her Enforcer voice.

"Milla," Tobias warned, and Milla called on the only intent she could think of.

Thrusting her hand at the mass of shadow, she drew the banishing ward with her fingers and rasped, "*Létat.*"

Fly!

A breeze kicked up out of nowhere, blowing the Shades back to the Dark Witch. They wrapped around his legs and crawled up his arms, clinging to him like a living shroud.

Darkly blinked once, slowly, and a cruel slash of a smile split his lips. She knew that smile, had seen that smile as he trailed his fingers down her body, and reveled in it when he disappeared between her legs.

She pressed her knees together, biting her lips to cut off a whimper at seeing his darker, scarier self. The heat of her Way intensified, kicking up the moths in her belly and urging her forward. Just a step. A hair closer to Darkly to seize that raw power and take it, him, all for herself.

Not. Yet.

Again, that foreign voice invaded, raising Milla's hand and crooking her fingers, twisting her intent and forcing it up and out of her throat.

"*Let', stín.*" Fly, Shade. "*A vrat' mi moji temnou čarodějnici.*"

Give me back my Dark Witch.

Darkly blinked again, a shiver twitching his shoulders as that glorious smile faded. The Shades siphoned into his figure, and he wavered in the grass, gazing at Milla in utter confusion before taking a step back only to stumble and land on his ass.

Twenty-Nine

"LOOK AT THIS DUDE." Milla flicked the edge of her phone, nudging it closer to Julie. "How much Botox does a man need?"

Julie cocked her head, winding a red curl around her finger and feigning deep thought. "I don't know, he's kinda cute if you narrow your eyes."

"Eww." Milla leaned away from her.

"Or if you like Ken dolls." Julie grinned at her, eyes twinkling. "At least they're non-threatening. You know." She straightened and flattened her hand, waving it in front of her navel. "Because they're smooth down there."

"Oh. My. *Goddess.*" Milla cackled and swept her phone away, turning off the interview she'd found with the CEO of Erlich Industries, Stefan Holfstaedter, aka her new landlord.

She needed this. Easy laughter, cruel mockery of a billionaire she would never meet. *Normalcy.*

After the casting range, she'd had the misfortune of riding home with Tobias and demanded to be dropped off at the store.

"Diego needs my help."

"Lou will want to debrief." His blue eyes met hers in the rearview mirror. Because obviously she refused to sit in the front seat. Let Rai take that one for the team. Which she had, playing on her phone and utterly oblivious to the bat-out-of-hell driving.

"Lou can suck my big toe. I did what she told me to do; I tended my demesne"—which she had, in the most terrifying way possible. What had made her think to spool up a hex like Dread Fire? Even Ezra had warned against using it, and Morgen had only let her practice the theory and sigils without stepping into her Way. Nine rings; maybe she *should* have dispelled the hex as Tobias demanded.—"Now I get to do what I want. That was the deal."

"That was not the deal." He adjusted his grip on the wheel, a warning that he was about to engage in some reckless driving. Milla pulled out her phone, hunkering down in the seat and staring pointedly at the screen. He had taken that as the signal it was: the conversation was over.

She tapped from app to app, finally opening the E.R.I.E. and waving it over Rai, playing with the scan function until Tobias dropped her off in front of the store, muttering something about the afternoon. Milla hadn't listened, and now she was here, relentlessly mocking a perfectly styled corporate mogul to stave off the burgeoning hangover and exhaustion.

"Have you heard from your current property manager?' Julie asked as Milla pocketed her phone.

"Nothing yet," she said. "It's only been a day; I'll bother him again tomorrow."

"I don't understand how this is legal." She shook her head. "Don't they have to wait until the end of the lease terms or whatever?"

"This is Florida." Milla waggled her fingers. "A lawless land."

Julie pinched her lips in a smile as she laughed quietly. "Just seems unfair." She nodded at the countertop where Milla's phone had been. "It's not like he needs the money or anything."

"I'm sure if we asked Stefan Holfstaedter, he would be happy to regale us with the generous girth of his portfolio."

At that, Julie outright laughed and made her way to the ICYMI display. Now down to a handful of racks and a séance table Milla had repurposed as a display, the remains of Julie's inventory and the Sanderson stash from Hattiesburg churned steady sales. Even working the store part-time, Julie constantly restocked the piles and draped new dresses and tunics on the racks.

Milla flexed her fingers at the memory of the leggings' greasy feel. Lou had re-bound her Way before they left the casting range, meaning all Milla could do was stare at the hideous clothing and daydream about removing the glamour. Until then, they made sales, which went toward keeping Southern Gothic right where it was.

"You know," Julie said after a moment. Her back was turned, face hidden behind a mass of red curls, but Milla knew the suggestion she was about to make.

"No, Julie."

"I'm just saying." She turned and put her hands up. "If you took my consignment off, you'd make more money, and that could help you keep—"

"Absolutely not." She slapped her hands on the counter. "Out of the question."

"But—"

"Not until we handle the credit card debt," Milla said, too harshly, if the blood rushing to Julie's cheeks was anything to judge by. "Shit, hey, no. Julie, I'm sorry, I just—I feel partially responsible for that whole mess."

"It's not your fault," she said in a voice too small for her personality. "I'm the one who got suckered, right? No more sorries."

"I got suckered, too."—*More than you can imagine.*—"We're helping each other out, okay? The lease isn't your fault, and it's not your responsibility to help me figure it out. If anything, even with the percentage that goes to you, those leggings are doing more to keep the doors open than my crap." She gestured to the rest of her store to demonstrate the point. Her occult collection sold about as glacially as it always had, but too much of the inventory had been sitting there for months.

At least the inventory she had procured. Diego's collection, on the other hand, could barely be kept in stock.

Julie scanned the shelves, again lingering on the ventriloquists' dummies above the register. She shuddered and sent Milla a big, blue-eyed look of reproach. "If you think so."

"I know so." And she did—this, at least. ICYMI had been a disaster for everyone involved, and the Loa had nearly ruined everything Milla held dear, but numbers, sales, and budgets were easy. They could get by, if only just, and Julie didn't need to know that Milla had stopped paying herself. "It'll all work out in the end," she said. "It has to."

Jangling bells kept Julie from arguing. Milla looked over, wrinkling her nose as Tobias stepped in. He nodded to Milla, scanning the store and halting midstep when he saw Julie gaping at him and clutching neon lycra to her chest.

"Oh wow," she said, lowering her arms slowly. "Wow, they make y'all tall."

"Y'all?" Tobias quirked an eyebrow, his mouth lifting in a smile.

"W—" She stopped abruptly. Her shock turned to panic, and she glanced at Milla and then back at Toby. "Um, Europeans?"

A tiny, disbelieving laugh left Tobias. He shook his head, still smiling at her, and Julie's cheeks crawled pink.

Milla darted her gaze from her friend to her guard and shuddered. *Ew.* "Did you need something?"

Tobias's smile fled, and he stared at Milla as if he'd just realized she was there. "Is Diego in?"

"He's in the back." She jerked her chin. "I think. The door's been shut since you dropped me off. Why?"

"You are needed at the duplex," he said, erasing any suggestion of the soft smile he'd sent Julie. "Both of you."

"Ugh." Milla dropped her head back and rolled her eyes. "It's been like two hours. Is she serious?"

"Deadly."

They heard the yelling through the door—a full-on blowout coming from the back of the duplex. Darkly's side, thank the Goddess, but Milla would have to smudge her half twice over just to get the bad vibes out.

Tobias muttered something under his breath, trying the knob and pushing the door open when it proved to be unlocked. Milla widened her eyes at Diego, moving them side to side to evoke a sense of, "What the fuck is happening."

He responded with a pantomime of a grimace. "I have no idea, but it is *awkward.*"

They followed Tobias in, stopping abruptly to avoid running into his back. He'd stopped a few steps into the middle of the hall, and Cyrus, Donmar, and Rai huddled in the front room. Their whispers fell off when they saw the witches in the hallway, and Rai pressed a finger to her lips, shushing them as Darkly erupted.

"It's bad enough you've got her on the team; I'll nae have her drinking that shite."

"Right," Lou sneered. "You'd rather keep rotting whenever she touches you, then?"

"That's nae—"

"Or rather, *if* she touches you."

Cyrus and Donmar each sucked in a breath, and Rai dropped her forehead into the crook of her hand.

Diego squeezed around Tobias, heading straight for Rai and whisper-hissing, "What is happening?"

"I made her tea," Rai answered through clenched teeth, jogging her head at Milla. "And it set him off."

"What kind of tea?" Milla asked.

"A restorative," she said. "I thought you might be tired after this morning and working your store."

"Goddess." Lou, apparently, was not done. "You'd likely prefer to have your dick fall off, wouldn't you? Some filthy kink you picked up from a—

"Dinnae." His voice dropped to a chilling low. "Dinnae talk about her like she's—"

"Like she's *what,* Keir? Another pathetic desecrant who made moon eyes at you? This is precisely why you were on probation for so long." Feet stomped across the linoleum, and a cupboard door slammed. "You think too much with your cock and not with that self-proclaimed clever mind of yours."

"Are we sure this is about the tea?" Donmar whispered.

"That's nae fair."

"What's not fair is how you can't see that I'm trying to keep you safe," she retorted. "It's all I've ever wanted, yet you are determined"—a cup slammed against the counter—"to find fault."

"If you wanted to keep me safe, you'd never have brought her on the team." Darkly backed into view, putting space between himself and his sister. He'd showered since that morning and donned a pair of gray joggers and a white V-neck. The glasses were back, his feet bare, and the outside fingers on his right hand were wrapped in tape. "You'd let me—" His shoulders sagged, the fighting wind falling out of his sails. "You'd …"

"All of this has been for you." Lou followed her brother across the kitchen, dropping her voice into a threatening calm. She had also changed and, in place of the exercise gear, wore Ponte pants, a pale blue cashmere blouse, and tan Oxfords. "From the first day, all I have done has been for you. To keep you from being cleaved, to keep my baby brother safe."

His throat bobbed, but he held his sister's glare. "Am nae a baby anymore, Lou."

"No." She spun around, throwing her hand over her shoulder. "You're a bloody fool who runs headlong into the most dangerous thing he sees." She stalked out of view and then lobbed, "What did you expect me to do?"

"Not slap a bleeding Soul Bind on my Death Witch, for starters."

Every witch in the front room gasped, and Milla glared.

"Rai," she said, drawing out the vowels. "That tea. It won't knock me out?" Rai shook her head, eyes wide and lips parted in a tiny o. Milla nodded. "Good. Fuck this shit."

She stalked around the corduroy couch, stormed into the kitchen, and located the cup and kettle on the counter. Darkly made a choking sound, and Lou had the good grace to look surprised as Milla filled the cup, spun, and looked them both in the eye as she downed the boiling concoction.

It scalded on the way down, but she refused to break. Her eyes watered, her entire chest felt hot, and she braced herself for the pain and stomach cramps. The deadening in her legs.

Instead, a cold suffused her body, crawling from her stomach outwards until the lingering headache and the pains in her joints were overwhelmed. Like she'd dipped her entire body in an ice bath.

Her eyes dropped to the teacup, snagging on the dregs swept against the side in the shape of a cross. Or was it a dagger? Milla narrowed her gaze, turning the cup and trying to read the conflicting meanings. Suffering and sacrifice? Or a warning of an enemy nearby?

"At least one of you has sense," Lou said. She swept the teacup from Milla's hands and dropped it into a pot of water soaking in the sink. "If you're finished?"

"Aye." He pinched the bridge of his nose under his glasses. "I suppose we are."

"Josh and Tammy were in Tallahassee a month ago," Diego told the room. He stood before the window, addressing the witches with a confidence new to Milla. Ordinarily soft-spoken, except with her, Diego was a witch who deferred and kept his head down. But something had changed in him while she was gone. He met the eyes of Lou's coven, answering their questions and arguing his point when pressed. It made him larger, somehow. More solid.

She loved seeing him command a room with his knowledge and cutting down criticisms with his no-nonsense sass. Still, she would have liked to be there to witness him growing comfortable in his skin and modernity.

"They will be back again this weekend to attend a campout arranged by the local coven."

"Did he give any reason why?" asked Lou.

"Part of the preparations for Beltane," he explained. His attention slid to Milla perched on the couch's armrest, where she had landed after being unable to sit still in a metal folding chair. Or against the wall. Or on the floor. Whatever was in the tea she'd chugged had soothed her headache and filled her with a need to fidget. Currently, she sat with an ankle propped on her knee, jogging it up and down so intensely that Tobias kept sending glares her way in a silent request to stop. "Aparentemente, the Witch of the Demesne has concerns about a neighboring territory and invited cults from around Florida to help him charge Tallahassee."

"What is his Way?" Lou asked. Diego shook his head, and Cyrus's keyboard clacked in the ensuing silence.

"Hippocromantic," he said after a brief moment. Lou chewed on that, and right as she opened her mouth with another question, Cyrus said, "Three of the six missing witches have been hippocromantics."

Donmar let out a low whistle while Lou dropped her gaze to the floor, darting it side to side as she thought. "Your source," she said after a moment, "can he be trusted? Cultists are notoriously fickle."

"I'll say," Milla snorted, covering her mouth and nose with a hand too late. Diego frowned at her and angled himself toward Lou. It stung. Why wouldn't it sting? He was her roommate, her tío, yet he'd distanced himself every minute she had been home, and now this?

"Sí." Diego nodded. "Every interaction I have had with Josh has led me to believe he can be trusted." He hesitated, angling his head and wavering a hand in the air. "He is out for himself, and his loyalty lies with his cult, but his guidance has never steered me wrong." A faint smile flickered across Diego's face, the response to some joke or a fond memory. "Only, be careful how you phrase your questions. He has an aversion to offering extra detail."

"Staid or Fae?" Darkly asked. He'd kept to a corner of the room, half-shrouding himself in shadow, which was wildly unfair. At any point, he could fall into the Neitherworld and leave all this awkwardness behind, while Milla was Soulbound and itching from the inside out. His question was a good one, however. Though Fae were uncommon since the gates closed, a few were rumored to wander the British Isles and Scandinavia. Mostly, they could pass as mortals but were notoriously cagey about introductions and giving straight answers.

"Staid," Diego answered. His brows pinched, and he pushed his mouth to the side. "And old. Whatever magick made him a cultist has him aging like a witch. He predates Morgen in Key West."

"That's impossible," Milla blurted.

Diego sent her a bland look and lifted one shoulder, letting it fall. "I am only sharing what I know."

At that, the chasm between them widened. Milla leaned back on the armrest, stunned by the coldness in his tone. She knit her fingers together and stared at her knee.

"What about the chicken egg?" Donmar asked.

"Come again?" Lou addressed her husband.

"The chicken egg the witchling spoke of." He gestured to Milla with a half-curled fist, and only then did she notice his swollen fingers and the abrasions on his knuckles.

"Chicken or the egg," Darkly clarified. He danced the vape pen across his fingers, drawing attention to his right hand and the tape on his ring finger and pinky. "Which came first."

"Considering the cultists have been preparing for this event in Tallahassee for weeks"—she sent a smile to Diego, hoping it would bridge the gap, even if only a little—"it would insinuate the cult comes first."

"But they were invited by the Witch of the Demesne," Tobias said. "What history do we have of him?"

"Not much." Cyrus opened the laptop on his knees, scanning a web page. "He has held the demesne for a decade and inherited it from his great uncle."

"So a standard succession." Lou crossed her arms and studied the ceiling for a moment. "Where are they meeting?"

"San Luis Mission Park," Diego replied. Cyrus's hands flew over the keys, and with a few brief gestures, a map came to life on Darkly's television.

"A little far from a demesne's heart for an empowered ritual," Rai noted. Milla scanned the roads and freeways, half-listening as she continued. "The witches and cultists will talk if we attend and make our presence known." She looked at Lou. "We risk blowing our cover if this is a run-of-the-mill cultist gathering."

"It is a gamble," Lou agreed. "And with the location being so far from the demesne's center, I am inclined to agree. Perhaps I could send Cyrus to—"

"No." Milla stood and approached the screen. "The missions in Florida predate modern city limits. Even ours is a half mile north of Tolomato." She named the cemetery just off the border of the

Colonial Quarter, recognized by the local witch population as the center of modern St. Augustine.

Silence filled the space at her back, and after a long moment, Milla twisted around to find Lou's coven staring at her.

"Care to explain?" asked Lou.

"Our mission, Nombre de Dios, where the first Thanksgiving mass was celebrated, is outside the old city walls." She looked to Diego, who nodded with a faint, supportive smile while the rest held vacant, albeit patient expressions. Bolstered by his approval, minor as it was, she continued. "Right, so none of you had to build one out of sugar cubes in Junior High. Okay, the missions were established by Spanish colonizers to convert the indigenous population of the Americas to Catholicism."

"Load of rot." Rai sneered.

"Pretty much. But they were cultural and commercial hubs of early settlements and the coastal ones were basically determined by the tides. Look." Milla spun around and grabbed Cyrus's laptop, swiping the map to St. Augustine and pointing to where the mission and the Shrine of Our Lady La Leche stood. "Think about tides, river flows, and the time of year. These guys landed in St. Augustine in, what, August?"

"September," Diego answered. Milla waited, letting him work through the memories and pull up the knowledge she sought—that, at least, they still had—the easy, near-immediate understanding of the point the other was trying to make. "It was a new moon."

"High tides, see?" She pointed to the river and the sand bars. "And the flow of the Matanzas would have pushed them inland, forcing a landfall here." Her finger jabbed the screen right where the Great Cross perched on a jut of land over the riverfront. "When the tide receded, their ships would have been stranded, forcing the Spaniards to head south"—she tapped the screen at St. Augustine and Castillo de San Marcos—"before properly settling." With a few swipes at the laptop, Tallahassee reappeared on the screen. "I'd be willing to bet that downtown Tallahassee was a swamp or a river plain five hundred years ago, and this mission was the original heart of the demesne."

"Westridge," Darkly read the name of a neighborhood on the map. "Griffin Heights, Holly Hills." He pointed his vape pen at Lou. "It makes sense, and an old sanctified space would be prime ground for a mass ritual."

"When was it built?" Donmar pushed from the wall and gripped the back of the sofa, peering over Rai's shoulder.

"1656," she read from her phone. "One of over one hundred built by Spanish settlers. And the principal village of the westernmost administration of Spanish West Florida."

"A place of old power, then." Donmar lifted his eyes to Lou. "The native magick in the demesne alone would be enough to charge a ritual Forbidden and Foule. And this is before accounting for the cult."

"Each previous ritual occurred in a similar area, except the Mabon rite in Refugio." Tobias scratched his cheek, eyes narrowed in thought.

"Right, that one was an outlier," said Lou. "Near a Catholic church, correct?"

Milla rolled her eyes, forever unimpressed with European centrism. "Refugio, Texas, near a Catholic church?" A few quick taps and the map re-centered. "Across the street from *Mission River Park*. Please."

Darkly snorted from his shadows. "She's got you there."

"Then what is the connection between Hattiesburg, Savannah, and Valdosta?" Diego posed. "If we are correct, Tallahassee is a return to form. But the most recent three…"

"Valdosta had a mission," said Milla.

"How on *earth* can you know that?" Lou eyed her from head-to-toe and Darkly chuckled.

"Spanish and European History." He ran a hand down his face, his eyes crinkling with amusement. "With a focus on Spanish Colonial History in the New World. I'll be Horned God-damned."

"Thank you." Milla curtsied.

"What is that?" Lou cocked her head at her brother, by-passing Milla altogether, which, rude.

"It's what I studied in college," she answered. "And Hattiesburg had a Loa." Darkly's amusement fell away while the other witches shared looks. "What? Anaisa worked on the huns there for months before coming to St. Augustine, and we just had this whole thing about magick clinging to people or whatever." She wafted the back of her hand at Darkly.

"And Savannah?" Lou pressed.

An uneasy quiet fell as each witch pondered her question. And it was a good question. From what Milla had learned, the most recent rituals were hasty, not following any particular cadence or aligning with any sabbat. A prickle began at her temples, and the room blurred as she unfocused her eyes and thought. Her tea came from Savannah, and she had visited the city several times with Ezra. It was an old city, one of the oldest in the southeast, but as far as she knew, Savannah did not have a mission.

"Even without knowing why Savannah was chosen," Cyrus spoke first, "five of the six locations can be directly tied to a place of old power. Perhaps the age of the city was enough for the rogue witches to try their ritual there?" He glanced around the room, and when no one argued, he added, "It is the best lead we have."

"It's the only lead we have." Lou sighed, scrubbing her face with her hand. "You're already proving your worth, Ludmilla."

"What is that supposed to mean?"

"It *means* were it not for Diego's connections and your bizarre knowledge of Spanish Colonialism, we might have overlooked Tallahassee altogether."

"Huh." Milla set Cyrus's laptop down, afraid she'd drop the technology out of shock. "When you mentioned my unique skillset, I figured you meant my Way."

Lou scoffed and smiled. "Turns out what we needed was a Floridian Witch."

Thirty

ONEIROMANCY The interpretation of dreams to foretell the future.
See: Divination; Vesticism

THE WEEK PASSED TOO quickly for Milla's liking. She had hoped for time to sit and reconnect with her demesne and Diego, but every minute of every day was filled with coven demands, sparring on the casting range or working the store while Diego kept to his sewing room. The only time she truly had to herself was at the end of the night when she drank her tea, but even then, those moments were brief and stolen by the death-like sleep.

She tried to catch him after the coven meeting, but Diego vanished when they were dismissed. She could hear his muffled voice as she made her tea, laughing on the phone. Whoever he spoke to, they made him smile, and that was all that mattered.

So Milla cuddled with a blanket on her sofa, drank her tea, and woke up on her bedroom floor.

Darkly waited for her on the front walk, dressed in his running clothes and looking as ragged as Milla felt. She greeted him with a quiet "good morning" and set off on her run, if it could even be called that.

Soreness dragged her steps; her pace was still abysmal, and Darkly's constant shadow didn't help. His presence was as annoying as it was comforting. Milla was beyond embarrassed that he was witnessing her terrible running but couldn't bring herself to tell him to fuck off. Even if she couldn't fully trust the witch, his quiet presence silently urged her on, subtly pushing Milla in that supportive way he always did.

By Wednesday, the run was easier, if still slow, and by Thursday, she felt strong enough to add in the loop of Eddie Vickers Park. As much as she wanted to credit her determination, she knew the praise belonged to Rai, whatever was in the tea she made, and Tobias.

He was a patient coach, which surprised Milla, but was no less challenging for it. Every day at two, he arrived at Southern Gothic to drive her to the casting range, where they lobbed low-level hexes back and forth until her muscles screamed and her head spun. Rai observed the first day, handing Milla a bag of root shavings when she teetered too far to the side and slurred her words.

"Angelica root." Rai shook the bag. "Tuck a few under your tongue and suck on them, it should help with your recovery."

"An' whaddabout the hi—*hic*—ups?"

"I'm afraid only water will suffice." She patted Milla on the arm and sauntered to the bench and her teak box.

The next day, Darkly, Lou, and Donmar joined them, keeping to the large field where the Simmons siblings put on another show. This one, however, Darkly lost to the sound of Lou berating him.

"You cannot be this distracted in the field, Keir."

"Am nae distracted," he hollered back, whipping out his arm and sending a series of shadeblades at his sister. She ducked and dodged each one, replying with a whirling pinwheel of light that left Darkly staggering and starblind.

Milla laughed, spinning around as Tobias barked her name and barely dodged a blue fireball.

"What the hell, man!" She spat hair from her mouth and swept overgrown bangs from her eyes. "You nearly singed me bald."

"But I did not." He lobbed a second fireball, and Milla snatched it out of the air, her Way rising to her palm with barely a thought. In the blink of an eye, she'd spun his magick into hers, holding the blackened orb in her hand before snuffing it out.

"Good work." He nodded.

"Warn me next time," Milla grumbled, but it was halfhearted. Something like pride warmed in her chest at his hard-won praise. The next day, he cast a cloud of smoke imbued with white-hot embers and sent it flying across the pit, and Rai introduced her to a new burn salve.

When she got home, the duplex was empty, which was not unusual, but the front door was unlocked, giving Milla pause. She stared at the handle for a long moment, wishing she could reach out with her Way and sense the demesne. Lou had closed her off when they were done at the Casting Range, explaining in her off-hand way, "I believe Cyrus has what he needs to re-write the E.R.I.E. parameters. We can work out an arrangement for your care of the demesne, but I'm not yet comfortable with you wandering around the city unbound."

"How come he gets to keep his?" Milla had jogged her chin at Darkly, standing nearby and playing with a stoat-like slip of shadow winding around his arm and through his fingers.

"I need him for a task," Lou said. "Speaking of—*dún*." Milla's Way snuffed out. She swayed at the sudden loss and the shackling weight on her wrists, stumbling forward as Lou walked away with Darkly following close behind.

He had not even looked back, following Lou to their golf cart and disappearing down the trail before Tobias put out the last of Milla's fires.

Now, standing on her front porch and staring down an unlocked door, Milla was tempted to knock on Darkly's, one hundred percent ready and willing to make up any lies necessary to sit in his half of the duplex and not be alone.

Instead, she took a big girl breath, shook out her hands, and entered her home. Her *home*. This was hers, and she wouldn't let any unlocked door, absent roommate, or coven of witches take that away.

The wad of blankets and random pillows were still stacked on her sofa, her checkered slip-ons where she'd kicked them off the night before. The only oddness she could identify was the open cupboard door in her kitchen and the row of neatly laid herbs and leaves on the counter.

Powdered hemlock, dried juniper berries, a pile of cloves, dandelion heads, purple hellebore petals, and a twig she knew would be hawthorn.

It was her tea, deconstructed, next to a mortar and pestle and a small vial of what she thought to be dried violet. The label read, "one teaspoon" in a clean, clear hand. Milla scratched her cheek, glanced around her duplex, and said aloud, just in case any not-Ghosts were listening, "I guess I'm making it myself tonight."

After dropping her bag in the bedroom, she dragged her comforter onto the floor, plugged in her phone, and texted Diego.

making my tea

It was their routine, after all. She was being responsible, which was all he had ever asked of her. While the tea steeped, she locked the doors and grabbed a trash can for when she was ill, checking her phone for Diego's reply.

There was none. At one point, three little dots began dancing at the bottom of the chat screen, and then they stopped, which Milla knew because she was obsessively staring at her phone. When that became depressing, she sat on the couch and drank her tea.

A sharp, shrill alarm threw Milla's eyes open. She dragged in a breath like a death rattle, willing feeling back into her limbs as the dregs of her tea-induced nightmare clung to the edges of her mind.

Masks and music, endless champagne. Faceless witches applauding her Way, calling for her to rot flowers and rejuvenate the blooms. A woman dressed as the sun and a man whose face was a blur, laughing with Ezra and clinking their glasses with Milla.

But the end, Goddess, the end of the nightmare had been the worst. Even now, she could feel the hard press of her back against a wall and Ezra's hand at her waist, the heat of his palm bleeding through that ridiculous bodice. She darted her tongue out as if she could taste the salt of his thumb teasing her lower lip and his mouth … the easily remembered warmth of it, the slide of his tongue against hers. The sizzling trail of his finger from temple to cheekbone to jaw…it had been so real. Too real.

A floorboard creaked, and Milla's door clicked shut. She whipped her head to the side, and the world spun, turning her stomach and sending black spots into her eyes.

"No, nono." She heaved onto her side, halting when the floor was two and a half feet further away than it should be and Milla was—"In bed?"

Hauling upright, she blearily took in her room, herself. She was under her comforter, mostly. It was tangled around her legs near the end of the bed, and she was over her bedsheets and still fully dressed in the yoga pants and cropped tank top from the day before. Her teacup was nowhere to be seen, and grayish-yellow light crawled through the curtains. She silenced the Horned God-damned alarm and read the time—just after dawn. Sagging over her legs, she groaned into her hands. How in the nine rings she was going to survive a run with Darkly, a shift at the store, *and* an afternoon sparring with Tobias, she had no idea.

Every muscle in her body ached, her limbs felt like they were made up entirely of sandbags, and her throat was as raw as an emery board.

"Coffee first." She rubbed the heels of her palms against her eyes, taking a few steadying breaths before standing. Her bladder protested, and she quickly revamped the plan as she shuffled across the room and down the hall. "No, bathroom first, then coffee. Then death. A long, unbothered death six feet underground where no one can …" Her words trailed off as she noticed the long, lanky witchy sprawled on her sofa. "What the fuck."

One long arm was thrown over Darkly's head, a leg had fallen onto the floor, and the rest of him was buried beneath the same pile of blankets that had occupied the end of her sofa for the last week.

Milla stepped closer and kicked his foot. "Get up."

He snorted awake, bolting upright and immediately assessing the room with bloodshot eyes before landing on Milla glowering at him.

"Milla." He tossed the blanket aside and, in a flash, had his knees under him, reaching for her. "What's happened? Are you alright?"

"Did you sleep on my couch?"

He blinked, looked down at the furniture he was kneeling on, then settled back, stretching an arm across a cushion to look cool, or natural, or whatever. "Yes?"

"Are you *stoned?*"

"Not anymore?" He said with a sheepish smile.

"Triple Goddess's Tits, Darkly, can't you go a day without getting higher than a kite?"

The last of the sleepy witch disappeared, and his jaw went hard. "We all have our coping mechanisms, Milla."

She glared at him, lost for words. That stupid smile returned to deflect the moment, so she said the only thing she could think of. "Why are you sleeping on my couch?"

"'Cos Rai's in my bed."

He said it so simply, as though it should have been obvious, but why in the nine rings would it have been?

"Why is Rai in your bed?" she finally managed.

"Because Toby's in the guest bedroom." His smile faded, and Darkly looked somberly back at her, waiting patiently, which she hated.

Milla swallowed, glancing at the blanket she kept re-folding and the pillows she kept putting away, her mind doing some very uncomfortable math. "How long have you been sleeping on my couch?"

"I'd really rather not answer that question."

"How long, Darkly?"

"As long as Rai's been in my room." He kept his face blank, and Milla stomped her foot. A growl crawled up her throat, and she knew she was throwing a tantrum, but he was being so cagey and obtuse, and all she wanted to know was *why*.

"How long." She forced the words through gritted teeth, putting as much frustration into them as possible. Darkly shrank back and dropped his eyes to his knee.

"Three weeks," he answered in a mumble.

"*What.* Why?"

"Already explained that." He looked up at her sheepishly, brows raised in a silent plea for her to pick a different subject. "Why are you sleeping on the floor?"

She snapped her mouth shut, not liking the turnabout one bit. "I didn't see you last night; where were you?"

Darkly sighed and ran a hand over his head, rising from the couch to stretch. Of course, he slept in low-slung plaid pajama pants and nothing else. His long arms flexed, muscles lengthening and bunching in his torso. Milla pressed her back against the wall to keep her gaze from traveling lower to where the v of muscle plunged beneath the waistband. Her mouth went dry—was dry. It was dry. From her tea and mouth breathing all night. Not from the stupid tall witch enjoying a luxurious stretch less than four feet away from her.

He finished his stretch and crossed his arms over his front, looking all too proud of himself, or rather, looking like *himself*. The cocky, arrogant witch she thought she knew.

"Ran with the cultists," he answered. "Lou wanted me to confirm some details before we drive to Tallahassee tomorrow."

"Right." She swallowed that obnoxious lump in her throat, eyes firmly pinned over Darkly's head. "Well, okay. Cool. I'm going for a run."

He nodded, half gesturing to a duffel bag on the floor. "I'll join you if that's alright?"

"What if I said it wasn't?"

Darkly smirked, and the dimple drove into his cheek, which was all the answer she needed.

For the first time that week, Milla did not feel as though she were trying to outrun him. Her body ached, muscles protesting every step, but Darkly was just as slow and lethargic as her. That knowledge alone sent adrenaline into her legs, pushing Milla faster than she had managed. For a few blocks, she felt like herself again. Powered by the demesne, by the strength in her body. It was as though a dark curtain had been lifted, and for the first time since the Soulbinding fell on her wrists, Milla felt like the scales had tipped, not so much in her favor, but at least finding a balance.

She glanced back at Darkly, three strides behind, and found him jogging with a peaceful expression mirroring how she felt. He nodded, a tiny smile kicking up his mouth, and Milla returned her focus to the road before them, ignoring the flurry of moths that had kicked up in her belly. Regardless of the knowledge that he had been sleeping on her sofa for close to a month, that Rai's clothes were in his bedroom because he'd given it to her to use while relegating himself to furniture, he was still Keir who jumped at his sister's beck and call and argued against Milla being on the team. He was still the Enforcer who had used her as bait for a raw-head.

But he was also Darkly. The ridiculous witch who had run with her morning after morning, teasing Milla until earning a hard-won smile. Darkly who took her out for lunches and struggled through the issues with her Way. The idiot Aural Insurance Adjuster who asked, "What do you need?" and ran her store and tended her demesne when she was gone, ensuring she had one to come home to.

Milla slowed as they approached the San Sebastian River, that last thought rattling in her brain. She stared out at the water, wishing she could feel the magick of St. Augustine coursing through her veins. The sigils on her wrists were like shackles weighing her down, and at her back stood an anchor. Panting lightly and watching her as he always did.

She took a deep breath and faced him, noting how his shadow pulsed and bled across the sidewalk. His head dropped back as he caught his breath, eyes hidden by his sunglasses, appearing for all intents and purposes like a man taking a moment to recover from a run. But the thoughts lingered. Everything Darkly had done, everything he was doing, and still, a piece was missing. Milla knew it in her bones, but what she did not know was *why*.

Darkly dropped his head, regarding her before speaking. "What is it?"

"Nothing."

"Isnae nothing," he argued. "I know that look, Milla." She tilted her head, brows rising in question. "There, that one." He pointed at her. "It's the one you get two seconds before you do something stupid like possess me with a Shade. Or hex me."

That said, Darkly took a hasty step backward.

"Oh, get over yourself. I'm not going to hex you." She bounced the inside of her wrists together. "Couldn't even if I wanted to. I was just thinking."

A dark look crossed his face, and he frowned. "What were you thinking about?"

She opened her mouth, the accusation on the tip of her tongue. A cool spring breeze blew in off the river, teasing the short hairs at the nape of her neck, and Milla thought better of it. "Nothing."

It was a thought, that's all. Unfounded and unproven. Just a wandering thought from the suspicious mind of a witch who had been too well taught not to trust anybody.

"Milla." He moved closer, and she shook her head.

"I said it's nothing, Darkly." Putting her back to him, Milla breathed in the air of her demesne and resumed their jog.

Thirty-One

"You do her a disservice," Tobias's voice floated through the open window. He crossed his arms, squaring his shoulders as he argued with Lou. "How can she learn to manage her Way if you will not allow her to access it?"

"And you think she is ready to run with a pack of cultists bleeding her magick everywhere?" Lou scoffed and shoved a bag in the back of her Land Rover. "Hardly."

"And Beltane?"

"What of it?" She slammed the trunk of her car and walked around the vehicle, out of sight from where Milla and Diego huddled in the window. Tobias followed, his voice dropping too low to hear.

"Goddess, I don't know which will be worse." Milla adjusted the electric candle in the window and twisted the blinds mostly closed. "Three and a half hours in a car with Lou or with Tobias."

Diego chuckled and cast her a sidelong glance. "I am sure it will not be so bad if you are in the same car as Darkly."

"Horned God, okay, nevermind. *That* is the worst scenario. If we ride with Lou, they'll fight the whole time, and if we ride with Tobias, he's gonna want to talk to me." She wrinkled her upper lip and gagged. "Or worse, sit next to me."

"I do not think you are being fair, pequeña bruja."

"I am being more than fair, considering all the bullshit he's pulled." She yanked on the curtain to punctuate the point and jerked her thumb at her sofa. "Did you know he's been sleeping on our couch?"

"Sí. Who do you think offered it to him?"

Milla stared at him, mouth hanging open like a fish. A tiny squeak came out as she processed what he had just said, and Diego was spared from her eruption by his phone ringing.

He pulled it from a pocket, grinning widely at the screen, and answered. "¡Hola mi amor!" Spinning away from Milla, he flashed two fingers at her and mouthed, "Talk to Darkly," before disappearing down the hall. "Sí, in the next few minutes. How was your drive?"

Four hours later, Lou's Land Rover pulled into the lot of a large greenspace west of downtown Tallahassee. Milla stifled a yawn, straightening in her seat and taking in their surroundings.

"I thought we were heading to the mission?"

"We are," Cyrus explained from the seat beside her. He closed his laptop and tucked it into a neoprene sleeve. "But the campground is here."

"We're meeting Diego's contact," Lou said from the front seat. "Apparently, the cultists congregate here while the Witch of the

Demesne lays his magick, and once he's ready, the pack will take off to stir things up."

Tobias's BMW pulled in beside them, and Milla wasted no time leaving the Land Rover. Donmar and Cyrus had kept a friendly chatter for the drive, allowing Milla to doze. She stretched, working life back into her limbs. Diego stepped out of the BMW, smiling at her and bouncing on the balls of his feet as he scanned the parking lot.

Darkly pushed open the passenger door, laughing at something Tobias or Rai had said, and hit Milla with a bright, easy smile. "Good ride?"

"Yeah." Seeing him so relaxed, laughing with clear green eyes and absent the strain that had taken up residence on his face, did something funny to Milla. She followed him to the rear of the BMW, freezing when he tugged off his shirt and tossed it into the trunk. Chatting with Tobias, he was oblivious to his effect on a handful of nearby cultists who stopped in their tracks, bumping into each other as they stared. Milla's attention, however, he noticed and returned tenfold, scaling his gaze from her face down to her running shoe-clad feet and back, his smile darkening with interest.

She wasn't wearing anything special. Just her running gear, but maybe she'd put a bit of effort into the ensemble. After all, she was a Witch of the Demesne, appearing in another witch's territory. She had an aesthetic to uphold and chose to do so with short lycra shorts and a heather gray tanktop adorned with a screaming raccoon and the words, "Life is trash." The deep cut-outs on the sides revealed a purple sports bra with a multitude of straps that she may or may not have dug out of her closet after seeing Rai wear a similar one.

Though no one could prove it, and she absolutely would not admit to it.

During the drive, she had woven her scraggly bangs into her hair and fixed the rest into a long braid dangling over one shoulder. She untied the end and re-tied it for something to do with her hands, pointedly looking away from Darkly as he tugged on a running shirt.

"You can stop now," Diego murmured from behind her. "He is not looking anymore."

Milla jumped, feigning innocence by cocking her head. "Hm?"

"Bruja idiota." Diego chuckled, raising a hand as a tanned, rangy-looking man wandered over from the campground. His sun-bronzed hair was pulled into a low ponytail, and from his beaded necklace and split-hem running shorts, Milla took him for a cultist. "Josh!"

"Hey, man!" He jogged the rest of the distance, a feat considering the flip-flops on his feet, and gathered Diego into a big hug, lifting the witch off of his feet and swinging him side-to-side. "Good to see you, D."

"Tú también." Diego grinned as he was set down. Milla gave them room, beyond weirded out by the interaction. She believed him when he said he had a contact; why wouldn't she? But this was more than just "a contact."

"And this is the rest of them?"

"Sí, the whole coven."

"Great, good. Awesome." Josh swept his gaze over the witches, hunger flashing in his eyes. No doubt they reeked of magick. Eight witches of eight disparate Ways, and two of them a rarity. He licked his lips and cleared his throat before spinning toward the park. "Follow me. I'll show you where to drop your bags, and then we're off."

Where Milla had expected tents set up around fireplaces and hammocks in the trees, maybe a handful of cultists sitting on logs singing "Kumbaya," the campground was anything but. Fancy RVs parked in a row boasted front porch areas to rival the wealthiest neighborhoods in St. Augustine. Chairs and rockers, outdoor grills, twinkle lights, and canopies decorated the space, and large, two-room tents were tucked in among the recreational vehicles, the front rooms open and welcoming.

Shouts and hollers echoed through the trees, and at one point during their tour, Tobias neatly avoided being beaned in the head by a frisbee.

"Horned God," Lou said, recoiling from a row of port-a-potties. "This reminds me of our childhood."

"I'll say." Darkly eyed the cultists gathered around a trio of kegs and a snack table at the center of the campground. He rubbed a thumb across his lower lip, barely suppressing a smile.

"Where the hell did you grow up, summer camp?" Milla cackled, her laughter dying away with Darkly's barely-there smile.

"In a caravan," he answered in a near-whisper. "Mum and Da were performers; they met when she joined a Galway troupe, then moved to a Highlands carnival when I was young."

The photograph in his bedroom formed in her mind: sullen teenaged Lou beside her grinning parents and a younger Darkly, a family portrait posed in front of an RV and tents.

He tipped his chin toward his sister, still speaking low enough that Milla had to lean in to hear him. "She trained in Grim Ness, so I wouldnae have to be uprooted." Almost as an afterthought, he added, "After they died."

"Oh." Milla walked silently beside him for a few steps. "I guess that explains the accent." And then, because Milla was Milla, and this all felt too real, "And why you're such a clown."

Darkly said nothing. Milla thought he'd gone back to listening to Josh's explanation of the camp and its intentional layout, ignoring her when she'd taken it too far. But then, he chuckled. "Aye, suppose it does."

"We'll end the trail here," Josh announced, calling attention back to himself. "Everyone will circle up around the kegs, and there will be a last push before we close out the night and the real party begins."

"Push?" Cyrus asked.

"Song and dance," Diego answered with a knowing smile. On cue, the cultists near the kegs broke into song. "¡Así!" His smile stretched to a grin, and he ran to join, moving faster than Milla had ever seen.

"What'd he say?" Darkly asked.

"Like that." She scanned the cultists and chewed her lower lip, unable to keep the worry from spreading from her face. "I should go see if he's—"

"He'll be fine," Darkly assured her. He gently pressed his hand to her back, keeping Milla walking. Her skin tingled at the soft press of his fingertips, and that wouldn't do. She needed to be focused on the cult and the ritual, and already, he'd distracted her from whatever Josh had said.

"Of course, he'll be fine," Milla snapped and skirted away from his hand. "He's a grown witch."

"You looked worried."

"I don't need you telling me how I feel."

"Funny thing, that." Darkly spun around, walking backward and smiling at Milla as he teased. "Knowing how others feel is a peculiarity of my Way."

"Then stop using it on me." She darted around him, jogging to catch up with Cyrus, who was facedown in his tablet, and the witches actually paying attention.

"One big circle," Josh was saying. "More or less. If you cross your eyes and squint real hard."

"But won't it affect the magick if your trail runs in a circle?" Rai asked.

"I sure as shit hope it does." Josh grinned at her. "Best damn high of the month if we run this right."

An idea sparked, and Milla raised her hand, earning a bemused smile from the cultist. "Ludmilla, right?"

"Yeah, um, do you always run these things at the same time?"

"Yup!" He nodded. "The pack's off at six o'clock sharp for evening runs. We'll chase the magick for about an hour, then be back here to stir up the fun before night fully sets in."

It made sense. The most potent rituals were those conducted at times of transition—twilight hours, the witching hour, the turn of the season, or a solstice or eclipse. Reaching the liminal edge of casting, at that moment in-between, when the world is no longer as it was, but not yet what it could or would be.

A skilled witch could hold her ritual in that moment, gaining power as the becoming stretched on and the being was delayed. Milla had relentlessly trained for that moment when the magick was almost too big to hold. The ritual at Lake Pontchartrain was one of becoming. A summons of the Baron and his Maman. A rebirth of wild magick in the world.

It was in that moment, when she had summoned the Shades, cleared a path to the Gates, and the world was all but torn open, that Milla had trapped Ezra.

All of that in mind, she asked Cyrus, "Have you been tracking the times of the rituals?"

"Of course I have," he said with more bite than her question warranted. "What good would I be if I wasn't?"

"Alright, calm down." Milla allowed herself a slow breath to keep from sassing him more. "Just wondering, what time did the burnouts happen in the other rituals? Or the largest surge of the Ways?"

Cyrus's face went blank. He slowly raised his eyes from the screen, staring at Milla for a moment before returning to his tablet and pulling up a flurry of reports, adjusting settings and data points. "Horned God."

"Thought so." She smiled, proud of herself for making the connection. He scurried over to Lou and showed her the screen. Her eyes widened as she took in the data and hissed something too low to hear. Whatever it was sent Cyrus running back to the Land Rover.

"I want to speak with the Witch of the Demesne," Lou told Josh. "Immediately."

"Yeah, me too." Josh frowned, biting his thumbnail as he scanned the cultists and witches hopping in circles on one foot. "He was supposed to lay this thing live."

"Lay what?" asked Donmar.

"The trail." Josh waved his hand at the cultists and the campground. "This is meant to help him get a nice little boost before Beltane next week, but it works best if the magick is fresh versus whatever drop casting he's decided to do."

"Why does he need a boost, anyway?" Milla asked. "It's just a performative rite, right?"

"Sure, yeah, to some. To other witches, it's the pinnacle of their year, a chance to feed into the regional power and get a little something back in return. Demesne lines have been known to shift with the power given to a major sabbat like Beltane." He winked at Milla. "And I guess there's a demesne to the east of here that worries him. Maybe it's performance anxiety; maybe it's territorial; who's to say?"

"Goddess." Milla feigned gagging. "As if anyone would want to steal Tallahassee."

Josh's eyes flickered and gleamed as he grinned at her. His gaze lifted over her head, and something old, far older than the twenty-something cultist, peered up at Darkly. "But that's not up to the witch, is it?"

Thirty-Two

LABYRINTH An elaborate, maze-like design prescribed in ritual use as a means of focusing intent.

"TWENTY PERCENT, AND KEEP away from Keir." Lou tugged on Milla's wrists, pressing her thumbs against the triskelions. "If you feel anything resembling a loss of control, if you catch the slightest whiff of rot, get as far away from the cultists as you can and find me."

"Are you sure about this?" Milla rubbed the tips of her fingers against her palms, squirming under Lou's grip. "It's only been a week."

"You've been drinking your tea?" Lou pressed down. Milla nodded, and she sighed. "Toby makes a good argument; we need you functional at Beltane or Constance and Dina will have my head and have you cleaved."

"M'already cleaved."

"You glean my meaning," Lou retorted. "Besides, it's a bad look to arrive in another witch's demesne and not leave an offering. Consider this a trial run. If you fuck up now, I'll keep your Way bound and let the steward assume control of your demesne."

She jerked her arms, more out of surprise than any desire to steal them back. "That's not fair."

"Isn't it?"

"I don't even know who this steward is, much less trust them to run St. Augustine."

Lou snorted indelicately. "Once upon a time, my brother reported that you thought of your demesne as a burden." Light gleamed in her eyes, the low, eerie foglamp glow of her Way. "What changed?"

"I grew up," she mumbled.

"Prove it." At that, she pressed down hard enough to curl Milla's fingers. "And a little advice? The Morgenhexe did not raise a weak daughter. This Way"—she tapped both thumbs—"belongs to you; you do not belong to it."

Her lips parted at the quasi-vote of confidence from the least likely witch. She nodded again, her posture relaxing, and inhaled slowly, steadying herself for the rush of her Way.

"But to err on the side of caution," Lou added, "keep to the back of the pack."

"No worries, I couldn't keep up with Darkly and the front runners if I tried."

Something resembling a laugh left Lou, and she whispered her intent. "*Oscailte.*"

A trickle of warmth bled up her arms, puddling in the crook of her elbows. It stopped there, pulsing lightly at her upper arms but unable to surge into Milla's center. She flexed her fingers, and when Lou let go, she crossed her arms tight across her front as if she could make the magick stronger through sheer will.

A cry rose from the cultists, and Darkly's voice sang over the din, "Pearls she wanted, a necklace she got!"

"Oh, I don't work there anymore!" The crowd joined in on the verse, laughing and cheering as he and Josh linked arms and skip-to-my-loo'd in a circle.

"I've never understood how he tolerates the spotlight, even with his Way." Lou shook her head, not bothering to hide the fond smile blooming on her face. Though it was rare to see Lou slip into emotion, it was something Milla had noticed about the Light Witch whenever she stepped into her Way. The stern facade retreated, and she became almost tolerable. Smiling and sharing confidences, where without her Way she was a stone-cold ice queen. Darkly was firmly the opposite. Arrogant, yes, but he was quick to smile and wore his heart on his sleeve unless calling on the Shades and revealing his darker, more terrifying side.

"I always preferred working behind the scenes," Lou continued, lost in a memory. Milla liked her like this. Her guard down, the tension in her face and shoulders eased. Confiding a piece of herself. *This* was Lou, she thought, a big sister in an impossible situation, tasked with keeping her idiot brother safe.

She did not envy Lou's task, especially now that she had Milla to deal with. Two Forbidden and Foule witches to keep out of C.R.O.W.'s sights. Goddess, no wonder the witch was constantly bitchy.

"Me too," Milla admitted. Across the green, the cultists flocked to Darkly, savoring his enjoyment. He beamed under their attention and let little ribbons of shadow, invisible unless you knew to look for them, slip free. A pulse filled the air, one Milla recognized on a deep, visceral level. He had done this in the swamp, using his Shades to bring them both pleasure. She pressed her thighs together at the memory, rubbing a knuckle against her breastbone at the uncomfortable pang of the memory.

Now, instead of feeding his arousal and pleasure into the crowd, he sent them elation. Joy. Giddiness. Rousing the pack and whetting their hunger.

"Never could keep him away from the clowns," said Lou. "Growing up, if we ever lost sight of Keir, we'd find him with the clowns."

A whistle blew on the far side of the pack, and Lou blinked, clearing her throat and settling her face into its trademark scowl.

"They're moving out." She gestured to Tobias, lingering on the fringes. "I'll be here if you need to hurry back. Your only role is to be seen supporting a fellow Witch of the Demesne, do you understand?"

"You're not running with us?"

"Please." Lou scoffed. "I only run from bears."

Milla settled into an easy jog, keeping the rear of the main pack in her sights and the walkers behind her. A string of cultists bridged the gap, like when she'd run with the St. Augustine crowd. Though most of the arcane symbols meant to hold the pack were solved by the time Milla reached them, a few had been freshly set.

"To zhuzh it up a bit," a cultist explained when Milla toed the fresh pile of flour. "Trail probably doubles back on itself at one point; the more we run certain key areas, the more we stir shit up."

"So we're not just running in one big circle," Milla asked, "but running in circles?"

"Pretty much!" The cultist chirped and ran off in the direction of a distant whistle. Twilight had fallen fast, thanks to a rush of thick, gray clouds that felt too purposeful not to be meteomantic.

Milla adjusted the headlamp Josh had given her, clicking it on and following the woman's bobbing ponytail.

As she settled into a steady pace, her worries and concerns fell to the side. Even her Way was satisfied, thrumming warmly beneath her skin in a happy reminder that it was there. Her wrists were still heavy, but it was tolerable, nearly forgettable the longer she ran.

True to word, the trail took a left and a left again, now running through the neighborhood they had been skirting behind. It reminded Milla of the labyrinth in Morgen's garden and the circuitous path she walked each morning.

She came up behind a pair of cultists on the next turn, speedwalking in a way that suggested they had just fallen behind the main pack. Not wanting to startle them, she slowed to a walk, catching snippets of their conversation.

"—friend said she ran with him in Glasgow a few years ago," one of them said. "Sheer luck; she had a layover with her fiance, followed the scent to a trail, and there he was."

"Jesus, can you imagine the high you'd get off that witch?" her friend asked.

"Girl, my panties were wet just listening to him talk, but, *god*, his magick."

They sighed in tandem, and Milla smirked. They weren't wrong, not that she'd admit it out loud. Darkly was a strong witch, and his Way was as unique as hers. With that thought in mind, she sped up a little, pooling what magick she could into her palms to give them something else to sigh about.

"You thinking about moving on to St. Augustine?"

"With a Witch of the Demesne like that?" the first cultist huffed. "I'm already looking at apartments. My girlfriend in Vilano says he shows up to *every* run."

Milla nearly tripped over her own feet as the words slammed into her. Darkly? Witch of the Demesne? *She* was the Witch of the Demesne. Sure, a steward cared for things while she was in that Horned God-awful cell, but she'd been tending St. Augustine almost every morning since. Not once had she felt any hint of another witch encroaching on her territory, much less Darkly.

When Anaisa stole the demesne, there was a sucking sensation down to the very roots of her Soul. The demesne had drained Milla, taking everything she was and demanding more, but every day she'd been back, it had been…

Temperate and level.

Balanced.

Except for that weird instance at the casting range when Darkly had knocked Lou on her ass with a shadowblind. He had looked for Milla, stepping in her direction, glancing at the ground in surprise, and in the same instant, she had felt a tug. Slight, faint enough to ignore, but all too familiar a sensation, and Darkly had noticed. He had felt *something* on his end of that and—

"Catch."

Tobias had lobbed a fireball at Milla's face, forcing her to react with a killing hex. And another that she spun into dreadfire before she'd lost control, summoning Darkly's Shades and making a thrall of the witch.

"Oh, Goddess." She fell still, the cultists' voices fading as they moved further away.

His second match with Lou strobed in her mind's eye. Every hex and allure his sister had flung, every hit he'd taken, and the weak shadows he sent in return.

He pulled his punches.

Now that she was thinking it, she couldn't unthink it. From her arrest to his actions in Constance's office, on their runs, and at the casting range. Goddess, even in their duplex—Horned God-dammit, *her* duplex. Getting higher than a kite to be useless for any Enforcer work, sleeping on her couch, driving her to the cult, Lou berating him for being distracted. All of it was because *he* was the steward of *her* demesne?

"Mother fucker." She broke into a run, fueled by too much anger to care about the Way bleeding from her palms or the giddy shrieks of the cultists as she sped past. She needed to find him, strangle him, smack him, call him on his bullshit, and demand to know what else he was keeping from her. How many more lies?

She darted across a busy road, flipping off a car as it blared its horn, and dipped under a low branch, skidding to a halt at a random intersection.

Forget the bottling. Forget that he wasn't fucking Rai in his black satin bed. Forget that he'd pulled his punches and kept from stealing her demesne outright. It was the principle of the thing. It was that he *kept lying*. Whether on purpose or by omission, he kept doing it.

She picked a random direction, kicking the pile of flour in the middle of one of the cult's marks as she sprinted by. Thin magick crackled over her skin, a faint static that rose the hairs of her arms like the aether before an oncoming storm.

The *audacity* of this witch to keep shit from her over and over again. Like he knew better. Like he was—

Like he was Ezra.

Heat shot up her arms, churning in her chest and burning in her palms, demanding a release. She followed the shadows onto a narrow trail, aiming away from the houses. As mad as she was, she couldn't risk losing control now. Not when Lou had finally trusted her enough to let her have some facet of her Way. Not when there was a Dark Witch to take her anger out on. The damn fool couldn't seem to stop himself from touching her, but this time—oh, this time, Milla didn't care if she rotted the idiot.

What was the point of keeping all of those secrets? Milla was reasonable. She was an adult. She wasn't some hair-trigger hex-lobbing witch.

Except for every time she was exactly that. Hexing Darkly, possessing him, summoning his Shade. Over and over again in those first few weeks. And what had she done when she was allowed to cast her magick again?

Summoned his Shades and enthralled the witch, proving she couldn't be trusted with her magick, much less any truths she thought she was owed.

A cramp pinched her side, and she cried out from frustration, from the pain of it. It slowed her sprint to a jog, down to a walk. Pine and oak blocked out stars and streetlamps, casting the wooded area in a deep twilight. Not a speck of flour or chalk marked the trees, but a tease of magick danced in the air. A subtle suggestion to turn her head, a breeze prompting her to walk in a certain direction.

She adjusted the beam of her headlamp to hit the trees rather than the ground and followed the trail. The faint crackle of energy grew to a buzz against her skin, a happy humming that danced over her limbs. Muffled voices carried through the trees from a cluster of cultists around a cache of magick, or so she assumed.

Ducking under a branch, she tripped over a low line of bricks, less than an ankle in height. It curved away from her in both directions, barely illuminated by her headlamp. She followed the arc to the left, straightening when she realized she was looking at a labyrinth.

Constructed of low grey and red bricks set in the ground, the arc of the outermost path circled a wide clearing before doubling back on itself and diverting in the opposite direction. A small mirror ball sat on a plinth in the center, humming with magick Milla could hear as well as she felt it.

Directly across from her was a small gardener's hut, a cement birdbath, and a wrought iron table where a man sat with his back to Milla, one hand gripping the table's edge. He dropped his head back on a gasp so full of passion that heat rushed up her neck. The beam from her headlamp reflected off of round glasses and illuminated the shoulder of—yep. That was a man on his knees.

"Oh, shit," she mumbled. "Sorry, y'all, I'll just—"

The man on his knees raised his head. Dark, shoulder-length hair tumbled free around his face, and though her headlamp half-blinded him, he stared at Milla in a way that made her want to die.

"Pequeña bruja?"

"Wha—" A choked little sound left Milla, surprise pinning her in place.

Diego wiped the back of a hand across his mouth as he stood. "Milla, what are you doing?"

"What am I doing? What are you doing?"

"A good job," the other man said, hastily tucking himself into fitted, cuffed chinos before facing Milla. Slender and half a head taller than Diego, the man was *weirdly* familiar, his face and build tickling a part of Milla's brain she had not accessed in a decade. His sandy, floppy brown hair was everything her 90s cartoon boyfriend dreams were made of, while the look on his face gave, "say one mean thing to Diego, I dare you."

He stepped beside Diego, twining their fingers and whispering something low in his ear. Diego glanced at him, the shock and—was that anger? What in the nine rings did he have to be angry about?—anger fading. He cupped the man's cheek, nodding and kissing him softly before addressing Milla.

"I did not plan for you to meet this way," he said with a sheepish shrug. "Milla, this is Trav."

"Trav," she said, squinting across the distance. "Who the fuck is …" Trav raised a hand to shield his eyes from her headlamp, waving his fingers in hello, and at the boyish grin he shot her, it clicked. She ripped her headlamp off to stop blinding the pair, blurting out a name she hadn't spoken or thought of, in years. "*Bergs?*"

"Hey, Milla."

Diego whipped his face to Trav, finally joining the dumbfounded party. "You know her?"

"Yeah." Trav cupped the back of his neck, cheeks deepening in color. "We were conversation partners."

"Senior year Spanish, what the *fuck*, Travis."

"Trav," Diego corrected with a glare. "And I would appreciate you not speaking to my boyfriend in such a way."

"Your—" She backed away, dumbstruck, dumbfounded, just fucking dumb. "I—" Her heel caught on one of the low bricks, and she tipped backward, about to land on her ass, when a firm, familiar set of hands grabbed her elbows. Cool strength rushed down her forearms into her palms. Milla tore free, whirling around to find Darkly there. Her shock vanished instantly, replaced by the anger that had brought her to this point, only for it to waft away, unable to take root.

"I can't—" She sucked in a breath, too thin, too shallow.

Number two: talk to Darkly.

But how could she talk to him now? Seeing Diego on his knees with a man he called his boyfriend had torn apart all the lies she had told herself over the past week.

Seven days. She'd been home for seven days, out of the cells for seven days, telling herself she'd made progress, that she was healing and moving forward. That nothing had changed, and everything was fine. Spending all her energy throwing her anger at Darkly for his lies and deceit when, in truth—

"Talk to me, Milla," Darkly pleaded, asking what she needed and how he could support her. Being the same damn witch he'd been from the very start.

"I *can't*." She darted around him, stumbling into a run and praying to the Horned God she didn't rot anything.

Thirty-Three

LYCHGATE A roofed gateway to a church or graveyard; traditionally used as the transitory resting place of a corpse en route to burial.

"MILLA!" HIS VOICE RANG clear and strong and far too close for comfort. She couldn't do this right now. Not ever. Never. She couldn't face the unraveling of her life and *him* at the same time in Horned God damned *Tallahassee*.

She darted around a tree, tripping over an upturned root as she ran because, of course, she'd dropped her headlamp in that labyrinth. Just a fuck up, all over the place. Not even a hot mess of a witch, just a mess, and her slow-rolling disaster consumed everything and everyone around her.

Darkly, with the bottling, being outed to C.R.O.W. and disappearing behind a haze of smoke just to cope. Julie, who she had forgotten about, again and again, and again, and Diego with his boyfriend.

His *boyfriend*.

When had that happened? And why hadn't he told her? They were a team, a pair. A lock-step set of witches. A coven of two, and now there was a third.

She'd been home for days; why hadn't he told her? Why leave Milla in the dark when she had been in the dark for so *long*? There had been more than enough time to let her in, to include her, yet he chose to cut her out, and, Goddess, hadn't she sensed it? That disjointed feeling, like she had done something wrong without knowing, blindly walking through her new routine and offending Diego with her mere presence.

"Milla, would you please stop?"

Her eyes burned. Goddess, they had been burning for days, and that lump in her throat had only grown bigger, making it hard to breathe. She slowed her run. Stopped. Horned God, she wanted to *stop*.

"*Leannán*," Darkly said. Too soft, too close. Why was he also so close? Milla sniffled, blinked, and the woods blurred, the burn in her eyes rising, but she would be damned before she cried in front of him.

She whirled around instead, channeling all of her upset, all of her pain, into something she knew. Into the anger and rage she wore as comfortably as a favorite coat, directing it at the closest target as she always had. "What the *fuck*, Darkly?"

He flinched back, hands raised. His headlamp was pinned to his right palm by two fingers, illuminating the trees and casting long shadows over the trail and undergrowth. Sweat beaded on his brow, and that annoyingly tight tech shirt clung to his torso, making it impossible to ignore the rise and fall of his chest or how the sleeves clung to his arms.

She hated that she noticed. Hated that she couldn't keep her eyes off him whenever he entered a room. How his presence alone soothed the constant ache, allowing her to breath for a second instead of pressing against the wall, every muscle tight, her entire body ready to flee at a moment's notice.

She hated how he made her want to be held and comforted like she was too weak, too frail to handle all of this when she'd been handling it just *fine*.

"Gonnae need you to narrow it down."

"My demesne?" Milla advanced on him, magick warming her palms. Not enough to rot him, thank the Goddess, but Horned God did she want to. "Was using me as bait not enough? Or leaving me every fucking day in that swamp? You had to go and steal my demesne, too?"

"Didnae steal anything, *leannan*."

"Sure, right. Keep lying, asshole." She curled her hands into fists to keep from jabbing his chest.

"Milla, I'm not—"

"Then why are they calling you the witch of *my* demesne?" Her heart tripped over itself, catching in her chest and beating fast. Too fast. "Is that what you were doing while I was stuck in that fucking swamp? In that cell?" she shrieked, unable to hide the panic in her words. "Wooing my cultists and stealing my home?"

"That's nae—" Darkly growled in frustration and swept a hand over his head, brows crashing low. He made the motion again, scrubbing his short hair as if he had forgotten about that stupid haircut. "That isnae what's happening here, Milla."

"Then what is it?" She threw her arms up, wincing as heat left her right hand. Brown, brittle leaves wafted to the ground, and she clenched her fist, backing away from Darkly.

Goddess, she wanted to tear her hair out. Wanted to turn and run and leave all of this behind, but there was nowhere left to run. C.R.O.W. had infiltrated every aspect of her life. They had her backed against a wall, and she'd bound herself to them for a chance at normalcy, only to find that everything had changed in her absence.

"Please," she begged. "Explain it because I can't fucking puzzle this out."

"I dinnae want your demesne, Milla. I want—"

"Then why are you still here?" She cut him off before he could say it. The way he was looking at her, the hurt and the anguish on his face—she could not bear seeing someone else hurting the same way she did. "All you do is complain about me, so why don't you leave?"

"Has it ever occurred to you that I can't?" Darkly finally snapped, raising his voice and straightening to his full height. Those long arms shot out, and the headlamp sent shadows stretching from the low, dipping branches of a massive live oak. "Did you ever stop to think, for a wee second, that I might be stuck here?"

"I—" she squeaked, backing up one step. Another. Stopped from retreating by a low wall. She glanced back, registering the rough-hewn stone base of a gabled gate.

"Whatever you did to me at the Fountain of Youth—when you summoned those Shades, you summoned *me*. Binding me to St. Augustine; to *you*." A cold lick of fear ran up her spine, and she shook her head, denying what she knew to be the truth the moment he said it. "I tried to avoid the demesne; Goddess knows I did. I wanted to let Lou handle the cleanup, and I tried to be careful when she made me step into my Way so I wouldnae steal it outright. I worked myself to the bone every Horned God-damned day to get back to you so we could … and then—then Lou got to you first, and you were gone, and I couldnae leave you behind. The call, the pull to you was—" His throat bobbed, and he held out his hands in supplication. "I leave, and all I want is to be here. With you."

"What," was all she could manage. Even by accident, the idea that she had bound them together was unfathomable. Meshing their Ways until one depended on the other? It … it …

Horned God, it made sense. How his magick surged around hers, how it powered Milla's Way, leaving her empty and useless in the burnout.

He had tried to tell her every moment they had together in that swamp. He had patiently coached Milla, training her to manage his Way and hers while keeping the distance she requested. And what had she done?

Summoned him, again and again. In the swamp, on the casting range. Tying him tighter and tighter to herself even as she pushed him away. A sob swelled against that lump in her throat. She cradled her casting hand to her chest, gripping her wrist and rubbing her thumb over the sigil. Darkly narrowed his eyes, following the movement.

"You seized those Shades. You ripped them from me, and now they're bound to the place. To *you*." His throat bobbed, eyes flicking up to meet hers. "As am I. But I dinnae want the demesne."

He took a step, hesitating before taking another. When Milla did not move, when she stayed pressed against that gate, he closed the distance in one long stride, gazing down at her with a look of such longing that it knocked the wind out of her.

"I want what I've always wanted," Darkly said, his voice firm. Final. "You were supposed to be my last job. Catch the wicked witch, and Lou was gonnae let me leave her team." *I need you,* he'd said on that first day. But he'd done what Lou wanted, so why was he still here? "I traded everything to get you out of those cells, Milla. I gave Lou exactly what she wanted because I thought it would help me get what I want."

His eyes, bright and green and feverish in the light from his headlamp, bored into her, heating Milla from the inside out. Her breaths came in tiny little sips. A dull ringing built in her head, curling around her mind and forming in her ears as an unspoken word.

You.

"You said—" She swallowed, tried again. "You said you didn't want me on the team. You argued against working with me."

"Because I want to date you." His fingers twitched at his side as if he were holding himself back from reaching out and touching her. And then he did, darting his hand out and snatching her wrist in a lightning-quick move. His grip was gentle, and the sweep of his thumb over the Soul Sigil even more so. An electric thrill shot up her arm, and the heat in Milla's veins erupted, her belly swooping in delight at his touch. She pulled her lips between her teeth to keep from gasping.

"I didnae want you working for C.R.O.W. or Lou because I didnae want her to put this on you." He swept the sigil again, took up her left hand, and did the same. Again, that thrill in her arms, the heat of her magick, but tempered now, as if her Way accepted his touch, *wanted* his touch, and recognized the same desire in her.

It should have been awkward, standing as she was with her back pressed against a Tudor-style gate, her wrists captured by a witch who crowded into her space. Instead, with Darkly towering over her, his words and gentle touch drowning out the world, a sense of safety descended over Milla. She inhaled, her chest expanding, her lungs filling enough for her to repeat the words Lou had used to convince her. "It's a lease."

"It's a leash." Darkly's gaze dropped to her mouth. He licked his lips, green eyes flicking up, and pressed both her hands to his chest over the triskelion he wore. She gasped at the rapid thudding of his heart. Heavy and strong, pounding beneath his ribs as though he had run a marathon to get to her. "Doesnae come off, Milla. The sigil is bound to your very Soul. She *owns* you like she owns—" His voice cracked. Darkly looked away, taking a moment to compose himself.

The gentle grip on her wrists eased further like he expected her to run and wanted to make it easy for her to do so. His shoulders dropped, and the defeat in his stance shone a new light on the witch.

He had said he needed her help and wanted to get back to his life, but then he had stayed. He had protected her, cared for her demesne, and helped Diego with the store, and Milla was terrified. This was real, too real, and one hundred percent why she avoided speaking to him.

"Everything changed," she whispered. Darkly jerked his face to hers, watching Milla intently as she spoke. "I went into that cell, and when I came out, everything had changed."

"*Leannán.*"

She curled her fingers into his shirt, shushing him. "I can't grab hold of it, Darkly. I feel like I'm a half-second out of time. Lou offered me a way to catch up. To be a part of my own life instead of standing on the side and watching it happen. Do you understand?" She searched his face, expecting anger or disgust or the pity or fear with which people often looked at her. Any of that would have been preferable to what she found: heartache. Need and longing and something else she refused to name. Not yet, not now. Not ever again.

Flattening her fingers, she slid her hands up his chest, breath catching when his eyelids fluttered closed as her fingertips brushed bare skin at the base of his throat. Warmth pooled in her palms, and she let it. Trusting herself for once.

"If the sigil means I can work my store"—she continued her slide up his throat, relishing his quick intake of breath when she curled her fingers, nails scaling the sensitive skin at the nape of his neck—"if it means I can touch you …"

She stilled as her palms cupped his cheeks. Days of stubble tickled her scars. His chest rose and fell beneath her arms, each breath bringing his body closer to hers. Smoke wafted over his eyes, but he held her gaze, fingers trembling where they still lightly circled her forearms.

"Milla." Her name rumbled in his chest, and the vibration of his wanting was the final straw.

"Shut up."

She popped onto her toes and crashed her mouth to his. No hesitation, no thought, only action, following the desire she'd been fighting since he walked into that office in his stupid, well-tailored suit.

Darkly let go of her arms, gathering Milla to himself as he returned the kiss. Soft at first and painfully tentative, as if she might change her mind. When she did not, when Milla clasped the sides of his head and held him to her, his tongue darted out, slipping between her lips.

At the briefest taste of her, all submissiveness in Darkly vanished. A rumble built in his chest, vibrating into Milla's bones. He gripped her waist, her hips, grabbing Milla's rear and hoisting her from the ground.

In a flash, her legs were around his waist, and Milla was a hundred miles away, back in that hallway in New Orleans, when he slammed her back against the wall. His kiss was just as hungry, just as frenzied, and Milla matched him in fire and fervor. She could not hold him close enough, could not touch enough of him at once, and she needed more.

He pulled away, snagging Milla's lower lip in his teeth as he allowed them a second to breathe, and then Darkly swept in, the thick slide of his tongue sending a heady pulse straight to her core.

Her nipples pebbled, scraping against his chest. She squeezed her thighs to gain leverage, to rock against him, seeking all of Darkly. His strength, his heat, his power.

Goddess, this could not be real. This was another tea-induced dream. A nightmare of longing and need, matched in the press of his fingers into her thighs and the teasing of thickness where she needed him most. They could not be here, finally here, after the touchless days and endless weeks in the dark where time made no sense. Where the hours passed in an instant, lasted for an eternity, and the voices in her head never ceased.

Those hours, days, and weeks spent thinking he had betrayed her when he had sold his freedom to gain Milla hers.

Darkly pressed a hand between her shoulder blades, crushing Milla tighter to his chest as if he heard her thoughts. He grounded her in the here and now with a too-hard kiss, a too-tight squeeze, setting every synapse in her mind aflame with the need in his demand. Lips, teeth, tongue. His thundering heartbeat, his mouth at her throat. Goddess, this was the kiss she'd ached for in Daytona. The embrace she had longed to forget in the cells. Passionate and all-consuming, erasing any errant thought beyond this.

Them.

Magick warmed her palms. A cool breeze curled lazily around them, their Ways waking and rising together as Milla and Darkly lost themselves in each other.

A faint chill crawled across her knuckles, distracting enough that she pulled away, eyeing the tail of shadow weaving through her fingers.

"Goddess, I missed you," Darkly rasped in her ear, sucking gently on a sensitive patch of skin. She arched into him, writhing at the sensation dribbling down her spine and into her hips. "Every day in that swamp was torture, *leannán*. Every night you were gone—"

"Don't." She forced his mouth back to hers. This was not the time to dwell on the weeks between them. Milla wanted to live in this moment for however long they were allowed, reveling in touching Darkly and not reliving her biggest fears.

She relaxed her thighs, brushing more against the hard length of him. Darkly groaned, the hand on her rear gripping tighter. His hips rolled, giving Milla more of what she sought, and Horned God-damned stars sparkled in her eyes.

"Please, Darkly," she moaned in a voice she hardly recognized. He rumbled in agreement, adjusting his grip and dropping Milla's ass on the slight ledge where support met beam. Stone scraped the backs of her thighs; aged wood replaced the press of his palm against her spine. Gripping her hips, Darkly tugged and angled Milla so he could rock against her. Pleasure rocketed through her body, and she dropped her head back. Splinters snagged her hair, and she vaguely registered the gabled roof and Tudor design of a lychgate.

She cocked her head, distracted by the oddity of a cemetery gateway hidden in the heart of Tallahassee, and then Darkly cupped her breast, thumb sweeping a nipple, and every cogent vanished.

"Can I?"

In lieu of words, Milla grasped the back of his head and guided his mouth to her breast. His dark chuckle shot straight to her core. He tugged her shirt and sportsbra low, freeing her breast. A lick of cold graced her peaked nipple. Milla hissed, further arching her back, and in one perfectly timed motion, Darkly lathed her nipple and rolled his hips, grinding his hard cock against her center.

A moan built in her throat, the pleasure of being touched too great to be contained. The hard press of fingers digging into her flesh. The grind of his cock and the heat of his mouth. The feel of *him*. It was too much and not enough, and Milla wanted more.

"Darkly," she pleaded, her voice a tight, needy whine.

"I ken," he murmured against her skin, kissing a line along her breastbone, down the swell of her other breast. "I ken."

"Please." She clutched his arms, wanting to hold the witch closer, tighter, never let go. Darkly's phone buzzed, the screen lighting up with a notification, and hers buzzed in the pocket of her shorts, the real world demanding their attention, but Milla only wanted to ignore her problems and the world to live in this moment as long as she could.

Darkly grunted, and whether it was from dismay or need, Milla could not tell. All she knew was that his hands frantically tugged at her shorts. He rocked her to the side, working a leg free. Cool stone met her heated flesh, but she had less than a heartbeat to register the sensation before his finger swept her folds. Sheer pleasure erupted, leaving her gasping, "Fuck."

"Too much?" He paused.

"Not enough." She wriggled her hips, seeking more touch, more heat, more warmth. "Nowhere near enough, Darkly."

He cursed, fumbling at his shorts and freeing his cock, all the while eyeing Milla hungrily—a look she knew mirrored her own. He was just as she remembered, thick and long, practically begging to be touched.

Her mouth went dry, fingers twitching where she gripped the stone, and a wicked grin stretched across his face. He gave his cock one long stroke, eyes dripping down her front, lingering on her bared breasts before dropping to her spread legs and sex. The dimple appeared, and his gaze darkened. He licked his lips, looking at her as if he would eat her up then and there, leaving nothing of the witch behind.

"Dinnae have anything." He angled closer as he stroked himself again, thumbing the head. Moisture beaded at the tip, and Milla whimpered, fighting the urge to grab him and haul him closer, the fucking tease.

"I'm a Death Witch." She cupped her breast instead, relishing how his devouring gaze focused on her fingers pinching a nipple. "I have it handled."

"There's a perk they dinnae list in any grimoire." That said, he grabbed her thigh and spread her further, sweeping the head of his cock through her folds.

A low groan forced its way out of her throat. Her pussy throbbed, clenching around nothing as he teased her again and again until she was writhing, nearly losing her balance on that narrow ledge. Until a tiny "please" escaped on the back end of a pant.

Darkly pulled away, still gripping her thigh to hold her open and wanton for him. With a glance at Milla and an even faster flash of that damnable dimple, he spat. The gob landed on his cock, and he stroked himself to the tip. That green gaze found her again, almost daring her to say something. To react. But what he had done, how he was holding her in place, precariously balanced and panting with need, it was all so fucking filthy.

She loved it. Loved that he gripped her too tight and pinned her in place, never afraid that she was weak or breakable. Just as in New Orleans, he handled Milla like the grown-ass, terrifying witch she was, and in that, the last of her restraint broke.

"Fuck me, Darkly."

The dimple deepened. Darkly slid his hand down her leg, spread her lips with two fingers, and thrust in. They groaned in tandem. Milla's head fell back with a thud against the wooden beam, and he buried his face in her neck. He held there, returning a hand to Milla's hip to brace her, giving her the time to adjust to his size. But in the tremor of his fingers, she knew he was holding back, clinging to his restraint and losing the battle.

She clenched around him, and his fingers squeezed tighter.

"Please," Milla whispered.

That one little word shattered whatever wall he'd been trying to build. He murmured something into her skin, sliding back and ramming deep, working his fingers into her braid at the base of her neck and hauling Milla's mouth to his.

Coarse stone scraped her backside, her scalp pinched. A decadent burn blossomed deep in her pussy as he filled her and fucked her with intoxicating abandon. She could barely breathe, barely hold on, and Darkly kept her pinned in place with his body, the hand at her hip, the fingers knotted in her hair.

Her nails drove into his shoulders and scraped his scalp, seeking any handhold. Darkly was relentless, hitching his hips to score against a place that had her whimpering a tight, desperate sound into his mouth and biting his shoulder when he let her breathe.

"Goddess, Milla," he grunted, slowing his pace and hitting her with a wild, manic look. Pupils blown out, color high on his cheeks, his lips swollen from the ferocity of their kisses.

"Harder," she demanded, and he delivered. The cadence of his thrusts grew frantic, and he drove a hand between them, thumb brushing Milla's clit as he pounded her into the beam of the lychgate. Fire erupted in her core, clawing up her front and bleeding into her arms. Stars danced in her eyes, and cool whisps teased her arms, her breasts, drawing Darkly and Milla closer and closer, as if the Shades could bind them together, body and Soul.

She fluttered her hands along his jaw, the heat building until it was too intense to think. She existed on the brink of absolute pleasure, winding tighter and tighter, and right when she would fall, Darkly withdrew from her clit, changing the cadence of his thrusts and leaving Milla dizzy and teetering on the edge.

"Please, Darky," she gasped, trying to lift his head to gain some reprieve if he would not let her come.

He grunted and snatched her wrists mid-thrust, hauling them over her head. She cried out in surprise as he slammed them against the wooden beam and locked them in place with one hand. With his other hand, he trailed feather-soft fingers down her jaw to her neck. His fingers spread wide, and he caged Milla's throat, lifting her chin so she could barely look him in the eye.

Euphoria rushed over her body from head to toe. The power, the control he had exerted with such ease, only to hesitate now. Waiting.

"Too much?" Deep and gravelly, his voice held a hint of teasing as though he knew her answer before posing the question. She gave the tiniest little shake of her head, and he frowned. Leaning closely, he pressed a chaste kiss to her lips. Wild, considering he was balls deep in her pussy and restraining her against a beam. "*Too much, Ludmilla?*"

That voice shivered into her ears, joining the tingling in her limbs and toes, the heat in her belly, and drawing an answer out with an unspoken demand.

"No."

"Good witch." He adjusted his grip on her wrists, glancing up quickly before asking, "Too far?"

Milla looked down her nose at him, clenching his cock as best she could to drive her following words home, lest there be any confusion. "Not far enough."

He grinned wickedly and increased the pressure on Milla's throat, sending another euphoric wave of sensation rolling through her mind. A cry escaped, her voice foreign to her ears. She sounded wild and wicked, wholly given over to pleasure.

Darkly latched his mouth onto her shoulder, teeth scoring her skin. The pain of it had her crying out, but the bright, burning sensation muddled with the pleasure of his cock, the dizziness from his hand on her throat. Goddess, had she known it would be like *this* …

She was his in this moment. Totally and utterly a fool for Darkly, and she wouldn't have it any other way.

A hitch of his leg, a pivot of his hips, and the orgasm she had been flirting with rushed forward. Her body flashed hot; sweat beaded at the base of her spine. Pleasure coiled tighter, turning her gasps into high, tight whimpers, and Darkly was no better off. His thrusts again took on that frantic edge as he chased his climax, fucking Milla hard enough to scrape her ass raw against the stone.

His mouth crashed against hers, stealing the last of Milla's breath, and the utter consumption had her tipping over the edge. Sound muted out as pleasure consumed her, pulsing the length of her arms and belling out like a shockwave from the very core of her. Distantly, she heard Darkly cry out and felt the slippery-sticky gush of release as he fucked through his orgasm, that delicious cadence slowing and ceasing.

Gently, he lowered her arms, panting with his face buried in her neck, murmuring sweet words and adulations as he massaged her wrists, palms, and fingers. Slipping out of Milla, he hoisted her arms onto his shoulders and gathered her to himself, kissing her throat and trailing the tender flesh with that feather-soft touch she adored, soothing the burn from his palm as they came down from the shared high of release.

Thirty-Four

BURNOUT Loss of magick due to excess use and lack of control. Commonly suffered in rituals where the casting witch holds the Ways too long in liminality.

"HORNED GOD," SHE MANAGED after a good long while.

"Mm." Darkly stroked her back, his low voice a satisfying rumble along her shoulder and down her spine. "You alright?" he asked after another long moment. Milla might have fallen asleep; she wasn't sure. Her body was languid and loose, all the tension, all the strain she had been carrying for, Goddess, *years*, gone and happily forgotten for the moment.

"More than," she said, leaning back to assess the damage. Her Way had risen so quickly, and she had been so lost in Darkly. Little by little, tension returned to her shoulders, that band tightening around her chest as she scanned his arms, his shirt, his lovely face and found—no rot.

Not a rash, not a blemish or a blister. Only the flushed cheeks and hazy stare of a sated man.

He blinked slowly at her, stealing a soft, sweet kiss and pulling away when the phone in his armband began buzzing. Lou's name lit up the screen, and he frowned, taking a quick step to keep his balance like he was walking on the deck of a ship.

"Are *you* alright?"

"Well fucked," he answered in a distracted voice. He pulled the phone free and sent Milla an apologetic half-smile. "I should probably…"

"Yeah." Milla stared dazedly at him, raised her palms, and assessed herself. Her Way was there, the pleasant, warm thrum in her veins, but it was—not dormant, but calm. Confused, she hopped off the stone support, wobbling on shaking legs. The ground at her feet seemed to swell and then settled as Milla regained her balance. Wincing at the raw scrapes on her ass, she pressed her palm to a cheek and muttered, "*Návrat.*" It was weak, but it sufficed, and the tell-tale tingle of healing magick bloomed against her skin.

"Aye?" Darkly glanced over, listening to whatever Lou was saying, as Milla healed the rest of her scrapes and pressed a palm to her lower abdomen. An eyebrow raised in question, and she turned away. Not that she was embarrassed. She had told him this was part of her Way, and he knew who she was. Still, a lady deserved to have her secrets.

"*Zemřít.*" Die.

She whispered the killing hex, wavering where she stood as the rush of her Way took her from sated to tipsy.

"Some park off High Road," Darkly told his sister. He angled his face in her direction, brow furrowing as she slapped a hand on the wooden beam where he'd just—wow, okay, that happened. "I've Milla, yes. What's happened?"

Millapet.

She whirled around, nearly tripping over her shorts and bat-printed panties, her buzzed mind blaming Darkly for the nickname. His back was turned, the witch deep in conversation with his sister, and the world beyond the lychgate was cloaked in shadow.

Tugging on her clothes, she stepped closer to the Shades shutting them off from the world, trailing fingers through cool, touchless smoke and fog. Faint murmurs could be heard through the mass, distant and far away. Edged in panic. Milla jerked her hand back, marveling at the privacy Darkly had cast Horned God knew when.

Millapet.

A whorl of smoke broke free from the mass, swelling toward Milla.

"Cannae be." Darkly raised his voice.

The shadow retreated, and a new voice broke through the muted silence. "Do you smell that?"

Darkly whipped his face to Milla, the startled look on his face enough to have her tugging her sports bra back into place and bracing her legs, ready for whatever waited on the other side of those shadows. Warmth pooled in her palms, a trickle of what she was capable of, but it would be enough. It had to be. Twenty percent of her strength, enough to heal scrapes and desecrate cells. Enough to cause a little hurt.

With a sweep of his hand, Darkly felled the shadows, and both witches staggered at the onslaught of—nothing.

Empty night.

Where before the air had crackled with magick, raising goosebumps and tickling their senses, now there was nothing. Only spent aether, the energy sucked from the atmosphere like oxygen at the striking of a match. Darkly staggered back, horror overwhelming the shock on his face, and Milla—Milla knew this hell. Had lived it for weeks on end in the cells and the moments following a ritual's end.

"Darkly—"

He threw out an arm, silencing Milla and scanning the trees as Lou spoke. "No one, just the two of us—aye, for twenty minutes at least. Lou, what's—" He glanced at Milla, eyes darting from her head to her feet, then higher. His eyes widened, and he staggered back. "A lychgate."

She twisted around, taking in the gabled roof and stone support. Now that he called it out, Milla recognized how weird it was to find a lychgate in Tallahassee. They were more common in English villages, meant to shelter a coffin or a body awaiting the clergyman and burial. Yet here one stood beside an old-growth oak, tangled among the low, sweeping branches.

Darkly's thumb pressed the screen on his phone, and he lowered his arm. "What're the odds we fucked under a lychgate?"

Milla huffed a laugh. She had to, or else she would start freaking out. "Can't say what the odds are, but at least it's on brand." A faint smile curled his mouth, and then he ran a hand over his head, the familiar motion more telling than his expression. "What's happened?"

"The ritual, a power surge, it—"

"Milla!" Diego's call shattered the empty night, echoing off the trees. "Pequeña bruja, where are you?"

"Here!" She darted blindly in the direction of his voice. I'm here!"

Darkly cursed and took off behind her. Soft white light from his headlamp illuminated the woods and, several paces away, Diego's stooped figure. Trav leaned heavily against him, head lolling and legs barely holding him upright. One long arm was draped across

Diego's shoulders, and her roommate looked wild and beyond terrified.

"Milla," he grunted, relief washing over his face when he saw her. "Help me, please."

Darkly rushed past, hoisting Trav's other arm across his broader back and easing his weight off Diego. The cultist groaned, mumbling unintelligibly, and slumped against Darkly, who staggered and adjusted his hold. "Mate…"

"Do you feel it?" Diego cast a wild look at the pair, the trees, then to Milla. "My Way, it's—" Flexing the fingers of his casting hand, he shook his head, stupefied. "It is gone. One moment Trav was fine, he was fine, and the next." He flicked his fingers outward, a motion Milla had seen him do whenever he stepped into his Way. "Nada."

"Burnout," Darkly said, scanning the trees.

"You've felt this before?" She did not know why it surprised her. He was an Enforcer and, from what she had seen of his sparring, damn good at hand-to-hex. She just had not thought of Darkly taking part in large rituals or pushing himself far enough to reach the dregs of his magick. That felt like more of a *her* thing to do. Except—she flexed her fingers, waving her hand through the empty, dead air—why did she feel the warm pulse of her Way?

Darkly must have come to the same realization. He frowned, raising a hand, and a slip of shadow bloomed in his palm. Trav gasped, head lifting, and blinked dazedly at the Shade. He whimpered and pressed against Darkly enough to have him snuffing out his Way.

"Aye, and dinnae fancy reliving the experience." His eyes bled black, and he jerked his head to the west, heaving Trav into a walk. "Come on."

He led them to an abandoned house tucked well back from the road and hidden among the trees. A handful of cultists staggered around what once was a front lawn, all of them dazed and morose, a far cry from the celebrant mood from the campground.

Headlamps and lanterns flooded the area with light, and Milla picked out the signs of a ritual scattered across the overgrown lawn: candles and black salt, focal stones, and empty vials. Goddess, the cleanup was going to be a nightmare.

A trio huddled together on what must have been the driveway. Donmar's large figure beside two smaller cultists. Josh, she recognized, but the woman was a stranger to her. Curvy and stern-faced, she shook her head at something Donmar said, her disheveled ponytail bobbing. Josh stooped into a crouch as they approached, examining a pile of clothing or blankets on the ground.

"Donny," Darkly hailed his brother-in-law, "have you seen Lou? Thought I tracked her here."

Donmar whipped his head in their direction. "Careful," he warned. Milla did not have a chance to wonder why—her next step had her swaying, knocked off balance by the absolute vacuum of power. The void was harsher here, a deep, hollow wrongness. Her Way flared, tingling against her palms and begging to be let out to feed the space. Diego grabbed her arm, cursing in Spanish as they entered the residual influence of whatever magick had been cast, while Darkly charged forward, unbothered, with Trav shuffling his feet to keep up.

"Where did it go?" he asked in a tiny voice. Diego squeezed Milla's arm, and she was struck by the intense worry on his face. He had not taken his eyes off Trav as they hustled after Darkly, his body practically trembling as he restrained himself from stealing the mortal man back.

"He'll be okay," she whispered, putting her hand over his.

Diego nodded, intent on the cultist as Darkly eased him onto a wrought iron bench choked with weeds and kudzu. Shadow trickled from his arm onto Trav, and he shot upright, blinking as though he'd just gotten a straight shot of adrenaline.

"Oh, God."

"Easy," Darkly said in a low voice. "Wee sips. Diego?"

With a tiny, tight sound, Diego darted over, kneeling in front of Trav and cupping his cheeks. He brought their foreheads together, speaking in too low a voice to catch. Darkly stepped aside to give them privacy, a Shade still circling his arm.

"How are you doing that?" The woman with the ponytail stormed over, glaring at Darkly, Trav, and the Shade. "How the hell are you doing magick?"

"I'm a witch." He straightened and glared down at her. "Who are you?"

"Cicerhoe, I'm helping run this shitshow." The woman stomped a foot, hands fisting at her hips. She lifted her chin, somehow managing to look down at the witch towering over her and immediately winning Milla over. "Who the fuck are you?"

"Keir!" Lou stormed around the side of the house, madder than Milla had ever seen her. Nostrils flared and cheeks flushed, she charged around Donmar and Josh, heading straight for her brother. "Can one of you two idiots explain to me what's just happened?"

"Lou—"

"Why were you off the bleeding trail?"

"I was following Milla." Darkly subtly put himself between Milla and Lou, and for once, Milla did not mind being protected. "Lou, what's happened?"

"The bloody Witch of the Demesne is dead; that's what's happened." She pointed at the pile of clothes at Donmar's feet, and only then did Milla clock the running shoes poking out from beneath the blanket she had mistaken for clothes. Josh, still crouched low beside the body, ran a hand over his face and covered his mouth.

"Horned God." Milla grabbed Darkly's hand without giving the motion any thought. He glanced down at her, lacing their fingers together and tugging her closer.

"Keir," Lou prompted.

"On it," he rumbled, eyes dripping a darker shade of black. He scanned the grounds and the body and shook his head. "No lingering Shades. I could shadestep …"

"Later." Lou shook her head. "We've too much to do here."

"How did he die?" Milla asked.

"The ritual." Tobias jogged up the driveway, not even breathing heavily, the maniac. "If I am interpreting my E.R.I.E. correctly. I suppose we can assume the same happened to the missing witches. Has anyone seen Cyrus?"

"At the campground." Lou sighed and looked at her brother, voice dripping in disappointment. "You'd better have a damned good reason for straying from the trail, Keir, or so help me—"

"Toby was on it." He jerked his chin at Tobias. "I left him with the front runners when I saw Milla dart into the woods. Forgive me for trying to keep one of our own safe."

"Oh, is that what you were doing?" Lou scoffed. "You had a task to attend to. The rogue witches were here, and now we've got a dead hippocromantic on our hands because you were distracted. Explain yourselves. What did you do?"

"Nothing," Darkly protested.

"The E.R.I.E. doesn't lie, Keir." Lou hauled her phone out and showed them the E.R.I.E. Only two signatures warbled across the screen, the rise and fall Milla recognized as her own and Darkly's. "You two gobshites are the only witches not suffering a burnout, and the Horned God damned demesne has no bloody witch at the helm; what did you *do?*"

"Nothing!" Milla shouted. "We were arguing, and then we—" She gestured from herself to Darkly, protest falling away when she noticed the faint black line curling around the tips of her nails. At the sight of it, she recalled the warmth of her Way responding to Darkly. The heat surging in her veins as he brought her to climax. Like in New Orleans, when she summoned that Shade. And the roadside motel. And in her swamp hut. "Oh."

"Oh?" Lou arched an eyebrow.

"Ah, nein." Tobias pressed a hand to his forehead.

"Um…" Milla looked over at Darkly, whose grip on her hand tightened. He had staggered, that quick little half step. And the ground had swelled when Milla hopped off the stone support. Darkly's throat bobbed as he swallowed, probably recalling the same thing, and in tandem, they looked at the ground.

"What. Did. You. Do." Lou leaned in close, her voice lowered but no less sinister.

"I don't know!" She ripped her hand free from Darkly's, putting distance between them. It was bad enough a witch had died, but if she was right, if they had done what Milla thought they had done, even by accident, this was going to get *messy*. "I was looking for Darkly because I found out he'd been moonlighting as the steward of my demesne, and then I saw Diego, and he—"

"We argued," Darkly interjected. "And we settled the disagreement."

Tobias muttered in German. From Darkly's quick scowl, it did not translate into anything nice.

Lou's mouth went tight, and she blinked rapidly at her brother. "Are you implying that by hate-fucking your *Death Witch* girlfriend, you two managed to not only protect yourselves from burnout but also *steal an entire demesne?*"

"I'm not his girlfriend," Milla protested. Darkly moved his scowl from Tobias to her.

"I don't want to hear it." Lou pinched the bridge of her nose. "Horned God knows we've all had enough of your relationship drama to last us a decade, Keir." She slammed her palm against his chest, snapping out her intent before Darkly could react. "*Dún.*"

He staggered from the sudden loss of his Way, grabbing onto Milla to keep standing.

"Hey, whoa." She planted her feet to keep from dropping under his sudden weight and glared at Lou. "How in the nine rings did you do that? There's no *magick.*"

"S'latent magick." Darkly dropped his forehead against her shoulder, panting to catch his breath. "Like a dispellation."

Latent magick. What was born in the witch, the truest form of their ability that, when connected with magick as a whole, became their Way.

"Managing the Soul is as inherent to me as breathing," Lou sniffed.

"But you can't just ground him like that," she argued.

"I can, and I will." Lou seized Milla's wrists with an alarming speed. She yelped, jerked off balance, and this time, Darkly reacted.

"Lou, no."

"*Dún.*"

The warmth in her arms vanished, and Milla stumbled forward as Lou dropped her arms, the Soul binding on her wrists like a heavy, weighted manacle. She gasped from the shock, barely registering Darkly's gentle grasp on her shoulders.

"We have a dead witch of the demesne," Lou kept on, walking toward Donmar and the cultists, her back turned now that Milla and Darkly were safely leashed. "A joint challenge for control of greater Tallahassee, Horned God help you both"—this was shot over her shoulder with a disdainful sneer—"and absolutely zero answers as to what or who we are facing. If I can resolve one of our issues, even if only for a moment, I will."

"That's nae fair, Lou."

"What's not *fair* is the amount of times I have had to cover your ass in the last three months, Keir." She stood over the body, staring down at the dead witch, and sighed. "We've a bloody crisis on our hands, and as the Elder Witch of this coven, it is my responsibility to handle it. Now somebody get Cyrus on the phone and Horned God help him if he hasn't parsed out this fucking data."

Donmar fumbled at his phone, and a moment later electronic ringing came over the speaker.

"Donny?" Rai's posh voice, tinny and frantic, cut through the tense silence. Donmar frowned, glancing at his screen. "Oh, thank the Horned God, Donny. It's madness over here. Do you have everyone?"

"Yes, mostly," he answered, still confused. "Why do you have Cyrus's phone?"

"He left it here to go find you. Goddess, these cultists have lost the plot. I don't have enough tea to go around, where are you? I need help—" she yelped, and a scuffle came over the line. "I said I *can't*," Rai hollered. "I've got no bloody magick, you wanker."

"Rai?" Darkly grabbed the phone out of Donmar's hand. "Rai, what's happened?"

"Cultists," she snapped. "They're desperate, where are you?"

"Where is Cyrus?" Lou stole the phone away. Her eyes tripped over the witches, and warning trickled down Milla's spine from the fear in her expression.

"He went to find you," Rai answered. "Twenty minutes ago, before whatever happened happened. Is he not there?"

"No." Lou exhaled, her gaze dropping to the body at her feet. She chewed her lower lip, and her expression was set and stern when she raised her head. "Keir?"

Darkly stepped forward without a word, eyes dropping to Lou's hand as she pressed the tips of her fingers against his chest.

"Do you need it all?" she asked. Darkly shook his head, visibly shaken by the news. The ritual had happened, and they had failed to stop it. A witch was *dead*, and one of their own was missing. "Alright. Be quick, and come back to me, wee yin."

"Aye, big yin," he said in a low voice.

Lou murmured her intent, and Darkly inhaled deeply as his Way was given back, his chest filling and shoulders squaring. "Find Cyrus," she said, then pointed at the body. "Find this dead witch; find *anyone* who can tell me what the hell just happened."

He nodded, mouth a tight line, black eyes narrowed. With less than a thought, he traced a sigil in the air. Smoke and shadow bloomed at his back, a whorling, contained stygian black cloud against the deepset night. As easy as opening an envelope, Darkly tore open a hole in the world and stepped through.

Thirty-Five

SHADESTEPPING

stepping into the Neitherworld, either with only my shade, or all of me. Can be jarring for onlookers.

— massive understatement

"YOU DID WHAT?" CONSTANCE raised her bejeweled glasses, perching them on her forehead. Even behind her massive desk, the witch was a force to be reckoned with, and that was before she accounted for the dual digital presences of Natje and Dina, the Third Head of the Tribunal, glaring at her from separate monitors.

"I lost control of my Way as a non-sanctioned ritual reached its liminal edge," Milla recited the practiced line, beat into her skull during the two-hour drive from Tallahassee. She kept her eyes pinned to a spot over Constance's head, silently praying to the Triple Goddess, Horned God, and whoever would listen that they took her words at point-blank value.

"We believe the ritual cost the former Witch of the Demesne his life," Natje said from her computer screen. It had to be close to six in the morning in Germany, and the witch was as cooly put together as always. Her gunmetal gray silk robe offset the sharp blue of her eyes, making her dark hair and blunt bangs all the more striking. She had taken Milla's call immediately and arranged for this web conference while demanding Milla appear in person before Constance. "A Terence Tonaby."

"Hippocromantic," Constance said with a nod. The skin between her brows bunched. "A good witch, old family in the local covens." She eyed Milla, full mouth pinched, and tapped the desk. "And in the instance of his death, you lost control, feeding Tonaby's Demesne with your Way—"

"And my brother's," said Lou. Constance glanced at her and on her screen, Dina laughed.

"I was under the impression Agent Simmons was acting steward of the St. Augustine demesne," Dina said with a smile. "Am I now to believe that a Dark Witch is not only sharing the duties with Ludmilla but that he *also* holds a claim to Tallahassee?"

"I'm pretty sure he'd rather not," Milla grumbled. Natje scowled at her through her screen, and Milla stared at her hands gripping her knees.

This would be easier if Darkly were here. He knew how to talk to these witches. Knew better how to play their games, but Darkly was … not Gone. He couldn't be Gone, but Milla had no idea where he'd gone. He had simply stepped into the Neitherworld—which, *WHAT?*—leaving Milla to manage this by herself. And then she'd been on the phone with Natje, lectured by Lou, and, finally, sat back in this leather seat to be interrogated by Constance and Dina.

She really needed to learn how to break free from negative cycles because this shit was exhausting.

"Section F, sub-section 14-c states that a witch cannot be held liable for theft, possession, or unlawful retention of a demesne whether accidental, intentional, or circumstantial in instances where a disruptive vacuum can or has been avoided," Natje stated.

"If my reading of C.R.O.W. legislation is correct, and I assure you it is, Milla is within her rights as a Witch of the Demesne to manage Tallahassee as well as St. Augustine."

Dina snorted, covering her mouth with a hand. She waved at the webcam and adjusted her fluffy pink robe. "Don't mind me."

"Well." The wicker-backed chair creaked as Constance rocked side-to-side, lacing fingers over her front. Though it was close to midnight, she was still somewhat dressed in a loose tunic top and capris. No rings or baubles adorned her person, and she must have been in the process of removing her makeup as she had walked into her office with a jar of cold cream in hand and a bonnet on her head. "All well and good then, so long as our Death Witch doesn't come for my demesne." She chuckled, and the laughter failed to move beyond her mouth. "There is the matter of Beltane, however."

Milla straightened, forcing herself not to look at Lou in the chair beside her. The witch had not settled. She was all hard lines and stress, her normally bright blue-green eyes dimmed by the burnout.

"What of it?"

"Ludmilla owes a tithe to the ritual as it is," Constance said. "We would have been happy with a small demonstration to reflect St. Augustine, but as we have no witch in the wings prepared to take on Tallahassee, and she has wrangled joint control of the demesne with a Dark Witch…"

She let the implication hang in the air, and Milla's stomach sank.

She owed more.

"Can't I just pay it? Like with cash?"

Constance pinched her lips in a smile, and Dina outright cackled. "I'll be booking my tickets tonight then," she said. "Wouldn't want to miss this."

"What does she mean?' Milla finally looked to Lou, whose face was grim. A bad sign, considering Natje looked just as somber.

"She means that you and my brother will need to put on one hell of a show."

Despite the late hour, lights blazed on both sides of the duplex. Lou burst into Darkly's half, storming down the hall without a word to Milla, and she stepped into her home. To her surprise, Tobias sat in her armchair, reading one of the fantasy romance novels from her bookshelf, and across from him, Darkly's long body lay stretched out on the couch.

"He came straight here," Tobias said in lieu of greeting. "I thought Trav would scheisse himself."

Milla lingered at the entryway, her heart doing odd flips in her chest as she took in Darkly's greying skin and sunken cheeks. Still in his running clothes, shoes and all, he looked diminished, almost frail. "What is he doing?"

"Shadestepping."

"The thing where his Shade leaves?" It was hard to explain, considering she'd only seen him do it a few times—in a voodoo graveyard, Dies-well's van, and again in the Fountain of Youth. She could still hear the sound of his six feet and change hitting the floor like a lifeless sack of meat and greatly wished she could not. "Isn't that dangerous?"

"Somewhat." Tobias closed the book and set it on the arm of the chair. "He can either sever his Shade and send it to do his bidding on this plane of existence or enter their realm to discuss matters directly with the Shades."

"It makes less sense the more you explain it," she said.

"Sí. Exactamente," Diego added from the kitchen. He appeared a moment later with a tray laden with tea, cheese, meats, and crackers, setting it on the coffee table. "Lavender," he told Milla. "Not that mierda Lou has you drinking."

"Thank you." She took the offered teacup, frowning at the tremble in her fingers. "How is Trav?"

"Upstairs," Diego answered, not looking at her as he handed a cup to Tobias. "Sleeping, I hope."

"Is he alright?"

Diego sent her a bleak look. "No sé."

"He slept most of the drive," Tobias added. "Lou?"

"Next door." Milla tipped her head at the wall and settled cross-legged beside the coffee table, right in reach of the snacks.

Tobias nodded, easing back in the chair. "Donmar knows everything we do, and Rai is there. With any luck, we will have a reprieve for the night."

Milla gripped her teacup in both hands, sighing as the warmth bled into her palms. "What have we learned?"

"Nothing regarding Cyrus's whereabouts." Diego sat opposite Milla, his back against the bookshelf. "Darkly could not find him in … there." He fluttered fingers at Darkly, gesturing to the Neitherworld, or so Milla supposed. "He unleashed a cloud of smoke in the living room about an hour ago, said he could not find him, and then he—"

"Keeled over," Milla cut him off, gathering what had happened, "and sent his Shade off?"

Tobias nodded. "He is attempting to gather the Shades of the missing witches."

"The dead witches," she said. But what else was she supposed to believe? With any luck, their Shades would still be lingering, and Darkly could gather information from them.

"Hippocromantics." Diego sent her a look she had no hope of translating. "At least, three of them were, from Cyrus's reports." He dropped his head back, staring at the ceiling. "How did it go in Jacksonville?"

"Well, I'm not going to be cleaved," Milla said. "Again."

"And?" Diego eyed her down the line of his nose.

"And, according to Natje, Darkly and I can legally run two demesnes, though I don't know how I'm supposed to do that from here."

"If you tend this demesne with Keir, he should be able to step to Tallahassee and tend that demesne as well," Tobias said as if it were obvious.

"Wait." Milla pressed a hand in the air as her weary mind put together what Tobias and Diego had just said. "Wait, wait, wait. He came straight *here* … are you saying you didn't drive him here?"

"Ja."

"Did you not hear me?" Diego pointed at Darkly. "He *unleashed* a cloud of smoke in the living room."

"I thought—I thought you waited for him. Not that he—" She fluttered an exasperated hand at the empty air over Darkly's body. "You know."

"Traveled through the Neitherworld?" Tobias raised his brows, sending Milla a fond little smile that was somehow more disturbing than the not-corpse on her couch. "I am more surprised he established your living room as an anchor." He swept his gaze over her travel posters and the potted ficus in the corner. "Or maybe it is the demesne?"

"I literally can't with this," she muttered into her teacup.

"How do you think he brought the motorcycle from Scotland?" Diego added with a tiny laugh.

"Shut up." The back door creaked, and the floorboards groaned, but Milla was too far gone to care about who might be sneaking into her house. "He took a *motorcycle* through the Neitherworld?"

"Goddess, I wish he would leave it there," Lou said, entering the living room with Donmar following close behind. She frowned at her brother's corpse-like figure on the couch, then looked to Tobias. "What do we have."

"Hippocromantics," he replied. "In Savannah, Valdosta, and the ritual outside of Houston."

"And the rest?"

"Josh and Tammy thought they were a vinefica and a chronomantic," Diego answered. "The third one they were not sure, and when I filtered the E.R.I.E. to account for social distortion, I identified a summoning."

"A summoning?" Milla clutched her tea. Every hair on the back of her neck rose. "How did you learn that?"

"Cyrus taught me," Diego said breezily. "Technomancy is similar to my Way." He waggled his fingers with a sly little smirk. "Different strands, lines of code, es lo mismo."

"Did he—" Milla glanced around the room and swallowed, struck by the absence of Cyrus. For a witch so easily overlooked, he left a large void. "Did anyone layer the E.R.I.E. from these rituals against the signature captured at Lake Pontchartrain?"

"I do not know …" Diego tipped his head in thought. With a twist of his wrist, one of the tablets Cyrus often worked on appeared in his hand. "But if that ritual was recorded in the database, I could pull it up and compare."

"What are you thinking?" Lou asked.

"What do you know?" Milla asked. Her situation was sticky enough without admitting to a room of Enforcer's anything C.R.O.W. might not already know.

In reply, Lou arched an eyebrow and glanced at her brother.

Donmar made a sound deep in his throat and shook his head with a wry look at his wife, then Milla. "There is not much Keir keeps from his sister, little witch."

"Alright, hate that." Milla chewed her lip, thinking through her next words. "I'm just wondering. We don't know what these witches are doing, but their intent mimics my Way—wait." She splayed her fingers in Diego's direction. "He was recording the other day when I summoned Darkly's Shades, right?" Diego tapped the screen, scrolled, and nodded. "Look for anything resembling that. It's what I did at the start of the Lake Pontchartrain ritual."

The number of witches Marie had gathered for that ritual, the *power* they had needed to amass for Milla to stand a chance of tearing a seam between worlds and successfully opening the Gates—that was one thing. But it was the first part of the ritual when she did the one thing a Death Witch could do that would require a full constellation of witches to achieve. If she was right, and these ritualists were attempting anything remotely similar, then that was where they needed to start.

Why else would you need to mimic a Death Witch for a summons if not to summon Shades?

Donmar cleared his throat, and Lou glanced again at her brother, likely remembering why Milla had been able to summon those Shades in the first place: he had been in a coma, and there was no one to stop her.

"You think they're mimicking New Orleans?" Tobias leaned forward, fingers laced between his knees.

"I think …" Milla paused, running through the words before she said them. It was a weak link, a thought she could barely grasp, but it was more than anyone else had, and she was a vestic. Even being half as strong as her mother, she could split the potentials and See. It would give them something, a heading, but in place of that, she had her instincts, and they had never led her wrong.

Okay, they had *mostly* never led her wrong, Ezra aside. And Darkly. And Anaisa.

Holy Horned God, we're fucked.

"I think," she repeated, "these witches need a Death Witch for their ritual."

"Death Witchual," Donmar muttered, mostly to himself.

"And Cyrus got some good readings on my Way at the casting range and probably tonight. While the earlier rituals in Texas were around sabbats, leeching off the power of Mabon and Samhain, the recent rituals broke the pattern. But what if they didn't?"

Lou narrowed her eyes at Milla. "Go on."

"What if it's a new pattern?" she asked. "Darkly and I were in Tallahassee earlier this year. Our escort out of New Orleans couldn't drive into the dawn, so we stopped at this roadside motel. The Flamingo something."

"There was a cache of magick tonight at the Flamingo Roadside." Tobias sat up straight. "Neon and pink?"

"That's the one." Goosebumps erupted down her arms as another piece clicked into place, one that did not have her coming out of this looking good. "What if the recent rituals are following me, and they're using the cultists to agitate the echoes of my Way into something they can use?"

A thick, wet blanket of silence fell over the room. Lou and Donmar shared a long look, and enough time passed that Milla began to doubt herself, but the inkling was there. A thin thread dangling from the mass she could almost reach.

"We were in Tallahassee, and both used our Ways. My old tea came from Savannah. I send charged talismans a couple of times a year. I think I saw an email asking for a new one from when I was gone. What if my signature was strong enough to attract this coven? Like how you read it off of Darkly."

Lou again frowned at her brother's body, lips pursed as she thought. "And Valdosta?" she asked. Milla exhaled, relief rushing over her. Lou believed her and, if not endorsing her reasoning, saw enough in what she suggested to entertain her logic.

"I'm not sure; I need to make a call." And hope the person on the other end was willing to talk to her, which was a problem for future Milla. "This is hella specious, but if I'm right, it would explain why they ran the ritual there."

"Make your call." Lou nodded and sat on the armrest by her brother's feet. It took Milla a moment to realize she meant now.

"It's midnight."

"And one of our witches is missing; make the call."

"Hah, no." Milla set her tea down with a loud tink. "Waking someone up in the dead of night is a terrible way to get information."

Lou opened her mouth to argue, and Donmar stopped her by dropping a large hand on her shoulder. "They are exhausted, Lou," he said. "You are exhausted. Let Keir work, and let the rest of us sleep. We cannot think straight when we are running on gas."

"Fumes," Diego corrected without looking up from the tablet. "Running on fumes."

The large Kazakh nodded his thanks and tugged Lou to her feet. "We can meet in the morning, but the team needs to sleep."

"We don't have time," she argued, following Donmar into the hallway.

"We need rest to recover from burnout." To elaborate, Tobias pinched his fingers together and splayed them quickly. A blue flame sputtered and vanished. "The ritualists will be in a similar state. It will take them days to recover enough magick to try again."

And another piece snapped into place.

"Oh, shit."

Every witch looked at Milla, and she really, really hoped she was wrong. But white spots danced at the corners of her eyes, and the room blurred suddenly as a potential unveiled itself—so obvious, so plain and under their noses that she should have seen it earlier.

She swallowed the lump in her throat and said, "Beltane."

"What?"

"Beltane. Next weekend." Milla glanced from witch to witch, each looking as sick as she felt, except for Darkly, who looked like death. "It's the largest gathering of witches in the southeast, and guess who just got signed up to display her Way in front of all of them?"

"They would not." Tobias's jaw went hard, and the stern expression she was so used to darkened his features. "To disrupt a ritual of that size is anathema."

"They've been dropping witches left and right." Lou pulled out her phone, typing a message as she issued orders. "They absolutely would. Ludmilla, keep talking."

"They've been mimicking my Way, but if they try at Beltane after I've paid my ritual dues, they won't have to mimic anything; they'll just have it."

"That is assuming they know you will be there."

"They will if they check their email," Diego said, holding up his tablet and showing the room a list of names. "Constance announced the attending witches yesterday."

Lou sat with that for a beat, blinked three times in quick succession, and groaned as she ran a hand down her face. "So we assume our ritualists know Ludmilla is paying into the ritual dues. That still is not enough to connect her with being a Death Witch." She paused and angled her face at Diego. "Is it?"

"Sí."

"Yes, it is enough, or yes, it is not?"

"Sí, it is not. No Ways are mentioned in the newsletter, only their demesnes, and Milla is still recorded as 'Vestic, unregistered' in the directory."

"There's a Witch of the Demesne directory?" she asked. Will wonders never cease.

"Of course there is." Diego flicked hair off his shoulder and tapped on his tablet, showing Milla an alphabetized directory of Gulf demesnes. "This is the twenty-first century."

"So." Tobias slapped his knees. "Assuming they know Milla is feeding into the ritual and will attend to take advantage of her Way, we have still not resolved the chicken-egg question."

"I understand that now." Donmar clapped his hands, grinning broadly. Milla could not help but smile back. For such a large, imposing witch, he certainly found it easy to laugh when the mood was dark. Must be how he survived being married to Lou. "Do they know Milla's Way will be at Beltane, or do they know that Beltane will create enough power for them to mimic Milla's Way?"

"Thank you, Donny," Lou sighed.

"Think about it." Milla sat up on her knees. "They've been popping up in places that tie back to me. It's too many coincidences, even if you aren't a witch. And like Cyrus said, there weren't any records of my Way in the E.R.I.E., so how would they know how to find the echoes unless they were already *familiar* with my magick?" She took a deep breath, or rather, tried to, but her heart was beating so quickly it felt like her lungs were atrophying. "Unless they were there that night."

"On the lake?" Diego asked. "How many witches were there?"

Milla pulled her lips between her teeth and shook her head. "Dozens, at Marie's. More on the water."

"Would you recognize any of them?" Lou gestured for Diego to, she assumed, pull up a directory with photos; damn C.R.O.W. and its desire to catalog the world.

"I—no." Milla leaned back on her heels, frowning. "Everyone wore masks."

"Any identifying features?" Donmar suggested.

"Tall? Dressed as the sun and moon? I remember a man in a red domino and a woman dressed like the dawn." Milla shivered, recalling her companion, his face a blur with the barest suggestion of eyes and a nose. Darker smudges on the fuzzy whole. An uneasy feeling stirred in her gut, the prickling suspicion she had seen him recently.

"You were there, Lou." Tobias sat back in the armchair, speaking low and slow as he assessed the Light Witch.

"On the lakefront," she said. "C.R.O.W. had Donmar, Cyrus, and I hunting hedge witches."

"Do you think this could be Marie?" Diego asked.

"I … no, I don't think so." Milla shook her head. "She's still a nightmare, but she seemed different when Darkly and I saw her. I think C.R.O.W. came down on her pretty hard, but she's too powerful a witch to take away from the demesne."

"New Orleans has been quiet since your ritual," Lou said. "And she tied my brother to a chair with willow. She has the connections, knowledge, and power to try again."

"Yeah, but she wouldn't."

"What makes you so sure?"

"Because the ritual wasn't *for her*." Milla dug her nails into the rug to keep from tearing out her hair.

Goddess, she was going to have to explain, out loud and to a room of Enforcers, what they had been doing on that lake. It was different when it was just Darkly. He had listened, and he had been furious, and he had nearly fucked her in the backseat of a minivan. But this was his sister. One, no thanks, and two, she held the reigns to Milla's Way. What if, after she heard the truth, she decided to keep her cut off from magick altogether?

She glanced at Darkly, lifeless and cadaver pale on the couch. At Diego hunched over a tablet, chewing on the ends of his hair as he fiddled with settings, and decided if they were willing to give so much of themselves to this, so could she.

"It was for Ezra." Puffing bangs out of her face to have an unobstructed view of Lou. "We wanted the Baron and the Maman, but they're locked behind the Gates with the rest of the old and wild magick C.R.O.W. shoved there. So Ezra put together a series of rituals to allow us access to the Neitherworld, where I summoned the Shades and cleared a path for him to get out there and open the Gates." She flicked her gaze to Darkly, again wondering about his absence and the circumstances around the coma. How coincidental it all was. "And to do all of *that*, we needed unobstructed access to the Neitherworld. As far as I know, or Ezra was able to find, no one had ever succeeded in doing that outside of a Dark Witch."

"One might argue they still have not." Lou arched her neck, extending the long, graceful line to look down at Milla … who was sitting on the floor, so the posturing was hardly necessary.

"I didn't fail," she snapped out. "Let me be abundantly clear about that. I left Ezra out there because what lurks on the other side is chaos, and I may be a witch, but I'm not an asshole."

When none of the witches argued, thankfully, or agreed, which was somehow worse, Milla continued. "I think the witches we're chasing were there that night. And now that all of C.R.O.W. knows I'll be at Beltane, I think they will try again. Only this time—"

"This time, they might succeed." Lou gripped the armrest and dropped her head back to groan at the ceiling. "Goddess, this is a PR nightmare."

Thirty-Six

 One of three major components of a ritual. Intent is the directive and meaning behind the appeal to the Triple Goddess or Horned God.

See: Desire; Sacrifice

EZRA HUNCHED OVER HIS desk, chewing the end of a pen and idly spinning a loc through his fingers. He'd wandered into the office with his French press and a bowl of oatmeal when Milla left for work, and from the empty bowl and muddied coffee grinds in the press, had been there all day, still in his plaid pajama pants and the white v-neck he put on while Milla showered.

"We'll run this evening," he had said, engrossed in a message on his phone. "Maman sent a new ritual for us."

Looking at him now, lost in frustrated thought and likely in a bad mood, a run was not in the cards. And if it were, Milla would have a terrible time.

She avoided the creaking floorboard in the hall and stepped lightly into the room, not wanting to startle him. He hated being surprised, and Milla had been dealing with elementary school field trips and feral tourists at the museum for eight hours. The last thing she needed was an Ezra tantrum. On quiet feet, she stepped up to the wingback chair and crossed her arms over the headrest. Better to be a presence that he *warmed to in the room. A knock on the door or a tiny cough would start a fight, and again, she was not in the mood.*

She read over his shoulder as he scribbled in a notebook. It was a translation, she thought, but in his mother's language of intent rather than Ezra's preferred French. She silently mouthed the words. Sometimes, if Milla said them aloud, she could glean the meaning, but this was gibberish. A glance at the ritual he worked on, a printout from an illuminated manuscript in swirling, decorative cursive, was even less helpful.

With a frustrated grunt, Ezra crossed out the line he'd written and tossed his pen down. He placed his elbows on the desk, massaged his temples, and let out a long, aggravated sigh.

"Why would you call me here for this?" He glared up at her, amber eyes blazing behind the skull mask.

Milla darted back, glancing around the office and stifling a cry when instead of the bay window and bookcases, a black nothingness stretched out in all directions. Boundless, limitless—a world of nothing, with Ezra stuck in the middle.

Nails gently scaled her scalp, fingers teasing through her hair. Soothing and soft, a gentle sensation easing Milla to wakefulness. Her neck hurt, and her ass was asleep from sitting on the floor with her back against the sofa. She blinked, groggily trying to recall when she had fallen asleep.

Lou and Donmar had left in a flurry of phone calls and she had opted against drinking her tea. Goddess, she wanted one night without the deadened sleep and heavy–limbed morning. She was sore enough from the week, and Tallahassee, the last thing she needed was a cup of poison.

Diego disappeared upstairs once the witches left, so she showered and pulled on her pajamas—a pair of loose purple and black striped shorts and a tank top; black, obviously—aimlessly wandering her kitchen until she could no longer deny she was waiting for Darkly to return. At some point, she sat down beside him, her shoulder brushing his elbow, and must have passed out from the exhaustion of the day, week, year, her *life*.

Still dark, the air held an otherworldly chill, the kind she felt whenever Shades lurked, which explained the fingers gently stroking her hair.

Milla stiffened, not wanting him to stop but startled all the same. When they were hunting the Loa, his return had been violent, his body lurching to wakefulness as his Shade took roost. This had been near silent. A hush of wind from the Neitherworld, a slight shift in the air, barely enough to wake her.

"You should get tae bed," Darkly said quietly. She twisted around, the muscles in her neck pinching.

"How long have you been back?" It was too dark to see if the flush of life had returned to his cheeks, but deep shadows clung beneath his eyes, and lines dragged at the corners of his mouth.

"A few minutes." He swept his fingers through her hair again, toying with the ends as a soft look came over his face. "No one's ever sat with me before."

It took her a second to make out the meaning behind those words, and when it hit, when the somber expression he wore and the way he was gazing at her made a little more sense, a piece of her heart broke. "Darkly."

He cleared his throat and sat up. "Dinnae fash."

"What?" She spun onto her knees, resting on her calves.

"Don't worry about it." He sat up, reaching for the blanket, and that wouldn't do.

Milla popped onto her feet and stilled his arm with a gentle touch. "Come to bed."

Darkly jerked his face to hers, eyes so wide the whites gleamed in the low, flickering light from her candles in the window. His throat bobbed, and he held utterly still.

"We need to sleep; it's gonna be a long day." She grabbed his hand and tugged. "Come to bed."

He didn't argue. What was there to argue? The weirdo had said he needed an invitation, and so she was inviting him. It wasn't a big deal. He was exhausted, she was exhausted, and no one was going to sleep well on the sofa.

He followed her without a word, taking Milla's hand and stepping over the creaky floorboard as they entered her room. Moonlight poured through the window, illuminating the wingback chair and her bed in a pale, pleasing blue. She stopped when she noticed how it also illuminated her nest of blankets and pillows on the floor.

"Right."

"Want to talk about it?" Darkly squeezed her hand, obnoxiously patient as ever.

"No," she said. "I just—the mattress."

When she did not elaborate, Darkly traced his thumb over her knuckles. "Aye?"

"It's too soft." Saying it out loud, she heard how silly it was, but what other words could she use? It was too soft. Too comfortable, too easy, and she couldn't breathe when she sank into the memory foam, tossing and turning while being cradled on a cloud. The floor was firm and unyielding, a punishing surface.

Darkly let go of her hand and settled on the edge of the bed, bringing their faces all but level. His fingertips dusted her arms, up to Milla's shoulders and down. A soft touch, a rapid sweep, and the feel of his skin against hers had Milla's body erupting in goosebumps.

"What are you—"

"Can I try something?" he asked, lightly tracing her arms again before catching her fingertips and lifting her arms away from her body. She nodded, unable to catch her breath. Darkly held still, bright green eyes boring into her. "Milla."

"Yes." The word scraped from her throat. Not that she didn't want him touching her. Goddess, now that he had and could, she wanted it terribly. But the blankets and her bed, and the why … she wasn't ready to face that. There was too much to do, too much to resolve and unpack, and they were running against a ticking clock. This could wait. Her time in the cells could wait. *Milla* could wait until she had a chance to—

"Breathe, *leannán*."

At his command, Milla gasped, burning lungs glutting themselves on oxygen. When had she stopped breathing? Her heart raced, her fingers tingled, and Darkly gently traced her arms, centering Milla in the moment, the room. Him.

"Breathe," he demanded. And she did. "Again." She timed each breath to the rise of his fingers up her arms, exhaling as he swept down to her hands. Until her heart settled, and there were no five things she saw or three she could feel. There was only Darkly.

"What does that mean?"

"Hm?" He gazed dreamily at her as if those light caresses were the only thing he wanted in this world.

"Leannán," she prompted.

"Milla—" Eyes darting over her face, his cheeks darkened with a blush, barely visible in her dimly lit room. Raising one of her hands, he lightly kissed the triskelion sigil. "Milla, *milenka*." And the other. Heat suffused her body as he raised his eyes again, staring intently at her. "*Moje milenka.*"

His voice shivered through her veins, that subtle command he wielded with the Shades sewing the truth of the words into Milla. It was no coincidence he chose to translate the word into Czech. Witches did not believe in coincidences, and Darkly was a clever witch, choosing the language of her intent to make his known.

My lover.

"I—"

"*Leannán.*" And repeated it in a soft, breathy *voice*, weaving his magick into the word. He slid his hands to her elbows, widening his legs to fit her between his knees.

"You've been calling me that—"

"For weeks." He set his hands on her hips and pulled Milla closer, resting his chin on her breastbone and looking at her with an absurdly innocent expression. "I slipped."

"Fell on your ass."

"Head over heels." This, he murmured into her breastbone. Milla gripped his shoulders to keep upright when her knees threatened to buckle. He lay a heated kiss against her skin, and she sucked in a breath.

"Darkly." She pushed weakly against his shoulders. "I need to catch you up. On the demesnes, and Beltane and—"

"Tomorrow." Another kiss.

"You need to call your sister." It was a weak protest, and she knew it, but there was so much to address, so much to work through before Beltane. They needed to know what he learned while shadestepping and whether or not he found Cyrus. They needed to keep moving, making plans to recover their lost witch and catch the ritualists before they unleashed nine rings of hell on the largest ritual in the Southeast.

Darkly's hands curved around her rear, and with a sharp tug, he hauled Milla forward. His strong legs gripped her thighs, his arms wound around her body, and his mouth—

"Dinnae mention my sister right now." Hot breath warmed her breast, the only warning before he sucked her nipple through the fabric of her top. Fire roared down her spine, her body responding immediately to the warmth and wetness.

"Darkly …"

"Too much?" He murmured, blowing a breath of cool air across damp fabric. Milla hissed, her nails digging into his shoulders, no longer pushing him away.

"No, but we—"

"You're tense, *milenka*." Goddess, the way his brogue rolled over the word. "Cannae do anything about the demesnes, willnae call my sister, but this …" His mouth came down over her other breast, sucking hard. A throaty moan tore out of Milla, and she dropped her head back. "This I can do something about."

His lips closed over her throat, traveling up to the sensitive patch below her ear as his hands roved her body. Gripping her ass and sweeping up her spine, hitching Milla onto her tiptoes until her options were to balance against him or fall. His approving rumble when she chose the former rattled her bones, setting off a low thrumming in her core.

"Earlier," he whispered softly in her ear, "it wasnae too much?" To clarify, he pressed a soft band of kisses across her throat, where his hand had been only hours before.

Milla shook her head, lost in the sudden rush of remembered euphoria. How the world had tipped on its side, and Darkly had taken total control, never shying away from his desire for fear of hurting her and fucking Milla the way she had always wanted to be fucked—like the idea of not losing himself in her was too much to bear.

His kisses stopped, and she remembered too late that he wanted words. "No," she forced out. "Not too much."

"And you'll tell me if I go too far?" The gentleness of the question and the way he held and kissed her had Milla raising her head. There was hurt there, an unspoken fear that made her want to gather Darkly to her chest and never let go. "I need—" He looked away, worrying his lower lip between his teeth and shuddering a sigh before meeting her gaze. "I need to know if I ever go too far, *milenka*."

"Of course." She cupped his cheek and Darkly leaned into her touch. In that, Milla would have given anything to see him smile. "Do we need to establish a safe word?" His eyes flew open, lips parting in surprise. "Or a red-yellow-greenlight system?"

"What?"

"Or I could tap your arm twice." She did so. "In case my mouth is full." At that, Milla rocked her hips into Darkly's groin. The shock left his face, and something darker bloomed.

"Think you're funny, aye?" Darkly practically growled, hands slipping down around her rear. Milla bit her lower lip in a grin as he hoisted her onto his lap. "What other jokes does this smart mouth have?"

Milla started to reply and Darkly seized her mouth in a deep, hungry kiss. His fingers kneaded her rear, teasing the hem of her shorts as his tongue swept against hers, denying Milla the space to breathe, to think. Her nipples scraped against the damp fabric of her tanktop, her breasts pressed against his chest, but it wasn't enough. Milla wanted his skin, his lips, his teeth. She wanted all of him, all over her at once. Rolling her hips, she squirmed against him in a silent plea that he touch her.

Her skin, her pussy, anywhere, just *touch her.*

He pulled away, teeth snagging her lip until Milla gasped at the burning pain. Canting his hips, Darkly ground his erection against her, moaning into her neck as she whimpered, caught in the bittersweet. He slid his hands to her upper thighs, gripping tight and holding Milla in place. The seam of her shorts rubbed wonderfully against her clit, his cock pressed against her sex in a delicious rhythm. "Nothing to say?" he panted in her ear.

All she could manage was a moan.

He chuckled and worked his hand between them. A finger swept her center, still over the Horned God-damned shorts, but even then, a thrill shot straight into her core.

"Good." His voice dropped into a growl Milla felt in her toes. "Then my witch is going to sit here and let me make her come until these beautiful shoulders relax." He kissed her shoulder and nipped the skin. "And she can sleep."

"Darkly—"

"Understood?" That devilish finger slipped beneath her shorts, teasing the crook of her thigh.

"Yes." How she managed to form the word was a mystery. She rolled her hips and Darkly squeezed her thigh tighter.

"No, *milenka.*" He pulled back, halting his finger and waiting for her full, hazy attention. "Be still."

Her lips parted, brain forming the words *controlling little witch,* but no sound escaped.

"One tap for yes." Darkly smirked, eyes glinting in the moonlight. He pulsed his finger once, teasing her slickened center, and Milla could not tap his shoulder fast enough. "Good witch."

He swept his finger across her sex, compounding the praise with the touch she craved. Light and teasing, summoning heat and pleasure to her pussy until it throbbed from each gentle pulse. Barely splitting her lips, avoiding her clit, and winding her tighter and tighter. Her arms trembled, the muscles in her stomach went taut, and it took all of her restraint not to relax her thighs and force that wicked finger into her aching cunt.

Darkly ducked his head, teeth snagging her tank top and tugging it aside to free a breast, matching the maddening pulse of his finger as he flicked her nipple with the tip of his tongue. A whimper strangled out of her throat, and her arms twitched at his shoulders.

"Can you come like this?" He asked, sucking her nipple as he awaited her reply. Milla was incapable of anything more than panting. Goddess, she wanted to come; she wished she could come like this. Her pussy throbbed, clenching around nothing because that fucking *finger* still teased her seam.

All it would take was the gentlest brush against her clit, and she'd be screaming, her legs turning to Jell-O.

"I think you can, Milla." Laying his finger straight down the seam of her lips, Darkly rolled the digit. Milla's breath caught, her body tight as a bowstring. He did it again, the base of his finger applying glorious pressure to her clit. Tears pricked her eyes. It was too much, the tease of this pleasure too great, and he'd barely done *anything*.

Lifting his head, Darkly studied her face, every twitch of her lips, the flutter of her eyelashes, and when her breaths came too tight, too close to one another, he drove his finger into her pussy, pressing his palm against her clit, and Milla fell apart.

Pleasure exploded in her core, shooting out to her extremities and leaving her in a deep, visceral groan. He chuckled, kissing her temple as Milla sagged forward, and that damned finger never let up.

"Again, Milla," he urged. "I can feel how *tight*"—a second finger joined the first, and she shot straight as he crooked against that place deep inside her—"you still are."

"Darkly—"

"Too much?"

She shook her head faster and faster as he scored that place, sending pulse after pulse of pleasure into her veins. "No, no, it's—" He angled his wrist, grinning widely as her inner walls clenched around his fingers, and a second orgasm crashed through her body. "*Fuck.*"

"Good witch." Darkly stood, praise thrilling along her limbs, and placed Milla on the bed. He pulled her shorts away and jerked his chin. "On your side."

Milla gazed drunkenly at him, her brain unable to parse the words. He ripped his shirt off faster than she could blink and raked his gaze over her, devouring every bead of sweat, the way her legs had splayed when he dripped her onto the bed, ready and open for him.

The sigil flashed emerald and moss green in the moonlight, each whorl and spiral curving along the lean muscle of his chest. The lowermost arcs of the triskelion dragged her gaze down the rigid plane of his stomach to the peaks of shallow grooves at his hips and the erection straining against his briefs. Milla's lips parted, finally understanding why the word *thirsty* was used reserved for moments such as these.

Darkly palmed himself with one hand and rubbed a thumb over his lower lip, heat darkening his gaze. "I willnae ask again."

"Didn't ask the first time," she said. Her tongue was thick and lazy, her head swimming, but she rolled onto her side, gasping when Darkly immediately pressed against her back, bare as the dawn.

"Punish me later," he rumbled in her ear, grasping Milla's leg above the knee and angling her how he wanted. His erection teased her pussy, sliding along her lips just as his finger had. He banded an arm across her front, slipping the other between Milla and the bedding to press down on her lower abdomen and hold her in place. Pleasure flooded her senses as Darkly teased her nipples and filled her head with filthy words. Begging Milla to come for him again, just once more, before he gave her what she wanted. It was all she could do to knot her fingers in the comforter and hold onto her sanity.

"Be my good witch," he cajoled. "I know you have one more in you, hen. Just one more."

And Horned God-dammit, he was right. As if summoned from the depths of her, another orgasm built. A slow burn that soon blazed across her body. She couldn't move, caught in his arms and imprisoned by the pleasure he gave her body. The head of his cock teased her clit, sliding easily through her arousal as her inner walls tightened and tightened. Clever fingers pinched and flicked her nipples; his teeth snagged her ear and those lovely, terrible *words*.

"Good little witches get fucked, Milla." His hips crashed against her ass, his cock hot and heavy between her legs. "You're my good little witch, aren't you?"

A word rose in her throat, caught on the back of her tongue as stars burst behind her eyes. The hand on her abdomen slid lower, those clever fingers finding her clit, and Milla screamed as she fell once more.

"Yes!"

Bliss fired from every synapse, drowning Milla in a sea of pleasure. Distantly, Darkly muttered, "Fuck," and too far away to reach, thick, delicious heat slid into her aching pussy, filling Milla until her eyes rolled back and her bones melted. He fucked her like the good witch she was, praising her with words that landed on deaf ears, but she was too far away, too blissed out to catch more than the passing, "*Moje milenka. Moje Milla.*"

Thirty-Seven

AS ABOVE, SO BELOW A common saying among Hedge Witches meant to imply a connection between the physical world and the spiritual realm. C.R.O.W. in no way endorses this belief.

funny how they don't speak against it. either...

MILLA DRUMMED HER fingers on the counter, watching the coffee drip into the pot and pondering the kettle. Did Darkly drink coffee or take tea in the morning? And if tea, did he drink it black? Was black even the right phrase?

Diego's door creaked open, and footsteps shuffled onto the landing. She was about to call out to the boys and ask if they wanted coffee when Trav said harshly, "Don't, Diego."

"Dulzura, please." Diego followed him down the stairs, hair in a messy bun and wearing one of Milla's silk robes. The black one with the gold embroidered dragon she had bought in Hong Kong.

I wondered where that went.

Trav jogged down the stairs with a tweed weekender slung on a shoulder, hesitating at the door. From her vantage in the kitchen entry, she glimpsed Diego's profile between the posts halfway down the stairs and the puffy, red eyes behind his glasses. He gripped the banister, leaning for Trav as though every atom in his body wanted to go to the cultist.

"I just—" Trav dragged a hand through his hair and let it fall to his side. "I need some time, alright?" Milla sucked in a quick breath, and Trav's attention skirted to her. He frowned and looked to the floor. "This is … it's a lot to unpack."

"Sí, I understand, but can we please talk? Will you stay?"

"I can't, D." Trav sniffed and swept his little finger at the corner of an eye. "I have the store to run, and I—"

"Trav." Diego eased onto the bottommost step, bringing his face level with Trav's. His fingers danced at his sides. Milla knew that gesture. He made it whenever he wanted to touch a particularly lovely ream of cloth or an occult item.

"I'm sorry, tesoro." And Goddess, did he look it. If hangdog as an expression had a poster child, it would be Travis Bergstrom. His mouth curved in a deep frown, and he dropped his chin, unable to meet anyone's eyes. "It's just that …" Two fingers flicked in Milla's direction, and she went ramrod straight, wondering how in the nine rings she fit into this. "She's a witch."

"*I* am a witch." Diego pounded a fist to his heart.

"I know!" Trav swept a hand through his hair again, fingers falling to the base of his throat. He scowled, glancing down briefly, then tugged on the collar of his button-down. "I know, D. But I *knew* that and Milla …"

A long, terrible silence stretched, ended by the soft rustle of his tweed bag hitting the floor.

"How long have I been this, Diego?" Trav finally asked in a weak, terrified voice. "How long has magick fucked with my life? Did I stay in Key West because of Martin? The store? Or did I stay because—" He stopped and sniffled. "I don't even know what's real anymore."

"Trav." Diego hurtled down the last stair, halting as his boyfriend backed away. Milla knew she shouldn't be witnessing this. She should disappear into the kitchen or her bedroom and give them some privacy, but Trav had named her, and she could not look away.

Darkly opened her bedroom door, sleepy-eyed and wearing nothing but his boxer briefs, but even that could not drag her attention elsewhere.

"You said this was real," Diego said in a hoarse voice. "After the mangroves, after everything, you said this was real. You promised me it was not the curse. That you—"

"I do, Diego. At least I-I think I do, but all this magick is fucking with my head, and she's a *witch*." He pointed down the hall, voice rising to a shriek. "I've known her since high school."

"Travis," Diego said his full name as a plea.

Trav's shoulders dropped. Someone knocked on the front door, and he stooped to pick up his bag, one hand on the knob. "I'll call you, Diego. I promise, but I need time to get my head straight."

He pulled the door open, and Josh, the cultist from Tallahassee, popped his head in. "Are you ready?"

Trav nodded, and Josh moved aside as he left the duplex and headed down the stairs. Cicerhoe, the short, curvy brunette who had been with him at the burnout site, waited on the porch. She looked at Trav and held out her arms, embracing him as he all but collapsed on her shoulder. "We've got you."

All Milla heard was a sniffle.

Josh nodded to Diego, reaching out to shake his hand. "We've got him, D. Just give it some time, alright?"

"Gracias, Josh," he mumbled in reply.

The trio drove off in a sedan, Diego watching from the curb. He stood there for a long while, and Milla waited on her porch beside Darkly, hands clasped over her heart. When Diego finally turned around, tears shone on his cheeks. He stared down the flagstone path at Milla, his eyes brimming with anger, hurt, and blame.

"Diego—"

"No," Darkly said in a low voice. He moved her out of the way as Diego stormed up the steps and into the duplex, feet pounding up the stairs. Only when his bedroom door slammed shut did Darkly let her pull away.

"What the hell?" Milla spun, batting his arm away and darting for the door. Darkly stepped in front of her. "Dude, move; I need to go talk to him."

"If he fancied talking, he would have." Though the words hurt, his tone was soft and weirdly gentle. Milla's glare died away, and she was about to argue when Rai popped her head out of the other front door.

"Ah, good, you're both up." She glanced between the pair and rolled her eyes. "Lou needs Keir to shadestep, and I need to harvest the Solomon's Seal from your yard, but the polevik won't get out of the way, the twat."

Unlike his sister and her million arguments, catching Darkly up on their theory took mere minutes. He simply listened to Milla walk through it, nodded, and asked how he could help.

"Find Cyrus," Lou said. "Find anyone."

Darkly nodded, and with less than a glance at the room, his Shade stepped free, and his body crumpled to the ground.

"Oh, Goddess." Rai threw her hands up and whirled from the room, looking visibly ill.

Donmar shuddered. "I hate when he does that."

"Right, so you're helping move him." Milla directed him to lay Darkly out on the couch. With his head in her lap and his body a cooling, lifeless weight, she took the rare moment of quasi-privacy to check her email and make her phone call.

Just as she thought, there was an email from Hostess City Tea and Spice asking her to send a new talisman charged with her Way. The skin at the nape of her neck prickled like spiders crawled out of her hair as she read the date—mere days before the Savannah ritual occurred.

"That's three." She took a deep breath, centering herself in a forced calm, and made her call. Tallahassee, Savannah, Hattiesburg. "Now for four."

The line rang twice, and a blunt voice answered, "What is it now?"

"Hi, Sarah?"

"You called me; who else would it be?" Sarah Sanderson snapped back.

"No, you're right." Milla relaxed into the sofa. The hedge witch, at least, was fine. Not that she had any reason to believe the woman would not be. The Loa was gone, and while Sarah's stepmother was still dead, she had made a decent amount of money off of Milla *and* was no longer stuck with glamoured leggings she could not offload. Winning all around, comparatively. "Look, I know this is really random, and it's been a few weeks since I saw you, but I remembered that your dad is a long-haul trucker, and I was wondering—"

"This about the burnout?" Aaaaand she sat right back up, nearly spilling Darkly to the ground. Sarah sighed. "Horned God, how did I know you would be involved."

A lanky arm fell to the ground, dragging Darkly's chest in the same direction. She slapped a hand down on him, grunting as a leg followed. "Shit."

"Milla?"

He tipped to the side, gravity hauling his useless body to the floor. "Double shit. No. Nonono!"

Tobias darted into the room, taking one look at Milla bent at an awkward angle, phone pinched to her ear with her shoulder, her nails clawed into Darkly's shirt, and the lifeless Dark Witch about to spill face-first onto the hardwood.

And he hesitated.

"Woman, what the hells is going on over there?" Sarah shouted.

"C'mon, man," Milla implored Tobias, who sauntered over, too slow to be useful. Cotton slipped between her fingers, and Darkly hit the floor with a heavy thud and a worrying crunch. Tobias grimaced, and Milla hissed, "Yikes."

"He is going to feel that later."

"Thanks." She glared at the flame witch, so quick on the sparring court and slow as molasses when it actually mattered. "For nothing."

"My pleasure." He waved a hand at Milla, disappearing into the hallway.

"Anything?" Lou called from the kitchen, where she and Donmar annotated maps of the Beltane grounds over cups of tea and mini donuts.

"Not yet." Milla prodded Darkly with her foot, wondering if the sudden collision would call his Shade back. It did not.

"Witch, I swear," Sarah said over the line. "If you don't start talking, I am blocking this number."

"Right!" She grabbed her phone, popping it onto speaker so she would not have to repeat the entire conversation. "Right, sorry, Sarah. What was that about a burnout?"

Lou's chair scraped against the floor, and Tobias's head popped around the corner. A step creaked, and Rai settled halfway down the stairwell.

"Happened a few weeks back, right around the time you were in town."

"While I was there?"

"No." Sarah clicked her tongue. "A few days later, hold on." A hinge creaked, followed by the clatter of a screen door against a frame. "I tracked it on my lunar calendar, you know how these things are."

Milla did not, considering she was a C.R.O.W. witch and had no idea how hedge witches managed things, but she nodded before remembering Sarah could not see her. "Right, yeah, lunar calendar."

"Let's see. Waxing gibbous, Mississip' on a retreat tide. Regulus rising in … Aquarius? No … no, you were here at the Pisces cusp. Ah, here it is." Something clacked, like marbles against stone, and a wind chime tinkled. "Just under eight weeks ago. The Saturday after you were here."

"The night of the Loa," Milla exhaled. "Oh, shit, okay."

"You sound like you know what this is." Sarah let the accusation hang. She was not wrong, but Milla was not ready to admit how big a part she played in all of this. The hedge witch exhaled heavily and lowered her voice to a conspiratorial level. "They followin' you?"

"Wait, what?" She jolted upright. Lou moved into the room, blue-green eyes gleaming. A faint vanilla scent filled the air, and Milla assumed she was leaning into her Way to glean the truth in Sarah's words. She circled a finger at Milla, prompting her to keep going. "How did you …?"

"We were down for two days in Hattiesburg, I drove out to my cousin's to recover, then three weeks ago, the same thing happened there."

"Where is your cousin?" Due diligence required Milla to ask, but she knew. How could she not? There was only one location they could not nail down, and here was that missing piece identifying the pattern she had recognized.

"Near Valdosta, you heard about that one too?"

"Yeah." Her knuckles went white from her grip on the phone. Goddess, witches were not supposed to believe in coincidences, but what were the odds?

"My cousin and her coven performed a cleansing on me while I was there, said I reeked of glamour and something worrisome. Scrubbed it out and sent me on my way. But you know how hedge witches are." Again, Milla did not. "News travels fast. The cultists hosted some campout, and then BAM." Sarah must have had Milla on speaker as well because a loud clap resonated through the phone like she'd slapped her tile countertop. "A two-day burnout."

"They performed a cleansing?" Milla was going to be sick. If Sarah reeked from the Loa and from her enough to require a cleansing, then that meant—

"As above, so below, bad intent, to the earth you go," Sarah sang and chuckled. "Hadn't heard that one since I was a girl, near lost it when they whipped it out."

It was an odd choice, for sure. A ritual no C.R.O.W. witch would perform. Hedge witches had a connection to the earth, to the land. They were outside of regulation and wild with their magick. Not quite dangerous enough to be considered Forbidden and Foule, but enough of a threat that Aural Insurance Adjusters gave them a wide berth.

"And when they cleansed you, they poured the energy into the earth?" Milla asked, to be sure. Lou gripped the back of the couch with both hands, and Tobias let out a low whistle.

"Where else would we send it?"

She couldn't take the phone off of speaker fast enough. Lou pushed away from the couch, shouting, "FUCK." and at the same instant, Darkly lurched back into himself.

"No Shades," he rasped in a voice like ash and gravel.

"What the hells—"

"Sarah, I gotta go," Milla rushed out, barely hearing the hedge witch's parting profanity as she hung up and tossed her phone aside. Darkly flailed on the floor, caught in a jumble of arm and leg between the couch and coffee table.

"Hey, ow." Milla grabbed his arm, too shaken by his jarring return to care that he'd smacked her in the face. "Hey, hey, it's me. You're back."

"Milla?" Smoke-stained eyes searched her face as if he were still half-caught in the Neitherworld.

"It's me, okay?" She slid off the couch to kneel beside him, gathering her Dark Witch close. His heart slammed in his chest, and he grasped her arms, clinging to Milla and the real world. "We're in your living room, which is still weird. I've got you."

Darkly swallowed and nodded, the green growing defined behind the smoke. "No Shades."

"How can there be no Shades?" Donmar asked.

"You're the bloody Master of Shades." Lou stormed around the couch. "Call them."

Milla shot her a glare. "Give him a minute. Jesus."

"Jesus has nothing tae do with this." Darkly hauled himself onto the couch and sprawled over the cushions. The vape pen appeared in his hand, and he pressed it to his lips. "They salted it."

From the way Lou tensed, Milla assumed that was a bad thing. "Salted what?" she asked.

Eyes closed, he blew out a long stream of vapor and let his arm fall to the side. Milla could not help but notice how his fingers trembled. "The Neitherworld."

"What?" She hopped to her feet. "How … what? How is that possible?"

"They got in." He opened one bleary eye. "Which means—"

"That whatever this coven is doing, they've managed to access the Neitherworld." Lou paced around the couch and loomed over her brother. "Did you bring any back?"

"Nae," he said around a mouthful of vapor. Lou snatched the pen from his hand.

"Then get back in there and bring us a sample so Rai can reverse cast and apply a signature."

"Am nae going back in there."

"Yes, you are."

"I almost *stepped* in it." Darkly sat up swiftly and planted his feet on the floor, chin lifted in challenge. "You want my Shade to get stuck out there as well? Where no one can reach me?"

Milla rose slowly and backed away from the siblings. "Black salt?"

"Black salt," Darkly confirmed.

She pressed her hands to her mouth, understanding now why he had lurched into himself so violently. Salt did funny things to magick. It was why witches avoided the ocean and only cooked with the iodized or kosher variety. Where white salt, like sea salt, was a magickal disruptor used in scourings, black salt was used to banish spirits and ill-will. Topside, it could banish haints and Shades to the Neitherworld. But if used in Darkly's realm…

He shuddered, a full-body shiver that left him looking even more haunted than he already did. "My Shade wouldnae have stood a chance."

"How did you find the salt?"

"Tried to follow Cyrus's anchor," Darkly explained. At Milla's blank look, he smiled softly. "It's easy to get lost in there, especially if it's just my Shade. Like calls to like, and all. Years ago, after I fell in the first time, Lou had me create anchors."

"Okay …" Tobias had said something similar the night before, failing to elaborate.

"Something or someone to call me back." Two fingers twitched in Milla's direction. "Some are easier to follow than others, 'specially if the emotional connection is strong enough. It's always been weak with Cyrus, but I thought if I kept at it …" He shook his head and drew on the vape again. "One of the other Shades, Lavelle. Nice woman. She warned me before I got too close."

"Lavelle … from the trailer park in Louisiana?" He nodded, and Milla huffed in disbelief. "You didn't send her on?"

"Nah, she likes me." He grinned, but it was half-hearted and fled quickly. "How did they get in?"

"Did any of the other Shades see what happened? The ones in there?" She wiggled her fingers at him to imply the boundless expanse of the Neitherworld.

"Aye, they said they were called." His gaze went unfocused, Darkly lost in thought. "But beyond you and I, who else could get in there? And what else can summon a Shade?"

Thirty-Eight

PSYCHOPOMP A guide of Souls and Shades from the physical plain to the afterlife. See: Ferryman

"VELES," SHE NAMED THE Slavic shepherd of the dead in a whisper. A door creaked open somewhere in the duplex, and Milla pressed her back against the wall. "Nepthys, Owuo, The Baron, Hel, the Valkyrie, Viduus," and any of the chthonic psychopomps she could think of. Those tasked as escorts and guides. Names she had memorized as a witchling, terrified of her Way and seeking a connection, a reason, coming faster and faster as terror overtook reason. "Aminon, Hecate, Hermes, Morana, the Horned God—"

"Not the Horned God," Tobias stated. "He slumbers below."

"Nae helping, Tobe," Darkly muttered.

Milla shrank to the floor, gripping her head and trying to breathe, but that Horned God–damned band was back around her chest, winching tighter and tighter. No one was supposed to be able to get into the Neitherworld. It had taken Milla, Ezra, and dozens of witches to do the impossible, but these ritualists had managed it and salted Darkly's realm. They had almost trapped him in there, and now they were summoning and capturing Shades.

Who were they summoning? How did they get in? What were they trying to achieve?

Was it more of Marie's witches trying to finish what she had started? She tried to think back, tried to bring any one of their faces to mind, but they all wore masks, and she'd been too drunk on Ezra, on champagne, on her Way.

Horned God, the room was too small, and the furniture was too big for the space. She needed to get out where there were no walls and no witches.

"I can't do this." The tight, tiny words left her like a wheeze, barely squeezing out of her lungs. It was the same thought she repeatedly had as they prepped for that Horned God-damned ritual, the one coherent thought she had when she Saw what came next.

Goddess, she had Seen it. Old Gods on earth, wild, unfettered magick, and the end of humanity as they knew it. C.R.O.W. had been founded in the aftermath of the Hundred Years' War, regulating magick and locking away the Forbidden and Foule after bloodshed had ravaged Europe. Uncountable witches had been slaughtered like pigs or burned on the pyre, and Milla had Seen what would happen if they unleashed that hell on the world again. She had Seen it, and she could not bear the guilt of success.

"Tobias, I need a complete list of all attending covens and third parties." Lou barked her orders, sending the witches into a flurry of motion. "Vampires, cultists, any desecrants approved to be on the grounds."

The Loa had only been the start. What was it Marie said?

Things long kept from this world slipped through when you failed.

But she had not failed; she had stopped. She had saved them all and sacrificed Ezra, and if she fed the ritual at Beltane, if they had her Way, backed by all of that power …

"I can't—" There was not enough air in her lungs, and the room was too loud, the lights too bright.

"Rai, pull every sanctioned ritual they expect to be performed. Every bit of magick, down to the intent the Mix Witches have decided to imbue in the alcohol."

Milla pressed her palms to her ears, burying her face in her knees, but the sound would not stop. The tingling in her fingers and toes would not stop, and when it did not stop, the world stopped, and she couldn't—

Shades fell around her, and Darkly followed, gathering Milla to his chest as he sat on the floor. "Sh, Milla. I've got you."

And that was the problem, wasn't it?"

"We can't feed that ritual." His arms tightened around her, and Milla sank into the embrace. "What if I can't control my Way? What if I'm the reason they succeed?"

"Keir, you're on interrogations. Pull whatever you can. I don't care how long they've been haunting the space; we need—are you listening?" Lou's voice carried across the room, and somewhere in the duplex, a door slammed. Darkly kissed the top of Milla's head, boldly ignoring his sister. He rubbed his palm up and down her spine, and she matched her breathing to the cadence, using every trick he had taught her.

Darkly, his arms, the rumble of his voice and steady pressure of his hand, the cotton of his shirt against her cheek, his lips against her ear.

"How are we going to do this?" A wave of nausea rolled up from her belly, drying out her mouth as she looked at Darkly. A smile flickered, there and gone again.

"Dinnae ken."

"Ugh, Goddess. Donny, you're on wards," Lou doled out the last of her orders. "Call the Panhandle Coven; I want to know everything they are doing to keep the grounds secure from prying eyes and the names of the casting witches."

"Of course," Donmar rumbled, the floorboards creaking under his feet as he walked the hall.

"What about us?" Milla pressed her cheek against Darkly's chest, knowing she looked pathetic and not giving a singular shit about it.

Lou cocked her head, eyes gleaming. Shining white hair slipped over her shoulder, sparkling in the morning light. "We run you at exhaustion," she said coldly. "And we drown her Way."

"Lou, no." Darkly stiffened. "You cannae keep poisoning Milla."

"I can and I will. She owes the ritual, and it's my reputation on the line. What happens when I can't deliver a Death Witch, hm? Have you considered what that means for you? Once C.R.O.W. decides I'm no longer fit to babysit their Forbidden and Foule pets, what do you suppose happens next?" Darkly's arms tightened, and he dropped his head. "Can't cleave yourself, can't cleave her. Fancy a visit to the salt and marble?"

He shook his head, stubble snagging in Milla's hair.

"Good." Lou sniffed. "Exhaustion and tea. We'll present her as weak, a non-issue, showing the covens she is no threat and giving these ritualists as little as possible of her Way. Now get up; there's work to be done."

Milla refreshed the browser, willing the number in Southern Gothic's account to be bigger. According to Rai, her tea would not be ready until that evening; something about hawthorn and the optimal time of day to grind cloves. With the rest of the team occupied, there was nothing to do but wait. She hated waiting almost as much as she hated Lou's idea. Weak was how Ezra wanted her. Broken and reliant on him to teach her, guide her, and train her for their ritual. Weak was what she had been hiding in St. Augustine until her Way burned, and weak was the witch who tried to raise her Gone ex-husband.

For the last year, Milla had worked to leave that weakness behind. She had the store, Diego, and Julie. She had the beginnings of something good, a strong foundation, and now she was back at square one: weak and at the mercy of C.R.O.W. And Lou and the billionaire who bought the building.

"It's about industry," Stefan Holfstaedter said in the video on her phone. "And the economics of the thing. Invisible hand and all."

She scowled at the billionaire in his perfectly tailored Oxford and tastefully undone buttons, then frowned at the depressingly small number in Southern Gothic's bank account. Goddess, she couldn't even fix this.

"Stop hyperfixating." Julie slammed the tablet face down, bright blue eyes intent on Milla. "You can't keep that silver fox from buying the building, so focus on something you can do."

"If they hadn't revoked my right of first refusal, I could have—"

"Bought the building with your ex-husband's life insurance policy." She rolled her eyes. "I know, sweetpea, you keep bringing it up. But they did, and you can't, and we just have to make it work. Which it won't if you don't fix whatever happened there." Julie pointed down the hallway, and they both turned their heads toward Celine Dion's muffled wailing. "If I have to listen to *All By Myself* one more time, Milla, I'm going to kick the door down and take one of your creepy railroad spikes to his stereo."

"They're not creepy." She crossed her arms. "They're locally sourced."

"Locally…" Julie grunted. Or maybe it was a scoff. It was sometimes hard to tell with her. "They're from an abandoned rail line that's haunted by the ghosts of little children who died on a bus. What is wrong with you." She swept the tablet from Milla's reach and waved it at the hall. It vanished, allowing Julie to cross her arms and hit Milla with a mom glare. "Go. Talk to him. Listening to power ballads that loudly is a verified cry for help."

"Where'd the tablet—"

"*Go.*"

Milla squeaked and scurried away, but not before glancing at the counter display, where the tablet was back in its dock.

Celine Dion's voice bled through the particleboard door, wailing about loneliness. That was heartening. Julie was right, if Diego was already drowning himself in power ballads, it meant he was processing what had happened and might be ready to talk about it, which gave Milla an easy in.

She rapped twice on the door and waited, silently celebrating when Celine's voice cut off. A moment later, the door cracked open. She took it as an invitation and pushed it wider as Diego resumed his seat at the sewing table, a needle pinched in his teeth. He had repaired the tiny room in her absence and replaced the carpet, but the edge of the table was still blackened and shriveled from the panic attack Darkly had barely been able to shield.

A long moment passed in silence as Diego threaded a bobbin and inserted it into his sewing machine. Milla cleared her throat, and when he did not look up, she said, "I wanted to see if you were okay."

Folding a hem on a swathe of flannel, he pulled the needle from his teeth and slid it into the fabric. "Why would I not be okay."

"After this morning," she prompted. "And last night, That was … a lot. I was worried that you—"

"I am fine."

"Diego, come on." She leaned against the doorframe. One look at the witch was enough to shatter the lie. He'd come to work in rumpled pants and a plain t-shirt, not a cuffed hem or accessory in sight, and she strongly doubted he had showered that day. His hair hung lank and a little greasy, which Milla had not seen since she introduced him to leave-in conditioner and blowouts. "Talk to me."

"Why?" He finally looked up, his red, puffy eyes magnified behind his glasses. "So you can make this about you, as well?"

"Whoa." Milla pressed a hand in the air, halting *that* before it started. "I never—"

"I, I, I—I am so sick of hearing you say 'I.'" He slapped the side of his sewing machine. "If *I* wanted to speak with you about this morning or last night, do you not think *I* would have done so?"

She opened her mouth, stopping the next "I" before it escaped. Diego choked on a bitter laugh, muttering under his breath in Spanish as he turned on the sewing machine. A hum filled the office, and he adjusted the flannel on the plate, feeding it through.

"Why didn't you tell me about him?" Milla had to raise her voice to be heard, hating how it sounded like she was shouting, but if Diego was so determined to be mad at her, she at least deserved to know why.

He stilled, foot leaving the pedal, and the humming died away. "Because he was for me," he finally said. "He was mine, and he was wonderful, and I did not want your influence decaying something so beautiful and new."

He might as well have reached into Milla's chest and squeezed her heart. "That's not fair."

"Is it not?" Diego glared at her, his eyes, normally so warm and inviting, full of cold, angry blame. "He is a cultist, Milla. When have you ever had a kind word to say about them? When have you ever taken the chance to get to know one? Never. You call them drunks and weirdos. You spit at any mention of them; why would I tell you about Trav when you hate the very thing he is?" He clenched his jaw, nostrils flaring. "When it is probably your fault he is one?"

"I didn't know!" She moved into the room, and Diego narrowed his eyes.

"Always your excuse," he hissed and pressed down on the pedal, shouting over the hum of the sewing machine. "You did not know, you did not think, you did not want—" He blinked, and tears streamed down his flushed cheeks. "You did not know those were my bones; you did not think that ritual would raise me. You did not want to take responsibility for your actions. You never have, and witches are missing, Milla. People are getting hurt; *I* am getting hurt because of it."

The flannel snagged on the needle, and he grunted, reversing the feed. It jammed a second time, and he flicked frustrated fingers at the fabric. A raw snarl tore out of his throat when nothing happened, and Diego threw his body back in the chair, slapping his hands on the table and staring at the edge.

"Everything I *am* is an extension of *you*." He spoke in a carefully calm voice, pacing out the words to ensure Milla absorbed every last one of them. "Do you know how that feels? My Shade is not even my own, Milla. It is a shred of yours. I only exist because of your mistakes, and I finally had something of my own, only to find out you tainted it before I even had a chance to—" His voice caught, and he pinched his mouth closed, bringing tear-sheened eyes up to hers.

Milla had no words. What could she say? Never in his second life had Diego yelled at her; never had he spoken a harsh word. A look, sure. A stern critique paired with a guiding hand, yes. But never this animosity.

The moment stretched, Milla caught in his unwavering, unblinking gaze. It filled the tiny room, drowning out all sound until all that remained was her heart thudding painfully in her chest. Her pulse was so heavy she felt it pounding in her temples and tingling in her fingers and toes, rushing in her ears like the quiet hiss of hushed laughter.

Diego's phone buzzed, and he blinked, releasing Milla from his pain. She lurched forward as the world caught up to the moment, and sound rushed in—a car horn blaring on Hipolyta, the jangle of bells, and Julie calling out, "Hello."

"Everything changed," Milla said.

"Aplicación estúpida," Diego scowled at his phone and cleared the screen before frowning at her. "Yes, Milla, things change. People change, and they adapt. You might consider doing the same." The pedal clacked as he slammed his foot down, and the sewing machine whirred to life. "Dejame solo," he said. *Leave me alone*. Adding as an afterthought, "Por favor."

She backed out of the room and closed the door, making it two steps down the hall before she froze.

Tobias leaned on the counter, a bright, broad grin lighting up his face as he watched Julie rambling animatedly about something.

"And this one?" He pointed at the glass without looking away. Julie flushed a bright pink and glanced down, pressing her fingers to her mouth as she giggled.

"That's the Victorian."

"Ja? With all those triangles?"

At her answering giggle, Milla palmed her face, sighing when Celine Dion resumed warbling in the sewing room.

Thirty-Nine

TASSEOMANCY The interpretation of tea leaves, coffee grounds, or wine sediments to foretell the future.
See: Divination; Vesticism

"Again!" Tobias barked, hauling her attention away from Lou and Darkly as he stumbled in the grass and teetered forward. "Enervate."

"I can't," she gritted through her teeth. They had been at this for hours. No water, no break, no breakfast. Lou had kept to her word, waking Milla and Darkly at dawn and driving them to the casting range. Hours later, her fingers were cramping, the tendons in her ruined right palm screamed, and if she had to rot and renew a clump of flowers one more Horned God-damned time ...

"You must." He crouched in front of her, eyes spitting fire. "There is no way around this. You owe the ritual. You must control your Way."

"What's the point?" she slurred, swaying where she crouched. The cost of her Way had been slow to appear, which might be the only upside to Tobias's relentless training. But after a full morning of teasing her magick, Milla was one hex away from falling over drunk in the grass. "They're just gonna steal it an' make the world all shitty."

Tobis leaned close, each word sharp as a knife's edge. "For weeks, I watched you fight in that cell. For weeks I watched you refuse to bend. Where is that witch now?"

"She's tired." Milla stood, listing to the side and barely keeping to her feet. "*Rozložit.*" A flick of her fingers splashed the decomposition hex against a cluster of flowers. Half of them dried and wilted, none of them rotting. Nausea sent her staggering, and she clutched onto the wooden post at the end of the court.

Across the field, Darkly threw a weak handful of Shades at his sister, and the whorling mass disintegrated three feet from their target. Lou thrust her hands on her hips and shouted something that had him dropping his head. Even from this distance, Milla saw how sharply he panted, pushed to the very edge of exhaustion. He shook his head at the grass, arms trembling, and collapsed onto his side.

Rai met them at the door with a cup of tea and Darkly's vape pen, and the rest of the day passed in a drunken haze, only to begin anew at dawn. And again the next day, until the world blurred and Milla could not walk in a straight line, much less see one. Tobias demanded more and more of her Way to rot flowers and tree trunks, making Milla score black marks in the grass and reverse the damage until her magick sputtered and fizzled out.

And at night, plans were made around them; discussions about Beltane, the ritualists, attending covens, and the rites being performed, but Milla was too tea-drunk to absorb any of it. By Wednesday evening, she could barely keep her eyes open, much less move her body. She slumped against the sofa where she'd collapsed hours earlier, staring down at her teacup. The dregs clung to the side, clustered like ants at a picnic. An omen? She closed an eye, focusing on the latent magick in her veins. The vesticism no tea could drown. A cluster blurred into the shape of a bear, but before she could decipher the meaning, the cup was swept from her hand.

Diego crouched in front of her, brow wrinkled and eyes gleaming hard behind his glasses.

"Why are you doing this, bruja?" He swept hair from her face, gently tucking the scraggly bangs behind an ear. His gaze lifted, and though Milla did not have the energy to turn around, she knew he was frowning at Darkly, lifeless and grey on the sofa, shadestepping as he did each afternoon at Lou's demand. To the Beltane grounds, to Tallahassee, Milla had no idea where he kept going, did not care, really, so long as he came back.

"Lou told me to," Milla mumbled through numb lips. Her head dropped to the side, and her vision blurred. "Didn't wanna make it 'bout me."

A bitter, angry sound left him, and he vanished from view.

On Thursday, Lou moved the meeting into the living room, presumably so Milla and Darkly could participate. She had made it to the couch this time, slumped against the pillows with her head resting on the Hygge blanket. Darkly filled the other end, his socked feet in her lap and higher than a kite on a breezy day.

"Check-ins will occur every thirty minutes, either in person at the landmarks I have noted on the grounds"—she pointed to the television screen, where a Beltane map was displayed. Different areas of the twisting, labyrinthine ritual grounds had been marked with tiny drawings of Roman statues, except for the monstrosity at the center: a three-faced, winged demon— "or by phone. Do *not* miss your check-in."

"Yes, ma'am," Darkly drawled in an exaggerated Southern accent.

"We leave first thing," Lou ignored him. "It is a six-hour drive to Mobile and another forty-five to the swamp where Beltane is being held."

Darkly raised his vape pen and pressed his index finger to his nose. "Dibs on ridin' with Tobe."

"Negative, Keir. I need you in the Neitherworld."

"An' I need you tae be less of a minge," he replied, devolving into giggles.

"Goddess," Lou sneered at her brother. "Get ahold of yourself."

"You did this to him," Milla said. No one responded, so maybe she thought it. Her lips had gone numb, and with every passing moment, her eyes grew heavier and heavier.

"—due at the center before sundown, make sure you aren't late."

"Aye, aye." Darkly fired off a heavy-handed salute, jostling Milla as he did. She grumbled and burrowed her face into the blanket.

"And keep it brief. You have to feed the ritual, but no showboating."

"Cannae promise anythin' in this state," he chuckled, and the gentle rolling sound lulled Milla into a heavy-limbed sleep.

The whispers woke her, teasing Milla to consciousness with their incessant demands in the pitch-black night. Not a seam of light bled through the curtains or under her door. Her heart thudded in her chest, struggling against an odd weight pressing down on her sternum, grinding her bones into a hard, unyielding surface.

"There she is," a trio of voices whispered near her ear. "It has been some time, magissa. Did you forget about me?"

Milla whimpered, trying to force her body upright, and the pressure increased, pinning her to the floor like a bug. Her arms would not move, her legs only twitched, the limbs and extremities tingling like her blood had been pinched off and flow was just returning.

"Still some fight in you, good." The voices hummed across her forehead and buzzed into her other ear. "You are going to need that."

Tears pricked her eyes, refusing to fall. She could not move, could not scream. It was the cells all over again when that witch had held her at his mercy, taunting Milla in the dark. How was he here? *Why* was he here? He was a torment designed by C.R.O.W., and Milla was out; she was free to do what Lou demanded and lead a semblance of life. Why was he *here?*

"Just a bit longer, magissa." The voices taunted, and the pressure increased, flattening Milla where she lay. "We almost have what we need."

Millapet?

The pressure on her chest eased suddenly as if in surprise, and a thin stream of air entered her lungs. She whimpered again, this time in relief.

"Who did you call?" Did she imagine spittle crashing against her cheek? The stink of stale of garlic and lemon? "Who else is out there, magissa?"

They're here, Milla. A new voice shouted. *You have to wake up!*

"No matter. He has wandered far enough, any moment now, and not even C.R.O.W. will be able to stop us."

Cannae get to you. Wake up!

A door slammed open somewhere in her duplex—and another, another—door after door, cupboards and drawers. The pressure eased, the voices murmuring in surprise, and then they vanished altogether.

Milla lurched upright, gasping wildly as she spun onto her knees, legs tangled in blankets. Her head spun, heart pounding relentlessly like it had whenever that witch left her cells. When time returned to normal.

But nothing was normal about this. The dark teemed around her, chilled like a thick fog. It crashed against her arms, her thighs, pawing at Milla's face and turning it to the left, the left, always to the left.

Cannae get to you.

She crawled forward, stumbling onto her feet and reaching out blindly for something to support her weight. Trinkets rattled on a shelf, and her fingertips brushed a row of books, their leather and paper spines grounding Milla in a time, a place. Every muscle protested, her limbs and bones heavy from the tea.

They're here. The warning from that new voice echoed in her mind, the timbre and tone so similar to Darkly's. And who else could it be calling to her when the Shades filled her room?

The Shades.

Milla whipped her head to the left, replaying the witch's words.

He has wandered far enough.

"No." Milla clawed along the bookshelf and reached for a doorknob that was not there. She swept blindly at the empty air, catching the faint groan of hinges before the Shades rushed in, crashing against Milla like a phantom wave and dragging her into their nothingness.

A floorboard creaked under her weight, and a sandy substance dug into her soles. The Shades heaved and relinquished their hold, sending Milla careening into the hall, where more Shades teemed around her legs and hips, keeping her upright as they urged her down the hall and into a room as black as the Neitherworld itself.

She crashed against her couch, and they receded enough to let faint light into the room, showing her Darkly stretched across the cushions. Eyes closed, cheeks hollow, his chest utterly still. One arm had dripped onto the floor, and the vape pen lay tangled in his fingers.

Cold slivered up her arm, matching the chill dribbling down her spine.

She knew what this was, knew what had happened at a glance. But last time, Darkly had woken himself. He'd come back, lurching upright in that motel bed and wrapping his arms around her, clinging to Milla as if he needed the reminder that there was a world outside of the dark, with warmth and beating hearts.

Cannae get to you.

A Shade caressed her cheek in a silent plea, and Milla lurched into action.

"Help!" she bellowed, collapsing to her knees beside Darkly. "Diego, help!"

Another door slammed open; footsteps pounded down the stairs. Milla grabbed the vape pen and tossed it on the table, running her hands over Darkly's face, his throat, his chest. Willing any warmth to bleed into her palms, any heat, *anything* resembling her Way.

"¿Qué carajo?" Diego cursed from somewhere behind her. "Why is it so dark? And what is all over the floor?"

"I need Lou." She tore Darkly's shirt up and away from his body, trembling fingers chasing the triskelion. Even that was deadened, absent the green shimmer. "He's not breathing, he needs his Shade. I need my Way; I need Lou!"

Diego ran, feet pounding down the hall. Milla pressed her ear to Darkly's chest, listening for and catching just the barest thumping—distant, far away, and fading.

"No, you don't." She crawled onto the couch, straddling his waist and laying heavy hands over the triskelion. Goddess, if she had access to her Way, she could summon his Shade, but she was useless, and Milla was beyond tired of being useless.

"She's not answering!" Diego called from somewhere deep in the house.

"Call Tobias," she yelled back and took a deep, centering breath. There was always a dispellation. And another deep breath. Latent magick, intrinsic to her. Goddess, if this worked, it was going to hurt, but it was the only thing she could think to do.

The tea had tried to tell her—the ant-like dregs an omen, the warning of the wolf and the bear when she closed one eye. Even Ezra had been warning her in her dreams, and she had not listened. They knew the ritualists had access to the Neitherworld, but never did she think they would try this in her demesne. In her *home*.

"Come back to me." Milla leaned over Darkly to repeat the demand in his ear. "Come back to me, Dark Witch."

Shades teased her ankles and crawled up her legs, cradling Milla as she straightened and closed her eyes, focusing on the deepest innermost kernel of *her*.

The Soul Sigil was magick, and all magick could be dispelled. A witch just needed to know how to do it. Diego could unravel the threads of magick. Darkly did whatever a Dark Witch did with a flick of his fingers, and Milla … Milla was a Death Witch, so there was only one thing she could do.

Sound cut out. Her body went limp, listing to the side, and right at the cusp, that liminal point of no return, shouts filled the room. Someone grabbed Milla's shoulders, tearing her hands away from Darkly and hauling her back to the present.

Foglamp eyes burned in front of her face, searching Milla, then dropping to the witch beneath her. "Ó, mo Dhia." Lou's thumbs dug into her wrists, an allure rolling from her tongue without hesitation. "*Oscailte!*"

Heat roared through Milla's veins, clawing out of her chest and tearing down her arms into her hands. She ripped free of Lou's grip, not wasting a single second, and slammed her hands down on the triskelion, hissing her intent.

"*Přijít.*" *Come.*

Darkly's skin warmed from her touch, and Milla repeated the allure, summoning the one damn Shade she cared about. It was a thin hope, but Milla had summoned the Shades of women stolen by a Loa, and spirits from beyond the Gates. She could summon one Horned God-damned Dark Witch.

"*Přijd' ke mně.*" *Come to me.*

The Shades kicked up in a frenzy, tearing at her hair and clothes. Lou backed away, shouting at someone as a sepulchral howl rose in the wind.

Darkly twitched once, twice, and shot upright, sending Milla crashing to the floor. She curled her hands into fists, clutching them against her chest and pressing her heels against the floor to shoot further away from him. He gripped the back of the couch and a knee, gasping like a swimmer at the end of a sprint. Shades siphoned back into Darkly, and soon the warm flicker of the candlelight brightened the space.

His black eyes fell on her, and Darkly let out a sob, spilling off the couch, reaching for her. "Milla."

"Keir, don't!" Lou shouted while Milla rushed out, "Don't touch me." She curled into a ball, fisting her hands in her shirt.

Cotton disintegrated at her touch, and her eyes pricked with tears. *Goddess be damned*; she was so fucking tired of the *crying*.

Lou moved closer, and Darkly shot out an arm, snarling at his sister. "Give her a minute."

"What's happened?" Tobias burst into the room in flannel bottoms and a white shirt, followed by Rai in a silk robe, her face covered in a green mask.

"Fell in," Darkly said. He knelt beside Milla, hands hovering over her. "Give me your gloves."

"My gloves?"

"Now, Toby." Darkly snapped his fingers, and a second later, Tobias tossed a pair of gloves at him. Pulling them on, he whipped the Hygge blanket from the couch, dropping it around Milla's shoulders and pulling her into his arms.

"I could just bind her again," Lou scoffed.

"No." Darkly glared at her and rose, not even struggling under Milla's weight. "Give her a chance, Lou."

When she did not argue, Darkly nodded and sat on the couch with Milla cradled in his arms.

"Someone had better start explaining what happened," Lou demanded after a far too brief moment. "And what is all over your floor?"

Milla lifted her head, seeing for the first time the sand-like substance she had stepped in. It surrounded her couch, and a line stretched the length of her hallway into her bedroom. "Black salt." Each witch looked down, and Tobias danced as far away from the salt as he could get. "Someone was here. There was this witch at my arrest and in the cells. He tormented me, and he was in my house tonight."

"Explains why all the doors are open," said Rai.

"There was no one in the cell with you," Tobias argued from where he had crammed himself in the furthest corner of the room. "It was my task to ensure that you were safe and alone."

"Bully job, there, buddy," Milla muttered. She wriggled against Darkly, ensuring the blanket covered her hands as she pressed herself upright. He did not yield as much as she would have liked, so she glared at him, halting when his weary eyes dropped to her chest. He pinched his lips together, raised his brows, and widened his eyes.

Milla looked down and quickly banded her arms tight over her chest. The straps of her tank top had rotted through, and the front fit like a stretched-out tube top. She cleared her throat, choosing to keep talking rather than flash the group.

"They know where we are, and they got into my house. We aren't safe, and your plan isn't working."

"Perhaps if you did not leave the doors unlocked," Lou replied, "they would not have been able to get in."

"Diego locked up," Darkly said. "Last thing I saw before passing out."

"From the weed *you* keep making him smoke," Milla added. Lou straightened, widening her stance. Her eyes began to gleam and Milla was having none of that. "You've kept Darkly too stoned to be useful and had me drinking enough poison to murder a royal family, and they got into my home."

"What are you implying, Ludmilla?"

She clutched the blanket and wriggled off of Darkly's lap. This time, he let her, reaching around Milla to lay a hand on her hip. In support, a shared show of strength, whatever it was, it bolstered her enough to keep going.

Because he was with her, he agreed with her.

"I think the ritualists are closer to us than we first thought," she said.

Lou scoffed. "Anyone could have broken in here and—"

"The wards are sound," said Tobias. Milla blinked in surprise at his weird show of support. "She learned them from the Morgenhexe; I would not expect anything less. I checked them on Sunday, and they are impregnable, just as they were at her hut in the woods."

"Someone would have to know where this house was to find it," Darkly said. "Walked right by that hut when she first brought me there."

"Where's Donmar?" Milla asked. Goddess, she hoped she was wrong because how could a witch get blindsided in the same way *twice*? And why was it always the friendly ones?

"With Diego," Lou answered. "They're scanning the house for signatures. Are you suggesting—" She blanched and backed up a step. "You're suggesting it's one of us?"

"What were you doing next door?" Milla fired back.

"Preparing for Beltane with Donmar." She checked her watch and frowned. "I had hoped to get a few hours rest before we left, but I suppose that is out of the question."

"We might as well try." Donmar entered through the front door with Diego right behind him. He flashed his phone at the group. "The wards are undisturbed, and the polevik claims no one new has been here."

"And the E.R.I.E.?" Lou pressed.

"If I read it correctly?" Donmar shrugged and sent his wife an exaggerated frown.

"No trace of anyone or Way not accounted for in this room," Diego answered. "Cyrus would be able to tell us more, but …"

A mournful beat passed, each of the witches looking away and honoring his absence. So, of course, Milla had to go and open her mouth.

"Really dicked us over by taking our technomantic."

Diego squinted at her, and Lou sent her a curious look, asking, "Technomantic?"

"Cut us off at the knees so we can't find them with the E.R.I.E." She gestured at Donmar's phone with a blanket-covered hand. "A simple plan. Effective." At the confused looks she received, Milla kept on. "I mean, it's not like they would need a technomantic to mimic my Way; why else would they take him if not to slow us down?"

"*Leannán.*" Darkly squeezed her hip twice to gain her attention. He leaned closer and murmured, "Cyrus is a chronomantic."

Milla froze, her brain struggling to process this new information.

Chronomantic.

That couldn't be right. Cyrus was obsessed with technology, constantly fiddling with the E.R.I.E. and hyper-fixating on reports and data, creating overlays, and tracking the times of the rituals. He was so obsessed with the latter that he had gotten defensive when Milla asked about it.

"Of course I have," he had snapped. *"What good would I be if I wasn't?"*

But, Horned God, did a chronomantic make sense if they were attempting her ritual from the lake. Milla could summon the Shades and hold the tear between worlds open; it was a specialty of her Way and one of the many reasons C.R.O.W. labeled her Forbidden and Foule. Couldn't a chronomantic achieve the same? The one in her cell and at her arrest certainly had. He'd held Milla in stasis time after time and again less than an hour ago.

Her stomach flipped, reliving the sickening lurch she felt every time he removed the hex, the prickling in her fingers and toes whenever she returned to the natural progression of time.

The ritualists burned through hippocromantics and vinefica, but there was at least one missing chronomantic. It stood to reason they had some means of tracking Ways, considering they had been tracking hers. They could have easily seen a chronomantic was with them in Tallahassee and grabbed Cyrus when the rest of the coven and cultists were distracted by the burnout.

But the polevik said no one new had been on the property, and the polevik was desecrant, and desecrants rarely lied.

She pressed her lips together, careful to keep her face blank. Darkly moved his hand to the middle of her back, and a kiss of cold followed, the witch preempting her panic and steadying her with his Shades.

"So, no one entered, no one left." Lou glanced from witch to witch, but none argued. She sighed and tipped her head at Milla. "Perhaps you are right about the tea," she conceded. "Rai's blends have been known to carry side effects."

"Hardly my fault," Rai replied. She pulled her silk robe tighter and cinched the ties. "If we're finished, I'm going to catch what sleep I can before someone tries to pin global warming on me as well."

"We have an early start," Lou said after Rai left. "Sleep, if you can. Donny?"

"On it." He waved his hand, and a wind tore through the house, gathering the black salt into a pile in the center of Milla's living room.

"If it's alright with you, we'll ring that in sea salt, and I'll have a team come by to package the sample." Lou cocked her brow, and Milla nodded, chewing her lower lip to keep from saying anything more. "Good. Sleep." Lou pointed to her brother, then Milla. "You're needed in, well, not top form tomorrow, but able to perform. Give me your wrists."

Only after the witches left, and they were safely in Milla's bedroom with their Ways both bound, did she open her mouth. "I know I sound paranoid."

"Not at all." Darkly stretched out on her bed, reached across the mattress, and flashed his fingers at her to join him.

"What."

"I learned my lesson in February. If you are suspicious, it is likely because something suspicious is happening."

"Again." She stepped up to the mattress, thighs pressing against the edge. "What."

Darkly rolled onto his side and propped his head in a hand. "Someone was in here, Milla, and they knew to wait until I fell in to try anything. They salted your threshold." He jerked his chin at her door. "And they ringed the sofa. You have every reason to suspect the culprit is someone close to us. Personally, my money is on the cultists."

"You are taking this far too well."

"It's been a strange year," he said with a shrug, "and I'm loused. Forgive me for not being clever." Dropping onto his back, he folded an arm under his head and again gestured for Milla. She crawled onto the bed, pressing in close and relishing his slow breathing and steady heartbeat. He cupped the back of her head, toying with her hair and lightly scratching her scalp, soothing his Death Witch in the best way. "Missed this."

"Mm." Milla let her eyes drift closed, losing herself in the moment, the touch. Thanks to the tea and the weed and Lou running them ragged, he had not been in her bed since the night after Tallahassee. She wanted to capture this moment of peace and bottle it for later use.

That had been close—terrifyingly close. If his sister had not been able to get to Milla in time, she did not know if she would have been able to call his Shade back. What she had been about to do was … a dispellation like *that* … it was desperate, and there was never any guarantee she would recover in time to act.

Darkly had survived having his Shade severed by luck alone. Luck and coincidence.

Milla popped her head up.

"What are you thinking?" he asked.

"Nothing."

He wound her hair around his finger and tugged to get her attention. Milla hissed at the sharp bloom of pain, jerking her gaze to Darkly. He waited, patient as ever.

"I was just thinking."

"About?" He stretched out the word.

About Lou and Donmar being next door and not answering their phones. About Rai and the tea, the weed, and her dreams. About Tobias, who knew too much about her Way and had been in the cells with her. How he had denied any other witch had joined them. About Cyrus being a chronomantic, and the cultists and the polevik claiming no one new had been through.

How would a desecrant define "new"? Trav had stayed in her home, Josh, and the woman, Cicerhoe, had slept next door. Was Milla willing to believe they had actually left? Three mortals addicted to magick with access to a house full of witches?

"About tomorrow," she half-lied. "And Lou's plan."

"You hate it." He slid his hand down her back, resting it on the curve of her rear. "Please tell me you hate it."

"Oh, so much," Milla admitted. That earned a chuckle and a gentle squeeze.

"And what, my wee disaster, is your plan?"

Milla could not help but grin at that. It was still more of an idea than a plan, but she needed Darkly on board if they were going to stand any chance of it working.

She grabbed her phone from the bedside table, pulling up a map of the festival grounds and zooming in on the center. "These witches want to steal magick, and they want to use my Way." She showed Darkly the screen and the landmark she had focused on. His eyes lit with interest, and he glanced at her, lovely lips parting with a question. "Lou wants me to present as weak. To pay as little as I can of my ritual dues and make it hard for anyone to steal anything. I disagree."

"Milla …" Though his tone was a warning, she did not miss the dimple driving into his cheek.

"I say *we*"—she pointed the phone at him, herself—"feed the ritual. Give everyone what they want. We went in blind against Anaisa, and she nearly outsmarted us turn after turn. We have an opportunity here to avoid making the same mistake."

Darkly blinked, and his lips parted as he laughed in disbelief. "You want to bait the ritualists?"

"I want to bait the ritualists," she agreed.

"After all that with the raw-head …" He shook his head. "Bampot."

Part III
Beltane

Forty

"THIS CANNOT GET BENT." Diego buzzed around Donmar, who was loading a large, shockproof case into the back of Lou's Land Rover. "It will mess up the calibrations, and without Cyrus here, I do not know how to fix the antenna."

Donmar frowned at the trunk space, then at the growing pile of luggage on the sidewalk. "I will put this in the backseat."

Milla dropped her duffel beside the luggage pile and adjusted the pillow under her arm, mentally tallying the bags against the witches. "This is a lot," she said.

"Sí, well, I have been thrown into a world of technomancy I hardly understand, forgive me if I practice an abundance of caution." Diego hoisted a crate and shoved it in the trunk.

She pinched her lips, counting to three before clapping back at him, spared by Rai adding her designer luggage to the stack. She wrinkled her nose at the Land Rover, and pressed a finger to the tip. "I am not sitting in the middle."

Milla laughed at the absurdity of the posh woman playing "Not It" like a witchling in school. Darkly glanced over at the sound, abandoning his task helping Tobias load the BMW, to saunter closer. "Fancy sitting in my lap?"

"I'm going to sleep the entire way," Milla replied.

"Alright."

"I drool in my sleep."

"Doesnae change my mind." Darkly grinned and took her duffel bag.

"If you two are going to be this saccharine for the next six hours, perhaps I am better off sitting with the equipment," Rai said. Though her tone was dry, her eyes twinkled and a faint smile curved her lips.

"We could demand Keir walk the Neitherworld and meet us there," Tobias added. "Save us all the nausea."

Darkly mock-scowled, but whatever retort he had was cut off by a car horn rendition of "Rule Britannia!" bouncing off the brick walls of Flagler and hammering down on the witches. Lou whipped around, hand out in a ready ward, and Donmar summoned a harsh wind.

Milla and Darkly could only stare as a deeply tinted, pristine vantablack minivan cruised down the road, coming to a slow stop directly beside them. The window rolled down, revealing a moon-pale vampire gripping the wheel. His shallow eyes were wide in shock, and his jaw hung slack.

Dies-well blinked at the steering wheel and slowly shook his head. "I assure you, I am just as surprised as you are."

"Dies-well." Milla blurted in surprise. "*What?*"

"Marie thought you might need an escort to Beltane." He grinned, flashing fang. "And I thought you would prefer to ride in style."

"What happened to your minivan?" She leaned back, examining the smooth paint and restored grille.

"British hospitality."

"Nae such thing." Darkly tugged on the handle, and the door slid open. He whistled as he examined the interior. "Spared no expense, I see."

"My fee for taking on one of the Madame's more peculiar jobs," Dies-well said over his shoulder.

"That bad?" Milla set her pillow on one of the pilot seats, effectively claiming it. Darkly picked it up and tossed it into the back with a wink. A *wink*, Goddess help her.

"To put it lightly," Dies-well said, "I met a fangling who made more of a mess in here than you two managed." He shook his head, a haunted expression crossing his face. "Still collecting dirt from the vents. Do you know how hard it is to count grains of sand?"

"A tragedy, I'm sure." Lou strode over, stopping a healthy distance away from Dies-well's open window. "What is this?"

"One of Marie's," Darkly answered.

"Ah, yes, the vampire chauffeur."

"You are *not* excused," Dies-well seethed.

"He prefers 'Vampire Detective,'" Milla said as she clamored into the backseat. Supple leather embraced her legs and back, and she wasted no time arranging her pillow and snuggling down. "Oh, Goddess, this is so much better than the Land Rover."

"Superior British Engineering, my lily-white ass," Dies-well muttered. Milla caught the briefest smile cross his face before Darkly crawled into the backseat, blocking the vampire's reflection.

⚜

Milla slept for the first few hours. There was nothing better to do since Darkly was shadestepping, and Rai had engaged Diego and Dies-well in a colorful conversation comparing the sixteenth and and seventeenth centuries. Darkly stirred somewhere outside of Pensacola, and she snaked her arm around his chest, snuggling close so he could feel her heartbeat when he stepped back into himself. It was quiet this time, and he spent a few minutes running his fingers through her hair before speaking.

"Could get used to this," he whispered.

"Me too."

"It is unnerving for a man to walk between the living and the dead as easily as stepping into a backyard." Rai turned in her seat, shooting a startled glance from one witch to the other. "I almost miss the death rattle."

"Rude." Milla narrowed her eyes at the vinefica.

"No, she has a point," Dies-well called from the driver's seat.

"Gonnae send Shades to haunt you both." Darkly sat up and pulled out his phone. "Need tae call Lou; there's news."

He dialed, rubbing a hand over his face and accepting the packed and warmed vape pen from Rai when she handed it back.

"Tell me you have something," Lou said in place of a greeting.

"Shades," Darkly said.

Milla shot upright. "You found some?"

He nodded, face somber. "Excited ones at that."

"Go on." Lou's voice flooded the minivan, her sharp tone coming from each speaker. Dies-well winked at Milla in the rearview mirror and mouthed "Bluetooth."

"Thought I would scope the ritual site and found a host of them clustered." Darkly closed his eyes, fingers dancing on his knee. Shades bloomed and wound in and around his knuckles, then vanished. "Due north. They were haunting a group of Staid, from what I could tell."

"Mortals? That close to Beltane?" Diego twisted in the passenger seat, gripping the backrest. "Could they be cultists?"

"Did your contact mention anything?" Lou asked.

"Josh will be there with a contingent of cultists," he said. Milla pulled out her phone, opened the map application, and searched the area around the ritual grounds. "But they have all been approved by C.R.O.W. and are quarantined to the Seventh Ring with the vampires."

Someone murmured on the other end of the call before Lou spoke again. "Tobias is telling me the same thing."

"The Seventh Ring was, what?" Rai asked. "Violence? With the illusionists?"

"And C.R.O.W. condoned vampire activity," Diego added. "He was distressingly excited."

"Right." Lou exhaled into the phone. "Keir, I'll need you to—"

"Go back in," he sighed but did not argue.

"Sway as many of the Shades as you can to block their ritual and deny their access to the Neitherworld, and call me back once you have confirmed the location. I'll have Donmar scope the area when we arrive."

"There's a campground a mile north of the ritual grounds," Milla said. She zoomed in on the map and showed Darkly. "Homestead Village RV park, could this be it?"

He squinted at her phone, frowned, and summoned his glasses, sliding them on before scrolling on the map. "I think so. What's this?" He tapped an icon on the screen. "Erlich Steam Plant?"

"Are you fucking kidding me?" Milla stole her phone back, jaw-dropping as she scrolled through the information. "This guy is *everywhere.*"

"Who?" Darkly asked.

"What is she going on about now?" Lou's annoyance came clearly over the line. If anything, Dies-well's state-of-the-art stereo system enhanced it.

"You're on speakerphone, Lou."

"I don't care, Keir," Lou snapped back.

Darkly nudged her arm. "Elaborate?"

"Erlich Industries," Milla said, scoffing when her declaration was met with blank faces. "As in the parent company of Homestead Commercial Real Estate, owned by Stefan Holfstaedter, the asshole who bought my building." Diego's eyes widened, but Darkly and Rai continued to look lost. "Erlich Steam is part of the Delta Power Clean Energies arm of Erlich Industries." A series of swipes brought up the chart of all Erlich Industries brands. She showed it to the van. "See? This dude owns, like, everything on the planet."

"What is it with you and this bloke?" Darkly asked with a bemused grin.

"Billionaires shouldn't exist," she replied, turning the phone back around. A business name on the screen caught her attention, and her heart skipped a beat. Refugio Clean Energy. "Diego ..."

"Sí?" he answered immediately, phone in one hand, eyes on Milla. She hesitated, wondering if she had misstepped. They were barely speaking; for all she knew, he was still pissed at her, but he sent her a soft, reassuring smile. "I know that voice, bruja. It is the one you use when you have figured something out. What do I need to look up?"

"Refugio Clean Energy."

"Un momento." He dove into his phone, and Milla scanned her screen. "Sí, I have it. It is a subsidiary of Erlich Clean Energies, and there is a news article from September of last year about an—"

He re-read whatever was on his phone, slowly raising his head. "An explosion."

"Now look up Tivoli Turbines."

"What does she have?" Lou demanded.

"A lead," Darkly said. "The power plant north of the Beltane grounds is owned by the billionaire who bought her building, and my Milla's obsession with him has got us our lead."

A deep, lovely thrill went through her bones at that, but she kept her focus on the chart, looking for any other names that would stand out.

"Tivoli Turbines in Texas?" Diego asked. She nodded. "All I am seeing is a larceny charge against an employee."

"Name?"

"David Aguilar. The article says he has fled authorities."

"On it," Rai said. Milla called out another business she found, Valdosta Lumber and Pine, but before Diego found anything, Tobias's voice came over the line.

"David Aguilar is one of the missing witches." Every head raised, the witches sharing startled looks. "A hippocromantic, registered to the Coastal Bend Coven.

In a quieter voice, Rai added, "Valdosta Lumber and Pine had a fire the night of the cultist campout."

Freeway rumbled under the minivan's wheels, and a silence as thick as a St. Augustine summer morning filled the cabin.

"Well," Dies-well finally said. "You jack-a-ninnies have certainly been busy in my absence."

"Don't blame me," Milla said. "I missed most of it."

Darkly put a hand on her thigh and squeezed, listening intently as Lou issued orders.

"I'll need whatever chart Ludmilla is looking at. Keir, confirm the location and seize the Shades."

"On it." He nodded, eyes bleeding black, and a second later, he slumped lifeless to the side.

"Diego, call your cultist. I want to know why he did not volunteer this information."

"You did not ask," Diego muttered and faced forward in his seat, already scrolling through his contacts.

"Tobias, I want any mortal records you can find on our missing witches, and Rai, see if you can match any more explosions, or fires, or what have you to the dates and locations of those rituals."

"I've already got one in Savannah," the vinefica said, copying a link on her phone.

"Excellent. Ludmilla?" Milla tensed, waiting for what she was sure would be a snide, dismissive remark about her obsession with rich men. Instead, Lou blindsided her with, "Good work."

"I—"

And the line went dead.

Dies-well followed signs for Ellicott Mound State Park down a narrow gravel road cutting like a scar through the dense overgrowth. Oak, pine, and maple trees bursting green with spring formed a tunnel that refused more than the most stubborn and persistent beams of sunlight to break through. Every fifty yards or so, they passed a broad cut through the trees, where towering metal poles, transformer blocks, and powerlines stretched to the horizon.

Darkly gazed out the window, eyes still black as he scanned the area for any errant Shades that could be bent to his will. Milla leaned close and, as he turned his attention her way, cupped his cheek and pulled him in for a kiss.

"How many did you grab?" she whispered against his lips.

"Two dozen." His breath was chilled, and she caught a hint of clove and winter spice. "There's an old cemetery near the campground. This change the plan?"

"Not at all." She started to pull away, and his fingers wormed into her hair, keeping Milla in place as he deepened the kiss from a means to hide their conversation to something far more real.

"Gross," Diego called from the front seat.

"Want me to roll up the partition?" Dies-well asked the van. "I've locked them back there before. It is the only way to manage the dandy pratts."

"Goddess, please," Rai laughed. "Let me crawl up there first."

Little by little, the gravel road widened to two lanes, belling out to the size of a modest parking lot hidden among the trees. Rai rolled down her window, and every witch gasped at the electric charge of magick in the air. A length of iron fencing disappeared into the woods in either direction and straight ahead, the gates of Beltane were thrown wide open.

Made of twisting, gruesome metal, the gates were barbed at the points and bulged in irregular, wart-like masses that dripped down each metal pole. The arch over the entrance was worse and all the more mesmerizing for the sculptures clinging to the metal. Gargoyles with their wings splayed perched on pillars supporting the arch and gates, eschewing a thick, purplish haze from open mouths that purled along the barbed peaks and wafted through the trees. Welded faces made up the archway itself, screaming and howling in silent attempts to escape their metal prison, and just beyond the entrance, a dusty Rhett Jones waited for them with a clipboard in hand.

Dressed for the Wasteland in a leather duster, vest, camouflage pants, a multitude of useless belts, and combat boots with mismatched laces, the Panhandle Coven vestic waved the van forward, pulling up his goggles at their approach. Dies-well rolled down the window, grinning broadly and barely stifling a laugh as Rhett's tanned cheeks paled and he leaned away from the van.

Milla clamored up to the front seat and pulled herself halfway through the partition. "Hey, Rhett."

"Ms. Lightner!" He thrust his arm in the open window to shake her hand, and Dies-well snapped his teeth, causing him to yelp and jerk back.

"Play nice." She smacked the vampire's shoulder.

"I'm cranky and hungry, and the sun is out," Dies-well replied. "So no, I don't think I will."

Rhett glanced between the pair, no doubt alarmed to see a witch treat a vampire like an obnoxious little brother. He rallied and tried again, summoning a manila folder, pamphlet, sheet of wristbands, and a parchment scroll. "These are for you and your party." Tentatively, he passed them through the window. "And you, sir," he addressed Dies-well, "will want the Seventh Circle. We have blackout tents and a blood bar for your convenience."

"Thank you, Rhett." Milla pushed Dies-well back against his seat and grabbed the stack, handing it all to Diego in the passenger seat.

Hopping onto the sideboard, Rhett swept dust from the windshield with the sleeve of his duster. He peeled a vinyl cling from a sheet, slapped it to the glass, and hopped down. "Is the Dark Witch in there?" His gray eyes sparkled at Milla, and he popped up on his toes, attempting to peer into the van. Darkly chuckled from the backseat, and Rai muttered, "Mind the ego, Horned God."

"Living and breathing," Milla confirmed, "and entirely obnoxious." Someone pinched her thigh, and by someone, she knew without any doubt it was Darkly.

"Oh man, okay." Rhett shook out his hands and nodded, like he was convincing himself to remain calm. Milla recalled his very strong and very loud reaction to Darkly's existence, but she did not track any of the hysterical fear he had shown in Constance's office. This reaction was more akin to nervous excitement. "Right, this year's theme is Inferno; your coven is in the Ninth Circle campground, late registration and all. Head to the corner of Purgatorio and Fraud, Canto 27, Line 133."

"Sure," Milla deadpanned.

"Everything you need to know about the demonstrations is in the folder. Don't be late, or the Elder Witches will be livid."

"It's that strict?" Milla wrinkled her brow. Demonstrations were demonstrations, and as far as she knew, they only had to report to the Elder Witches before sunset.

"It's *Beltane*," Rhett stressed. "Don't be late; it'll make us all look bad—you most of all." He waved them on, and Dies-well dutifully rolled the minivan forward through the gruesome gate.

"Canto 27, Line 133," Rai said. "Did that mean anything to anyone?"

"We onward went, I and my leader, up along the rock," Darkly recited. "Far as another arch that overhangs the foss, wherein the penalty is paid of those who load them with committed sin."

Diego turned in his chair to stare blankly at him, along with the rest of the car. "I do not suppose you would translate whatever it is you just said?"

"Welcome to hell," he replied.

"I've got it." Rai unrolled a parchment scroll so long it hit her knees and fell to the floor, revealing a map of the outer rings curling around the labyrinthine ritual grounds. "There's a map. Turn left at The Red Death."

"The what?" Dies-well whipped his head up to the rearview mirror.

"The that." Milla pointed out the windshield at the massive twenty-foot-tall statue of a skeleton in red frayed robes wielding a scythe. "Holy Horned God, this is going to be awesome."

Forty-One

OSCAILTE *"Open": counter allure to waybinding hex. Need to touch target. update: can allure/hex Keir from a small distance. Test further.*

ONCE PARKED, DIEGO AND Milla were ordered to stay out of the way as the Enforcers set up camp. Eight-foot tall tents were pitched, a kitchen area set up under a canopy, and a workstation, complete with a wireless hotspot and a technomantically powered generator, was up and running in record time.

Milla spent the time witch-watching, noting the outfits worn by attending covens. The Steampunk Wastelander aesthetic was most prevalent—worn leathers, boots, goggles, frayed vests, tank tops, and silver facepaint shiny and chrome. But there was a strong showing of the Fleetwood Mac crowd, mostly young women in Boho-chic dresses and knee-high leather pirate boots, with floppy felt hats and long, flowing hair. A neon presence was speckled in and among the leather and beige, bright, cheerful rompers, cat ears, furry boots in electric hues, nipple pasties, and shorts that were closer to underwear than anything else.

One look at her mesh-panel cut-out yoga pants and Siouxsie and the Banshees crop top told Milla she was woefully underdressed.

"Here." Diego tugged her into a tent by the elbow, directing Milla to the pile of bags and parcels in the corner. He handed her a tightly packed bag and swiveled his wrist, summoning Milla's chunky-heeled, knee-high boots from her closet at home. "You are being presented to all of witchdom as a Death Witch today; I want you to look the part."

Milla clutched the bag to her chest, at an absolute loss for words. "Diego …"

"Not now." He handed her the boots. "Later, when all of this is finished. You are my pequeña bruja, and te adoro. Even if you do drive me mad." He grabbed a few more parcels and made to leave, stopping at the tent's entrance. "Oh, and whenever you are complimented, tell them I am the master behind the craft."

Milla hugged the parcel and boots tighter, wishing it was Diego. He might not be ready to talk about, well, *everything*, but this was his way of saying he would be. Later, as he said, when this was all over. "I will."

"Bien. Now get dressed." He stepped through the flaps, then popped his head back in. "And whatever it is you and Darkly have planned, let me know if I can help."

The outfit Diego had designed for Milla landed squarely between Boho-chic and Wasteland:

A black bandeau top and low-slung, high-cut compression shorts, a gauzy scrap of deep red fabric fashioned into a skirt she tied at the hip, and a leather belt embossed with skulls, athames, and intricate whorls dangling with gold coins. Her dreamcatcher and amethyst necklace was replaced for the day by a long silver chain affixed with the curved blade of a pocket boline knife, a finger bone that she hoped was fake and knew at a touch was not, and a silver pentagram.

It was an absolute nightmare, and she adored it.

She tugged her stacked-heel boots over knee-high black stockings and wound thin leather straps affixed to the topmost eye holes around her leg, tying them off as bows on her upper thighs.

Rai had entered the other half of the tent to get dressed and called through the divider as Milla unfurled a long black macramé vest that finished her outfit. "You decent?"

"Yeah." She slid her arms into the vest, swiveling and walking in a circle to get a feel for the garment. Diego had worked embroidered skulls and bones into the design, and when she walked, the ends billowed menacingly behind her.

The zipper sang, and Rai let out a low, admiring whistle. "Holy Horned God, Lady Death."

Milla glanced over to grin at her, doing a double-take as the vinefica stepped fully into view, hooking the last of the enclosures on a green satin bodice. Paired with shiny black shorts, fishnets, and matching green combat boots, Rai looked more serpentine and deadly than usual. "Me? You look like the ringleader of an underground hand-to-hex death match."

"I know." She shimmied her hips and flipped a long sheet of glossy hair over her shoulder. "Your Diego is a wonder; I love it. Here, let me." Milla held still as Rai reached for her head, freeing the braids she had wound and bound while her hair was still damp.

Gentle fingers worked the waves free, fluffing Milla's bangs before Rai plucked a tube of lipstick out of the air. She pulled the cap off to reveal the deep, decadent, Cabernet-red hue and handed it over. "Fatal Kiss, perfect for you."

"Thanks." Milla took the tube and applied the lipstick, half wondering if she'd just entered into some sort of fae bargain.

"My pleasure." Rai sauntered past in her boots and held the tent flap wide open. "You'd better come along before Lou has a fit."

Milla followed her out of the tent, making it all of two steps before she was stopped in her tracks by six feet and change of half-dressed Do Not Fuck With standing under the canopy.

Like Milla, Darkly had been dressed to represent his Way and role. But where she was intended to present as a Death Witch, his was a mix—the tactical, multi-pocketed Enforcer blacks hung low on his hips and clung to his legs, and he'd traded the C.R.O.W. issue boots for a well-worn pair. In place of the tight woven belt was a simple length of treated leather knotted in a Celtic loop at his hip, drawing attention to the v of muscle disappearing below his waist. With no shirt on—and, really, was that necessary?—the triskelion was half obscured by a tartan scarf lazily wrapped around his neck and shoulders, made of the same flannel Milla had seen Diego struggling with a few days earlier.

To finish the look, he had cleaned up the neckline of his stubble, leaving the perfect amount of shadowy beard to highlight his sharp jaw and ludicrous cheekbones. And Diego must have attacked him with clippers because his fuzzily regrown hair was now a sleek, faded mohawk.

"Oh, Horned God," Milla said on a lusty exhale, thrilling at the sight.

Darkly looked up from the printout in his hand and hit her with the Dark Darkly grin. He turned toward her, and a thin slip of shadow was revealed, twining around his left arm in a lazy helix. The final effect was striking, and Milla just about died.

He prowled closer, eyeing Milla like a hungry predator, and stopped mere inches away, taking in every bit of her not-very-modest clothing. Running a knuckle across her bare stomach, just above the line of her belt, the Dark Darkly smile sharpened as goosebumps rose at his touch. Milla swayed, her pulse quickening as her body responded to his nearness, his caress. He repeated the track, this time adding a brush of Shade, and she shivered, struggling to hold his hungry gaze. He hooked a finger in her belt to tug Milla forward, erasing the inches between them.

"I both love and loathe that lipstick," he said in a low, rumbling voice.

"Why?"

"Because it makes me want to kiss you." Smoke wafted in his eyes, and Milla lifted on her toes, bringing her mouth within easy reach. "And when I do, everyone's gonnae know."

Lifting her chin, Milla pursed her lips slightly, pleased when his tongue darted out to wet his. "Is that a problem?"

"Nae," he whispered. "The only problem is I willnae stop at the kissing."

Moths winged madly in her belly, sending jitters into her lungs and dancing down to her fingertips. His hands clamped around her hips, keeping Milla raised on her toes. She let a wicked smile bloom. "Then why stop?"

Darkly's fingers at her hips pressed harder, and he leaned closer. "Ah, *leannán*."

"¡Oh por Diosa! Look at you both!" Diego stepped out of the other tent, delightedly clapping his hands. Milla jerked back, Darkly's hold the only thing keeping her from toppling over.

"Impeccable timing, Diego," Rai said, applauding him in a light golf clap. "Spared us all."

Diego bowed in a flourish, straightening and giving Milla a good look at his chosen outfit. She could only describe it as Pirate Chic. Black leather pants hung almost as low on his hips as

Darkly wore his, though these were a bit baggy in the crotch, too tight in the rear, and featured off-center gold buttons embossed with a Spanish Rose. Knee-high suede boots with an overlarge cuff complimented the breeches, along with a maroon and gold unbuttoned vest embroidered with black roses and far more belts than were necessary.

On his stomach, chest, and arms, the Stitch Witch had applied a vast amount of glittery sheen to mimic a sea salt spray. The overall effect was striking, a Conquistador Out of Time, and it pleased Milla to the tips of her toes to see Diego de Gregorio Bimini in all his glory.

"Lady Death and the Living Shade." Diego clasped his hands together and sighed. "Que encantadora."

"The covens are in for quite a show," Tobias rumbled, following Diego out of the tent. In brown pants and his Red Wing boots, the spalování shrugged on a worn, heavy brown leather coat that dropped to his mid-thigh and boasted an overly large fur collar, an obscene amount of buckles, and deep pockets.

"Then let's get this farce started." Lou strode over, dressed in her Enforcer blacks and a fitted tanktop crackling with anti-hex magick. She handed out papers to each witch, speaking quickly. "Donmar is scoping out the campground Ludmilla identified. Keir"—Darkly straightened to attention, the sultry witch gone in an instant and replaced by a soldier. "Be ready; if Donmar sees an opportunity, you will need to shadestep immediately."

"Understood." He nodded, jaw hard.

"We have until dusk to sweep the grounds and gain any intel. Check-in with the covens I've identified; each has at least one witch working for a subsidiary of Erlich Industries." Her eyes flitted to Milla as she said this, and Lou gave her a tight, terse nod. Acknowledgement for making the connection and giving them a heading. "Blend in, be as covert as possible. Do not draw undue attention to yourselves. Except for you two."

She faced Milla and Darkly, barely suppressing her disapproval of their outfits. "I suppose it's for the best you look the part," Lou muttered. "Be seen. Mingle, and make yourselves the point of conversation to allow Toby and Rai the space to work. If Constance's lackeys have done their jobs, the rumors will swirl about a Death Witch and a Dark Witch at Beltane. Confirm them." At that, she gestured for Milla's wrists. When she hesitated, Lou huffed impatiently. "The Elder Witches you meet today will expect to feel a hint of your Way." Pressing down on the sigils branding her wrists, Lou tugged Milla closer and whispered, "Do not make me regret this."

"I won't." When Lou did nothing, Milla added, "Stick to the flower trick, right?"

"Right." She pressed harder, a gleam building in her eyes. "If we've done our jobs, you should not be a threat, even with access to your Way. Come running to me if even the slightest thing around you begins to rot." Milla nodded, mouth pressed firmly shut. "*Oscailte.*"

Darkly steadied her by the shoulders as the unbinding hit. The weight on her wrists fell away, and warmth flooded her palms, climbing up her arms. He hummed dreamily, and magick pressed against her shoulders, cool and calming. Bolstering Milla without responding to the call of her magick. Not yet.

Curling her hands into fists, she closed her eyes, relishing the feel of his magick, the heavy crackle in the air, and her own Way pulsing happily in her veins.

"Too much?" Darkly murmured. Milla opened her eyes, locking gazes with Lou.

"Not at all."

Forty-Two

SPRAWLING ACROSS A BEND in the Mobile River, the ritual grounds were a mix of forested and cleared land bordered by the magick-disrupting running waters of Sisters Creek to the north and Cold Creek to the south. According to the map Milla studied, the Panhandle Coven had spared no expense on the entertainment, attractions, and exhibits.

Keeping with the theme, the grounds were laid out in a series of concentric rings meant to mimic Dante's Inferno. The outermost ring, Limbo, consisted of the campgrounds, a thin warded barrier shielding the witches inside from the Staid world, and an area for basic conjurations and summons, which bubbled and popped in the air as they crossed the campground and approached the official entrance.

The more personal and intimate rituals encompassed Lust as the Second Ring, and to keep all the attendees sated and refreshed, the third ring was filled with food trucks, BBQ tents, pop-up bars, and beer gardens as representative of Gluttony. Artisan booths and coven tents comprised the Fourth Ring, Greed, and all witches in attendance had signed Forms of Consent to account for the Fifth, Sixth, and Seventh rings.

The Eighth Ring, Fraud, housed the audiomantic tents for music and dancing, and the mound at the center of the grounds representing the Ninth Ring and Treachery featured the main stage and Elder Witch tent where Darkly and Milla were scheduled to demonstrate their Ways.

Their tiny coven plunged through the campgrounds, joined by Dies-well clutching a large black umbrella and carefully avoiding the sun. Excitement welled with each step. It had been years since Milla had attended a C.R.O.W.-sanctioned mass ritual, a Mabon held at Poverty Point in Louisiana. She had been little more than the quiet, black mini skirt and crop-top-clad witchling on Master Lightner's arm, too afraid to be seen and all too happy to hide in Ezra's shadow.

Now, witches stopped mid-sigil, hands held out before them and eyes wide with a mixture of fear and wonder as Lady Death and the Living Shade passed through the campground. Darkly lifted his chin, walking tall and proud, almost defiant, as the Shade on his arm writhed and whirled, happy to see and be seen. But the silence that followed in their wake worried Milla. She half expected to be tackled or hexed to the ground at any moment.

Sensing her discomfort, or perhaps feeling his own, Diego fell into step beside her. A silent show of support that did more to heal the rift between them than the clothing or the promise of later. So Milla took a chance.

"Hey." She nudged him with her shoulder. In the periphery, she saw a witch at a nearby campground run into a tent pole in shock. A Death Witch touching a Stitch Witch, the horror!

"Hola," Diego said quietly.

"I was wondering," she said, pulling her phone out of the leather pouch attached to her belt. "Could you run me through the E.R.I.E. real quick?"

He arched an eyebrow at her and cocked his head. "¿Por qué?"

"I'm just curious. If I wanted to filter out the social distortion … the noise from all the other Ways," she explained, "and track a certain a specific Way to a location, like how they found me off of Darkly." Milla wiggled her fingers at their surroundings. "Could I do that?"

"Which Way?"

"Chronomancy."

He tripped over his own feet. It was subtle, and he recovered quickly, but that was obviously not what he expected her to say. "Why?"

"A hunch."

"A hunch," he asked, "or a 'hunch.'" Diego pinched his fingers in the air.

"Both." At his sharp look, Milla amended. "Later, I promise."

Diego searched her face. "Is this about your visitor in the cells?"

"And at my arrest." She nodded. "Also, could you show me how to pull up old reports? And filter them for a specific Way or witch?"

"Ya veo." He nodded and pointed to her phone. "Sí, let me show you."

The crackling charge of the barrier tingled along her arms long before she saw the sheen in the air. Like Lou's ward, it flew up as a shimmering transparent wall into a barely discernible arc doming the festival. Darkly slid his fingers down Milla's arm, interlocking their hands and giving a squeeze as they passed through the shimmer. Static danced down her arms and over her scalp, raising the fine hairs and setting little sparks dancing over their hands as they stepped into a world turned upside down.

Revelry, she had expected. Laughter and song and merriment, absolutely, but Milla was wholly unprepared for the riot of color and sound and the wild rush of magick accosting the senses from every discernible direction.

The Mabon at Poverty Point had nothing on Beltane. Where the covens of Louisiana practiced structured rituals following a tight schedule, the Panhandle ritual was an onslaught on the senses. The closest she had ever come to this mad swirl of unrestrained Ways had been the large-scale skirmishes on Big Torch Key and exposition tournaments Morgen hosted. Even then, there had been a martial bite and organization to the explosion of ritual magick.

This was an intoxicating ecstasy all its own. Milla swayed at that first step, laughed at the second, and felt her Way kindle to life at the third, responding to the overabundance of visceral energy in the air.

Svítilna bursts of neon light strobed the trees in pinks, purples, and caustic blues, illuminating obnubilari cast illusions of fae and cryptid creatures. Milla spotted duendes with their bright white eyes and colorful caps darting among the trees, and a seven-foot-tall female figure in dark clothing swayed back and forth beside the path, silently screaming at the witches from beneath her wide-brimmed straw hat. Overhead, hopping from branch to branch, were a bevy of long-armed creatures that Milla recognized as Floridian Skunk Apes. On the ground, loping after them, tongues lolling and ears pert with excitement, ran a pack of shifted rougarou, tumbling into one another with joyous yips and playful growls.

The edge of Limbo was marked by a creek illusioned by obnubilari to appear far wider than it was. Dies-well tipped his baseball hat to a witch stationed beside a small dock floating on the water. Cloaked as a ferryman, he traded minor spells with witches waiting to cross on a barge. For those not wanting trade for passage into the next ring, a wooden bridge had been conjured over the creek, the cost of crossing a simple secret.

Milla gripped Darkly's arm, giving over to her excitement and all but dragging him up and over the bridge. She paused in the middle, feeling the secret bubble to the tip of her tongue, a heady compulsion intent on dragging the most inane truths from any witch that fell under its influence.

"I adore Taylor Swift," she stated, grinning at Darkly's unconstrained laughter.

"I had a poster of the Spice Girls on my wall as a boy," he replied, waggling his eyebrows, "for five very bonny reasons."

"Oh, my Goddess."

Giggling, they stepped off the bridge and followed the path to the left. Occult circles marked the entrance into the First Ring, the volume of the various intents and incantations controlled by audiomantics stationed every dozen feet.

"Reminds me of Samhain at Ord Hill," Darkly shouted over a ritual chant. "But less sinister."

"Less sinister?" Milla glanced at twelve witches gathered beside the creek, each chanting in a guttural tongue and laying sticks in a perfect circle while a thirteenth cast her bones into the center. "They're literally casting a drought."

Darkly watched the coven, nodding when the grass at the center of their circle brittled and browned. "They're Delta witches; what do you expect?"

"More." Milla grinned wickedly at him and joined their circle. The intent washed over her, sharp and dry as a desert weed. Falling into step beside a Green Witch, Milla studied the cadence of her hands, marking the sigils and trying them on for size. As the ritual chant repeated, she joined in, appealing to the Goddess and the water in the skies, the earth. Their desire was to keep the waters at bay, their intent to ensure a strong growing season for the Delta crops, absent the floods brought on by a strong hurricane season, and their sacrifice was the moisture in their skin and their hair.

Gallon jugs of water sat outside the sphere of influence, ready for the exhausted witches once their ritual was cast.

Milla added her sigils to the next repetition, mimicking the witch beside her and bolstered by a friendly smile. Her brow furrowed as she eyed Milla, realization dawning as to who cast beside them. Then that smile bloomed into a manic grin as the magick caught, and the grass beneath their feet withered and died. Milla's phone buzzed at her hip, and before the next round began, she fell out of the circle, caught by Darkly, and whisked away.

"Well cast." He kissed her temple and guided her down the walk, a stone-faced Tobias walking right behind. "How are you after that?"

"Gonna need a drink to hide what I'm doing."

"I think we can manage that."

Rai waited at a turn in the path, eyes darting from Milla to the witches behind them before she continued on. The rituals changed in tone as the path doubled back on itself for a few hundred feet before turning again, wandering deeper within the barrier wards. Lodgepole pines became maypoles, hedge walls sprung up on either side of the trail, and Green Witches manipulated flowers to burst and bloom on the vine.

To speed their progress, throughways were cut into the hedge walls every few turns. Tobias, Diego, and Rai disappeared into one, waving to Milla and Darkly as they headed off on their assignments.

The crowd grew thicker at the official entrance to the Second Ring. Housed in a meadow, Green Witches dropped ivy crowns on the heads of witches seeking entry into Lust, kissing them on their cheeks and murmuring "Blessed be" from berry-tinted lips. Darkly ducked his head, accepting a crown and a kiss before snatching an ivy crown for Milla from the Green Witch's hands. The brunette smiled, sweeping her hand as she backed away and turned to crown the next coven passing through.

"Blessed be," he murmured. Shadow bloomed in his palms, weaving in and among the ivy. He set it on her head, and Milla reached up, her fingertips just brushing his own crown to wither a strand of ivy, marking his festival regalia as he'd marked hers.

"Blessed be, Darkly." She smiled at him, closing her eyes as he kissed her forehead and grabbed her hands.

Head spinning and feet light, she let herself be pulled into the Second Ring, where the more intimate rituals were performed, less than surprised when he stopped to watch a fertility rite.

"Fancy a go?" Darkly rumbled in her ear as he slipped behind her, hands firmly on her hips. She craned her neck to look up at him, somewhat disappointed when the copulating witches within the occult circle held his attention. Bright eyes tracked the balletic act, their moans a luscious, decadent song.

"I doubt this is what Lou had in mind when she said 'be seen.'"

He replied by brushing hair away from her ear and nipping the lobe, eyes still trained on the act before them. Milla gasped as he worked his hand under her macramé vest, trailing knuckles up and down her spine while dusting kisses along her neck. She shivered, not unpleasantly, and pressed her hips against him. A trio of witches to their left dropped their voices and stared at the Dark Witch and the Death Witch. Milla met the eyes of a tanned Ink Witch, his Way apparent in the sigils painted on his skin, who openly scowled.

"Witches are watching."

"Thought that was the point." Darkly's chest pressed against her back, his hands sliding from her hips to her waist. The low rumble of his voice rattled among her bones. "Do you want me to stop?"

The Ink Witch leaned over to the woman beside him, another Green Witch from the flowers wound in her hair and earthen tint at the tips of her fingers. He whispered something, and she made a gagging noise before cackling and turning away.

"No," she angled her neck, silently asking him to continue. "But it's your turn." Darkly chuckled in her ear, his palm sliding higher up her stomach until the tips of his fingers brushed the bandeau top, tugging gently. Milla's breath caught in a tight gasp. "You're awful."

"You love it." He cupped her breast, his other hand splayed across her stomach. Her skin heated despite the blooming chill in his palm, and she bit off a moan as he teased her nipple and ground into her backside. Other couples began pairing off, giving over to the libidinous nature of the rite and feeding the ritual with their intent. Bodies twisted and twined within the occult circle while onlookers caressed and fondled their partners. A witch somewhere cried out with a low, guttural moan of pleasure and Darkly spun Milla to face him. His skin was a sea of goosebumps, and thick whorls of smoke drifted over his heavy-lidded eyes. "Enough?"

"Almost." She ran her hands up his chest and under the tartan scarf, nails lightly tracing his skin. Darkly bit his lower lip, eyeing Milla hungrily as she danced fingers down his front and palmed his crotch, licking up the center of his chest. He groaned, muttering a curse under his breath as he clamped his hands at her waist. Winter cold wrapped around her, falling like water down her legs to disappear into the earth.

Milla flicked her tongue over his nipple, smiling when he spasmed against her. So she nipped the sensitive flesh.

"Ach, Goddess, too much." He gripped her arms, hands warm once more, and pinned Milla against his chest, grinning wickedly down at her. "Keep going, and I'll never last the day."

"Poor baby."

Forty-Three

THE PASSAGE FROM LUST to Gluttony was swift, which seemed appropriate. Once a sinner, as Alghieri would argue, always a sinner. The slide was easy once you'd begun the fall.

Food trucks and beer tents lined the passage, tempting the senses with kebab carts and taco trucks, sno-cone vendors, and cotton candy twirlers. Any food a witch could want, any beverage they could wish to slake their thirst, was available in Gluttony. The ring was a carnival of scent—garlic, onion, and herbs, sweet and savory spiced meats spinning slowly on sticks. Tropical sweetness and the sugarcane burn of rum. Milla laughed in surprise as her stomach rumbled and her tongue dried within a few steps into the ring.

Darkly smacked his lips, eyeing the offerings. "A witch could get well fat in here."

"Moderation is key." Her eyes snagged on a stone-fired pizza vendor, her fingers slipping from Darkly's as she drifted closer. "Not sure how I can play this one."

"Grab a bite first." Darkly pointed to a slice of Margherita, already pulling up the wallet app on his phone. "Use the crust; no need to ruin everyone else's appetite."

They found Tobias lounging in a beer garden near the throughway into the Fourth Ring. With his back against the narrow table, his long legs extended and crossed at the ankles, he eyed the passing witches and sipped from a massive beer stein. His phone was held loosely in one hand, the E.R.I.E. lens displaying a sinuous warble of magickal signatures.

"Working hard, I see," Darkly said as they approached. Tobias's brows lifted, and he sat up. The front of his coat fell open, revealing a cut physique that rivaled the Darkly's, save for faint, wave-like bands of paler, puckered flesh licking his ribcage and crawling up from his hip.

Burns, Milla realized with a start.

"Worked my list through the Second Ring," he answered. "All witches accounted for, but I drew some attention. I thought it best to blend in."

Darkly snorted. "Of course, she sent you through Lust."

Tobias smirked and waved his full beer at Darkly. "One of us needed to have eyes on the covens in there without getting distracted."

Darkly looked down and flushed a lovely shade of pink that almost matched the lipstick marks Milla had left on his torso and nipple. She cackled as he tugged on the scarf, trying in vain to hide her handy work, then scowled at her. "You're a menace."

Milla curtsied, wavering slightly off balance. Grumbling under his breath, Darkly headed to the bar and returned with a beer for Milla and a cocktail for himself. His eyes were a little hazy, and he had a sloppy smile on his face. "Witches at the bar bought me shots," he said.

"I'm sure you had nothing to do with that," said Milla.

"No one could prove it." He grinned at her, and maybe she grinned back a little too knowingly because Tobias cleared his throat and knocked the base of his stein against the table to get their attention.

"Something I should know?"

Darkly broke away first, allowing Milla a chance to exhale. It wasn't that she did not want to trust Tobias—Darkly certainly did, and that was enough for her—but he had been in those cells with Milla, held by the same witch who held her, and denied it.

"Bought me a drink, too." He swirled his drink before taking a sip, and Milla caught a whiff of rum and ginger.

"Is that a Dark and Stormy?" she asked. Darkly nodded, his lips pursed around the straw. "A little on the nose, don't you think?"

He hit her with a disarming, not-at-all sober grin so cheerful and innocent that it pulled a matching smile from her.

"Idioten," Tobias muttered into his beer, shooing them along with his still running E.R.I.E. Milla glanced at the screen, noting the low chronomantic thrum, and smiled.

The deeper they wandered into the Fourth Ring, where the Coven Tents and artisan booths popped up, the more witches noticed them. By them and by design, it meant Darkly, not Milla hiding in his shadow. This ring would be the trickiest; they would be passing by the most experienced and sober witches at the festival. If one of the ritualists were here, they would clock Milla's intent immediately, so she kept behind Darkly and let him take the lead.

Showboat of a witch as he was, Darkly drank up the attention like a flower starved for the sun. Every coven wanted to claim that C.R.O.W.'s Dark Witch had stopped by their tents and met their *čarodějnicez*, and none of them were prepared for the grand reveal.

It was cheesy and downright embarrassing, but it was what Lou had wanted, and Goddess forbid they let her down.

A bevy of Whaler's Wives in mourning gowns asked to take pictures with him, and Darkly gladly obliged, hauling Milla into the frame at the last second. They were stopped by two couples from the Cahokia territory with feathers tied in their hair and swathes of brown smudged on their cheekbones and across their eyes, who asked if Darkly wanted a drink.

He hit them with his most disarming smile, thickening the brogue to illegal lengths. "Aye, something tropical if ye've got it. Though I wonder …" He stepped aside to reveal Milla. Shades stretching unseen from his feet and winding around the ankles of his targets. "Have ye a tait o' whiskey or the Lady Death?"

The sun was nearing the tops of the trees as they came upon the Elder Witch of the Pine Curtain Coven in East Texas. Tall and robust, he wore a ten-gallon hat, fringed brown leather ass-less chaps, a red speedo, and cowboy boots with golden spurs and a five-pointed star in the center. He introduced himself as Cal, a shepherd witch with a Way with animals, reaching to shake Milla's hand with thick, tanned fingers decorated in all manner of sigil-warded rings. Resting over the burst of golden curls on his chest was a gold pentagram crowned in a pair of miniature longhorns dangling from a thick, braided gold chain.

"So this is our li'l Lady Death." A bear paw of a hand clamped around hers, and he winked as he pulled the hat from his head, revealing a thick mess of golden blonde hair pulled into a bun. "All the witches have been atwitter 'bout y'all."

"Aye, and a wicked thing she is too." Darkly rolled his brogue, meeting the Texan's drawl as if he couldn't help it.

"It's always the sugar-sweet ones that'll knock you on yer ass, ain't it?"

Milla liked him immediately.

He led them through the last of the Fourth Ring into the Fifth, Wrath, where more invasive and dangerous rituals were performed under a careful eye.

"Consent or Crossing?" A security witch at the barrier scanned their wristbands, gesturing to the ritual path to his right and the warded through-way that would allow quick passage to the Sixth Ring, Heresy, to his left, where another Consent check posed the same question to the witches gathered there.

"Consent," Cal stated with a lusty wink, holding out a swarthy wrist. The security witch swept a willow wand along the inside of his arm, and a golden arrow appeared in the wake.

"Welcome to the Order, sir."

Cal sauntered into the Fifth Ring, thumbs hooked in his belt and a shit-eating grin on his face.

Darkly turned Milla to face him when the security witch posed their question. "It's getting late. Do we have the time?"

"We need at least two of the consent circles." She gestured to the throughway. "I'd rather skip the Vamp Camp in the Seventh Ring." Darkly nodded, accepting her answer, and she faced the security witch. "Consent."

"Welcome to the Order, ma'am." He swept the wand against her wrist, a tingle following the lazy swipe, and a golden arrow appeared, granting Milla passage.

The might of Wrath hit Milla like a wet blanket slap to the face the moment she crossed the barrier. Where in the preceding rings, the air was crisp and clean as fresh cut grass, the Fifth Ring breathed a heady miasma. Milla's belly swooped, and Darkly's fingers slipped between the belt at the base of her spine and her skin, tugging her closer. Even Cal wasn't immune, taking off his cowboy hat to fan himself. The motion sent a cloud of leather, musk, and a sweet, floral scent to envelop Milla, pooling heat in her belly.

"Shall we find a tent?" Cal glanced at them, wearing a slick smile full of wicked promise. "Or sidle up somewhere private?"

Darkly tightened his grip on her belt, jerking Milla flush against him. "Dinnae share."

The pooling heat in her belly rose to a simmer, leaking into her limbs. She fisted her hands, closing her eyes and taking deep breaths to calm her Way. But each breath meant inhaling more of the candlesmoke and ritual intent. Her core throbbed, and she licked her lips, fighting the urge to wrap herself around Darkly and bring him to the ground.

Cal gave them a wary look, and Milla dug her nails into Darkly's thigh instead. He bit his lower lip, black eyes drifting over Cal, and unleashed a wicked, sensual smile. "Though if the lady obliges, I'm down to take you for a ride."

Milla choked in surprise, while Cal was quicker to recover. He bellowed out a laugh, slapped Darkly on the back, and pulled him in for a side hug that jostled them both. "Boy, you couldn't handle this bull."

"I'd be willing to take that bet."

The deeper they walked along the Fifth Ring, the headier the intoxicating magick in the air became. Every lurid glance from Cal traced her body with dark promise, and each touch from Darkly intensified. Magick sizzled over her skin, coiling deep in her belly and between her hips, tighter and tighter and tighter until she had to pause.

Darkly pulled her out of the main flow on the path, and from the smoke-stained look he gave her as he adjusted his pants, the feeling was mutual.

A ragged cry exploded from the tent to their right, and they whipped their attention toward the sound. A manifestation ceremony was just visible over the heads, or rather, bodies of the crowd. On a raised altar in the center of the tent, a coven worked each other, channeling their telos—the focus of the ritual, the intent they sought to bring to fruition—for all to see and participate as they would.

The female witch in a harness rode her partner, head thrown back as she rocked her hips. She took the finger of another witch into her mouth, who was in turn being pleasured by a witch on his knees. Yet another sucked at the ritual leader's breasts while her partner in the ceremony adjusted their grip on iron rungs, chanting as their mistress cried her pleasure.

The charged energy of the ritual crashed against Milla at the same moment Darkly's hand cupped her ass. The simmering heat pooled in her belly rose with frightening intensity, stoking an ache she'd all too willingly ignored.

The witches around them were just as affected. Moans rose as heads dropped back against chests, tops were pulled aside, and legs spread. Cal disappeared into the throng, his broad shoulders and ludicrous hat led away by a man and a woman illusioned to appear as centaurs.

Milla whirled to face Darkly, slapping her palm against the center of the sigil and marching him away from the tent until his back hit a tree. "Now, Darkly."

"Yes, ma'am," he drawled. The smoke in his eyes deepened, and his hands clamped down on her hips, pulling Milla against him and holding her there. His erection dug into her belly, and he ground against her, capturing her mouth to drink her moan.

He slid a hand up her spine, pressing her into him, and wrapped lean fingers around her neck, hauling her deeper into his mouth. It was that reckless crashing of teeth and tongue in Tallahassee all over again, just as furious and impassioned and ill-timed, but they needed this. Needed to lay their trap in this circle, and *Goddess*, did they want it.

It was evident in the drag of his teeth along Milla's lower lip and the frantic path of his hand as he grasped the hem of her gauzy skirt, setting the gold coins jangling against one another in search of her thigh.

His fingers finally dug into her flesh, hoisting Milla's leg, and he thrust, teasing her until she moaned, "Oh, Horned God."

Darkly pulled away to look at Milla with eyes as clear and jade green as she had ever seen. "Me or you?" he panted, clinging to a desperate edge.

"Both."

"Thank the Goddess." Black flooded his eyes, but before he could act, Milla dropped to her knees, frantically tearing at the Celtic knot and undoing his pants. "Milla—"

"Shut up." She freed his erection, taking one selfish moment to marvel at the sight, and then swallowed him down as much as she could manage.

Darkly's head hit the back of the tree, his fingers knotted in her hair, but it was the desperate whisper of "Fuck" that did her in.

She rolled her tongue, hollowing her cheeks and rearing back, flitting her eyes up his long, lovely body. The lower whorls of the triskelion danced and shimmered in svítilna cast light, and Shades bled from his shoulders, slithering down his arms in search of her.

A dangerous heat built in her at the sight of this witch, undone by her lips, her tongue, her touch—hers. She tongued the slit on his head, groaning at the salty taste, and swallowed him down again, fisting his cock and spinning her wrist, slamming forward and relishing the tears that bloomed in her eyes until Darkly was trembling from her touch. His hands alternated from grabbing her hair to guiding her head to caressing her cheek.

And when the heat became too much to bear, when she thought she might lose control and ruin them both, Milla stretched her arm up his body, just barely managing to tweak one of those gloriously sensitive nipples.

Darkly damn near flew off the tree as he came, shouting loud enough to call any witch who cared over. Hot spurts coated her tongue and throat, doing nothing to quell the need churning inside of her.

And he knew or suspected because the moment his cock ceased its eruption, Darkly hauled Milla to her feet, spun her around, and blanketed her back with his body.

"Heinous witch," he snarled in her ear, spent but no less exhausted for it. He cupped her pussy, dragging his middle finger along the seam of her shorts before working the hem to the side and doing the same against bald flesh. Milla whimpered, held in place by his weight, his heat. "Grab the bark," he demanded, and she did, digging her fingers into the coarse ridges of the green oak. "Dante."

"What?" she panted, wriggling her hips as his finger trailed her lips.

"Too much or too far," he sang in a low, sinister voice. Cold bloomed in the wake of his fingers, and he cupped her breast with his free hand, teasing her nipple. "Say 'Dante.' Understood?"

"Yes." She said it fast, too fast, but Holy Horned God, the teasing alone was going to drive her to lose control. Bark crumpled beneath her hands, the heat in her veins on the verge of boiling.

"Good witch." Darkly dipped his finger into her pussy, sweeping through her folds to gather arousal before tracing her clit. Milla arched against him, teeth ground together to keep from screaming. He did it again, driving her to the same trembling state she had brought him. A hand of shadow bloomed at her throat, gently easing Milla's head back. Wisps of cool air caressed her exposed midriff and pulsed against her pussy, wrapping around Milla until the chill seeped into her bones, tempering her Way and lessening the burn while at the same time every other sensation coursing through her body intensified.

Darkly gasped, and though she could not turn her face to see, she knew it was in surprise. His cock twitched against her backside, and he dropped his head against her shoulder, moaning as he thrust between her thighs. "Goddess, *leannán*."

She did not know what he had just done or how. How could she when there were no thoughts or questions in her head? She was nothing but bliss, reverberating along a taut wire. Ecstasy shot from one end to the other until all she knew was the feel of Darkly's fingers sliding deep inside of her in their wicked summons. The grind of his cock against her skin. The pinch of his fingers and roll of his Shade. Yet through it all, faint on the other end of that wire, was the sensation of cool sweat and soft flesh. Of need and wonder, and slick heat clenching down.

"Too much?" he asked, yanking Milla back to earth, if only for a moment.

"More," she demanded, and he gave. His fingers slid from her pussy, and he jerked her shorts down, fumbling her skirt out of the way before sliding into her in one delicious thrust. Her palms sank into the tree, bark falling as ash to her feet. Darkly relinquished her breast to grab her hips, hitching Milla to a better angle before driving into her again. Shades cushioned her cheek against the tree bark, teasing her nipples, her clit, and Darkly fucked her in her favorite Way.

Hard, like she was unbreakable. Impervious.

Like she was a Death Witch.

She cried out, not caring if anyone heard. Pleasure swelled in her core, heating her skin. She gripped the tree, moaning as her Way built higher, fed by Darkly and his Shades, and when release was within reach, she pressed her hips back, and he pounded forward.

Stars burst behind her eyes, and pleasure overrode sense. Searing heat left her hands, pouring from Milla into the oak, along with a ragged, wild cry from her throat. Darkly pulled out on a curse, dancing away from Milla and leaving her to collapse against the tree. The trunk juddered from the dead weight of her body, branches quaking and dropping brittle, autumn dry leaves all around them.

It took a moment to regain herself. To realize where she was and what they'd done. When her vision cleared, she saw Darkly mere inches away with a worried look on his face.

"Dante?" he asked.

Milla grinned, panting as she replied, "Fuck no."

Forty-Four

"You'll want to freshen up," Rai called from near the tent, her tone indifferent and bored.

Darkly muttered a curse under his breath, tucking himself back into his pants before turning around. "Lou send you to babysit?"

"Do you think I would if she asked me?" Rai cocked her head. She'd added a jaunty, undersized top hat and half veil to her ensemble, and the red lipstick had been traded for a poisonous green that smudged into a sinful black. "It's almost sundown. Constance Abernathy's assistant is about to have a heart attack looking for you two."

"He can deal," Milla grumbled. She tugged her shorts up and fiddled with her skirt, trying to get it to sit correctly on her hips.

"Also, there's the matter of what in the nine rings you two have been doing all day."

"Being seen." Darkly yanked on his belt, easily looping the Celtic knot.

Rai blinked calmly at him and looked pointedly at the ashen husk of an oak tree he had just fucked Milla against, then back to him. "Sure."

"Rai—"

She raised a hand, silencing him. "Neither of you is weak, Keir, and frankly, it was insulting for her to insinuate as such. I am only worried about what happens next."

"Gonnae tattle?"

"Please." She skirted around him and plucked a satchel from the empty air, opening it up and offering it to Milla. "Angelica root. I don't know what this is all about"—she waved a vague hand at the tree, Milla, and Darkly—"but you are expected to perform for the Elder Witches. We can't have you dawdling drunk about the stage."

Milla shoved a root shaving under her tongue, head-clearing almost immediately. "Thank you."

"And you." She wheeled around and examined Darkly, lips parting in surprise. "You're not …"

"Rotted?" he finished for her. "Aye, nifty trick I've picked up."

"But how?"

"Yeah, seriously." Milla moved closer, stopping her hand a hair's breadth away from his chest. "I'm unbound, and you were still on me when my Way … how are you not rotting?"

"La petite mort." He winked at her. It took Milla a second to translate, and when she caught up, her neck and chest flared with heat. The little death. She stared at him in shock, and Darkly grinned. "Had me wondering how Lightner survived you." He booped her nose, and Milla swatted his hand away. "Your magick wants to be used, *leannán*. Even better, ken it fancies bein' used on me."

"Oh, Horned God, really? Magickal orgasms?" Rai vanished her bag and stalked toward the tents and the narrow passageway between them. "I literally can not."

This deep in the ring, it was a bit of a hike to the throughway that would lead them into Heresy. Milla caught glimpses of the rituals they passed, marveling at the ingenuity of the witches as manifestation rituals and libidinous displays evolved into more fetishized performances.

At their heart, rituals were all the same—first came the establishment of the telos, or the objective purpose of the ritual, the intent.

Next came desire. A witch must want with all her mind, body, and soul the thing for which she appeals to the Triple Goddess. Desire was fairly easy to achieve where sex magick was involved, but in sex magick, desire was wound in with intent and established through the act.

Sacrifice was the tricky one. In the traditional sense, the sacrifice taken was one Milla knew well. One she had fallen back upon with Ezra time and time again and now with Darkly. It was easy to lose oneself in carnal pleasure, and wasn't loss a sacrifice? While Milla never leapt to that as a first choice, it was hard to deny the appeal of la petite mort, and clearly, Darkly had made the same connection.

But as with all things witchy and weird, the Ways were many, and the means plentiful.

Sacrifice could be of the flesh. It could be pain given or received. It could be the emotional loss of self above the physical or be as simple as taking away one's freedom and will. All of this illustrated by the final rituals they passed. In one, a woman perched on the lap of a witch, her legs held apart while he played her like an instrument and savored her moans. Near the through-way, a pair of witches in clunky, iron shoes were led by their harnesses in a circle, their legs hobbled and horse-hair plugs bobbing. A striking image to hold in mind as they entered the Sixth Ring.

"Flinging or Flying?" the Security Witch asked, gesturing to the casting ranges within the ring.

"Flying," Milla sighed, following the witch's pointed arm to the through-way. It did not stop her from flinging a subtle hex or two, withering a Green Witch's vine and reversing a chronomantic's offensive allure.

Crowded tents filled the Seventh Ring, Violence, housing everything from the Vamp Camp to live paintings of torrid scenes to spoken-word open mics. Witches illusioned to appear as creatures of myth wandered the ring, and Rai led them easily through the installations, handily avoiding the vampires.

Thumping bass and electronic wails welcomed them to the Eighth Ring—Fraud. Milla kept her eyes sharp, scanning the crowd for Diego while knowing the likelihood of spotting him was slim. The crowd in this ring was thick at the end of the day as witches made their way to the center of the festival, all of them blind to the extra shadows clinging to the trees and tents.

The barrier between the Eighth and Ninth Rings was thin and guarded by the massive landmark Milla had pointed out to Darkly on the map.

Larger than the Red Death or any of the other sculptures and statuary speckling the grounds, every passer-by slowed to marvel at the towering winged terror. Red eyes lit with spalování flame scanned the crowd from a head pivoting left to right. Clever mechanics twisted each of his three mouths in a cycle of pain, malice, and rage. Both hands gripped limp bodies dressed in rags, and a third dangled half-chewed in one of the mouths.

As they approached, Milla lightly caressed the thin casing wrapped around the statue's leg.

"Leather." She moved to the beast's cloven hoof and pressed her hand against the heel. Life whispered back at her, and she jerked her hand away, mystified. "And bone and fur, Holy Horned God."

"The Panhandle Coven spares no expense," Rai advised from somewhere over her left shoulder. "The pamphlet described it as iron reinforced bone and chronomantically hexed leather and fur to maintain the Mystique of the Real." Milla glanced at the Vinefica, and Rai's lips spread smugly. "You two are clearly up to something. I trust this will do?"

Milla whipped her face to Darkly, who looked just as alarmed as she felt.

"What do you mean?" he asked, all innocence.

"Please, she rotted an oak tree, and you've been dropping Shades since Limbo." When Darkly's mouth formed a startled little o, Rai shook her head and sent him a fond smile. "I can still sense your magick a kilometer away, Keir. A witch doesn't easily forget something like that." She patted his arm. "Anything else I should know?"

"Be ready," Milla said, checking her phone and sliding it back into the pouch. "If this works, the ritualists are going to be caught bare-assed." At Rai's blank look, she clarified, "They'll be out in the open."

"They'll need tae act quickly," Darkly added.

Rai's gaze drifted from Milla to the organic construct looming over them. "How many of the rings did you manage?"

"All but the Seventh."

Rai nodded, contemplating the three-headed statue and, no doubt, the Ways of the witches she escorted.

"M'gonnae need something to keep me grounded," Darkly said in a low voice. "No weed, a stimulant."

Rai whipped her face to him, worry creasing her brow. "You're sure?"

"Need my wits about me." He brushed Rai's arm. Took her hand. "Lou's gonnae expect me to be functional."

"Lou's going to be livid." Rai squeezed his fingers and pulled away, looking between the pair. "You're positive about this?"

"Deadly," Milla confirmed. "And you should put up a ward; with any luck, this will take out the entire festival."

"Well, alright then." Rai fluffed Milla's hair, straightened the fingerbone and boline on her necklace, then did the same to Darkly, tugging his scarf into place as she smiled sweetly at him, carefully avoiding the Shade looping his bicep. "I'll go find Toby."

"Oh, thank the Goddess, there you are!" Rhett bustled up beside them, eyes frantic and curls tousled. Dust clung to the creases at the corners of his eyes, aging the young Vestic by a handful of years. "Ms. Abernathy hoped to meet with you before your demonstrations, but we don't have the time now. The svítilna can light on the fly, but the audiomantics are beside themselves."

"I'm sorry, what?" Milla stumbled a step, half-tracking Rai, who slipped away as Rhett pressed on.

"You're up first; I'll need some idea of what music they should play," the vestic fussed over Darkly. "Will you talk? They can cast your voice easily enough. And where have you been? You were supposed to be here half an hour ago."

Darkly smiled a shark's grin, eyes bleeding deep black. "Got waylaid."

The main stage of Beltane was separated from the crowd by a narrow moat of cleared ground guarded by Enforcers. A trench had been dug beneath the stage, allowing more clearance for the taller witches. Darkly halted at the entrance, an earthen ramp guarded on both sides by sound-dampening wards and a slew of look-away hexes that Rhett dispelled with a lazy wave. Dropping hands on his hips and rocking back on his heels, Darkly scanned the crowd beyond the Enforcers, the angle of the sun, and the mound rising over the curve of the stage. A broad grin lit up his face; the fool of a witch was thrilled by what he saw.

"Let me guess," Milla said, "reminds you of your childhood?"

"Aye, that it does." He scanned the stage and the gathering crowd, completely at ease with their circumstances, while Milla's belly was a riot of nerves and anxiety. "Mum used to breathe fire in the main ring." Of the carnival he'd grown up in, she assumed. "Da worked the lights."

"Svítilna?"

"I—" He closed his mouth, chin tucking and lips pursing. "Actually, dinnae ken what—"

"There you are." Lou popped out from under the stage, eyes blazing as she examined them both. Her lip curled at the lipstick stains on Darkly's chest. Milla's disheveled skirt. "Goddess, are you even sober enough to cast?"

"'Course I am." Darkly pressed a hand to his chest in mock affront. "Wee Milla, on the other hand."

"Had a li'l fun in the Fourth." Milla hiccuped and pressed a finger to her chin, swaying slightly. "Or wassit the Fifth?" She flexed the fingers on her casting hand, forming a wobbly sigil. "Can still do the flower trick. I think."

"Abysmal." She prodded them under the stage, Rhett following close behind. "The Elder Witches are seated here." Lou pointed to a short staircase leading to a lowered portion of the stage.

"Did Dina make it?" Milla asked. Lou's brow bunched, and she clarified, "She said she wanted to be here." Swirling a finger in the air, she swayed for good measure, forcing Lou to back away. "Wouldn' wan' her to miss the show."

"I'm sure she's here somewhere." Lou directed them to the stairs. "There's a vase on stage. I'll be on hand to bind your Way the moment you're done. We wouldn't want you rotting anything unnecessary."

"Got it."

"Keir, you're expected to bring on the night. With any luck, the crowd will be too stunned to be disappointed by Ludmilla."

Darkly's drunken grin widened, and glee crinkled his eyes. He clapped his hands and rubbed them together, plumes of deep, black smoke rising with the motion. "Excellent."

"Is that them?" Constance descended the short flight of stairs, bustling over. "Thank the Goddess, I thought we were about to miss the window." She bustled over, necklaces and bracelets clacking, and swept Milla into a hug. Pendants and beads dug into Milla's front, and the cat-eye point of bright purple glasses pierced her temple. "Two demesnes, my girl, Morgen is so proud!" She gripped Milla's shoulders and leaned back, beaming a bright, gap-toothed smile at her. "She can't wait to see you."

"Morgen's here?"

"Of course she is. What sort of mother misses her daughter's first Beltane?" She released Milla and faced Darkly. He grinned, dimple and all, and offered his hand. Constance batted it away and hugged with as much vigor as she'd hugged Milla.

The smoke drained away, and startled green eyes widened over the Elder Witch's head. He was over a foot taller than Constance, undoubtedly stronger and heavier, but the woman rocked him side to side with as much ease as she had Milla's slight frame. His shock melted away as quickly as it had risen, and Darkly hugged her back.

"A witch could get used to such greetings, Ms. Abernathy," he said, all charm and smiles.

"None of that. You're one of ours now. Call me Auntie." She let go, checking her watch, and jerked into motion, ushering Darkly to the stairs. "Five minutes, is that enough time?"

"More than." He ducked to avoid a beam and alighted the steps with Connie right behind him, glancing back at Milla before ascending out of sight. "It's showtime."

Lou, Rhett, and Constance followed him up to the viewing platform, and the crowd erupted as Darkly took the stage. Milla closed her eyes and counted to three. Her nerves were a jangle, and, absent an audience, she took a moment to internally freak the fuck out.

This would work. It had to work. They had primed the ritual grounds, Darkly would bring on the night, ensuring Milla had everything she needed in place, and they would light their figurative beacon, drawing all of the attention and all of the magick to themselves. It wasn't her best theory, but Goddess, it was better than rotting flowers and waiting for something to happen.

Charge the field, draw the magick, starve the ritual. Turn down all of the noise, erase the confusion of Beltane and distortion of the Ways, and clear a path to locate the witches pretending to be her.

She only hoped it would be enough.

Shadows flickered and stretched beneath the stage, drawn to the stairs. Her phone buzzed, and she pulled it out, reading the E.R.I.E. and its reassuring chart, doing exactly what she expected it to. The light winked out, plunging Milla into utter darkness. The Beltane crowd shrieked in delighted terror, and a deep, rolling chuckle trickled through the boards to Milla's ears, dying away as the light returned and she came face to face with the Voodoo Queen of New Orleans.

Milla yelped, jerking out of Marie's reach. The vampire did not move. Dressed as impeccably as ever, her deep crimson wrap dress clung to every curve. Liquid shadows dripped from ruffles at the neckline and along the asymmetrical slit in the skirt. Gold adorned her fingers, wrists, and neck, glinting rich and wicked in the salt lamps beneath the stage, and nestled in the wild curls of her hair was one of those little dreadfuls Milla despised.

The doll waved a stumpy appendage at her, and it was a struggle not to hex the damn thing into a pile of decaying burlap.

Despite the utter fear curdling her blood, despite all wisdom screaming at her not to, Milla spoke first. "I'm surprised to see you here, Marie."

"This is a celebration of the Ways, is it not?" She pursed her lips in false innocence. "I had not been made aware Voodoo was no longer considered acceptable." When Milla had no response, Marie flashed her fangs. "Is this any way to greet me after so long apart, Little Lightner?"

Milla's heart seized. Just plumb stopped in her chest. She willed herself not to flee, not to lash out, managing enough poise to stare at the vampire with her lips pursed together. The Voodoo Queen had never called her by Ezra's name, and Milla did not want to unpack the implications of her using it now.

Marie laughed again, throwing her head back. "Terror is lovely on you, Ludmilla."

"My being terrorized doesn't tend to end well for you and yours," Milla replied. That sobered Marie enough to have her move closer. Milla held up a hand, showing her the blackened tips of her fingernails. "One question." Shallow eyes darted to Milla's hand. "You know about these rituals, don't you?"

A long, loaded moment passed, heavy as a held breath. Marie nodded, relinquishing a few inches of space between them. "What have you done?"

"Rigged the deck." Milla faced the stairs, boldly putting her back to Marie. "Is the Vamp Camp warded?"

"By the best, naturally."

"You should leave." She tipped her head to the side, angling it enough to see Marie's face. Was that a hint of pride she saw there? "Get behind the wards and keep the cultists inside."

"And the witches in the Seventh Ring?"

That had Milla twisting around. "How many."

"A handful," Marie conceded. "And one Stitch Witch."

Fuck. She knew Diego had been assigned the Seventh Ring, but she had thought he would be smart enough to avoid Marie. Who was she kidding? No one could avoid the Voodoo Queen. The Horned God-damned woman was inevitable.

"Can you—" she swallowed thickly, hating that of all the witches in the world, she was about to ask Marie this favor. "Can you get him behind a ward?"

"It is going to cost you."

"Whatever you need." A fool's bargain, but this was Diego they were talking about. What else could she do?

"It is less about what I need and more about what I want." Marie let that sit for a singular heartbeat. "*Who* I want."

Milla closed her eyes, dropping her chin to her chest. Like the witch, her request was inevitable. But this was a question of Diego, and in that there was only ever one answer. She raised her head, hoping her expression was as determined as she felt. "Whatever you need."

Marie smiled, the Shades plunged them into darkness, and a cold, vice-like grip seized Milla's wrist. She cried out as fangs plunged into her arm, the sound drowned out by the roaring crowd. Marie sucked once, dragging at the very essence of Milla, and released her arm. When the light returned, she was a dozen feet away, wiping her thumb across her lower lip.

"Await my summons," Marie stated. The stage was plunged into darkness again, and Milla knew before the lamps flickered to life that the Voodoo Queen was gone.

Forty-Five

SHADES POURED OVER THE edge of the stage, rising as a fog and wafting westward over and through the crowd, gathering around the massive devil guarding the entrance to the Ninth Ring.

From her place on the viewing platform, Milla scanned Darkly's work, noting the crowd mesmerized by his every move, an utterly captive audience. She pressed her hand against her phone, half telling herself and half pleading with the app she'd left running.

This will work.

Her phone buzzed in a show of support.

"Any minute now," Constance said from behind Milla. "Goddess, he's something, isn't he?"

"Millamäuschen has excellent taste," Morgen's crisp voice answered. She sat in the front row of chairs beside Cal of all witches and greeted Milla with a tight nod and tiny smile when she joined them on the viewing platform. Her casting hand danced in a series of sigils, and she had one arm raised, projecting an illusion in the sky to show Darkly paying his ritual dues to every witch in attendance.

"The vase is there." Lou pointed at a small table on the stage, several yards away from Darkly. "One quick enervation and you'll be done."

"Got it." Milla did not take her eyes off Darkly, and honestly, who could? The witch was a born showman, flinging shadows and playing with the crowd. He spread his arms, summoning a stygian cloak like a vaudevillian. "Any word from Donmar?"

Sweeping an arm to the side, Darkly whirled in a circle. The cloak billowed behind him, casting out over the crowd. They cheered, and he did it again, blinding another swathe of witches with his Way. A slice of his hand sent the cloak flying over the crowd to tangle in the devil's horns.

"Staid campout," Lou said. "Some corporate event, no sign of the ritualists."

"Hm."

The sun was well below the trees, the sky to the east deepening toward night as the western horizon gleamed in goldenrod and blush pink. On the stage, Darkly spun in a slow circle as he moved to the edge, where he dropped into a wide-legged stance, his right arm stretched to the east, his left reaching west for the construct. The crowd and the Elder Witches cried out as the shadows cast by the beast's wings swelled and throbbed, whorling as a midnight storm. With less than a breeze tangling in Milla's hair and tickling her cheek, Darkly clapped his hands together, summoning the Shades and bringing on the night.

Black sped across the sky from the east, rushing to the roiling mass he had summoned and plunging the Ninth Ring into a starless black. Magick filled the humid air, heavy and electric. A charged aether at the ready for any witch bold enough to reach out and take it.

Milla closed her eyes, curling her hands into fists and taking three quick breaths before mounting the stairs to the stage.

As swiftly as they were summoned, the Shades vanished, taking with them the crackle of excess Way Darkly had drawn from every witch in attendance. Darkly swayed as she stepped beside him, the magick filling his person. His eyes were wide and fevered, a glistening opalescent black. Veins pulsed in his neck and temples, and faint, worming ashen streaks crawled along his arms. She grabbed his hand to keep the quake in his fingers from being seen as salt lamps flared to life at the base of the stage, lighting their world in grays and greens.

There was a moment of silence. The crowd inhaled as one, and then deafening and riotous applause erupted. The audiomantics beneath the stage dampened the sound, and Darkly raised their joined hands, drawing all the attention to Milla.

"Hope you're ready, *leannán.*" His words came out hollow and distant, not quite the *voice* he sometimes used, but she heard the restraint as he spoke. "Nae sure how long I can hold on."

"Like you said, milenec," she used the masculine Czech, calling to him as he called to her. "It's showtime."

Darkly grinned, releasing Milla's hand. The crowd fell into an uneasy silence, taking in their first glimpse of the Death Witch. Small, slight, pale. In her costume vest and dark makeup, she was everything they expected and still fell far short of the mark. It was in the hushed whispers and mocking whistles. In the silence bleeding from the viewing platform at the back of the stage.

Milla sashayed in front of Darkly, circling the flowers on the table and rotting them with a touch. The crowd gasped, her small act of magick projected by Morgen for all to see. She brought them back to full bloom, and a witch on the viewing platform muttered, "I never get tired of seeing that."

The phone in her pouch buzzed. Milla feigned a yawn and made a show of checking the notifications.

"Got the time, witch?" Darkly jeered.

The chart on her screen was a mess of signatures, wavy lines, and sharp peaks and valleys. She glanced at the crowd, Darkly, the phone, then turned her face to the mound behind the stage. Darkly followed her look and smiled sharply. At his nod, Milla slipped her phone into the pouch.

"Time to go."

He was fast. Goddess, he was so fast. He strode across the stage and took Milla into his arms, uttering nothing more than a rushed "Hold on to me" before the world opened up and arctic winds swallowed them both.

He stepped them out on top of the mound, keeping Milla tight against him as he formed a sigil with one hand and closed the seam. The winds of the Neitherworld still howled in her ears, and for a second, Milla thought he had miscast.

"Darkly!" She yelled over the sound to gain his attention, but he kept his gaze pinned over her head. "What happened?"

Hollows had begun to creep into his cheeks, and a faint bruising grew beneath impossibly dark eyes that crinkled as he showed Milla the crowd.

The screaming, cheering, riotous crowd.

Every witch in attendance whooped and hollered, losing their minds as they surged for the Enforcers holding the space before the stage.

"We have to do this now," Darkly said, no louder than a whisper, but she heard it clear as a bell as if he had slipped the words directly into her head. "Cannae hold on much longer."

A faint tail of smoke drifted from his mouth, whipping around Milla, and for a moment, the world went hazy and gray, clearing just as quickly.

That's new.

"Right." She shook out her hands, took a deep breath, and stepped further into her Way than she'd gone in years.

She focused her intent on the demonstration. In the shock and awe. On impressing the assembled covens. Showing them what a Death Witch could do and keeping the attention on her. Her desire was in line with her intent: be the distraction Lou demanded. Never let them know what was coming next. Darkly had done his job well; now it was up to her.

And sacrifice, well, considering the requirements of *this* specific ritual, this was certainly going to hurt.

"Are you ready?" she asked.

"Goddess, I hope so." Darkly wrapped an arm around her front, steadying Milla, and a jolt went through her body. Her veins lit up, heat flaring higher and brighter than ever before.

No. Not quite. It was the Loa all over again. The surge of power from her demesne and from his Shades, pushing Milla over the finish line. But this time, it was given power. Desired power. *Intentional* power and Darkly was not the sacrifice.

Lifting the curved boline blade on her necklace, Milla dragged it along the length of her left pinky.

"Holy Horned God," she hissed from the pain and hooked the blade at the last minute to slice off a chunk of her flesh. Blood welled and dribbled into her palm, pooling over the scars and drowning the slice of skin. She pressed the fingerbone on her necklace to her palm with two fingers, mingling it with her flesh and blood, and began chanting.

"Probuď se, probuď se do tohoto falešného života."

Wake. Wake to this false life.

Milla swayed as her intent immediately caught. She staggered to the left and Darkly grabbed her by the shoulders to keep her upright.

"Nahoru a natáhnout křídla. Nahoru a natáhnout křídla."

Rise and stretch your wings.

"Gonnae give them all nightmares," Darkly muttered in a voice gone guttural and raw.

"Probuďte se a dýchejte."

Wake, and breathe.

Goddess, the intent was strong, the magick in the air high and charged, yearning to be seized. The vein-worming pain of the funeral mask shot out from her temples, grounding Milla in the ritual and urging her on.

She raised her palm to the massive sculpture at the rim of the Ninth Ring, bidding the triple-mouthed beast to wake. To stretch his wings in a simulacrum of life.

"Dýchat."

Breathe.

Her voice went sepulchral, echoing as a rasping moan the audiomantics did not bother to adjust. Morgen's projections flickered overhead, doubling the greyish-green light from the salt lamps on the stage and casting an eerie pallor over the mound. Milla allowed herself one greedy glance at the projection floating over the crowd, and Horned God was it terrifying.

Her eyes glowed an incandescent purplish pink. Pale smoke wafted from her sclera, heightening the horror of the decayed lacing of her veins clawing across her cheekbones, above her eyebrows, and knotting together at the bridge of her nose. Her little finger and ring finger pinched the fingerbone to her outstretched palm, and blood flowed from the wound, running in a crimson line down her forearm and dripping from her elbow.

At her back stood a King in Smoke and Shadow. Tendrils of flame-like Shades fanned and danced around them, and the pale, harsh angles of his face stood out in sharp relief against wickedly narrowed black eyes. A cruel sneer parted Darkly's lips, and a Shade wreathed his head as a crown with smoking tines. He held his casting hand beneath her elbow, pooling her blood in his waiting palm. What he did not catch fell to the earthen mound, where it ate the dirt and grass, sending the scent of sweet-rot to cloy and tease her nose.

At the sight of them, deep in their Ways and joined by his Shades, his arm, her blood, Marie's words burned in her mind: *Do you know what you both could do? Together?*

Milla faltered, her arm shook, dropping slightly, and Darkly's lean fingers curled around her elbow in Death's own grip.

"*Continue,*" he ordered in that *voice*. She shuddered at the sensual roll of mercury in her veins. The heat of him at her back intensified as he curled fingers around her hip, stepping so close she could smell the wintry spice and smoke scent that was all *him* mingling with the sweet rot of the earth. "*Summon them.*"

Milla swallowed. This was a theory, one he had all too willingly agreed to test. And why wouldn't he? It piggybacked off of the theory he'd been working with all along. His Way, to quote herself, was a "freaky battery" for hers. Instead of drowning it or avoiding it or working themselves to exhaustion just to ignore this peculiarity of their Ways, why not *use it.*

Milla braced her feet and dove further.

"*Dejte mi pozor.* "

Heed me.

There was a sickening pull on her Way as a tether unspooled from her gut and connected with the Shades swarming the sculpture. She jerked forward, and only Darkly's grip at her elbow and hip kept her on her feet. A wicked and low chuckle escaped the Dark Witch as the statue's wings twitched and curled in, swallowing the magick he had sent there. Summoned from every cache he dropped throughout the ritual grounds, from every witch who cheered and applauded as he paid his ritual dues, who bought him a drink or asked for a picture. From the oak tree he'd imbued with the power of the telos they fed in the consent circle. All of it hoarded in plain sight for his Death Witch to use.

All of it now at her command.

Milla gasped at the influx of power, and the beast shivered, rolling his shoulders with the creak of metal and snap of bone. He tilted his triple-faced head back before thrusting out massive wings and releasing a grinding, metallic roar.

His wings flapped, expelling the Shades. They burst out and swept low over the crowd like the ghouls and ghasts from Bald Mountain in the old orchestral Disney film. Her fingertips blackened and ached, her hand cramped from holding the bone and sigils. She focused on the pain to keep from being terrified. No amount of tea or sparring could have prepared Milla for this amount of magick, and she was about three seconds away from dropping the ritual and passing out.

A low, rumbling chuckle built in Darkly's chest. He slipped his hand to Milla's wrist, circling lean fingers around her bones to keep her steady and connected to the beast. The hand at her hips slid up and splayed across her stomach, and Darkly jerked her back against his chest with a word she didn't know.

"Cothaigh."

A manacle of cold flashed at her wrist. She jolted as the Dark and Death Ways connected and joined. Cold bled into her bones, deeper than the chill of the cells. Deeper than a winter night. The cold of the Neitherworld where none lived save for the King in Smoke and Shadow and the lone witch at the Gates. A flash of arousal coursed through her body, and Milla knew where she had felt this before—in her hut as he plied her with his Shades and again at the tree in Wrath.

Darkly guided her arm, and the Shades followed the swipe of her hand. He swooped them low over the crowd, pulling her hand back to draw them close, then swept her arm to send them crashing over the witches in a wave. Conducting an orchestra of Shade through his Death Witch.

Her phone buzzed in her pouch, one alert after another. Milla tore her eyes from the Shades and the construct, scanning the crowd and almost missing it—a deep red, so deep it was almost black against the night sky, blooming of light.

"Darkly."

His smooth, sweeping movement faltered just enough that she knew he had seen it, too.

Their idiot plan had worked, and the ritualists had taken the opportunity Milla presented. The magick Darkly had pumped into Beltane, the intent, desire, and sacrifice Milla paid to her ritual. The beacon they lit atop the mound drew all eyes onto themselves to allow the ritualists a chance to work, and it had *worked*.

"*A little longer, Death Witch,*" that *voice* crawled out of Darkly again, and for the briefest moment, it felt as though he were conducting her as he conducted the Shades.

"When this happens, we need to be fast."

"*Lest you forget, Ludmilla,*" he teased, breath chill against her ear. "*I can leap tall buildings in a single bound.*"

"Alright, Superman."

Darkly chuckled. The beast stretched and furled his wings, rushing an arm down low over the heads of the crowd and roaring its three mouths into the night sky. Their terror, the fury of the Shades, turned his rumbling chuckle into a laugh that grew into a full-on villainous outburst.

His laughter bubbled over into Milla, drunk as she was off her Way, and soon they were both cackling mad on top of the mound, masters of the terror they unleashed on the mayhem of witches below. Wreathed in voided flame and looking like the Forbidden and Foule things they were.

Darkly quieted and sent one last surge of power into Milla, "*With me now, love.*"

His hand left her front and gripped her other wrist. He held their arms out, muttering quietly in Irish over her head and circling their arms to gather the Shades as a teeming hurricane. Tightening the whorl until it was a flat disc of impenetrable black. A thin circle of Shades surrounded them, protecting Milla and Darkly from what came next.

"*Charge the field, Milla,*" he murmured. Breath hot and voice full of dark, delicious promise. It licked up her spine, heating the marrow in her bones and winning a small, needy whimper. "*Burn them out.*"

His fingers unfurled one by one by one from her wrists, leaving Milla in control of their Ways. Though he kept his arms outstretched, ready to catch her, he let her close the ritual. Let her have this moment.

"*Živit.*" Feed.

Her voice boomed out over the terrified crowd, and she brought her hands together, clenching her fingers until her knuckles blanched white. Power vibrated in her bones, trembling her arms, but Milla held until she thought she would fly apart. Held until the teeming mass in the sky threatened to burst and consume them all. Held until she was certain, beyond a shadow of a doubt, that this charge would take everything she was, everything Darkly had fed into his Shades, everything the witches had given over to Beltane. Until she knew in the rotted, knotted, Soul, Shade, and body of *her* that in the absence of magick her casting left behind, the ritualists would have nothing left to steal.

"*Živit!*" She cried again, throwing her hands apart, thrusting the palms down and directing all of that emotional energy, all of the life and death she and Darkly had doled out, all the power of the Southeastern Covens down down down into the field.

It left her arms in a rush, draining Milla beyond the precipice. The Shades came crashing down, plummeting into the crowd and the earth to dissipate in lazy whorls of smoke. The bone fell from her hand, and the construct froze in a menacing half crouch, wings high and outspread with an arm reaching out over the crowd.

Utter silence met them as a sea of stunned witches gazed up at the mound. Milla held her breath as the last of Darkly's shades wafted away, waiting for them to realize what she had done.

The phone in her pouch erupted. Buzzing and buzzing and buzzing until the leather burned at her hip. At that same moment, Darkly jerked Milla back against him and pointed out across the field. "Milla, look."

She followed the line of his arm, clapping a hand over her mouth. A cry rose from the crowd, and another, as the witches realized what Milla had done: total burnout, their Ways hauled into a ritual and exhausted to power the magick of a Death Witch, save for those safely tucked behind wards.

Milla was deaf to the cries and blind to the chaos down below. Every fiber of her was intent on that deep red bloom of light, now a crimson star with a voided center pulsing in the night sky.

"We found them."

Forty-Six

DISPELLATION To undo the effects of a hex or allure cast by an opposing witch.

sever the shade, call it back

"WHAT DID YOU DO?" Lou screeched at them when they hit the viewing platform, falling into stride next to Darkly, who carried Milla in his arms. She was too Waydrunk to walk, much less keep up with him. As far as she was concerned, this was the best of both worlds. Close to her Dark Witch and getting a ride down the mound?

Nine rings, yes.

"What the piss-shitting hell did you do?"

"Found the ritualists." He ducked under the stage, dodging a sprinting Elder Witch and aiming for the exit. Though the *voice* had gone the way of the Shades and all the magick at Beltane, he still spoke in the cold, distant way of a Dark Witch deep in his magick. "Where's Toby?"

"Here." Tobias stepped beside Darkly as he cut across the grass, following the curve of the stage. He had changed, donning Enforcer blacks and the leather gloves, and clutched another wooly-pully in his hand. "Was all that necessary?"

"Found them, aye?' Darkly snarled and stopped, scanning the fleeing crowd and deaf to the panic filling the ritual grounds. "Rai?"

"Just over here," said Tobias. "She was putting up a ward the last I saw her."

"Does one of you want to explain what the fuck just happened?" Lou put herself in front of Darkly, walking backward.

Milla held up her phone, showing her the map function within the E.R.I.E. "Got 'em."

Lou read the screen, eyes flitting to Milla, then Darkly. "The campground? But—Donny …"

"No time, Lou."

"Make time," she snapped.

Darkly ignored her, charging past his sister. Behind them, Tobias explained what he had pieced together or learned from Rai.

"The social distortion made it impossible to locate the ritualists; Ludmilla and Keir resolved the issue."

"By causing a massive *burnout?*" Her voice rose impossibly higher, and Toby pointed to the sky. She looked up, faltering as she saw what Milla had from the top of the mound.

A pulsing, crimson star. In the few moments that had elapsed, the summoning had gained ground. A humanoid shape now visible, if only just, at the heart of the dread star, its head haloed by prismatic rings, the limbs too long and far too familiar.

"A brückengeist," Tobias stated. That one, Milla knew—a bridge ghost, to translate the old German phrase directly. It was a shell, an illusion, a temporary manifestation housing whatever elder power was being summoned from beyond the Gates. The mark of a ritual so Forbidden and Foule only the biggest idiots would attempt it.

So Milla and whoever these chucklefucks were.

"Holy Horned God." Lou drew a warding sigil in the air, and Tobias jogged ahead of Darkly, calling over his shoulder, "This way."

Safely tucked in a copse of oak and pine, Rai hunched over a picnic table, chanting with her voice pitched low.

"Where is it, where is it, where is it?" Her hands flew over herbs, sachets, powders, and pills. A kettle on a camp stove whistled quietly beside her mortar and pestle, and she'd drafted a metal pail to serve as a makeshift cauldron.

"Is it ready?" Tobias called out. She whipped her head up, throwing out a hand at their approach.

"Don't come closer." Scanning her work surface, she fisted a handful of black powder, swept around the table, and tossed it onto a ring of salt laid in the grass. The rotten egg stink of sulfur hit their noses, and Tobias gagged, pressing the extra woolly-pully over his mouth and nose.

"Sorry, Tobes," Rai muttered. A twine-bound broom appeared in her hand, and she swept away the brimstone and salt, dispelling the ward and allowing them to enter. Before they could, she rushed forward, tugging Milla from Darkly's arms and guiding her to the table. "Sit, drink."

A cup of tea was shoved into her hands, and Milla wasted no time getting it down. The astringent burn brought tears to her eyes, and she recognized the green, celery-like taste of Angelica Root. Near immediately, her head cleared, and the wooziness from her Way dissipated.

"Keir, for you." Rai finished packing the vape pen and pressed it into Darkly's hand. "Larkspur, witch's herb, dragon's blood, and ava pepper."

"Ava pepper?" He twirled the pen in his fingers, lifting a brow at Rai.

"I can't find the comfrey." She frowned at the table and her box of herbs. "It's the best I could do under the circumstances."

Milla's mind tripped over the ingredients, recognizing most. Witch's herb was basil, used to dispel confusion. Larkspur for health and dragon's blood as the stimulant he requested. Ava pepper threw her, but comfrey was frequently used for protection during travel. Considering how skilled a vinefica Rai was, it was probably safe to assume she had used the spice as a substitute.

"I could put together something with mugwort or damiana..."

"Too distracting," Darkly muttered around the pen, inhaling and unleashing a vapor cloud. "This'll have tae do."

Tobias shoved the wooly-pully into his free hand, glancing at Milla as he asked, "Are you sure you're ready for this?"

"Gonnae have to be," he replied, tugging the tactical sweater over his head.

"Does she know?" Tobias pressed.

Whatever Darkly replied, Milla did not hear it. Lou filled the space in front of her, eyes burning foglamp bright, her face pinched and angrier than she had ever seen the Light Witch.

"I told you to give them a minor display," she said in a cold, furious voice. "Rot the flowers and move on, and you decided to hijack the entire ritual?"

"Goddess, let it go," Milla said. "We needed to find the ritualists, so I did."

"There are thousands of witches out there suffering the largest burnout this region has ever seen! There are rules in place, Ludmilla. Regulations and statutes we must abide by!"

"And there's a pack of witches at that campground using my magick to summon something from beyond the Gates." She thrust her phone in Lou's face again, showing her the E.R.I.E. reading she had attuned to the ritualists.

"Fuck me, how are they still—are they warded?" Rai asked. The screen's light illuminated the finer details of her face, and fear widened her eyes, giving just a hint of the whites. "Why is it increasing?"

"Better question, where is Donmar?" Milla tucked her phone away. "Why didn't he call this in?"

"The campground is full of Staid," Lou argued.

"Cultists?" Tobias offered. "They have been known to attempt rituals from time to time."

"They could never manage a casting of this size," said Lou. "It would—"

"What, burn them out?" Milla stood, bringing herself to her full height, which was still six inches short of being intimidating. "Can we get going before that thing gets here?"

She thrust her arm in the air, pointing to the brückengeist. Larger now, its limbs more defined. Lou's nostrils flared, and she darted out both hands, grabbing Milla's wrists and jerking them together. The empty teacup fell to the ground, and she barely caught herself as she was hauled forward. "*Dún.*"

Darkly darted over to Milla. "Lou, stop."

"It's done, Keir." She threw Milla's wrists aside. The heavy weight of the binding had her stumbling two steps, but she waved Darkly off. "Goddess, you've made a mess of this."

"Berate him later." Rai appeared at Darkly's side, tucking sachets into the pouches on his pants. "He needs to get over there if we're to stand a chance of stopping this."

"Just him?" Milla asked.

"It's what he does," Lou answered, putting herself between Milla and Darkly as she issued her orders. "Toby, you're support. Head east-northeast, hold at twenty paces, and keep out of sight." He nodded and darted away, breaking into a dead sprint across the now abandoned field. Lou turned to Darkly. "Keep to the Shade, drop within the wards. I'm no longer as concerned with assets as I am with stopping this ritual, whatever it takes."

Darkly's lips flattened to a line, and a flicker of disgust flashed over his features, there and gone. He nodded, closing his eyes when Rai slid her hand into his, interlocking their fingers and muttering under her breath in Cantonese.

Lou pressed her palm flat against the center of his chest where the sigil lay. "*Oscailte.*"

Darkly shuddered, ripping his hand free from Rai's. A surge of magick that far outweighed what he'd released on the mound shivered around him, and a rush of cool, spiced air followed when he exhaled as if the Dark Witch had just charged the air with ready Shades. Milla snapped her attention to Lou, following the line of her arm and where her palm was pressed, and realization struck her back a step.

"That wasn't everything?" Goddess, what they had done, what they had achieved, and that was Darkly still bound?

"I've told you before, *leannán.* The Neitherworld is boundless."

"Enough with the dramatics, Keir." Lou stepped away, massaging her wrist. "That campground is just over a mile away. Donmar should still be there; anchor onto him if you can. Dear Goddess, I pray you can, and don't fuck this up."

"What about me?" Milla asked, which seemed redundant. She already knew Lou's answer and had already come up with a reply.

"What about you?" Lou summoned an e-grim to hand, tapping furiously on the screen. "Put some clothes on and let the grown-ups work."

"Lou," Darkly warned. He formed a sigil with his left hand, pressing it against the air. This time, now that she was looking for it, Milla *felt* the fabric of the world stretch and tear. Black smoke exploded from the Neitherworld, churning as a self-contained mass.

"Go. *Now.*"

"Hold up, he's going by himself?" Milla moved toward Darkly, only to be cut off by his sister.

"Correct," she said.

"Like hell he is."

"Milla, please." Darkly slid his fingers through hers, intending to give her a, what, goodbye handshake? "This is my job."

"One he'd rather you not witness," Lou added. "Keir, so help me, Goddess, if that thing steps into our world, I'll cleave you myself." She jerked her chin at the brückengeist, now sporting seven fingers on each hand. "*Go.*"

The air behind Darkly churned, and he rotated his wrist, widening the Way and preparing to step through. Body, Shade, and Soul; a piece of him already lost to the dark.

Which meant there was only one thing she could do. It was a bad idea for countless reasons, considering what and who waited out there, but the phone at her hip kept buzzing, and if that meant what she suspected it did, then where he was going was where she needed to be.

His fingers twitched in hers as he tried to pull away, so Milla clutched the front of the wooly-pully, popped onto her toes, and hauled his mouth to hers.

Intent she'd not traveled in years flared in her mind as if it had been waiting for her all this time. His arms banded around her on reflex, and she clawed her hands at the back of Darkly's head, swallowing his surprise with her mouth and dragging the witch flush against her. His magick strained to join with hers, and the fabric of the world tore further.

Milla pushed off of her toes, tipping them both backward. The ground rushed towards them—

—and Milla and her Dark Witch plummeted through roiling black clouds.

Shrieks and howls pierced her ears like shards of ice, deafening her to Darkly's shout. Wind tore at her macramé vest and turned her hair into vicious whips lashing her cheeks and neck.

They fell forever and for no time at all, rocketing into the depths of a boundless expanse. Milla wrapped her arms and legs around him like a clingy koala bear and held on tight. The last time she had done this there was no Dark Witch, and the Shades had bent to her command. Now, they rioted against her presence.

It was less a fight and more an internal brawl to control the terror of falling into nothing in the arms of a Horned God-damned Living Shade.

She thought of the Bridge of Lions, of two laps around the track at Flagler, and of a quiet street in a village near Český-Krumlov where a black-and-white dog had once run, relying on all of her old tricks to force the boundless expanse into something that could be overcome by sheer will alone.

The formless black billowed around Darkly as he slowed their descent and positioned himself to land on his feet. Milla buried her face in his chest, the wool from his sweater tickling her nose, the hex-resistance patch over his heart burning against her cheek. One of his hands moved to the back of her head, forcing Milla to look up at him. She was too focused to fight him and too busy trying not to scream to care about the death glare he sent her. Which, by the way, not fair. Death-anything was her whole deal.

His left arm shot out, fingers dancing in wild sigils, and solidity formed beneath her feet as if they had never been falling at all.

Darkly yanked her arms away and staggered back, separating them in the nothing, which was a terrible idea. Any Death Witch worth her Way knew that. But maybe Darkly didn't. He did seem surprised to see her here, so it was safe to assume that maybe, no, he did not know it was a bad idea to separate from the living when they wandered into the Neitherworld.

His black eyes bugged wide like marbles, and then he darted forward to grab her arm with both hands as if afraid she'd vanish before his eyes.

So maybe he did know.

"*What!?*" He shouted at her. Smoke curled out of his mouth, and Milla almost felt bad for the poor thing. It was not his fault he was in a coma the last time she did this.

"Hey." She wafted a tiny smile and waggled her fingers in greeting. He sputtered and tightened his grip on her arm. "Which way?"

"*What?*" he repeated.

"Which way?" She pointed all around. "Where do we go? Can you find Donmar?"

That knocked the shock right out of him. Darkly stared at her for a beat, then slid his gaze to the side, expression going somber. He blinked and shook his head, then tried again. "Cannae."

"Yikes." Milla widened her mouth into a grimace. "Let me try." Taking a deep breath that came with more rattle than she was comfortable with, she dropped into her latent magick and let the Forbidden and Foule summoning call to her across the void. A chasm opened in her mind's eye, tearing off into the distance. Milla jerked her arm out of Darkly's grip, grabbed his hand, and dragged him to the left. "This way."

"*What?*" He asked again, and Milla ignored him again. Something silken brushed her legs in greeting, and she shuddered to a halt. "*What are you—*"

"Seriously, if you can't think of something else to say, this is going to be a terrible time."

"*What are you doing here is what I was going to say.*"

"My job, obviously. Lou hauled me out of the cells, and you bottled yourself, idiot, to catch these ritualists. So, we're catching the ritualists. Catch up." She rolled her eyes and resumed her stomp. Or tried to. Darkly did not move, which meant Milla made it all of one step. She tugged, and still, he did not relinquish a single inch. "Ugh, Darkly don't make me drag you out of here."

That struck something in the witch. He shook his head rapidly, taking a half-step back, which, come *on*, was not the aim. Only this time, when he repeated his new favorite catchphrase, it came with a sense of startled awe. "*What?*"

Whatever had struck him in her words was enough to jolt the witch into action. He cast one last confused glance at Milla, then stared out across the nothing, nodding, taking her hand, and breaking into a run.

Hand in hand, they crossed the formless expanse. Darkly following some internal compass only he possessed as the master of his demesne, while Milla was drawn to the Foule magick bleeding across the boundary of worlds.

"*There,*" Darkly pointed after what felt like half a mile, that *voice* guiding Milla's eyes. "*This might hurt. You. Or it might not. No way to tell.*"

He flicked his wrist, withdrawing an obsidian blade from nowhere. Stabbing the haze above their heads, he sheared a hole in the air, dropped Milla's hand, and stepped through without a glance back.

"Right." Milla pulled her lips tight, steeling herself for what came next. This had been the hardest part to learn, and from everything Milla put herself through for that ritual with Ezra, the most useful tool in her arsenal. It would take everything she had, everything she was, but it was a latent skill tied into her very being.

She had almost done this in Marie's hall when a circle of salt kept her from Darkly and again in her living room just before Lou arrived. Unlike each of those times, this was Milla alone, and there was no avoiding what came next.

Burrowing down, she dove as deep as she could into the kernel of heat that was her Way. Not in her arms, not pooling in her hands. This was Milla at her core, the defining magick that made her a Death Witch. It was latent.

She muttered a one-hundred percent illegal hex. Her vision tunneled, her limbs went numb, and her body teetered forward through the churning mass of clouds.

Forty-Seven

SACRIFICE One of three major components of a ritual. Sacrifice is the willing cost paid in appeal to the Triple Goddess or Horned God.

See: Desire; Intent

DARKLY CAUGHT HER BY the arm as she snapped back into herself, easing Milla onto her knees, blind in a world of chaos. Wild magick pulsed and sizzled around her, setting the hair along her scalp and arms on end. She squinted and blinked, squeezing her eyes shut and opening them wide. This was always the risk. It took a minute for everything to come back online, but Milla did not have a minute. She needed to be fully functional *now*.

He released her arm and moved away, leaving Milla groping blindly where she knelt. Dirt, grass, dry tufts, rocks. Outside, cool. Probably the campground, great. Sitting back, she raised her hands, nearly clocking herself in the face from how freely they moved and how light her wrists were. A blink of surprise revealed the fuzzy outline of her fingers, the tips dark and pointed. She turned her hands over, marveling at the near-weightless feel.

She was unbound.

Unbound.

Milla whipped her face around as if she could see the seam to the Neitherworld. But it was closed, the access to a dead realm gone and Darkly nowhere to be found.

Wait, shit.

Milla clamored to her feet and staggered forward on half-dead legs, her vision still blurry but clearing by the second.

"Darkly?" she hissed in a whisper. A dark figure hovered a few feet away, and she aimed for it, reaching out to grab his arm, his hand, his leg. Her phone buzz-buzz-buzzed in her pouch, and the figure twisted, ducked around her, and pulled it free faster than Milla could follow. Goddess, he was fast. The buzzing ceased, and he pressed the phone into her hand.

"Shouldnae be here." He sounded almost mystified, black eyes flicking to Milla, then scanning wherever it was they had landed as if he were looking for someone. Or making sure they were alone?

"Well, I am, so get over—"

A scream cut her off, jerking them both ramrod straight. Milla followed where Darkly looked, squinting and making out a coven of witches in a ritual circle partially obscured by trees. They were deep into their casting, roughly thirty feet away and ten feet below. She leaned forward, trying to gain a better view, and Darkly shot his arm out.

"Careful." He pointed to the slope in front of them, and Milla belatedly realized he had stepped them out of the Neitherworld onto a low mound. Satisfied she would not fall, Darkly dropped his arm and glared down at her. "How?"

"You want to do this now?" She brought her phone close to her face, tracking the signatures on the E.R.I.E. Hippocromantic, vestic, chronomantic, and – "Corpomantic?"

Darkly startled back, jerking his face to the coven. "What?"

"That's what it says, see?" She showed him the screen, pointing to each Way as she named it. At Darkly's suspiciously arched brow, she explained, "Diego gave me a crash course earlier. And see these two? They're the signatures for a summoning and a conjuring; no way to tell what Way it is."

"Which do I aim for?" he asked, anger vanishing to make room for direction.

"Um." Milla bit her lip, scanning her phone, the coven beneath them, and another scream rose over the clamor or chanting and sizzle of magick. "The fuck, is that …" Milla squinted at the ritual, making out a naked figure on its back. Tied to a … slab? "A sacrifice?"

"Triple Goddess's tits." Darkly cursed. He threw his arms down, tight at his sides, and twin obsidian blades appeared in his hands, wafting thin plumes of smoke.

"Holy shit," Milla breathed.

"Who do I aim for, Milla?" he demanded, already moving away from her.

"Um, shit, the—" she scanned the E.R.I.E., cursing herself for not spending the last two weeks getting to know the technology. She shot her eyes skyward, intending to appeal to the Triple Goddess, the Horned God—nine rings, she would call on the Baron if she thought he would help—and spotted the sickening pulse of that crimson star instead. The brückengeist loomed larger, closer to being summoned in full. "The-the summoner!"

"*Stay here.*" That *voice* ribboned through her, locking Milla in place.

"Darkly—" she started to protest, the words dying out as that black-eyed gaze looked at her, through her, and his *voice* unfurled in her mind.

"*Dinnae fash.*"

An absurd calm washed over her, suffusing Milla's veins with an alluring sense of peace. It was a Living Shade that stalked down the hill, his purpose clear and deadly. He disappeared among the trees, and still Milla held in place, not really sure why. He was going to need her, and someone had to do something about that sacrifice on the slab; that was obvious. But she should probably stay put. Donmar was in position; he would help Darkly. And Tobias had taken off running like a maniac. He would be here any minute to back up the Dark Witch. Better to stay out of the way.

Her phone buzzed. She looked down at it, head foggy. Someone screamed somewhere. Not her problem, nothing to worry about.

It buzzed again, and she frowned.

Chronomantic.

That seemed important. Why was she tracking a chronomantic? She drifted her gaze to the ritual, entertained by the deep shadows bleeding from the trees and reaching for one of the ritualists. They engulfed him, dragging the witch, kicking and screaming into the dark, then moved on. A body lay in their wake, lifeless and gray—still as death.

She smiled, her Way thrilling at the sight and the new, dark power coursing in the air.

Nothing to worry about at all.

A neon-red bolt of lightning shot to the ground, landing beside the body. And another, closer to the trees. A third bolt lingered longer, tracing over the undergrowth like a tendril or tentacle seeking a handhold before it, too, retreated to the sky. Milla followed it back to the brückengeist, cocking her head at the massive, terrible figure in the sky.

Someone should do something about that.

A wet, frantic cry called her back to the ritual, where Darkly darted out of the trees and dropped into a lunge. Arms flung forward, fingers clawed, he curled his lip and tore a Shade from a witch.

"Huh."

Another tendril shot from the sky, landing to the left of Darkly, lighting him up a bloody red. It crawled over the ground reaching for the witch, and, at the last moment, he vanished into a puff of shadow. The tendril retreated, zipping over the fallen body like the filaments in a plasma globe before returning to the sky.

"That can't be good." Milla toed closer to the edge of the mound, a thought needling in the back of her mind. Something about summons and rituals and sacrifices. About Dark Witches and what they could do. How they were used.

She shrugged it away, searching the shadows for Darkly, when a strong, smooth hand gripped her arm and yanked her around.

"What have you done?" Tobias yelled in her face. Blue flame blazed in his eyes, yet the air around him was frigidly cold.

"Nothing." She batted his hand away, shrugging lazily. "Don't worry about it."

Tobias straightened. "Do not …" His gaze drifted past her to where the shadows swelled and swallowed witches, then dropped back to Milla. "Gott im Himmel." He snapped his fingers in her face, momentarily blinding her with a bright blue fireball. The crackle of magick vanished, along with the warm, fuzzy calm, and she staggered back, swiping in front of her face. Another cry rose above the chanting and the magick and the roar of the brückengeist overhead. This one angry and oh-so-familiar.

Panic rushed in, whipping Milla into action. Which was good because if she didn't do something right now, she was going to hex the shit out of Darkly for alluring her like that.

Dinnae fash, he said. "Don't worry." Don't worry her ASS.

She scanned the ritual—three ritual witches and the sacrifice on the slab remained. The witch at the head, their face hidden behind a mask—Horned God dammit, why were they always *masked*—raised both arms high. They gripped a sinuously curved boline in one hand, blood dripping from the blade, and formed a Vestic's divining sigil with the other.

A sigil Milla knew as well as she knew there would be a human bone licked clean of valerian dust lying at the witch's feet.

The memory of that cloyingly sweet herb made her gag. Gray light bled from the Vestic's eyes, their mouth never ceasing its chanting even as a pale white smoke purled like dry ice from their lips. Milla knew firsthand the pain of the intent they spoke. It had taken weeks for her tongue to heal from the blistering poison of those words.

A witch at the base of the altar moved quickly, drawing Milla's eye. They flung their arm, and an acid-green hex shot toward the trees.

Darkly darted to the side, barely avoiding a direct hit. Right hand pressed to his side, he flung out his left. Sharp bullets of black sped across the distance, colliding with the witch, one-two-three, and Darkly vanished into shadow.

She stepped back, shaking out her hands, and collided with Tobias. He grabbed her elbows, and she threw him off. "What is he doing?"

"His job," Tobias answered easily. He moved beyond Milla, flame dancing at his fingertips as he scanned the ritual. "You were not supposed to see this. It was not part of the plan."

Part of her brain recognized that he'd covered a mile at an ungodly pace and wasn't even breathing hard—which, unfair—while the other part of her brain screamed. So she screamed right along with it. "What 'plan'?"

"His." He looked back at her. "And Lou's."

"And is this part of the plan?" she asked, throwing her arm at the ritual, the seething shadows, the bodies on the ground.

"Almost always."

Random pieces fell into place, and Milla really should have known. Should have seen it coming.

He hated his Way, and he loved his job in Florida, lazing in an Adirondack and chatting up a Death Witch.

I need you, he'd told her. To get out, get away. He was supposed to sacrifice her to free himself and this was why.

You don't know what he's like, Kayleigh's Shade had screamed.

You're going to learn things, Lou had warned.

We all have our coping mechanisms, Darkly had said of his weed.

"Oh, Goddess." Another red tendril zipped toward the ground, and another, prying the shadows as though seeking entry while the sacrifice thrashed and writhed on the altar. Milla was going to be sick—all over herself, the mound, and Tobias—and she didn't care. "Larkspur, witch's herb, dragon's blood, and … Tobias, what is ava pepper?"

"Kava kava, why?"

"Horned God fucking DAMMIT." Milla launched past him, running over the edge of the mound.

Larkspur for protection and dragon's blood for energy. Witch's herb, to dispel confusion and fear, but then there was Triple fucking Goddess kava kava. Rai had called it ava pepper and Milla hadn't known what that was, but kava kava she knew well.

When steeped and the steam inhaled, it kick-started visions in Vestics. Ground into a poultice or powder, it promoted protection in travel and astral work, necessary for a witch about to traverse the Neitherworld. But when smoked or disbursed in a censer, it lowered inhibitions to dangerous levels, and they had let him go all Dark Witch and wander the Neitherworld with Horned God-damned *kava kava* in his bloodstream.

Another howl of pain had her skidding to a halt halfway down the mound, Tobias sliding and crouching low beside her. A witch fell to their knees, heaving the contents of their stomach and the ritualist beside them kept one hand directed at the altar, the other at the trees.

"Where is Donmar?" Tobias asked in a low voice.

"Not here," Milla answered, flashing him the screen of her phone. "No meteomantics."

"Scheisse." She started to flip her phone around, and he grabbed it, staring with wide eyes at the screen. "Is that a corpomantic?" Milla nodded. He handed her phone back and lifted his gaze to the ritual. "He hates corpomantics."

"I'm sure there's a story there." When Tobias took a breath, as if to tell her, Milla cut him off. "Holy Horned God, later." She crept forward. "You witches have the worst timing."

The witch on their knees cried out again, their arms spread wide and chest arced forward as if hauled upright by a rope bound to their ribs. Ribbons of shadow stretched from their body, drawn to the dark.

The ritualist beside them shifted their sigil, and whatever hold Darkly had on those Shades severed. The witch fell back as their Shades snapped back into place, and Milla pointed at the ritualist.

"The summoner," she told Tobias. "And a damn strong one. Now that Darkly knows, he'll—"

Red lightning streaked from the sky, crashing against the earth with new fury. Aether crackled in the air like a live wire, and Darkly stepped out of nothing. He clawed his hands at the witch and the summoner and wrenched their Shades apart.

The fallen witch let out a wet-sounding cry, going terrifyingly still, and the summoner crumpled. Their head slammed against the edge of the altar with a sickening crack, and the body hit the ground.

Before she could even begin to process what she had just seen or the vicious, cold-bloodedness of Darkly's Way, a flash of bright color from the head of the table jerked her attention to the ritual leader and the sixth witch hidden behind them. Short, slight, and maskless. Blonde chin-length curls gave her the appearance of a frightened cherub. She spotted Milla, meeting her glare—an appropriate death glare, not that half-assed attempt Darkly had made—with terror in her eyes. She slammed the massive grimoire in her arms closed, turned, and ran.

"I see her." Tobias started to rise, ducking immediately as another tendril struck the ground like a live wire, shrieking and scouring the earth between the mound and the ritual. "Horned God." He dropped low again, blue eyes burning purple beneath the light of the dread star.

Another tendril scraped the altar's base, reaching for the sacrifice chosen to host whatever horror the witches had summoned.

"The summoner is down," Tobias stated. "Why hasn't this stopped?"

"Because there's more than one." Milla felt outside of herself despite the crackle and sting of wild magick against her skin. This couldn't be real, it couldn't be happening, and yet—"Lou said 'whatever it takes.'" She blinked, swallowed a rush of nausea. The bound man wailed as the tendril danced over his form and bent to the shadows. In the crimson flash, Milla spotted Darkly prowling along the fringes of the ritual circle, aiming for the leader at the head of the altar. "He's not going to stop, is he?"

"No," Tobias straightened and met Milla's question head-on. "He will do whatever it takes to stop this ritual."

"Well, shit." She counted the remaining witches, glanced at the spectre in the sky, and made a decision. "You get the ritual leader, I'll spare the sacrifice."

Tobias nodded as the next tendril struck the ground at Darkly's feet. He darted back, barely avoiding the strike.

Milla jerked her face to the sky. The brückengeist loomed close enough she could make out vague features on its face. Over-large hollows scanned the mound and the ritual circle, dismissing the sacrifice and leveling the weight of their desire on the Dark Witch.

It reached out with an over-long limb. A tendril burst from splayed, multi-knuckled, extra-long fingers, scraping across the sky toward Darkly.

He disappeared at the last second in a burst of shadowsmoke, oblivious to the threat, and reappeared behind the witch on the opposite side of the altar. Obsidian blades sped from his hand, catching them in the back. They rattled a bone-shuddering gasp and flung out a hex. Milla's phone buzzed in her hand, and the hex hit Darkly over his heart.

He stumbled back, stunned, and Milla was moving before common sense could stop her. She tossed her phone to the side, tearing down the mound. Tobias grabbed her shoulder, and she ducked, spinning out of his grasp. "New plan. Get him out of here."

"What?"

"Now!" She pointed to the sky, the brückengeist, and the next tendril forming in its hand.

"Nein, he can handle this." Tobias reached for her again, and she snarled.

"No, he can't, and I can't *do this again*." Heat flooded down her veins, pooling in her hands. "*Zastavit!*" The flash-freeze hex hit him in the stomach, and he jerked still. Tobias could dispell her hexes as quickly as Darkly, but it was enough to give her a head start.

She charged for the ritual, skidding and sliding on humid-damp grass while pooling vicious intent in her hands. Trying not to think about what would happen if that tendril found Darkly and latched on to him. The brückengeist was nearly formed, the summons a success even with a summoner down.

It had gone too far, and with Darkly fully unbound, Milla knew as well as she knew this Horned God-damned ritual that the sacrifice on the altar would not be enough.

Not when she had yet again delivered the perfect vessel.

I've really got to stop helping these people.

Forty-Eight

bloody blood witches

CORPOMANTIC A witch with an affinity for bodily organs and sanguine humours. Previously categorized as Forbidden and Foule, corpomancy was established as Fine and Faire by the 41st Tribunal Convention in 1996. House of Aragon.

A BRIGHT BLUE flash lit up the trees, showing Milla her path in harsh, stark clarity.

Hands slicing through the air, she sped down the mound, across the flat, magickally charged earth, and tackled the witch who had dared to hex Darkly—the witch who had flung a hex that set off her phone—the *chronomantic* who had made her life a living hell for weeks on end.

They hit the ground, rolling and clawing at each other until they collided with the altar. Milla drove her knees into the witch's waist and slammed her hands against their chest.

"*Frigidní.*" She spat the hex Ezra had named Morgue Frost. Frigid cold bloomed from her palms, coating her hands, and she put all of her weight into her arms, pressing harder. "*Frigidní.*"

Slick warmth met her touch as she sent flesh-eating frostbite into the witch, astral fingers driving between their ribs, prodding their lungs. Good Goddess, did C.R.O.W. hate this one. Ash spewed from her lips, the funeral mask around her eyes pinched, and she hexed them again. "*Frigidní.*"

A terrified, pained wail left them even as their casting hand worked a rapid sigil and gripped her right arm. The cold sped from her hand, replaced by a crushing, withering pinch. She yelped, and the chronomantic bucked their hips, throwing Milla off. She rolled onto her hands and knees, pushing against the ground to rise, and her arm buckled, pain clawing up the limb.

She spared a glance at her casting hand, gagging at the sight of withered fingers and leathery skin tight against bone, the tips blackened around jagged nails.

Useless.

Not a great look overall, still, not her worst. Shoving to her feet, she whirled around and barely dodged a second hex. The edge of the altar behind her exploded in a cloud of dust, and she lobbed a fradey-hex at the witch—"*Boj se mě.*"—with her left hand, twisting around to make sure the sacrifice had not been hit.

Writhing on the altar, he appeared unharmed. If one forgave the fact he was naked, bound, and caught in the rapture of a ritual at its liminal edge. Muscles strained against his bindings, the veins in his neck stood out taut, and perfectly veneered teeth gnashed as a blood-red tendril traced his naked body.

Milla blinked. Blinked again, and blurted, "Holy shit, it's—"

A hex like acid hit her in the shoulder. She screamed, slapping a hand down, working a rapid return to heal what she could, and pooling a decaying hex in her left hand as she turned.

Darkly got there first.

Face twisted in fury, he reached for the chronomantic. Shades bled from his eyes, and his mouth worked an intent she could not hear. The chronomantic choked, hands flying over their figure as if they could keep their Shade intact. In a final effort to avoid the punishment of the Dark Witch, they prodded their mask, shoved their fingers under the rim, and ripped it off.

"Please!" Cyrus shouted, throwing the mask aside and begging with his last breath. "Please, Keir. Help me!"

Darkly faltered, his hold on the Shade slipping, and Cyrus ran his hands in a rapid sigil, blurring out of sight.

"That *FUCKER!*" Milla darted to where he had last been, reaching blindly, needing to grab him, choke him, *ruin him.*

Cyrus, the little shit. In the swamp, in her cell, *in her home.* Fucking with her head and time, making Milla believe she was going mad while helping her and teaching Diego. She should have known, but she'd been too stupid to recognize the evidence staring her right in the face. But the E.R.I.E. did not lie, and she'd left it running after drinking her tea. It caught his signature, and she had assumed it was an echo. The residual of his Way once she'd learned what he was. Again, choosing to believe the lie she told herself rather than face the painful, hideous truth: she got played.

Goddess she was so tired of getting played by these witches.

Trust among us is necessary, Lou had said.

Trust, my ASS.

"Where are you?" she bellowed, lobbing hex after hex in a circle—rotting, festering, noxious hexes—praying one would land and show her where Cyrus, the coward, was lurking.

"*Where are you?*" Her eyes burned—Goddess, they burned—and she tasted ash. Her right hand was useless and deadened. Her hexes off-target, and he was there but not, and she needed to ... needed to ...

Lighting cracked. Red crashed against the earth in front of Darkly, illuminating his sharp, terrible features, and the sacrifice screamed.

Stay focused, Millapet.

Focus. She needed to focus. Focus on rotting that tiny little witch to nothing.

She flung another necro hex, rotting a patch of grass near the woods. Nothing. And again. Nothing. Not a yelp, a gasp, a blur in the air.

Sobbing in frustration, she grasped the boline at her throat, sliced her arm, and flung her arm at the nothing. "*Moje čepel!*"

A scythe of blood flew across the empty space. A voice cried out, the grass crumpled, and Cyrus's stooped figure blurred into view.

"You." She advanced, hands flying in sigils, ash drifting from her lips. "You were there that night. Who else?"

"Please," Cyrus burbled, hacking blood in the grass. "You do not—"

"Don't *what?*" Milla switched intents, drawing on all of her anger, her rage. "Don't understand? Then explain it to me. Who else was there?"

Cyrus hung his head, panting in wet, bubbling rasps. He raised his head and grinned at her, that utterly unforgettable face searing itself into Milla's mind. Blood dribbled from the corners of his mouth, staining his teeth. His dark, dull eyes wheeled in their sockets, and his laugh—that laugh. It rattled in her skull, threatening to draw her back to the cells. A band tightened around her chest, fear lodging itself in her throat as his face began to blur, the features vanishing behind whatever chrono-magick he had just cast.

"So close, magissa," he taunted, rising slowly to his feet. He wrapped an arm around his front, limping toward her. Bursts of deep red and bright blue lit up the woods and the ritual grounds, illuminating the spreading bloodstain on his shirt. Even with her left arm, Milla's aim had been good—she'd struck him on the side, slicing deep into his ribs and lungs. "Better act quickly. Time is not on your side."

He dropped his arm and blurred more. Milla's fingers tingled, her toes. Her belly lurched, but now that she knew it was chronomancy, that it was *him*, she was ready.

"*Nehýbejte se.*" She pressed the sigil in front of her. *Don't move.* The blurring ceased. Cyrus stood before her, less than an arm's length away, smudged around the edges, his face frozen in shock. Milla mimicked his grin, acid spittle burning her lips as she pressed her palm over his heart and gave in to the witch she was. "*Rozložit.*"

Rot.

Cyrus choked out a cry, eyes flickering, tears falling. Rot crawled across his front, and black veins wormed up his throat, cupping his jaw, climbing into his mouth. Teeth blackened, his lips shriveled. His body flickered—blurring and twitching through time, but the rot was too far gone. Milla's intent too sound, her desire too great, and her sacrifice the weeks upon weeks she spent in that cell at his mercy.

A dry, brittle laugh escaped, and she restrained the hex, cocking her head to the side in invitation.

"She's going to get what she wants." Cyrus wheezed. His eyes, dull and shimmering with the gray of advanced cataracts, gazed at nothing.

"Who." Milla did not ask. The Death Witch demanded. Multiple bolts hit the ground, lighting up the entire ritual grounds a terrible red. Cyrus's laugh breezed out of him, the last gasp of a drained bellows.

"Too late."

Millapet.

She twisted, searching for the other voice that lived in her head as Cyrus hacked and gasped. A terrible silence had fallen, blanketing the glade so the dying chronomantic was the only sound.

Why did you call me here for this?

"I didn't." She released Cyrus, searching the dark for Ezra, but he was Gone—Gone because of her, because of this ritual, Gone at the Gates.

What did you do?

And the Gates were opening.

Tobias's clean, bright flame shot across the dark void behind her, painting the scene in a master's oils:

The sacrifice bound on the altar, his back bowed, hips striving upward, mouth wide open in a scream. A ghostly light rose from his body, attaching itself to the ritual leader, lowering their blade. Their eyes gleamed behind a mask as they mouthed their never-ceasing chant.

And Darkly.

He loomed behind and beside the ritual leader, far gone into his Way. Every angle of him was keen as a blade, his eyes murderous black, his mouth a slash. Shades whipped around him, cloaking the witch and crowning him as their master. He reached for the ritual leader, and black smoke seethed from their arm, heeding his command.

What did you do?

"I left you there," Milla said. She turned her back on Cyrus, drifting toward the altar in a daze. The world was beyond dark. Shadow wafted like dense fog with her every step, clinging softly to her legs and whispering through her hair. "I left you at the Gates where no one could reach you."

Why?

"We went too far," she admitted the truth—the point of her failure. She was not weak. She was not afraid of the witch that was her husband. They had gone too far, and though she could stop the Gates from opening, Ezra, in all his wisdom, had never accounted for this one point of failure. "I couldn't bring you back. The tether broke. The Baron had been summoned, and you were the best available vessel—the only vessel."

Tobias's mouth moved in a shout, the sound carried away by the Shades. Red tendrils shot to the ground, connecting with the altar and the earth. He deflected what he could, sending fireballs and plumes of liquid flame at the bolts, but there were too many, coming too fast.

They slithered up Darkly's legs, around his waist, painting that lovely face electric-red, and the damn fool witch was oblivious.

"We went too far." Milla raised her face to the sky and the pinpoint of dreaded light bleeding through. "I had already lost you to the Baron, and the tether was broken." Milla was a Death Witch. Realms of the dead welcomed her with open arms and were loathe to let her go. But for the living … the living were never meant to traverse the Neitherworld. Never meant to gaze upon the Gates, much less open them. "Our connection was severed. If I summoned you home, I would lose you all over again." Her eyes burned, and she let the ashen tears fall. "I couldn't do it."

Millapet.

"I can't do this again."

She blinked, and time screeched back into place. Sound rushed in like a tidal wave, battering Milla back against the shore of her failures.

Another tendril streaked toward Darkly, and Milla's intent blazed to life:

Get Darkly out of here, stop the summons, spare the sacrifice.

"Tobias!" Milla shouted, tongue thick in her mouth. "If he tears out that Shade, he kills them both!" She thrust her arm out, lobbing a weak enfeebling hex at a descending tendril and pointing at the ritual leader.

Tobias snuffed out his flame, face jerking between Milla, the tendrils, Darkly, and the altar. He cursed in German, shook out his arms, and they erupted in a crystalline blaze.

"Can you stop him?"

"I don't know," she yelled back as she jogged up close.

"Well, try." He threw his fist at the sky, sending a punch of flame at a new tendril. And again and again, jabbing one and sending another careening into the dark with a right hook. It was metal as hell, and Milla didn't have the time to appreciate it.

Darkly curled the fingers of his outstretched hand, and Milla jolted into action, darting around the altar with every intent of tackling the oblivious witch to the ground. The Shade seething from the ritual leader tensed, tightening like thread caught in fingers, and they swayed, stuttering over their chant.

Tongues of scarlet and neon magick lashed at the ground, seeking a foothold in one of the three witches now bound by Shade, granting Milla and Tobias a slim reprieve.

"Darkly!" She sent another tendril sizzling away from the altar, calling out to her Dark Witch. "Keir, please, you need to shadestep!"

He twitched a lip at the sound of his name and wrenched the ritual leader's Shade. Drawn to the surge of his Way, the brückengeist latched onto his casting hand, sizzling down to his wrist and worming beneath the hex-resistant fabric.

"No!" She flung a desecration hex with her left hand, and for once, it didn't go wild. The hex splattered against the tendril.

Wool burned, burning flesh filled her nose, and Darkly released a soul-sundering howl of pain. But the tendrils slipped away.

Her world went blurry from the amount of magick she'd just used in short order, her body catching up to the cost. Head spinning, stomach heaving, the hurt winnowed into bones. It was too much, too soon after the ritual. The tea had helped, but it was not enough, and that thing was going to take her Dark Witch if she did not act.

Darkly was going to kill that witch and their sacrifice if she did not act.

Milla clenched her teeth, dragging the depths of her Way. Darkly had survived a blight from her before, so she flung one now. The hex splattered against his desecrated left hand, and his skin withered further, tightening over the bones of those clever fingers.

The Shade snapped back into the ritualist, and it was a King in Smoke and Shadow who raised his right hand against the Death Witch.

His fingers clawed, and in the deepest, darkest places of her, he tugged, wrenching what remained of Milla's Shade free. It splintered through bone and burned through her pores, dragging the last breaths from her lungs.

A whisper of a shadow pulled from her arms and chest, hovering as Milla watched, helpless to the command he held over her, unable to think of anything but the pain, the cold, and how in the sickest way possible, this felt a little like coming home—and he released. Her Shade snapped into place, and Milla hit the ground, wheezing and gasping.

Blue flame erupted to her left, searing the ends off another tendril winding around Darkly's waist. Tobias moved into the field of her vision, snapping out a whip of cold blue fire at the lashing red vines. At the sight of his Way out in full force, Milla remembered three things in rapid succession:

Tobias had survived the burnout at Beltane and was the first to recover after Tallahassee.

His flame burned cold, unlike any *spalování* she had ever known.

And Darkly had suffered a burnout before.

Dinnae fancy reliving the experience.

A burnout caused by Tobias.

"Tobias," Milla gasped, pushing at her knee to rise. In the cells, when he dispelled the illusions, and just now on the mound with Darkly's allure, Horned *God*, she was blind. She teetered to the side, hardly able to stand. "Burn them off."

"What?" he shouted over the altar.

"That's your job, isn't it?" She gestured around them with an angry, withered hand. "Burn off the shadows, take him down."

"Are you certain?"

"One hundred percent," Milla lied. She readied a hex in her palm. "I've got the ritualist; you save my Dark Witch."

To his credit, he wasted no time.

Blue flame flared in his palms, burning brighter and brighter until Milla had to look away. Darkly was lost to his wretched work, already summoning the ritualist's Shade. It was going to be a near thing, a close thing, but Milla had faith in Tobias, as unforgivably weird as that was.

"Close your eyes, Milla," he warned.

The burning blue erupted into a blinding white. Tobias's silhouette imprinted behind her lids as she clenched her eyes and ducked behind the altar. Clamping her hand over her left ear, Milla pressed her right against the stone as a high-pitched whistle screamed from his flame, ascending beyond mortal pitch.

All sound belled out of the world, and the boom of a thunderclap rattled her bones. She might have been screaming, her mouth was open, and her throat was raw, but there was no sound. No way to tell. A flash sweat broke out over her skin, darkness soothed the burning in her closed eyes, and it was time to move.

Milla lurched to her feet as Darkly collapsed, smoke curling from his body and joining the haze of disrupted magick. She flung out her left hand with the last dregs of her Way, striking the ritual leader in the chest and throat with a wicked blight. They screamed, the high-pitched shriek of a woman in pain, and the summons finally ceased.

The ritualist dropped her boline to the ground and clawed at her throat as if she could tear the blighting hex away. Milla's stomach lurched. She gagged and staggered forward, the ground heaving and roiling beneath her feet.

And then she stopped.

Just ... stopped.

Her feet froze, her legs seized, and her lungs stopped their bellows. Milla was no better than a living statue with a very short lifespan. Blood slowed in her veins, and her heart beat out one, two ... three .... four .....

When the fifth beat never came, Milla finally remembered the corpomantic.

Her panic was immediate and immediately stopped. She had no heartbeat to be frantic, no pulse to skyrocket, no breath to come in sharp little bursts, and the strain on her body was immense. The dam of her rising hysteria placed a splintering pressure on her bones that would have earned a wail had Milla a mouth to scream. Each joint felt brittle as eggshells, her kneecaps ready to shatter. Every muscle and tendon drawn taut enough to tear, and there was no release, no relief. She was trapped, held by the whim of someone else, and she was going to die.

She was going to die.

Unable to breathe, unable to scream or close her eyes or fling a hex. Unable to fight, Milla was going to die.

So she did the one thing she could still do. Burning through the last of her reserves, she dove into that burning kernel of latent magick at the heart of her.

And she killed herself.

The world flickered out, darkness fell, and Milla felt a presence in the nothing. A weighted gaze and the suggestion of curved horns rising in the dark. She drew a ragged breath as her lungs started their bellows. Her fingers and toes prickled, the muscles in her extremities spasming as blood rushed back into her veins. She pushed herself up from the ground, her right arm still useless but enlivening with each beat of her renewed heart. Her eyes took in a haze of blurry gray light bending to define shapes by dimension and then color as the corpomantic hex was fully dispelled.

A whirl of sound and movement drew her attention to fleeing robes disappearing through the trees with Tobias in swift pursuit.

She stood on wobbling legs, too fast for someone who was just dead and half-collapsed against the altar. Pale moonlight washed over the stone, not the sickening red pulse of the brückengeist, and no wicked intent filled the air. Instead, she heard crickets.

Groaning, Milla flexed the fingers of her right hand and rolled her shoulder. Dispelling hexes and curses was decidedly not an enjoyable experience, and she had just done it twice in the span of, what, ten minutes? Less?

Grasping the edge of the altar, she retrieved the ritualist's boline, dropped dangerously close to the sacrifice's head, and leaned heavily against the stone.

"And they say Imma creepy witch." Milla slurred to the man tied on the altar, inebriated beyond the point where she should be handling a blade. He blinked bleary brown eyes at her, mouth working to form words but wholly unable to do so. Gripping the handle, she brought the blade against the leather strap. Her eyes focused on the bones in the man's wrist, at his pulse fluttering there, and a drunken laugh burbled past her lips. "Probly shouldn' be usin' a knife rihhnow."

"What was that?" The man tried to flinch away, unable to move more than a centimeter.

"Ah-ah-ah," Milla shook her head, clicking her tongue and waving the blade in his face as she sang, "If you move, I'll cut you."

The warning sounded more like a gleeful threat, and the man whimpered, pressing his head against the stone to get as far away from the boline as possible.

Milla muttered an apology and pinched the blade in her fingers. Terrible idea, but better than slipping and cutting his wrist as she sawed the strap. The thick rope fell away, and she sent the poor man a sloppy smile, hiccuping as she slid the handle into his freed hand. He made quick work of the other strap, then pushed himself upright with a groan.

"Are y'all witches?"

"Yessir." Milla blinked at him, still amused and bewildered by what she was seeing. He split into three blurry versions of himself, and she blinked again, settling the fractured image into one very startled, very recognizable face. "Yer nekkid," she hiccuped again, "and yer Stefan Holfstaedter."

He sighed, ran a hand through his hair, and splayed his fingers between them. "It's pronounced *Steeeven*. With a long 'e'."

"You bought my store," she informed him, teetering forward. His crotch rose to meet her, or maybe it was the other way around. Either way, Milla became well acquainted with Stefan and his long "e", informing him, "I hate it," before passing out in his lap.

Forty-Nine

MATRILINEAL LINES The flow of magick and genealogy of the Ways through female ancestry.

a male witch cannot begat a witchling upon a mortal partner.

#thefutureisfemale

"*WHAT IF I FAIL?*"

"*You've never failed me before,*" *Ezra said, pinching her chin.* "*Now would be a terrible time to start.*"

He kissed her, quick and fierce. He made promises and told Milla that he loved her. The slice on her arm stung, the tether snapped into being, and then Ezra marched deeper into the lake, the water churning at his legs.

Summoning the Shades was the easy part, the most practiced bit of magic in the whole endeavor. Countless flies, rats, and toads had found themselves with new passengers over the years she had been with Ezra. Confidence thrilled through her as she let her vision fracture, seeking out the potential of death, luring those Shades to heed her call, and opening the way between realms.

Black smoke rose off the water, thin curls at first, whorling tighter and tighter until they coalesced into a thin seam, stretching beyond its bounds until the world split wide open. Arctic winds churned waves in the lake; they tore at Milla's cheeks, and she saw Ezra pushed back a step. And another.

"Now, Millapet!" he yelled, the words edged in fear. She doubled her intent, tripled, and quadrupled. Her knees shook, and her calves cramped. The pinching of decayed lace grew at her temples, but Milla kept on with her call, her summons.

Something tugged at her heart; a return summons beckoning Milla closer. One she was powerless but to heed. She took a step, another. Out of the occult circle, down into the silt. The waters lapped at her thighs, and that ludicrous skirt pulled in the tide, threatening to sweep her away.

A tendril of silken midnight slithered out of the Shade realm to coil around Milla's wrist, and a small, inquisitive voice said, "I know you, you know."

Clouds.

Milla was asleep in the clouds. Puffy, soft white clouds billowing in a cornflower blue sky.

The wrong clouds.

Her clouds were stormy and black, smelling of winter spice and smoke. They rumbled low like thunder in a spring storm and took up altogether too much space.

These clouds were clean and crisp and boasted the highest Egyptian cotton thread count money could buy. The wrongness pried her eyelids apart, and she regretted it immediately. Even with curtains drawn and lights out, the room was too bright and too clean. Everything was sharp angles and flat surfaces, absent a Shade and a Soul.

She rolled over, half expecting to see Darkly, but there was only the empty expanse of the bed she lay in.

In a room she didn't recognize.

She bolted upright. The motion shrank her skull about five sizes, and the pain of it matched the rest of her body. Her right arm screamed when she moved it, her left muttered annoyed protests, and every muscle in her legs strongly considered throwing its hands up and leaving her body altogether. She croaked, tongue dry as ash and throat ravaged.

A bleary glance showed Milla one scrap of personality in the shape of a bedside table hosting a tall cylinder of fashion water, a bowl of exotic fruit, none of which she recognized, a packaged moist towelette, and her phone plugged into the wall.

"What the—"

Three terse raps on the door cut her off. The stainless steel handle rattled, stopped, and then turned ninety degrees as the door opened. She yanked the down comforter to her shoulders, half registering that all she wore were her shorts and the bandeau top, which had slipped below her breasts. She tugged the black elastic into place, and her eyes landed on the ashen streaks her fingers left on the sheets. And then the dried blood, mud, and what looked embarrassingly like drool.

"Hey there, kiddo, how are we feeling?" A pleasant tenor sang-spoke as the door opened, revealing Stefan Holfstaedter in chinos, a casual short-sleeved button-down, and leather moccasins with no socks. He balanced a mound of towels in his arms and looked Milla over with that cultivated smile plastered on his face.

"What," Milla croaked as pieces of the night came back to her in flashes. The brückengeist, bodies hitting the ground, Darkly,

Tobias and the burnout, and Milla slurring something at the CEO of Erlich Industries before—

"Ohmygoddess, I passed out in your lap." She clapped her hands over her mouth and stared wide-eyed at Stefan over her fingertips. His smile dropped a little, and then something more genuine bowed his lips, showing the creases at the corners of his eyes from years of laughter. It softened the corporate mien and made him all the more relatable.

"Well, kiddo, I'd be lying if I said it wasn't the first time."

"It was for me." Milla scrunched her eyes closed and then clarified, "With a billionaire CEO, I mean."

Because that helps.

Stefan chuckled, and the end of the mattress dipped under his weight. When she opened her eyes, he was perched on the corner, close enough to be cautiously friendly, but nowhere near inappropriate.

"You did pass out pretty hard back there." She blinked, fingers trailing down to her chin, and he kept on. "Now don't worry, nothing untoward happened. That big angry fella helped carry you in here, and no one has touched you since. Well, minus the band-aids." He gestured to her hand, his eyes fell to Milla's shoulder, and then he frowned at the stains on the sheets.

Milla examined the beige bandages wrapped around several of her fingers. A glance at her shoulder revealed a giant, medical-grade bandage covering her skin where Cyrus's hex had landed. She sniffed, catching the scent of lavender and calendula.

"Big fella dropped off a change of clothes, if you'd like to shower." Stefan wafted a hand at the wall and a series of small depressions that were almost like handles. "You cut yourself working on that leather tie-down. I had our camp nurse tend to you. Don't worry about the sheets, kiddo. You saved my life, which is worth far more than my bedding."

The laugh lines appeared again with his grin, and though it seemed genuine, Milla had a hard time believing he wasn't actually freaking out over her filth on his fancy sheets.

"Where am I?" she asked.

"Now, don't freak out."

"That tends to have the opposite effect on people," Milla wheezed. Stefan frowned a little and rose from the bed. Grabbing the fashion water from the side table, he showed her that the bottle was sealed before twisting the cap and holding it out for her to take.

"No more talking until you drink up, kiddo."

"Where is Darkly?"

Stefan waggled the bottle, tapping the bottom of it against her knuckles. Milla relented, took a small sip, and swallowed with a grimace.

"Darkly is the big fella's name?" he asked. She nodded, draining more of the bottle. "I'll go let him know you're awake. You sit tight."

Stefan left, the door clicking quietly closed behind him. Milla drew her knees up to her chest, running through the night before. Everything she had done and learned, and settling herself in the knowledge that Darkly had gotten her here, which meant he was alright, and not the meatsuit for whatever those ritualists were attempting to summon.

The door handle jogged again, and Milla sat up straighter. Her heart flipped over at the prospect of Darkly standing on the other side and thudded like a stone when Tobias entered.

He closed and locked the door behind him, facing Milla and running his hand through filthy hair. "You were not supposed to be there," he said.

"Gathered that." She waited for him to speak. He must have something to say, some explanation of what he was and how he could perform a burnout on command. Instead, he dropped his eyes to the bottle in her hands. "You should drink. Beyond the magick you cast yesterday, the burnout has a tendency to dehydrate survivors."

"That's … ominous."

"It is," he agreed.

The door handle jogged again, and Stefan muttered something to himself before knocking. "Y'all want omelets?"

Tobias stared at Milla, Milla shrugged, and he unlocked the door, opening it a crack. "A moment, bitte."

"Sorry, sorry," Stefan ducked away, and Tobias closed the door.

"May I sit?" He gestured to the bed. When she nodded, he took the same place Stefan had and stared at his knees before saying, "I need to get the story straight before we leave here."

"Where is here, exactly?"

Tobias's mouth twitched into a smile, and he shook his head. "Herr Holfstaedter's private recreational vehicle."

Milla's jaw dropped. "His … his fuck wagon?"

He chuckled, true mirth in the sound, and then he shook his head. "No, just a normal, ehm, RV."

"Seriously?" Milla sent a wide-eyed look to the sheets and the sparse room. "You're telling me this isn't a fuck wagon? He's probably got thousand thread count Shangri-la silk tie-downs that retract into the wall."

Tobias pulled his lips between his teeth, and she suspected he was trying not to laugh. He cleared his throat instead. "Lou has questions, primarily around how you got to the ritualists."

"I don't know," Milla said too quickly.

"Yes, you do, and you are going to tell me," he said with the patience of a man who is used to being lied to. "Or you are done."

"What?" Milla goggled at him. "She can't do that."

"She can, and she will, Ludmilla." Tobias pinned her with that blue-eyed stare. "What happened last night … you hurt her brother."

"*She* sent her brother into a dangerous ritual. Alone."

"And he saw Cyrus, who has vanished once more, and your Way is all over the site. She has questions."

"He … what do you mean *vanished?*" Milla hugged her knees tighter, a chill creeping down her arms. "I left him rotted three-ways to Sunday, lying in the grass. How could he vanish?"

Tobias pursed his lips, his gaze wandered over Milla's head, and she became acutely aware of the fact that he did not know. He sighed and met her gaze again. "Lou will not be the only one with questions."

The anger in Milla's chest bottomed out, replaced with something far more timorous.

"How is he?" she asked in a quiet voice.

"Sleeping it off." Tobias set his hand on the bed between them as if reaching out to comfort her, even though he knew she wouldn't accept. "Burnout tends to be a harsh recovery."

"You say that as if this is a common occurrence." He remained silent, and Milla closed her eyes, her heart panging.

"I, too, have a question. If you are willing to answer it."

"Hit me." Milla met his piercing gaze.

"How did you know?"

"That you could take down Darkly?"

Tobias shook his head, mouthing, "Nein."

"Oh." Milla filled in what he didn't say and took a steadying breath. "I didn't," she admitted. "Not really. I knew it had to be someone close to the team or with access to us, but honestly? I thought the chronomantic in the cells and my house was Dina."

"The Third Head?" Tobias hopped to his feet, looking genuinely surprised. "Why her?"

"Lou said she was a close family friend and that she—" Milla pressed her lips together, realizing she had gone too far. But there were too many questions around Lou. Where was Donmar? Why had she been so willing to send Darkly alone, and how did she know about the flower trick?

"You think this goes that far?" Tobias asked.

"What do you mean this?"

Tobias's face hardened, and those clear blue eyes drilled into her. "How many witches were there that night, Milla? On the lake, and at Marie's ball; whose faces do you recall?"

"I don't—what? What do you know?"

He rose and regarded her before speaking again. "This will never work if you cannot trust me, Milla."

"How can I trust you?" she asked, raising her voice. "You work for Lou."

Tobias scoffed as if that were the most offensive idea in the world. "Whoever said I work for Lou?"

"Who wants fresh squeezed orange juice?" Stefan knocked again, harder this time. Both witches jumped, and Tobias shot an annoyed look at the door.

"Find out what you can," he ordered, leaving before she could reply.

The shower was blessedly hot. She washed her hair three times and only whimpered in pain twice when she forgot about the hex on her shoulder. When the steam cleared, Milla leaned close to the mirror, eyeing what remained of the funeral mask. It had retreated to a cluster of blackened veins at her temples, easily hidden by her hair. Her fingertips were still blackened, which was a minor problem, but it was her eyes that had Milla staring at her reflection for a good long while.

Where before, the deep brown held just a spraying of tombstone gray, now the mark of her magick burst around her pupil, thinning as it reached for the edge of her iris.

Ripping the bandage on her shoulder away with a quick jerk, she studied the delicate lacing of skulls and bones wrapping around her shoulder like a tattoo in red, ashen ink. The wound was still new, and Milla had no doubt the color would fade to something less obvious. She ran her finger lightly over the raised flesh, muttering to her reflection, "At least it's kind of cool."

Careful of the wound, she pulled on the stretchy purple sports bra and grey muscle tank Tobias had brought by and shimmied into the yoga pants before entering the RV's main room.

Stefan sat at the kitchen table, reading a tablet with his ankle propped on a knee, looking for all the world like a suburban dad on a Sunday morning. Or so she assumed. Milla hadn't spent many Sunday mornings with her dad or anyone else's, so the image that came to mind was entirely drawn from television shows and cereal commercials.

And Stefan Holfstaedter was a perfect rendition of that Hollywood ideal.

Thick, wavy brown hair trimmed on the sides, long on top, and shot through with salt and pepper at the temples. Stylish scruff dusted a square, all-American jaw, fitting when paired with broad shoulders on a fit body. The man looked as comfortable in his chinos and button-down as he did in a slim-cut suit on national television. Milla was pretty certain he'd look just as at home in pajama pants and a bathrobe.

Or a smoking jacket.

A cup of tea sat beside a folded newspaper and an empty plate on the table, and the news was playing on a television somewhere out of sight. The curtains were drawn, blocking Milla from the real world, and she stood in the narrow hallway for a second, trying to figure out how to sneak past Stefan without him seeing her.

She settled instead on saying, "This is all very weird."

Stefan looked up at her and laughed, a warm, genuine sound that immediately put her at ease.

"Sit, sit." He rose and gestured to an empty seat at the table, where an omelet waited for her on a pale yellow plate.

Milla sat and stared at the omelet. And then she stared at Stefan.

"You're shorter than you look on TV."

"I get that all the time." He had the grace to laugh, and again, those crow's feet crinkled his eyes. "Can I let you in on a little secret?" Stefan waggled a moccasin-ed foot. "Camera angles and big shoes." He nudged the plate closer to her, then pinched the edge of a rolled napkin to reveal a fork and knife. "Bell pepper, swiss, mushrooms, salt and pepper. Big fella said you're vegetarian, right?" Milla nodded, dumbfounded. "Please, eat. I won't talk until you've got something in your belly." His smile sharpened, and he winked. *Winked.* "I usually buy a woman dinner before she ends up with her face between my legs, so please allow this gentleman his delay in manners."

Milla's cheeks heated, and she grabbed the fork, fingers fumbling around the metal. She focused on the omelet, shearing off a corner and popping it into her mouth. It was Horned God-damned delicious, and she struggled to swallow the moan that came with the bite. "Oh, my Goddess."

"How do you take your coffee?" Stefan asked as he rose and faced the kitchen nook. "Milk? Sugar? Cream?" He held up a goose-neck kettle.

"Sweet and pale as snow," Milla replied, shoving a forkful of omelet into her mouth.

"A girl after my own heart," Stefan hummed. Milla's cheeks flamed hotter, which was just embarrassing. She was blushing like a schoolgirl. Or Darkly. When had that started?

He poured hot water from the kettle over the grinds in the dripper, humming as it filled her cup. He finished it off with a heaping spoonful of sugar and a generous dollop of cream and set the concoction in front of Milla with a flourish.

She took a sip, mentally preparing herself for subpar coffee made by a man who probably employed a different cook for every meal and two sous chefs for snacks. Her eyes flew open at the decadent, silken drink that met her tongue.

It was good.

Horned God-damned good.

"I wouldn't have assumed a man like you to make his own breakfast," Milla said in lieu of thanks. Stefan's friendly smile faltered, and he took a seat, swiping at something on his tablet before fixing her with a warm, brown-eyed stare.

"Wouldn't have assumed a wispy thing like you to be a Death Witch."

Coffee sprayed over her omelet and the table, and Milla sputtered, "What?"

Amusement again crinkled his eyes as she blotted the coffee with her napkin. He waited until she was recovered before he explained.

"I come from a long line of occult-obsessed Texans," he started. "My great Memaw was a witch, at least as far as Papaw tells it." A well-practiced chuckle had him shaking his head at the memory. "The matrilineal line died out around World War Two. Big shame, really," he shrugged, "but what are you going to do?"

"How did the line die out?" Milla sipped her coffee, wondering if it were appropriate to ask. But she needed to have *something* to give Lou whenever CEO Soccer Dad let her leave. Stefan glanced at her, but he didn't seem offended. He seemed resigned more than anything else.

"Momma would say it's a curse; the Holfstaedter Sons are a bit of a running joke where I come from."

"Is that how you got involved in that ritual?" she asked.

Stefan puffed out his cheeks, and Milla realized she may have overstepped. The man had almost died, or worse, been possessed by Goddess knows what. He exhaled, eyes on Milla, and then ran a hand through his hair. As he did so, she noted a burnished gold alumni ring on his right hand. A musket and sword crossed over a cannon were engraved on the side, and the deep, garnet blood-red stone in the setting was easily the size of one of her knuckles. A wayward lock of hair flopped down over his forehead, making Stefan look younger, more rakish, and then he chuckled.

"As far as my people can figure." He slid his eyes to hers, grinning into the rim of his teacup. "Knocked me out when I was leaving a meeting." He took a sip. "I woke up on that table and the witchy lady in the mask started ramblin' on about my blood being the power or somesuch. Never really followed that mambo-jambo on a good day"—he waggled his fingers at 'mambo-jambo,' and Milla inwardly winced at how crudely he referred to the Ways— "much less when I've been stripped down to my skin and tied to a table. But my Memaw, she was the last, mind, always said we came from a powerful line of witches."

"And your Memaw was a witch?" Stefan nodded. Milla narrowed her eyes. "I thought you said there were no daughters."

"She was the last girl born into the family." He swept a hand in the air, dismissing her suspicion. "As I said, the Holfstaedter Sons are a bit of a running joke, cursed with a football team's worth of boys since nineteen-twenty."

Milla finished her coffee and set the mug down. "Well, you're handling being the survivor of a ritual sacrifice really well. Most mortals would be tearing at their hair or calling up the National Enquirer by now."

"Part of being an internationally recognizable CEO." He grinned at her. "It's a bad week in business if there isn't someone calling for my head. Rest assured, kiddo, my therapist earns his paycheck." That said, he tapped on his tablet and spun it to face her, watching Milla closely. "This your store?"

She frowned at the Yap! Reviews page on the screen. The main image was a street front shot of Southern Gothic, and the late Kayleigh Masterson's slanderous words still crowned the reviews as her highest-rated comment.

Milla rubbed her temples. "I am never going to get rid of those reviews."

"I knew it!" Stefan slapped his hand against the table, rattling the dishware. "Thought you looked familiar!" He snatched his tablet back and opened another app—the occult bidding website she and Diego used. "I got myself into a fierce bidding war a while back over an antique séance table from London." His eyes twinkled at her, and Milla's stomach fluttered. "Rumored to be the same table Sir Arthur Conan Doyle used when trying to summon Agatha Christie."

Milla knew the exact table he meant. It was sitting in the main room of her store, serving as a display for piles of hideous leggings.

"Lost on a generous bid from a store owner and collector of antiquities in St. Augustine. Been wonderin' for a while who the person behind the handle 'xBlackxParadexPrincess95' was."

Milla's ears blazed hot and she unwound the towel from her head, dragging fingers through her hair to hide the blushing. Honestly, it was getting out of control. "My co-worker keeps telling me I need to change my screen name."

Stefan chuckled, shaking his head as he scrolled through the reviews, lingering on Kayleigh's. "Well, that's not nice, nor is it representative of the witch who saved my life."

"I crossed the wrong hun," Milla explained. "She sent her horde after me."

"Ah, yes, the ICYMI Banner." Stefan put his tablet down. "We've been trying to clean up that mess since the acquisition."

"Erlich Industries bought ICYMI?" He nodded. Milla curled her lip in disgust. "Why? Those leggings are hideous."

"I know, I know, but the board raised a compelling argument." Stefan rolled his eyes and shrugged in a manner that said, 'What can you do?' "Sales are trending net positive and poised to grow. The year-over-year was too irresistible to pass up, and due to some nastiness around their quarterly conference in your neck of the woods, the price was right."

Milla pinched her lips, and a knock on the door spared her from having to explain all of *that.*

"Ludmilla, we need to get moving," Tobias called through the door.

"Alright, big fella, alright." Stefan threw his hands up in surrender and leaned towards Milla. "Kiddo, it has been a pleasure." He extended his hand and Milla forced herself to keep her eyes on his. It seemed rude to read his palm, considering he'd almost been a human sacrifice. Especially after he'd gone out of his way to make sure she was alright. She gave the CEO a firm shake like her father had taught her to do, and Stefan smiled in a way that caused a weird little flutter in her chest. "Now that's a businesswoman's handshake."

"Thank you for the omelet." Milla pulled away, averting her eyes. She picked up the damp towel she'd pulled from her hair and folded it to busy her hands, looking around for somewhere to place it. Stefan hopped from his chair, grabbed the towel, and headed to the bedroom. "I'm sorry, again, about your sheets."

"No worries, kiddo!" He returned with a canvas bag. "Belt, socks, the remains of one ruined vest … thing, a little pouch, and your boots are by the door." Stefan pointed over her shoulder, and sure enough, there were her boots next to a familiar pair of well-worn checkered slip-ons. "You saved my life. Least I could do."

Milla slung the bag over her good shoulder and stepped into her slip-ons. A last thought occurred as she grabbed her boots and noted the red clay clinging to the soles. "What were you doing in backwater Alabama, anyways?"

The corporate mask slid into place, his eyes gone carefully friendly, and the cultivated smile reappeared. "Had a meeting, like I said," Stefan replied. He leaned a hip against the counter, perfectly casual. "My assistant arranges corporate retreats whenever we finalize an acquisition."

"You're … camping?"

"Glamping," he winked. "I'm not a savage." He jounced from the counter and crossed the RV to open the door for Milla. Sunlight poured in, and she scrunched her eyes against the burn. "I like to drive myself to these meetings when I can; keeps the head clear and the body humble."

"On one-thousand thread count Egyptian cotton sheets."

"Like I said"—his smile widened, and Milla looked away before he could see the blush that smile pulled into her cheeks—"I'm not a savage."

Fifty

TOBIAS ESCORTED HER THROUGH a blended campground of RVs, tents, and small one-room cabins circled around shared fire pits. As Stefan had implied, the campers all appeared to be men and women in a mix of ages from early twenties to late fifties. Many wore gray fleece vests over their long-sleeved thermals and flannels, with the bright green Erlich Industries logo embroidered over their hearts.

To her disappointment, Lou and Donmar waited at the entrance with the silver Land Rover. Still in his Enforcer blacks, Donmar looked as though he'd spent the night in a ditch, where Lou, dressed in jeans, a white t-shirt, and her hair in a ponytail, wore not a hint of what had passed the night before.

Milla stared at the Light Witch for a long moment, a hundred accusations dancing on her tongue. Lou's arms were crossed, her back against the driver's side door, and she waited. Her stance and expression daring Milla to speak what was on her mind.

It wouldn't end well for either of them. Milla knew it with a confidence that was a little startling. She had seen something she wasn't supposed to see and learned a little about how Lou ran her team. Milla was fairly certain C.R.O.W. had not sanctioned the sending of a Dark Witch to cleave Shades to the point of death, and she was absolutely certain that she hated the Light Witch for asking Darkly to do so.

No, not asking. Where did consent exist in the power differential between the Simmons siblings? Lou controlled his Way. She treated her brother like a sultry teen at best and a tantrum-throwing toddler at worst, shutting Darkly off from the very thing that made him *him*.

There was no asking, no polite requesting that he cleave Shades.

She made him do it.

And all of that before the wealth of her other suspicions about the witch.

Milla remained silent, offering her wrists to be bound. If she were right, this was just the tip of the iceberg. The opening round of a game. Milla barely knew the rules, but she knew how to play this.

Lou lifted her chin in a smug, close-lipped smile. "*Dún*," she said, releasing Milla's wrists. It took every bit of restraint she possessed not to marvel at her wrists and the lightness there as Lou patted the rear door. "Get in."

They rode in silence, creeping through the woods and onto a small country road. Milla tipped her forehead against the window, letting the sun-warmed glass burn away the lingering chill in her bones. Across the road, they passed the entrance to Barry Power Plant, where a large banner read, "Now an Erlich Industries Clean Energy Plant!"

Lou started talking then, filling in Milla on the key details she had missed with no small amount of judgment. "Donny couldn't get close enough for solid readings, meaning all we have are the distorted signatures before Keir's insertion, and Horned God knows he never turns his E.R.I.E. on. Toby pursued one of the assets through the woods but couldn't catch her. Keir, at least, was more successful. He secured three Shades for interrogation, even with your little interference."

Milla snorted. "I was just doing my job."

"And what is it you think your job is? Distracting one of my Enforcers to the point of injury?" Lou's tone told Milla she wasn't talking about the bandages on her fingers.

"To help you catch the ritualists," Milla replied.

"Your job is to do whatever I tell you to do," Lou snapped back.

Milla sat up, digging her nails into the upholstery. "How can I do that if you don't tell me anything?"

"It is a fair point—"

"Shut up, Toby."

"Don't tell him to shut up; Tobias is the only one willing to tell me the truth."

"It is not your place to know the truth, Ludmilla. You are a junior member of this team, and Keir has a job to do. One he excels at."

"One he hates." Milla raised her voice to meet Lou's. "You've seen what it does to him and what he needs to do to cope. Why make him do any of this if it so obviously kills him to do it? How can you be angry that I'd trip into the Neitherworld with him when you know—you've *known* the toll it takes."

"About that—"

"It's a Death Witch thing." Milla brushed the half-formed question aside. "If C.R.O.W. weren't so hell-bent on burning or cleaving us the moment we're born, maybe it would be more widely known."

"It is useful," Donmar offered. Though he spoke quietly, his tone had a bit of resolution directed at Lou. She met his stare, nodded, and turned her eyes back to the road.

"What did you learn about the main asset?"

"CEO of Erlich Industries."

Donmar snorted. "That had to make you smile, little witch."

"On the contrary," Milla said. "He told me he lost a bidding war to Diego, then read the reviews for my store. He's probably going to use it as grounds to evict me." Tobias laughed at that, quickly covering his mouth with a hand. "He says he's from an old witch line," she continued. "And that the ritualist Tobias chased mentioned he was the power behind the ritual or something."

"Any daughters?" Lou glanced at her in the mirror, drumming her fingers on the steering wheel.

"None. Apparently, the Holfstaedters have been cursed with sons since the 1920s." Milla chewed her lips, thinking through the night. "Cyrus was there."

"So Tobias informed me," Lou said. "Though he could not corroborate the claim. And there was a corpomantic?"

She sat back, staring at the ceiling. "Froze me right at the end."

"I told you," Donmar sang at his wife, needling her with a finger. "Donmar Bolatov does not fall asleep on missions."

"I did not accuse you of falling asleep," Lou sniffed, adjusting her grip on the wheel. "I accused you of severe ineptitude and the reckless endangerment of my brother."

The large meteomantic swallowed, his shoulders hunching as he dropped his head. He muttered something under his breath that earned a soft look from Lou. Milla rolled her head along the backrest to ask Tobias, "You think it was that girl you chased?"

"It is possible," he shrugged. "She vanished into the trees, and I circled back for Keir." He cleared his throat and dropped the next bomb. "The ritual leader also vanished after the burnout."

"We'll have C.R.O.W. subpoena a list of registrations from the Panhandle Coven," Lou said, "and see if we can narrow down our ritualists to those unaccounted for over the next few days."

"You should compare it against a list of Barry Power Plant employees as well," Milla offered. "The whole campground was some corporate retreat to celebrate the acquisition."

"Good thinking." Lou tapped her hands against the steering wheel and sent Milla a tight smile through her reflection in the mirror. "If Diego is willing, I can have Rai help him; she's decent with data."

"I can help after tending to the demesne—"

"No need," Lou said. "You and Toby will be needed to assist Keir with his conversations once we've settled on a specific pursuit."

Tobias cursed under his breath and glanced at Milla, who couldn't figure out what was so terrible about a conversation that it warranted German expletives.

And that was that. Donmar got on the phone with C.R.O.W., Lou drove, and Tobias fell asleep.

The trees blurred into a haze of green outside her window, and soon enough, they were in Tallahassee, and she was hobbling across a parking lot on insanely sore legs to use the restroom. At some point, they'd caught up with the minivan, and Milla waved to Dies-well, pumping gas under his umbrella.

"What are you still doing here?" she called out. Dies-well replied with a blank look, shallow eyes boring into Milla. She raised her eyebrows, and he relented with a haughty snort.

"Protecting the Madame's assets." He tapped two fingers to the inside of his forearm, just below the elbow, then asked in a softer voice, "Are you sure that was wise, goody witch?"

"No," she admitted. "But it was necessary."

Diego's head popped up on the far side of the minivan, eyes widening when he saw Milla there. He glanced at the far end of the parking lot, where Lou was storming in a circle, yelling at someone on the phone, and gestured for Milla to hurry over with a cartoonishly wide sweep of his arm.

"¡Apurarse!" he mouthed. She hustled across the parking lot, hissing and wincing as she did. The clunk of doors unlocking greeted her, and Milla tugged the handle, waiting impatiently for the sliding door to open enough for her to slither in.

"Oh sure, do not ask if there is room or anything," Dies-well grumbled as he climbed into the driver's seat. Milla stuck her tongue out at him and climbed over Rai, hesitating when she spotted Darkly's long legs. Stretched between the pilot seats, she followed their length to a gaunt, haggard face, sunken closed eyes, and a rear window full of shadow.

"Horned God." She settled on the edge of the empty pilot seat, looking at Rai. "How long?"

"It's nothing to—"

"You fed him that kava kava, poison witch."

"For protection!"

"How long." Milla demanded, her face inches from the vinefica's. Rai glanced at the front seat as if Dies-well or Diego could save her from the pissed-off Death Witch. Dies-well unsubtly began rolling up the partition. "How long has he been in there?"

"A few hours."

"Son of a bitch." She crawled over Darkly's legs and into the backseat. "What is it this time?"

"Solomon's Seal, pollen, clove," she rattled off quickly. "Barberry and—"

"Weed. Got it." Knowing he'd retreated to his usual blend was somehow worse than if Rai had given him something different.

He'd changed into clean clothes: his gray joggers and a white V-neck with short sleeves that revealed the gauze wrapping his forearm. White bandages wound around each finger, and another peeked over the collar of his shirt. The scent of ointment hung fresh and clean in the air, and Milla could have cried.

She had done that to him. Hexed him without a second thought.

Again.

After losing control and desecrating him in a moment of panic. *Again.*

She bit her lower lip as she grabbed Darkly's injured hand, cradling it in her palms and swallowing a cry at the lifeless chill before curling up on the bench seat beside him.

Milla looked up when Diego climbed inside, settling in the pilot seat beside Rai. "We should go," he said to Dies-well.

"Happily," the vampire replied.

Diego twisted around to examine Milla, smiling faintly as he checked her over. His fingers twitched at his side, and the smile lost most of its strain.

"You warned Marie," he said.

"I did." Her arm throbbed, the pinpricks of Marie's fangs long gone, but the ache remained. "Did she find you?" He nodded, and she could have cried. "I needed you and the cultists to be safe."

Diego looked away as he blinked rapidly, sniffing and raising his glasses before wiping the heel of his palm at an eye. "Josh wanted me to tell you—whatever you need, they owe you a favor."

"Good." She looked down at her blackened fingers thin and brittle between Darkly's knuckles. "I could use a favor right about now."

Dies-well chuckled. "You certainly could, goody witch."

"What are you going to do?" Rai asked.

"My job."

Dies-well had them on the road before Lou was off the phone. Milla let the bump and sway of the freeway lull her to sleep beside her Dark Witch. She woke when his hand twitched, lifeless fingers curling around her palm as warmth bled back into his skin. She lifted her head from his shoulder, watching Darkly open his eyes.

No death rattle marked his return, no sepulchral moan to give warning, just a seamless stepping from one world to the next.

When the black had withdrawn and his pupils were their normal size, Darkly rolled his head along the headrest to look at her. "Too much?"

Milla shook her head. "No, Darkly. Not too much."

His fingers twitched, and he frowned, throat bobbing before he asked, "Too far?"

Milla focused on the road and the landscape speeding past: swamps and marsh, the rise and fall of a panhandle town, and the blur of Spanish moss dripping from the trees. They had come so far since that first day, and as she let her vision blur and the world split into three, she saw just how far they had to go.

"Leannán?" The lack of power, of his Way, of that delicious curl of mercury teasing down her spine whenever he said that word called her back.

"No," Milla said, accepting the potentials for what they were: potential. Not set; undecided. A multitude of paths laid out before them, as broad and boundless as the Neitherworld.

"What do we do?"

She tore her face away from the potentials, gazing at the witch who kept choosing her for some maddening reason, weighing his question against all she knew and all he could have intended in those four little words.

What do we do?

About C.R.O.W., his sister, the missing ritualists, and the faceless witches haunting Milla's every step.

What do we do?

Or maybe he spoke only of them.

"I don't know," she admitted, heart aching in more ways than one as she pulled her attention back to the potentials and chose. "But we do it together."

THE NEITHERWORLD

He falls in darkness.

Tipping back with his eyes closed and trusting the Shades to catch him.

The wind is a soft comfort after the last few days. Weeks. How long has it been? Time has always been odd for him here, where the horizon stretches without end. He no longer feels the cold. In truth, there are days when he feels more at home here than he does topside. Here, the Shades obey him. Here, the landscape crafts itself to his will. Streets form beneath his feet, and paths stretch before him, away from the light. Away from C.R.O.W. and their laws and the life he can't escape.

Where are you going?

But this, his little shadow, he can never escape, nor would he want to.

"Away."

A slither of smoke twists up his arm, settling over his shoulders with a familiar not-weight, her voice a pleasing, musical tickle in the back of his mind.

Why?

"Don't I deserve a break?" He waves a hand, and the darkness splits before him, revealing the low rise of a hill and the barest silhouette of a black tent against a black sky. A safe retreat in the world only he can enter.

Except, that's not true anymore, is it?

Can we go back? Please? Little Shadow bunches against his neck, her voice taking on the suggestion of a whine. *I want to see her again.*

He pauses at the edge of the field, glancing at the Shade on his shoulder. "Her?"

Yes! She slithers down his arm, puddling to the ground, where smoke kicks up in a tiny plume. *I saw her!*

"You did." He crouches, elbows resting on his knees. The dervish of her excitement brings a smile to his face and he thinks it might be the first time anyone has smiled in here.

She was in here. With you! The tiny shadow slows and coils tight, vibrating with excitement. *Can she come back?*

"I–" Something like pain, or regret, pinches his chest, and that isn't right. There's no pain here. No sorrow or joy, the Neitherworld just *is,* and that's how he likes it. Safe and calm and still and empty, except for the Shades that obey his every whim. A place he can come to escape, not *feel.* "I dinnae ken."

Why?

"Dinnae think she's too happy with me."

Why?

That makes him pause, and in the pause, a new voice echoes through his realm. "Horned God *dammit*, Darkly, did you fall in again?"

Her! Little Shadow bounces onto his knee, whipping around his arm and whirring onto his shoulders. *She's here. Can we go? Please say we can go. Don't make me drag you out of here.*

And for the first time in its unfathomable existence, a laugh rings out across the Neitherworld. It is sharp and cold, but laughter all the same.

"Ye ken, Little Shadow, I think one of these days you just might manage to do so."

Milla and Darkly will return in

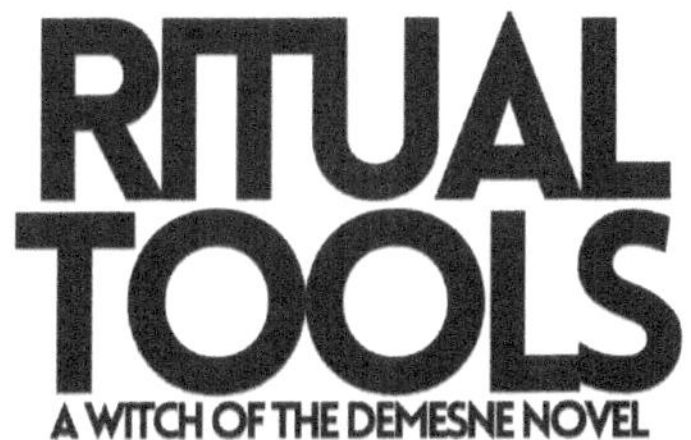

Elsewhere, in the World of C.R.O.W.

*A witch running from heartbreak, a merman who hunts the stars,
and the Shade which binds them both.*

Keir Simmons, a bounty hunter for the Coven for the Regulation
and Oversight of Witches, has made a career of running away
from his problems. Blindsided by a break-up, he leaps at the first
assignment he's offered, one that will take him far away from his
ex: chasing a rogue lorelei to the edge of the European continent.

When a chance encounter with a midnight diver leaves the pair
inextricably linked, Keir is caught between his responsibilities as a
C.R.O.W. Enforcer, his past as a questionably wicked witch, and
his broken but beating heart. With C.R.O.W. breathing down
his neck and the lorelei continuing to evade capture, it becomes

harder and harder to turn away from his unlikely ally — a man
with a secret lurking just beneath the surface.

<u>AVAILABLE NOW</u>

Every witch has her Way

Milla is a witch who wants to hide. Grieving the loss of her
mentor, she retreats to St. Augustine, where her only goals are
to run her antique store and tend her demesne into obscurity.

But C.R.O.W. has other plans for the formerly wicked witch.

As if being saddled with a new apprentice and trying to get rid of
the Aural Insurance Adjuster sent to observe her isn't enough to
deal with, a pack of multi-level marketing huns sets their sights
on Milla, intent on burning her store to the ground. When a
threat to the demesne and the witches and mortals under Milla's
care raises its ugly head, it is up to her to decide:

Is living out her days as a nothing witch in a nowhere demesne what she truly wants, or is the formerly wicked witch ready to rejoin the witchy world of C.R.O.W.?

<u>AVAILABLE NOW</u>

Greed is a curse.

Diego Gregorio de Bimini needs a vacation.

After his roommate stirs up trouble with the Enforcers of Witch Law, he leaps at the chance to head down to Key West, lounge in the sun, and cruise the Conch Republic for reliable cell service. When a run-in with a rogue chicken lands him in the care of a handsome pawnbroker, Diego thinks this forced vacation might be just what the witch doctor ordered … until he stumbles upon evidence of an occult artifact housing a curse. The same curse that killed him in the 16th century.

Calling on all he knows of the Ways and his own Stitch Witch magick, Diego must race against the clock to spare the mortal world from an ancient threat.

<u>AVAILABLE NOW</u>

Witch of the Demesne
Ritual Income
Ritual Dues

Witches of C.R.O.W.
Shady Depths
Stitching Palms

Camp Cryptid
Faun Over Me
Shifting Hearts

Beerhall Brides
Ravished by the Rasselbock

THANKS, Y'ALL

With every manuscript that makes it to a published work, the list of people I have to thank grows. This is exactly the sort of problem I love to have. Writing is sometimes solitary, but bringing a world and characters to life takes a village. This is my village:

Oliver — You told me to "shut up and write" without truly understanding what you were unleashing. I love you for that and so many other things.

Ana — The World's Best Hype Woman™. Thank you for listening to me ramble over uncountable glasses of wine. I am the luckiest person to have you in my corner.

Molly — Thirty+ years of friendship, and all you got was this witchy book for your birthday.

Kel — MA'AM. You're the best thing TikTok has ever put on my fyp. This book features at least one less instance of the word 'necrotic' thanks to you.

Megan — for being my witchy font of knowledge and ginger sister from another mister.

Kourtney — you are a champion of edits and authors. Thank you from the depths of my black heart for embracing these broken characters and helping me shape them into enjoyable chaos.

The Ladies of Fort Smut — Over the years, we have added four tiny humans, survived a pandemic, group-read numerous terrible and not-so-terrible books, and crafted the most rewarding and routinely hilarious group chat. Sorry for all the TikToks. I love you all. Where are we going next?

My Beta Team, Amazing ARC Readers, and the divinely talented authors of *Blood and Pulp* and *FaRo*.

You — you lovely, lovely human being who read this book. We frequent the same corners of the internet. I feel like we could almost be friends. I hope you stick around for more.

Britta is the worst. She doesn't even publish under her real name and responds to things like, "Mom", "B", and "Brown".

As B. L. Brown, she publishes urban fantasy and paranormal romance. Her debut novella, *Shady Depths*, was released in April 2023, and her short fiction can be found in *Tails, Trysts, and Tentacles: One Monstrous Summer*, *Fireside: Modern Legends and Lore*, and *The Future of Us, A Moms Who Write Anthology*.

As Britta, she is a human-wrangling, word-wielding, musical theatre and beer-loving runner with a passion for fairy tales and folklore. She can be found under a pile of digital literature or begging her academic friends for their JSTOR logins.

Otherwise, she is in no particular order: lost in the woods, scanning the shelves at the bottle shop, flicking through a classic cookbook, or chasing a kiddo around the neighbor's yard.

You can follow her on Amazon, Goodreads, Twitter, Instagram, and TikTok. For less obnoxious updates, join her infrequent newsletter at www.brittawritesthings.com

* 9 7 9 8 9 9 0 0 6 3 4 3 3 *